DESERT WINDS

J. M. TAYLOR

SCREAMING EAGLE PRESS

Also by J. M. Taylor

Lost Key
Missing Sticks
Gulf Winds

This Special Edition includes

The Image of Christ

This book is a work of fiction. All of the characters are products of the author's imagination. Certain real organizations and locales are used in the settings, however, none of the fictitious events described in the book occurred with these organizations nor at those locales.

Any resemblance to actual events or persons, living or dead, is entirely coincidental.

Printed in the United States of America
This is a revision of
Behind the Green Water
Originally published in 2004
by
Hard Shell Word Factory

ISBN: 1-879043-07-6

EAN-13: 978-1-879043-07-7

TURKEY
SYRIA
LEBANON
Euphrates River
Mosul
Sinjar
Irbil
Tigris River
IRAN
Palmyra
Damascus
Golan Heights
Baghdad
Amman-Baghdad Highway
IRAQ
Amman
Al Jouf Special Operations Forward Operating Base
JORDON
SAUDIA ARABIA
ISRAEL
KUWAIT
Red Sea
Riyadh

CHAPTER 1

Amman-Baghdad Highway, 1991

The dirty yellow ball of fire grew to a brilliant white pillar of iridescent flame, searing a trail up into the night sky.

"Everybody down!" Devon shouted, dropping as he squeezed his eyes shut against the glare of the rocket motor climbing into the desert sky. He dug his fingers into the sand as the ridge rumbled and shook, rattling his body like a tambourine. Underneath his gut the ground rippled as the shock wave from the rocket launch dissipated into the desert.

As Devon forced his eyes open a Scud missile slowly lifted from the cloud of desert dust and smoke, balanced on a tail of fire over the barren Iraqi desert. It accelerated, rising faster and faster, all too like the grainy films of the Nazi V-2s on their way to London.

This one angled into the heavy clouds to the west, toward Tel Aviv.

"Get the damn Hog down here before they get off another one!" Devon yelled at Baker, still struggling up the sandy slope. Devon craned his neck and searched overhead for the A-10 Wart Hog and its Maverick missiles. The glare of the rocket motor had completely wiped out his night vision.

He shivered, his heavy desert battle dress uniform sweat-drenched after leading his kluged-together four-man Special Operations team at a dead run from the helicopter drop point to the top of the sand ridge. He quickly scanned all around their position. To the south, the Night Stalker Blackhawk helicopter scuttled low over the tops of the dunes toward Saudi.

Staff Sergeant Wilbert Baker fell to his knees beside Devon, breath coming in deep gasps as he slipped off his heavy rucksack. He unfolded the satcom-mode antenna and tested the transceiver with a couple of quick squeezes of the handset. Baker softly clucked into the microphone, listened for the return echoes, and switched to air-to-ground mode. Soft bursts of static confirmed they were on the air.

Sergeant Larry Tuggle, the third American soldier on the team, pointed toward the highway, his freckled hand barely visible in the reddish gleam of the climbing rocket. "Rag-heads crawling all over the desert, Chief. Can't stick here too long."

Pinpoints of light flicked around the mouth of the *wadi*, a ravine cut into the desert floor by the infrequent torrential rains, where the highway bridge formed a shelter from the sky.

"Look over yonder," Tuggle continued. "'Rackies got no light discipline."

"It's like they's hanging out a sign sayin', Come on down," Baker added, nearly invisible in the dark as he hunkered low behind the top of the ridge.

On the far side of Baker, Aragon, their French Coalition member, scanned the distant highway with a pair of binoculars.

A quarter of a mile across the desert, movements of the individual Iraqi soldiers teased Devon's eyes. He scrubbed the sand from his face and yanked the laser designator from its carrier. Hands shaking, he flipped off the lens covers. If the Iraqis had another Scud, they'd try to quickly launch, almost in salvo with the first—if for no other reason than to confuse the Patriot missiles at the other end of the ballistic arc.

Devon swung the scope over the area, blinking to regain his night vision. He ignored the clinging particles of grinding sand, pressed the eyepiece back against his face and centered the invisible beam.

Sharp in the magnification of the scope, a gaggle of bodies waddled around a second missile teetering in the erector. The missile slowly moved toward a vertical position.

Baker's deep voice rumbled in his ear. "Hog's in firing position, Chief. Mark 'em...now!"

Devon triggered the laser beam, holding the center spot on the missile as the launch crew locked the tube in its firing position, then ran out of his peripheral vision.

Devon flinched as a fiery streak crossed the sky. Suddenly, the infrared amplifier overloaded and a green bloom filled the lens. Devon took his eye away from the scope and looked up to catch a faint blur against the stars. The Hog's turbines whined overhead as it pulled out, chased by flaming debris catapulted from the exploding Scud. Devon dropped back to the ground as the glare and roar of a secondary explosion washed over their exposed position.

Devon, heart hammering, pressed his face into the cold grit of the ridge until the glared died.

"The fuel truck!" shouted Aragon. "*Extraordinaire*!"

The fire silhouetted Aragon dancing on the top of the ridge.

Baker shook his head. "That Frenchie—he's gonna get us in trouble."

"Let him prance." Devon pressed the eyepiece back against his face and searched the darkness behind the flaming tanker. "For now, the Iraqis are too busy to care about us." The wavering flames across the desert floor blurred in the scope.

"If they got any sense, they'd be watching for the Hogs," replied Baker, referring to the A-10 ground attack fighters patrolling high in the fading light of the quarter moon.

The sour odor from Devon's sweat gradually dissipated in the cold wind as he searched the desert for new targets. The low moan of the wind singing across the *wadis* brought a chill up from the damp sand. Devon grinned into the darkness. He had always enjoyed night fighting. Seemed what he was born for, to creep across the desert, flashing blade in hand, instead of bouncing around in an air-conditioned missile hauler.

This war gave him another chance to be what he really wanted: a warrior. He belonged away from the research labs and algorithms, out in the open desert. Like a big owl, tonight he was ready to swoop. Devon zipped open his desert parka.

"Why don't you leave it on, Chief? Ain't got a hint what kind of glasses they got out there." Baker's soft Savannah Geechee drawl came from somewhere deep in the big black man's chest.

"Yeah, you're right." Devon left the parka on, accepting Baker's reminder that the green crosshatch pattern on the parka supposedly confused the old infra-red night vision devices sold to the Iraqis with all the other obsolete Soviet weapons. He scanned the length of the *wadi* that stretched across the sand to the highway. *Finally!* Devon slowed his breathing, steadying the sight picture on the blunt nose of a third Russian missile on its transporter-erector-launcher. The TEL's massive shoulder-high wheels were barely perceptible under the thick rocket body, just like in the news clips of the lines of missiles parading through Red Square on May Day.

"Jackpot, Bert. Another one." The long-nosed Condor II, an Iraqi variant of the Soviet Scud missile, nestled on the TEL's back as it rolled into sight. Nash Devon, an Army Air Defense captain on special assignment with the Special Forces to hunt out the Iraqi Scuds, had studied the photos enough to recognize the additional length, just enough extra fuel to boost the warhead to Tel Aviv.

"TEL's coming out from under the overpass, Bert. Get the Hog ready for a run." Devon stared through the scope until his eyes blurred. The TEL stopped—a mouse poking its nose out of a hole.

But it was night and the owl could see.

Baker pulled the radio handset back to his dark face. "Enfield flight, this is Paris thirty-one. Confirm one Scud kill. Spotter's got another one hiding under the bridge."

Funny. Baker used his nothing-but-a-good-old-Savannah-colored-boy voice in conversation. Yet, on the radio he had the accent of a midwest announcer. *We all play our games…me trying to decide if I'm white man or Injun—Baker, homeboy or professional soldier.*

Ever since he had sat by Grandma's fire and listened to her tales, impatient while she packed her cheek with Tube Rose snuff pinched out of a tin, Devon had wished he was pure Iroquois Tuscarora, not a mongrel mix of Scot, Irish and Lumbee Indian. In her scariest stories, the fierce Tuscarora warriors rampaged across the lowlands, terrorizing the Lumbees peacefully farming on the edge of the Carolina swamps. He'd always wanted to be the boogey man like in Grandma's stories. Tonight he would get to be the Tuscarora.

The TEL suddenly reversed and disappeared.

"Damn!" Devon searched the backside of the overpass, but the TEL remained out of sight.

A flat voice whispered back from the radio handset. "Paris, Enfield twenty-two. Roger the new target, but I'm bingo gas. If the Eagles are up, I'll tell AWACS to send them over. Good spotting and good night."

With that call, the faint buzz of the A-10 melted into the desert night and the TEL slowly rolled back out into the open.

"Aragon, see anything else out there?" Devon asked.

Sub-Lieutenant Tristan Aragon, attached to the U.S. Army Special Forces team from the 1st RPIMa, the French Marine Commandos, scanned the black desert around them. "Only milling Iraqis, waiting to be killed."

Baker tapped the handset against the metal frame of his rucksack in frustration. "Damn, Chief. The Hogs bagged it."

Devon nodded. "We'll wait. A flight of F-15s is supposed to be on station. The Iraqis haven't figured out we're out here. Yet." He rolled to his side and searched the ridge for Aragon. He had objected to the Frenchman's assignment to their team, but politics had overruled common sense. *Damn!* Aragon was nowhere in sight. "Tug, where'd Aragon get off to? This isn't the time for a stroll in the desert.

His outfit lost a whole team last week. You'd think your buddy would be a little more careful."

"Aragon ain't my buddy, sir. He's an officer." Tuggle swept his glasses across the flat desert. He stopped and pointed in the direction of the burning Scud. "Shit, I take back anything good I never said about the bastard. He's heading toward the underpass."

A pair of headlights bounced across the desert, circling around behind them. "And the Iraqis are cutting between us and the pick-up point." Tuggle stuffed the glasses back into the pack and looked at Devon expectantly. "Five minutes and the rag-heads cut us off from the helicopter, Chief."

Without a Hog overhead, and the Eagles God knew where, the decision was easy. "Bert, call back the Blackhawk for pickup. We're through. Get the bird back here, pack up and head for the rendezvous." Devon handed Baker the laser designator. "Tug, I'll wait here. You drag Aragon back, and we'll follow Bert to the pick-up point."

Tug waved and trotted toward the *wadi* leading toward the bridge.

Baker made a short call to the Blackhawk crew waiting across the Saudi-Iraq border, slapped the folding antenna together and shoved it into the bulging rucksack along with the radio. He slipped the rucksack straps over his shoulders. "I'm heading down to the pickup point." His grin showed in the flames from the burning fuel truck. "Don't hang around taking no scalps, Chief."

"We'll catch up with you as soon as Tug polices up Aragon." Devon picked up his rifle. "They'll have me under the jail if anything happens to the Frenchman." He scanned the desert floor with his pocket binoculars. Neither Tuggle nor Aragon was anywhere to be seen.

Devon stood and looked over the desert. Tracer fire sprayed out from the Iraqi position—random firing. The Iraqis still didn't know what had hit them.

He trotted down the exposed side of the ridge toward the highway bridge and the remaining Iraqi mobile missile erector. He yanked the charging lever of the M-16 back and let the bolt fly. Desert sand ground into the bolt carrier, jamming it half-shut. A ricochet twanged past his ear. He slammed the bolt home with the heel of his hand, picked out a darker lump on the desert floor and ran toward it, crouched, low to the ground.

He hummed a low chant. Hell of a heritage. His ancestors were all farmers, white and red. Out in the desert he felt more akin to the Apache. But no time to take *coup*. He trotted down the slope. Find Tuggle and the damned Frenchman, then out of here.

CHAPTER 2

Tracers silhouetted two figures running ahead of Devon, closing on the distant Scud. Devon followed, cringing under his soft cap at the whine and snap of bullets passing overhead. The gunfire was louder as he neared a low mound. A man raised up, rifle at his shoulder, silhouetted in the flames. Machine gun fire raked across the mound and the man went down. Devon couldn't tell who was shooting. Was that Tug, Aragon or a 'Rackie?

"Tug," Devon yelled. When he reached the mound, he stumbled over a body, face down in a sand drift. When Devon rolled him over, Tuggle's soft cap came away sticky and matted with blood, gritty with sand. Devon felt Tug's throat. No pulse.

"Aragon!" he shouted, oblivious to the Iraqi soldiers across the desert. Aragon was nowhere in sight.

"God damn Frenchman!" Devon eased Tuggle's body back to the ground and slogged through the loose sand toward the muzzle flashes. He spotted Aragon beside a large boulder, silhouetted by the flames, and dashed toward his position. The French Marine knelt behind a limestone boulder, a bulky Milan rocket launcher propped on his knee. Devon grunted as he plopped to his belly beside Aragon.

"You son of a bitch, what the hell are you doing? Come on! Let's get to the rendezvous before the Iraqis spot us."

Aragon ripped open a field dressing and wrapped it around his wrist.

"You hurt?" Devon asked.

Aragon shrugged. "*Non*. A bullet took but a bite."

"And Tuggle's dead, trying to cover your ass. Now let's get out of here."

"The boy sergeant? I'm sorry, but I didn't ask him to follow. First I will finish our mission."

Devon pulled himself up to his knees to peer over the boulder. "Even these Iraqis aren't stupid enough to think the Maverick just dropped out of the sky."

Aragon let the launcher slide from his shoulder. "I disagree. The Iraqis are just that stupid." Aragon smiled across the tube at Devon.

"The Scud must come back out, either to launch or to run. Either way it is mine, *mon ami.* We French aren't impatient like you Americans. We don't go home until the fight is over, even when men die."

Devon resisted the urge to reach out with his knife and finish Aragon on the spot. "Then you French are all balls and no brains."

"You wait here in the sand. I will destroy the missile without your airplanes and Mavericks." Aragon stood and ran toward the culvert.

A single report echoed from within the shadows, followed by a burst of automatic fire, the flat pops unmistakably AKs. *Son of a bitch*! Devon scrambled to his feet and ran after Aragon. Orange muzzle flashes preceded the crack of bullets flying overhead, sprayed from the mouth of a shallow *wadi* to the right. Devon kept running, swerving in an impromptu zigzag across the flat sand. He sprinted across the open for the cover of a dark boulder mass ahead, leaving him only a couple of hundred meters from the missile transporter and the Iraqi shooters. He slid to a stop in the shadow of a low rock pile.

Aragon rose from between the rocks.

"Ah, *mon capitaine,* I thought you might leave without me."

Devon leaned against the boulder to get his breath then pulled up to peer over the rock. "Not yet." The limestone crumbled under his hand, flimsy protection from the Iraqi bullets. "I'll wait till you've finished being a hero."

A line of green tracers raked across the sand. Devon crouched to press his face close to the rock. He squinted, trying to see beyond the flames, and searched for the Scud missile. The sooner they spotted it, the sooner he could get Aragon out of this kill box. A burst from an automatic weapon splattered grit in his face, chewing great chunks of limestone away from their cover. He dropped flat to the sand and slithered around for a better look. His blood raced as he caught a glimpse of the transporter edging from the ravine.

"Clear the back-blast," warned Aragon. He stood, large Gallic nose profiled in the flames, looking over the boulder. A burst of gunfire roared overhead and Aragon dropped down. "I am a Frenchman, a Commando. We have our reputation, you know. Just like your Delta Force. Except we succeed." He stood back up at a lull in the firing and slid the launcher sight to his eye. "*El momento de verdad*, the moment of truth, as my Spanish lover would say—for a different reason." He traversed the Milan and yelled, "Stand clear!"

Devon rolled to the side and the Milan whooshed away, immediately followed by a massive explosion where the transporter had been sitting just a moment before. An answering barrage of gunfire spit out from the shadows.

Aragon threw down the empty Milan launcher and shouted, "Direct hit, right on the Scud. Now you can run, *capitaine*!" He raced toward the distant ridge, green tracers ricocheting around him. The tracers seemed to converge on Aragon, sprinting across the desert, then he was gone.

The Scud's liquid fuel flowed into the *wadi*, and burst into flame when a line of tracer fire raked across the desert. Devon gritted his teeth at the scene in front of him and sprayed the melee with a full magazine from his M-16 rifle.

Devon emptied a second magazine, this time on single fire, aiming at the muzzle flashes, target practice on the range at Fort Bragg. He slowed his breathing and squeezed off the shots.

Nothing trembled. For some reason, the fear hadn't hit yet. Everything seemed so deliberate. Iraqi soldiers dropped to the ground, then sprang up and began running toward him in ones and twos. As they came closer faceless targets resolved into men, soldiers like him—soldiers who wanted to kill him as he had been doing to them

He picked out individuals, focused on where they dropped, then fired at the spot whenever one climbed to his feet and tried to rush forward. He fired and men went to the ground. The Iraqis continued to edge closer. Machine gun fire again swept toward him, chewing the boulder down, forcing him to slide back to a prone position. The faint *whap* of approaching rotor blades reverberated between the snap of bullets around his head. The sound moved to his rear, then faded.

What the hell was he doing? He hadn't been sent out here to massacre the Iraqi army by himself. If he didn't get his wits about him, the Iraqis would soon have him surrounded. *Do they take scalps?*

Devon fired at a hurtling body and slid back behind the boulder. He scanned the ground in the direction of the ridge. Aragon was either gone or down. Devon searched behind him, picked out an escape route by the half-light from the burning debris and gathered his nerve for the sprint. Two steps and a bullet snapped by his chin. A second tugged at his sleeve. A swarm buzzed and cracked over his head and sang against the sand.

He ran for all he could muster for the next boulder. A bullet tore at his pants and a second grazed his thigh like a burning ember. He flopped to the ground behind the boulder. For an instant he thought he saw Aragon dash across the sand.

Devon sprayed a covering burst until the rifle bolt locked back, empty. He rolled across the sand, back to the dwindling safety of the boulder. Sweat-slick fingers popped out the old magazine and slammed a fresh one home. The last one in his pouch. One more chance.

In the dying light of the fire, a tracked vehicle pulled clear of the *wadi.* A Soviet-era ZSU-23 anti-aircraft gun, it depressed its four barrels to their minimum elevation and rocked to a stop, belching fire. Devon pressed his face to the sand and covered his head while the desert exploded around him. Fragments of rocks pelted his bare hands and wrists. The incoming fire shifted to explode across the desert to the ridgeline, tracers cracking the desert sky. He shook the sand from his face and looked up.

All those waving flashlights. The damn Iraqis had tried to pull the A-10s down into an anti-aircraft ambush.

They had been too slow to catch the A-10. Now the ZSU-23 had settled for him!

Another burst sent a stream of high explosive shells his way, eating away at the soft rock, digging shallow craters in the desert around him. A soldier popped up from a depression, so close Devon could see the fear on his face as the shells cracked overhead. The soldier stood, oblivious to the 23mm rounds sweeping the sky, and charged toward Devon's boulder. Devon pulled the trigger on his M-16. The man staggered and fell, disappearing into the desert as quickly as he had appeared.

Devon scuttled back from the crumbled rock pile, keeping the chewed-up boulder between him and the ZSU-23. *Time to go.* He stumbled to his feet, turned and ran, head down into his shoulders while ricochets screamed around his ears, beginning to drag his wounded leg across the packed sand. Devon kept running, afraid to touch his thigh for fear of what he'd find.

His desert camo flop hat flew off as he ran. The desert air blew cold through his short stubble of black hair as he gathered speed. *Fucking pride.* The Frenchman had worn his beret on this mission, true commando-style, so Devon had left his Kevlar helmet back on his cot. *Lot of damn good it does me now.*

The ground suddenly sloped out from under his feet. He slammed into the bottom of a depression. Crawling to the lip of a shallow gully, he realized he had stumbled into a shallow ditch running along the edge of the road. A dew-damp layer of pot-holed asphalt glittered in the flames, snaking out across the desert. In the distance, a pair of headlights careened toward him.

"Turn the truck around, Akmed," he whispered. "Nothing here any good for Injun, white or Iraqi."

But the truck continued toward him, steady on the asphalt. Balloon-sized tracers floated over Devon's head as the ZSU slewed around. Devon willed the truck to stop, but knew the Iraqi gunners would shoot at anything moving across the desert. Closer and Devon could see it was a civilian pickup wandering where it shouldn't be.

Cannon fire raked into the truck, exploding parts into the air. The rear wheels seemed to disappear, then the cargo compartment disintegrated into fragments. What was left skidded directly toward him, leaving a trail of sparks on the road. The riddled cab slid to a stop about ten meters away, then toppled onto its side.

Devon scrabbled backwards and huddled on the bottom of the ditch. The hair on the back of his neck stood stiff as the heavy smell of spilled gas flowed down into the depression.

A final burst of machine gun fire raked the underside of the truck. Green tracers ricocheted, screaming off the asphalt, and ignited the spilled gas. Flames licked along the sand, then, with a *whoomp*, the gas tank exploded. Devon threw his hands over his head as a wall of fire roared overhead, singeing the hair from his arms. He gagged as a dark cloud of smoke followed the flames over the ditch. Smoke obliterated the stars, replaced by the green snap of tracers slicing through the boiling smoke.

Small-arms fire from the Iraqis behind him intensified. Time had long since run out. Devon crawled back to the edge of the ditch closest to the highway.

Two people rushed toward him from the dark side of the truck, blocking his escape. One was a blur of flowing robes, the other a silhouette in shirt and pants. Devon triggered off a quick burst from the M-16, downing the one in pants. The remaining one hurtled toward him.

His rifle stopped firing, jammed or empty. He flung it to the ground. When he looked up, folds of the robe blotted out the stars. Devon reached for his knife.

Finish this one the right way, he thought.

His heart raced as the robed one dove on top of him with a high-pitched scream, arm swinging in a great arc toward his head. A brilliant flash strobed through his head and a kick to his side took his breath. Devon twisted and turned, trying to avoid the pelting blows, tangled in the robe.

His fingers finally closed around his knife, but the desert night had gone totally black. Was he blind from the blow? He blinked at the sandy grit in his eyes and shoved his attacker away. Maybe he was nothing more than a desert mouse after all, and the owl had come to feed him to her brood.

Devon worked his knife free and, half-blind, stabbed out. He connected, ignoring the numbness creeping toward his hips, then slashed upward against the falling figure. The serrated blade slid through flesh and grated over bone when he twisted and pushed the blade. Feeling his attacker pull back, he grunted with the effort, jamming home the blade, slicing through the folds of cloth until the screaming stopped and his attacker fell away against the other side of the gully. Devon shoved himself up and looked around.

The scream wasn't right. He shook his head and wiped at his eyes until he could see through the flickering firelight and blur of pain. A woman lay across from him, her robe bunched up around her waist, long, dark hair twisted around her face. He crawled across the sand and leaned close to her face.

A smell of burnt flesh, no sign of breath, and a stillness that spoke death.

Devon scrambled on his hands and knees up the bank to the other body lying in the road, the one he had cut down with the rifle.

All he found was a boy, a child, lying on the cold asphalt, still breathing.

"*Ummak?*" The voice was so soft, like the boy was asking for a glass of milk.

Devon picked him up and stood, looking around for help.

A burst of machine gun fire from the Iraqi position dug into the ground between him and the burning truck. He ran back for the ditch and slid down beside the dead woman, the boy in his arms. Devon coughed, stifled by the smells in the depression.

The boy's eyes shimmered in the firelight, dilated, huge circles of white with unfathomable darkness in their centers. He turned his head toward the woman, then reached out to touch her face.

"*Ummak,*" he cried again. The cry turned to a shriek, then a wail that cut through all the background cacophony of gunfire and exploding fuel tanks and burning trucks.

"Dear God, please, help me." Devon stared down at the boy. The boy's small hand clutched at the woman's hair. "Don't let him die."

The boy shuddered in his arms and murmured something undecipherable. His hand fell away from the woman's face and his eyes turned back to Devon.

"*Walidak?*" His voice was a wisp of the wind. The boy trembled in Devon's arms and then became very still, eyes wide, staring past Devon up into the night.

Devon looked up into the sky. “No...no, God, no...” His appeal turned to a scream of his own.

A deep voice interrupted. “Let him go, Chief. He’s dead.”

Devon shook his head. He couldn’t see clearly though his left eye. He let Baker take the dead boy from his arms, then lead him at a stumbling run across the ridge and around to the waiting helicopter.

After the Blackhawk had transitioned into level flight, Devon leaned forward on the canvas seat. He let the wind blow the tears and grit from his eyes as the Blackhawk flew over the desert back to the *Al Jouf* Special Operations Forward Operating Base.

Tug. A boy. And the boy’s mother. All dead.

At that moment, Devon truly wished he were back in the swamp, a medicine man with a chant and dried mouse bones, who could bring them all back to life.

He grimaced and raised his hand to his face as he swung his feet to the ground. His forehead was tender with a long, tacky wound where the woman had hit him. The field dressing Baker had wrapped around Devon’s leg was crusty with blood, but he wasn’t sure if it hurt or not, his mind was too numb. On the floor of the Blackhawk, Tuggle’s empty eyes stared into the long night. Devon touched the still face. “How’d Tug get here?” he asked.

“Aragon brought his body to the rally point,” Baker replied.

Devon climbed out of the helicopter, nauseous. “Jesus, I can’t even take care of my own,” he muttered.

Baker grabbed Devon’s arm and pulled him away toward the line of tents. “Come on, Chief. We can’t help Tug anymore. Let the medics take care of him. I know where there’s a case of beer. Aragon will tell the debriefers all they need to know. The rest is war shit. It’s just gonna happen.”

Aragon walked by with an American officer in tow, both laughing as the French lieutenant made shooting motions. Apparently there were no dead sergeants or civilians in Aragon’s account, just heroes.

Devon wished he could dance around, whoop a little, celebrate the kills, but all he could think about was Tuggle’s freckles, the boy’s cry into the dark night and the smell of burnt flesh.

“You pray much, Bert?”

“Shore. Every time I get back to Savannah, my daddy tries to make me a deacon or something in the AME church.” Baker chuckled, a low rumble in his gut. “But I always get too busy with Clara—she’s my wife, you know—trying to make my Junie Bug a brother to spend much time down at the church.

"'Sides, the chaplain out at the Hunter Army Air Field married me and Clara, so I don't got too much invested in the old AME." Baker smiled at him. "But you gotta pray, Chief, just in case, you know." He pointed up into the desert night. "The Lord, He looks down all of us, black, white, Muslim or good, old African Methodist Episcopalian, don'cha know." Baker took a deep breath. "Damn war. I need to get home. Junie, she's going to be finished with high school soon. But the Lord will see us through this."

Overhead, a single star shown through the gathering clouds. "Your God ain't mine, Bert, not no more." Devon pulled off the bloody parka and pitched it in a trash barrel. *Enough of the desert.* He wished he were back in the Carolina swamps with his grandma's pine tar remedies. Anything to clear the smells out of his head. Dead soldiers, dead kids.

God damn the Tuscarora, their chants and war dances. He went prancing out on the battlefield, and what happened? He lost a man. He would never be a warrior, just another country boy out where he shouldn't be.

CHAPTER 3

Riyadh, Saudi Arabia, 2001

Drunk and in an off-limits area. If he cared, he couldn't remember why. It was a party. He couldn't even remember who invited him; how he had gotten past the guards at the entrance to the King Fahad National Guard Hospital.

When the Patriot Battalion Intelligence Officer slid her brown T-shirt up over her head, her body heat washed down over Devon like smoke from a fire. Devon tried to think through the bourbon haze. *What's her name? Susi? No, Susanne, Susanne with a southern lilt.*

Now he remembered. He had been invited by an advisor to the Saudi National Guard, a civilian contractor, ex-armor guy. Somehow Devon had been swept away from the main party by Susanne and her bottle of bourbon.

He looked up from where she had him pinned to the narrow bed in the nurses' living quarters, his blood rising as the muscular woman arched her back, reached behind and unsnapped her bra. She let it fall, then leaned forward, sweeping her breasts across his chest.

"Are your wife's as nice as these?" she asked, voice husky in the dim light filtering through the heavy drapes. She reached down and unbuckled his belt.

Devon took a warm, soft breast in each hand, thinking back as the nipples firmed against his touch. "No. Rachel's kinda thin. Skinny. And she's an ex. She divorced me, years ago, not long after the war."

The contraband bourbon had taken control as he let Susanne pull off his pants. She pressed against him, warm body soft, pushing him down into the narrow bed. She kissed his upper lip, then his lower, brushing her tongue over his, satiating him with the smell of bourbon, a distant reminder of fermenting corn mash. Susanne's hot breath reminded him of burning oak, with smoke drifting soft in the before-dawn gray light of the swamps where the Lumberton moonshiners fired their stills.

"Couple of drinks and y'all not much help, are you?" Her soft voice was distant, almost apologetic as she slid her fingertips along his cheekbones.

"Sorry, Susanne." His time to be apologetic, but his body couldn't warm to the task after all the booze the woman had poured down him. "Thought I could do better." Her Charleston drawl had intrigued him at the battalion party, and blinded him to whatever else was going on.

He waited naked, numb—at least in body—as she leaned over him.

"You ain't going to be no fun at all." She got up and gathered up a handful of clothes. "Sorry, Nash. Thought maybe there'd be something in this for both of us before we had to get down to business."

Somewhere far off he imagined hearing her unlock the door and whisper in the dark.

Suddenly, the door flew open, and hands grabbed him and slammed him, naked, to the floor. Several men in American desert fatigues stood over him pounding, kicking. He tried to fight back, but knew he was in the Lumberton jail and the bootleggers had finally caught up with him. Someone screamed out in the hall. Just as suddenly, the men left.

Arabic voices boomed through the partially open door as Devon struggled into his clothes. Cold sober, he yanked on the window. No luck...it was sealed shut against the blowing sand. He peeked into the hall. *No one. Yet.* He thought he had come down the hall past a tall ficus in a pot, remembered it brushing his face.

In the opposite direction, a fire door slowly creaked shut. He sprinted down the hall and kicked the door open. A burst of desert heat and blowing sand cleared his head.

Outside, like most of Riyadh, he stood on the edge of the desert. Someone behind him yelled. He turned to catch a fleeting glimpse of two men with long staves, untrimmed beards and calf-length robes. The *muttawas*, Saudi religious police, burst into the room he had just left.

Images of the long runs across the swamp floated through his head as he stumbled down into a *wadi*, disconnected to what his body was doing—memories of the Locklear boys, his full-blooded Lumbee second cousins, all screwed up after a night on 'shine, bruised and beat up after being thrown in the Lumberton jail.

After seeing them dumped off at his house by the sheriff, Devon, all of ten years old, had pretended he was some kind of avenger with his one-boy, early dawn, still-busting raid. He had slipped through the swamp, silent as any snake, and sneaked up to the big still gurgling over an open fire. He'd pulled the vat plug, then ran like the devil while the fermenting mash spewed across the black swamp humus.

Bellowing 'shiners had crashed through the woods behind him, adding speed to his barefoot sprint along the winding game trails that led from the deep swamp to the cornfields. Hungry and briar-scratched, he'd hidden astraddle the cross tiers in the top of a deserted tobacco barn until the cursing 'shiners gave up the chase.

He had been so proud—one kid fighting back against the boot-leggers nobody else in the whole county seemed to care about—sheriff or preacher. He'd summoned the black bear from within his own Injun soul, unleashed the avenger, and spilled the evil spirits before they could make it to their Mason jars.

Now he was on the run again. Not in the swamp, where the black bear raged. Tonight, he ran through the desert where he had lost his soul to the crow. Maybe, if he ran far enough, he would find the hawk, soaring free in the desert. He stumbled down into a palm grove and stopped, feet damp as he splashed through a shallow stream. An oasis.

Dear God. He watched a snake slither onto the bank and away from him. *I've fallen to the land of the snakes to pay for my sins.*

He wasn't sure of the time. Someone had crunched his Timex between their heel and the King Fahad National Guard Hospital's polished marble floor. He had made his way back to his quarters just before sunup and showered, just in time for a knock on the door.

A sleepy-eyed duty officer stood in the hall. "Major, you got a message from the military attaché over at the U.S. Embassy. Wants you to see him first thing."

Devon thanked him with an inward sigh of relief. After last night's escapade, he had expected the military police. With luck, his new assignment had finally been approved. At least at the embassy he should be safe from avenging boyfriends or whoever the hell had given him such a beating.

The Saudi police who screened the entrance to the diplomatic quarter didn't give him a second look when he drove past. The Filipino guards manning the outer gate to the American Embassy compound just smiled and told him to wait.

Apparently access was by invitation only. His dusty uniform and military ID weren't enough, even after the call from the attaché's office. Finally, the guard at the embassy's outer gate waved him toward the main entrance. There a second guard kept him waiting in the shade of a tall palm. Devon gradually desiccated in the dry heat until a swarthy Marine finally came out for him.

He followed the Marine through the embassy's main entrance. Inside, he had to lean his thigh against the edge of a table to steady himself and take several deep breaths to flush out the remaining alcohol fumes stagnating his lungs. He blinked back the swirling spots, head down, until he realized a pair of glossy, black shoes had come into his range of vision. He rocked back on his heels, comparing his scuffed desert boots with the shiny shoes of the young Marine in dress uniform until a voice boomed into his head.

"Ready to go, sir?" the Marine asked.

Devon slowly looked up so his head wouldn't fall off his neck and grinned. "Sure. Lead on."

The Marine waved him through the metal detector screening further access into the embassy. Suddenly, it screamed at him, high-pitched beeps piercing deep into his hangover. He reached into his pocket and handed the guard his pocketknife, his old single-bladed Case, then automatically stepped back and forward again through the detector.

"You can pick up the blade when you leave, Major." The Marine ran his hand under his desk edge, mercifully quieting the alarm, then dropped the knife into a drawer.

Devon nodded. He'd give up the old knife if that's what it took to turn off the alarm. "No problem. Sorry 'bout that."

At least the lobby was cool, with a deceptive view of running water splashing over dusty plants and tall palms in the garden on the other side of a tall glass wall. His previous knowledge of Saudi was all sand and desert, hot days and cold nights. Inside the lobby, the whisper of the air conditioning held the hundred-plus temperature on the other side of the glass at bay.

"Major. Over here, sir." Another Marine behind a plate glass ticket window called him over, waving a card behind the partition like a ticket seller at a movie. "Here's your pass, sir. Return this when you leave and exchange it for your ID." The Marine slid a numbered card under the partition in exchange for Devon's military ID and pointed at a buzz-cut Marine waiting by an open door, the one who had first brought him inside. "Corporal Gonzales will show you to Colonel Houston's area. Have a nice day, sir."

Corporal Gonzales led him up a set of stairs and through a locked doorway. Devon wondered if the kid knew what was going on. The enlisted grapevine was always better than a bulletin board.

"Saudi pretty good duty, Corporal?" Devon asked.

The swarthy Marine shook his head. "Sucks, Major. No women and no beer—that you can talk about. Only good thing we got here is downtime in Europe. R and R'ed to Spain last year, sucked up a whole lotta of wine and talked Castilian like my momma always wanted." He held open another door for Devon, now completely lost in the maze of offices, and glanced up at Devon's swollen cheek. "You box, sir? We got a pretty good bunch here to spar with." The Marine dropped into a fighter's stance and feinted a left jab, dancing down the aisle. "Probably a few in your weight class…what, one-seventy-five or so?"

"Nope." Devon had to laugh, even though it hurt his ribs. "Getting too close to one-ninety for comfort, plus I never was much with gloves. Lately seems like I ain't been too good without them either." *Especially after being stomped against the concrete floor.* "Besides, I think I'm on my way somewhere else."

Corporal Gonzales grinned and shook his head. "Ain't that always the way, sir." He pointed toward a receptionist guarding a row of doors. "Colonel Houston's down the hall, through the open door, just past the good looker. Your lucky day, Major."

The receptionist smiled up at Gonzales. He snapped to attention and grinned at Devon.

The receptionist's blond hair was in a twist, pinned tightly to the top of her head, not a strand out of place. Her makeup was so subtle she looked like a natural beauty, until Devon stopped in front of her desk. Then he saw the too-broad nose and weather lines around her eyes and wide smile.

"Major Devon." Her smile slid away as she read his nametape on the dusty fatigues. "Colonel Houston's waiting for you." Her accent hinted at Jersey and smoky refineries, with maybe a touch of Harlem.

Without a look back, she led the way down a narrow side hall. Gonzales gave a tiny shrug and a grin that implied Devon was in officer's quarters now, out of his hands.

Devon returned Gonzales' grin and followed the woman. Nice tight skirt. Too tight to wear off the diplomatic quarter where the religious police would rap her butt with their canes, or maybe worse if they took a notion. Saudi was not for the carefree. He had gotten an unexpected reminder the night before.

"Hi, I'm Nash Devon." He held out his hand when she stopped at a closed door. She was a head shorter than he, full-busted, maybe a little too heavy, broad across the shoulders, with dusky skin like she spent a lot of time in the sun. Her hand was soft as she gave his a quick shake, then dropped it like he might have some illness.

"Birdi Flowers, glad to meet youse," she answered, her voice echoing a bit of a chill to match the air conditioning whispering from the vents.

Oh, my goodness, Devon thought. The "youse" was definitely Jersey City.

Devon sensed she might be glad to meet him, but she probably didn't want to know him. And now he had confirmed her Jersey accent, he wasn't as interested either. Big boobs and tight skirts weren't quite everything. But times might change. Flowers motioned him into the next office, flashed an official smile, and left him standing inside a ten-by-ten office. A desk dominated the center of the room, surrounded by safes and file cabinets. A familiar face grinned at him.

"Hi, Nash. Sit down. Be just a minute." The man seated at the desk ran his hand over a perfectly slick head as he talked to someone over a red secure phone.

The plaque on the desk said Colonel Ronald X. Houston, USAF, with navigator wings on each side. In-flight photos of Air Force heavy cargo aircraft—a C-141 over the Egyptian pyramids, massive C-5s and KC-10s—covered the short wall, floor-to-ceiling between two file cabinets. On the desk next to the secure telephone was a close-up of the crew posed under the front hatch of one of the National Emergency Airborne Command Post—NEACAP—birds, converted Boeing 747s specially suited-out for the president back when the Cold War was still overt. A younger, but still bald Houston's head in the center of the photo made him easy to identify, kneeling in front of President Bush, the elder.

Devon wondered if the attaché job had been a promotion for Houston or, like Devon's pending assignment to the United Nations Special Commission in Iraq, an end-of-the-road assignment for screw-ups. Nice enough desk and sex pot secretary so, for whatever reason, it had to be tolerable.

Devon doubted his assignment to the newly formed UN Monitoring, Verification and Inspection Commission, the acronym a Slavic-sounding mouthful—UNMOVIC—would be as tolerable. Searching for nuclear weapons wouldn't be a lot of fun—especially in a place where they hated you. Even more than the Saudis did, deep in their white-robed hearts.

"You're late, Nash." Ron Houston stood and held out his hand. "Enjoying the party circuit? You look like you've put on a little weight since Norfolk."

Devon looked up from the photos. Houston would be one to remember how trim he had been, not so many years ago. His bruised shoulder silently screamed at him when he reached out to shake Houston's hand. "Yeah, having a real good time here. Sorry I'm late. Busted my watch last night."

Devon felt a hint of a blush under his collar as he tried to match Houston's neutral tone. At least the purple boot marks didn't show, and the pillow party hadn't taken out any teeth.

"How's Rachel doing?" Houston sat back down behind the desk. "Still with Defense Intelligence Agency?" he asked.

Devon took a deep breath, knowing he had to get past this, and nodded. "Yeah, she's gone career with them, GS-11 the last I heard. You couldn't get her out of DC with a bomb." Might as well say it, since Houston probably already knew. Spooks were like that—talked all around what they knew, just to see what you would say. "But we're divorced. She left me three years ago, so you probably know more about her now than I do."

Houston's eyebrows went up. "No? That right? Well, at least I don't have to get personally excited about last night's report from the Riyadh police—at least about the adultery charges. But the police superintendent himself queried the embassy security liaison this morning about a drunken brawl in the nurses' quarters. Women of loose morals, alcohol, all the things that ring the *muttawas*' bells and get the royal family's attention."

Devon took a deep breath and let the blush rise up from his desert fatigues.

"But you really have screwed up your chances of going to the weapons inspection team. Moot point, though. Iraq's still not accepting the new team. Seemed they had their fill with the old USCOM guys. Between pressure from the French, the Russians and the chicken-shit guys advising the old White House, State Department gave up on the original team. So you think they are going to take you? No way," he said with a grunt that passed for a laugh if you knew Houston that well.

Houston's eyes never wavered from Devon's face; his neutral look never deviated toward smile or frown. He was a good navigator—and a better poker player. On his side, Devon knew he wore his soul on the surface. Hiding emotion was never in him; that part he inherited from his Scotch-Irish grandfather. So yeah, he drank and screwed around, and a hell of a lot of the rest of the world knew it. But he still hadn't figured out what had happened the night before.

"State kicked back your assignment this morning. With all the crap they're going through in Iraq, they don't want a drunken pussy-hound dancing around Baghdad, if Hussein should ever decide to let them in. Which really leaves you in limbo."

Devon closed his eyes at the verbal slap, then relaxed and finally nodded in agreement.

"What went wrong, Nash?" Houston asked. He finally frowned—at the cold coffee he had just sipped. "When we were at the Staff College, everything seemed fine. You were a war hero and Rachel was as proud as she could be of you. Seemed to me like she was even in love. Now you're divorced. Hard to believe."

Devon shrugged. "Those were good times. But Rachel wanted kids." He tried to wash the grimace from his face, pained by the words. "I didn't. Simple."

"So now you work out your frustrations on female Patriot battalion staff officers." Houston shook his head. "The way I read the report, you'll be lucky if she doesn't file charges." He flipped though a thick file. "Be glad your assignment came from the State Department, not the Pentagon. You better hope the Central Command crowd doesn't figure out your chain of command before I get you out of here. The prince that heads up the National Guard and the Interior Minister are probably debating who'll get the biggest chunk of your ass."

Devon didn't answer. He didn't know exactly what had happened either, and, in fact, had wondered the same thing ever since he woke up, bruised and battered after the one-sided drunken brawl following the party. Or what he thought was a brawl. All he could remember was getting the crap beat out of him, and high-tailing it through the desert. Past that, he didn't have a clue. Or who had sicced the *muttawas* on him.

"And you look like shit," Houston added.

Devon didn't need Houston to tell him. He could feel it.

"Hair's so damned long you'll be able to braid it pretty soon." Houston wouldn't let it be.

Devon clenched his jaw and ran his hands through his black hair, shaggy on the sides, but still not as long as most Air Force wienies wore theirs. If they had any.

"You letting that Cherokee thing get to you?" prodded Houston.

"Lumbee, not Cherokee. And it's not getting to me," Devon shot back.

He fought to keep his face neutral and looked into Houston's eyes. If Houston wanted him to lose his composure, he was pretty close on target. Devon bit off the rest of his angry reply and waited for Houston to get to whatever the point of this meeting was.

"Ever see *The Godfather*?" Houston held up a folder, Devon's name written in broad felt-tip across the front. "I've got an offer you can't refuse. You sure as hell can't stay here in Saudi. As soon as the folks down at the Ministry of Defense and Aviation hear about an American in a drunken brawl in their backyard, you're out of the country.

"If anyone cares, you'll be enjoying the facilities at their social reformatory facility over by King Khalil Air Base." He threw the folder on the desk. "And believe me, they probably already have the hooded guy who chops off heads warming up. If you were a woman, they'd have you in the park stoning you to death already."

Devon nodded in agreement. He wasn't drunk now, and he knew how the Saudis dealt with inebriated Westerners. "What happened to Susanne? Is she in trouble?" asked Devon.

"Her boss got her on an Air Force bird heading to Frankfurt last night. She was long gone before the Saudis could latch onto her. I had our folks looking for you last night, too. You better think about yourself, buddy." Houston paused for a moment and looked at him. "I do have a quick way out. Special deal from the ambassador. Bypass the Army brass and the Saudis. You up for it?"

"Ron, this is bullshit. Some gal I'd never met before dragged me into a dark room and boozed me up. Don't I get to say my piece?" Devon tried to keep the pleading out of his voice.

Houston shook his head. "The feedback I get is that the lady in question…Susanne, you called her? Oh, look." Houston held up a sheet of paper. "Susanne has been convinced she should file charges." He smiled for the first time, half a grin, half a grimace. "Something like date rape."

"God damn it!" Devon cut off his rebuttal when Houston held up his hand.

"Nash, I don't want to even hear about it." Houston folded his hands and leaned back in his chair, waiting. "This is straight from the ambassador. You get a choice. Take my offer, his offer, or you're *persona non grata* under guard and on the next Air Mobility Command flight out."

Devon knew someone had stacked everything too high for him to even see over. He swallowed down some of the bile and irritation. "Okay. Whatever you say, Ron. I'm good to go."

"Fine. 'Go' is the operative word. Now let's get you ready." Houston pulled out a sheaf of papers.

"Don't I get to know what? Or where?" Devon held his hands out, palms up, half in surrender, half-questioning. "With whom?" he asked.

Houston's smile began to spread across his face. "Only if you agree to accept."

Devon was trapped. A trap of his own making. "Pig in a poke?"

Houston's bald pate wrinkled with his growing grin, obviously more amused than Devon. "Our Muslim friends might not think too highly of your analogy, but the short answer is yes."

Devon stared down at his scuffed boots. Boots were all he had worn since he was a kid—work boots, combat boots, jungle boots, now desert boots—with very few exceptions. Like the all-too-short stint at the Armed Forces Staff College where he and Rachel had truly enjoyed being together in the Army and meeting people from the other services, like Ron and his wife, short-lived as that happiness had been. But bootsville was all he really knew or desired.

Houston waited, elbows on his desk, fingers steepled under his chin as Devon searched his mind for any but the obvious answer to where he was going. Hell, Ron wouldn't send him to Siberia. He was a friend. Devon felt a nervous grin blossom. "Sure, why not?" he finally said. Friends took care of friends.

"Good decision. Now let me tell you what a great deal I've got for you." Houston shut the office door, then pulled a map out of the desk drawer and spread it over the desktop.

Devon frowned. It wasn't a military topographic map, all meters and contour lines, but one of the guides you could buy at a street stall, hotels and museums. The label on the slick cover said "A Tourist's Guide to Mesopotamia."

"A tourist guide?" Devon shook his head. "I don't really want to go on a tour." The map started at the edge of the Mediterranean Sea and outlined the rivers and roads over to where Iran touched Afghanistan. "Especially to those countries."

"Just listen, Nash." Houston pulled a pair of glasses from the clutter on the desk, slid them over his nose and leaned close to the map. "See this town at the end of the rail line?" Houston traced a heavy line running northwest from Baghdad to where the colors on the map indicated the mountains began, finally thumping the map at a small dot at the end of the line.

Devon bent his head down next to Houston's, squinting at the small print beside the dot. "Irbil," he spelled out. "Then next to it the map says 'Arble' with an 'A.' Can't they make up their minds? What's there you care about?"

"Your future home. At least to start." Houston leaned back in his chair. "The UN High Commission for Refugees has an operations center there. Primarily support for the Kurds. Refugees have been flocking there for years, running from Turks, Iranians, Iraqis, and now the fundamentalists streaming in from Afghanistan, these Taliban guys. UNHCR's charter is to provide support for the refugees."

He bent over the map again to slide his finger along a dashed horizontal line just below Irbil. "This marks the thirty-sixth parallel, southern boundary of the no-fly zone, officially the northern Iraqi safe haven zone. The Iraqis aren't supposed to conduct military operations north of the line, so we shoot at anybody who paints one of our birds. Therefore, in our own way, we manage to add to the refugee flow."

Devon wondered what all this had to do with Houston and airplanes and, most importantly, him. "So? What do you have to do with Iraq? What do I?"

Houston tapped the bright floral print tie partially covering the food stains on his white shirt. "Your duty, partner. Comes with the uniform." He smoothed the crease from the map sheet with his index finger. "I was counting on you understanding. Or at least recognizing the consequences." The smile was completely gone.

Devon nodded. And understood. Or thought he understood, especially since Houston wasn't wearing a military uniform, but the button-down shirt and tie of a good military attaché. Houston was referring to the Duty, Country, Honor, supposed to be inside all soldiers, even if Devon had blown the honor part. He bent over the map and tried to focus on Houston's words.

"See this string of hills stretching across from Irbil to Mosul to the Syrian border?" Houston brushed his hand across the top half of the map.

Devon found the color contours indicating high ground on the glossy map and nodded.

"Somebody in DC thinks the Iraqis have hidden a WMD facility in the mountains," Houston looked up to see if Devon was paying attention.

He was.

"Weapons of Mass Destruction. Nukes, biologicals, chemical weapons? WMD—that's what the UNSCOM guys were supposed to find. I was nixed for the assignment. From what you said, I thought the whole weapons inspection business was dead."

Houston folded the map and slid it back into a desk drawer. "Your background suits you perfectly for the job. Field experience with the Pershing Missile Brigade in Germany, research and development at Fort Sill on the improved accuracy warhead for the Pershing II—"

"Before we traded it off to the Russians to cool down the arms race," Devon interjected.

"Yeah, and it worked—with them. Now we're dealing with Hussein and our old friends the Pakistanis, both trying, for separate reasons, to build the better bomb—and missile to carry it. You're the best short range missile expert in town, and a trained killer to boot." Houston waved his file at him. "Hell, you know Scuds better than anybody outside of Iraq, even blew one up, if all those citation write-ups weren't bull."

Devon waited. He was pretty sure he wasn't going to like life above the thirty-sixth parallel. Mountains too high, temperature too low, and he'd still be in the land of the Koran and prohibition.

"Look," said Houston. "You want to go home? Maybe face charges, if the ambassador has his say. You sure as hell don't want to stay here and let the Saudis get their hands on you. Or do you want to go help the refugees, and maybe kill another even nastier Scud before it gets born?" Houston punched his finger into the desk. "UNMOVIC is dead. God only knows what Saddam's son Qusay and his Apparatus of Special Security have hidden away—nuclear, biological, or chemical. We've run out of ways to find them. Sad as it may be, you seem to be our best hope."

Houston's chair creaked as he leaned back, fingers now steepled over his chest, apparently dead serious.

Devon thought through the alternatives for an instant, then glanced down at his feet. "Do I get to wear boots?"

"Yeah, long as they're work boots and don't say US Army. And you've got to trade those scummy desert fatigues for jeans and denim shirts. It's definitely not a coat and tie job, if that's what you're worried about." Houston ran both hands over his bald head. "Well?" he asked.

Devon shook his head in disgust. He had laid the perfect trap—and caught himself again. "Sign me up," he said.

Houston picked up the phone. "Good." He punched a button. "Birdi, bring in the travel packet for Mr. Devon. The one labeled Walter Raleigh." He laid down the phone and grinned at Devon. "The one with the feathered hatchet on the cover."

As soon as she had delivered the folder and returned to her desk, Birdi Flowers picked up the phone and dialed the Pakistani embassy. "Colonel Khan, please. Tell him Robin calls."

Despite the cool air from the air conditioning vent blowing across the room, she had to pull a tissue from the desktop dispenser and pat the sweat from her upper lip as she waited.

"Yes," a guarded voice answered.

"The American officer's assignment is confirmed. Travel will begin tomorrow."

"Is it Devon, the Pershing missile expert we expected?"

"Yes. He will be traveling as a civilian—a circuitous route to Baghdad, then on to Irbil."

"Excellent. The information will be welcomed in Islamabad. He will receive a proper welcome. Thank you for calling." There was a pause, a slight change in tone. "Will you and I have the opportunity to meet soon?"

She frowned at the phone, then closed her eyes, picturing in her mind the surf breaking along Jersey's Sandy Hook, gulls soaring, the wind in her face, her older brother splattering water in the shallows. Her brother's grin firmly fixed in Flowers' mind, she smiled and replied in a soft voice, "As soon as I can get away. Very soon, I hope."

"I also," replied the voice on the phone.

She looked at the phone in disgust as she hung it up then turned back to the computer to type the request into the intelligence back-channel system to New York. In moments, the system confirmed the assignment of Mr. Nash Devon, dated exactly one month earlier, as an agricultural advisor to the UN High Commission for Refugees, for further duty in the northern Iraqi safe haven zone. And into the hands of the Pakistanis.

She wondered if the sacrifice of the brash American was worth her continuing friendship with the Pakistani colonel. She hoped so. She closed her eyes for a moment. Foolish. She knew it to be so. Any measure that could assist in the compromise of the new *Ahad* was worth many lives, including her own.

Buried deep in the National Security Agency complex at Fort Meade, Maryland, one of the analysts sitting in front of a computer jerked his head up from the *Washington Post* sports section. Several lines of text flashed on his monitor, just above two new message windows. He folded the paper and stuffed it under his monitor, then called out across over the hum of hard drives and CPU fans. "Mr. Allen, come look at this, please."

Russell Allen, NSA's Echelon Operations Center Duty Officer, walked over and stood behind the analyst. The first alert window tagged an internal tap of a telephonic exchange in English originating from a known Israeli intelligence operative buried in the American Embassy in Riyadh.

An intercept of the satellite link of one side of a call from the Pakistani Embassy in Riyadh to Islamabad, the capital of Pakistan generated the second.

The analyst pointed out the words 'Robin' and 'Pershing' flashing red in both of the side-by-side windows. At the top of the screen the code word 'Rosemary' popped up, with a terse set of instructions.

"We don't want to get bit on the butt over this one again," Allen muttered as he scanned the two intercepts and checked the standing instruction in regard to that particular combination. He leaned over and pointed out a name mentioned several times in the call to Islamabad. "Add the surname 'Olanti' to the Rosemary alert list. Looks like another member of *Ahad.* I expect our friends over at the National Military Command Center will want to see this one."

The analyst highlighted the name and added it to the data list on the sidebar, then carefully scanned the messages for anything else of interest. He pointed at the instructions. "Pop it on over to the NMCC—to the Defense Intelligence Agency desk?"

Allen shook his head. "Let me finish reading. We damn near lost our ass over the Indian-Pakistani weapon test thing. National Security Advisor wienies, CIA…none of those jerks paid attention to their mail, then blamed us for missing the underground test.

"One DIA desk officer, Major Lester Fowler, was the only uniform who paid attention, and no one listened to him. Les seems to be the expert on the new Islamic brotherhood, this *Ahad* bunch." Allen, finally satisfied with the results, tapped the analyst on the shoulder. "Send it."

The analyst clicked the block firmly attaching the code word 'Rosemary' to the two messages. The next click forwarded the intercept record to the Defense Intelligence Agency desk fifty miles south around the Beltway in the NMCC officer buried in a sub-basement of the Pentagon.

Allen waited for the acknowledgement line to flash, then picked up his telephone, made sure it was in the secure mode and punched the number for the NMCC desk officer. While Allen waited for an answer, he vividly remembered his personal embarrassment, not so much at the damn reprimand, but that he had blushed beet-red in front of the director. The director had very quietly stared him in the eye and told him that, as far as the White House was concerned, the DIA's failure to provide early warning had seriously jeopardized out-year funding for the Echelon project.

Allen didn't need the director to remind him money was the key to all secrets, and, in the case of the National Security Agency, his job. This time he wanted to make sure the seldom-used code word was recognized.

"Not on my watch—again," he muttered, waiting for the secure phone to synch with its mate in the Pentagon.

The phone finished its warbling and made the connection. "Les. This is Russ Allen, Echelon Ops. Got something on your Rosemary coming over. Something important."

CHAPTER 4

Immediately after noon prayers, one tick on the clock around which all Muslim activities revolved, Corporal Gonzales drove Devon to the *al Batha souk* and led him through the maze of stalls to buy a soft duffel bag, work boots, old American jeans and threadbare chino shirts at designer prices. Devon paid for the jeans and looked at the wad of riyals left over.

"Know where I can get a cheap watch?" Devon asked. Not that he needed to make reveille or anything, but he missed his old Timex, and it would be nice to know what time it was.

"In here." Gonzales led him to a small shop off the alley. Glistening watches lined the display case, glittering under the overhead lights. A huge Rolex dominated the display.

Devon shook his head. "Nothing this expensive. Does he have something plastic, digital?"

Gonzales laughed. "They're all knock-offs, Major. The works are supposed to be made in Switzerland and assembled in South China or somewhere."

Devon pointed at a Rolex, a Submariner with a big, black face. "How much?" he asked the shopkeeper, a young Saudi in flowing white robes.

The shopkeeper pushed back his *ghutra*, the traditional checkered red-and-white headdress, as he looked back and forth between Devon and Gonzales, then nodded, very seriously, as if this were a major transaction. "Three hundred riyals." The price was a statement, but with a lilt of a question, enough that Gonzales apparently recognized the invitation to haggle and jumped in.

Gonzales shook his head. "Nah. Way too much, man." He took the watch from the shopkeeper and turned it over. "This looks like one of them cheap twenty-one jewel tickers." He held it up to his ear, then handed it to Devon. "If you like it, offer the gentleman two hundred, 'bout thirty-three US dollars. It'll keep time, but ain't any big deal."

Devon held the watch to his ear. Heavy, he would have never suspected it to be counterfeit. So much for his clandestine credentials. "A copy, huh?"

"Oh, no, no. This is a very nice watch. It will keep excellent time," the storekeeper argued and pointed at the band. "See. The classic Rolex safety latch on the clasp." He took the watch back, held it for a moment, and then smiled. "Okay. Two-fifty."

"Got to get rid of this stuff somehow." Devon pulled out a wad of bills.

As they left the shop, the courtyard filled with men hurrying toward the nearby mosque.

"Prayer time. We got to get out of here before they close the gate." Gonzales led him back to the parking lot almost at a run as the call to prayers wailed came from the speakers high overhead. Gonzales steered the big Suburban out of the parking lot and down an empty *Al Malek Abdul Aziz* Road as the call to prayer echoed through the city.

The corporal glanced over when they passed the big Ministry of Defense and Aviation complex, Saudi Arabia's equivalent of the Pentagon. "You aren't on a wanted poster anywhere, are you, sir?" Gonzales's face was dead serious.

"Not yet. Or at least nobody warned me if I was."

Had Gonzales picked up something he hadn't? Was somebody in a strange uniform going to be waiting between here and the airport?

They pulled past the guard into the compound and parked by his billets. The sun burned a fiery red over the compound wall—a fitting end to a shitty day. Normally sun-baked, today Riyadh reflected his mood, black clouds building overhead, an unusual dampness in the air.

"I won't be long, Corporal. Give me time to change into these civvies and we'll be on our way."

Gonzales joined him on the sidewalk with an empty box under his arm. "Sorry, Major. Colonel's orders. I stay with you. Excuse me for saying, sir, but you must've got yourself in a pile of shit."

"Yeah. You pretty much got it right," Devon replied.

Inside the room, he pulled his uniforms off their hangers and started to throw them into the bag.

"Hold it, Major. The colonel said just the civvies. Everything else stays." Gonzales flashed his big smile and held out the box. "'Course you get to keep the watch."

"You do much work for Colonel Houston?" Devon had quickly realized Gonzales was a lot more than just a driver.

Gonzales grinned. "A little—special assignments. He promised to hook me up with the right people the end of this hitch. I love the Corps, but not embassy duty so much. The colonel gives me a chance to get out in the streets, move around, get stuff done. You know...kind of on the edge of black ops, clandestine stuff."

Devon wondered what Gonzales knew about black ops. No use trying to work the kid. Gonzales only knew what Houston wanted him to know.

Devon changed into jeans and a polo shirt, tossed his fatigues into the box and watched Gonzales pack away the rest of his military career, topped off by his desert boots. When everything was cleared from the room, Devon let Gonzales lead the way into a rare rain that had dropped the temperature from over a hundred down to the nineties. He wondered if this would be his last trip to Saudi. He hoped so.

Quickly, the weather turned uglier, unleashing a heavy desert April rain. Gonzales had to search for the seldom-used windshield wiper switch to clear the sheets of water from the Suburban. The black water swirling along the Saudi roadway reminded Devon of the spring-swollen Lumber River, meandering through the flooded bottoms toward the abandoned Carolina rice fields and salt marshes, and on out to the Atlantic.

Devon patted his shirt pocket. Grandpa's old pipe—the one part of Devon's life salvaged from Gonzales's watchful eyes—was reassuring, the closest thing to family remaining. The stem was Lucite, a '90s replacement, but the bowl was the original, hand-carved briar, gouges and scrapes polished over the years by his grandfather's callused thumb.

Slowed by the flooded underpasses on Riyadh's ring road, midnight and flight time were approaching by the time Gonzales turned into the departures lane at King Khaled International Airport. The box-like Patriot launchers squatting alongside the access road, snouts in the air, mocked Devon in a silent farewell to the Arabian peninsula and another bitter reminder of his loss of control of his life, his future.

Gonzales hurried him through customs. Devon had the distinct feeling the guards were ignoring him, right up to the point the agent took the ticket from Gonzales and saluted him onto the big plane. He sat back into the narrow seat toward the rear of the economy cabin with the mass of workers returning home with their hard-earned wages.

By sunrise he, his seatmates and the rain would be gone from Saudi.

The midnight flight out of Riyadh put him in Heathrow at first light. Outside the sun darted in and out of the clouds, a brilliant day by English standards, he figured, but foggy and chill by his. The dreary atmosphere added to the exhaustion brought on by the midnight flight. After pork-less Riyadh, he queued up for customs, then stopped to indulge himself with an English breakfast complete with eggs, toast, marmalade and greasy link sausages, washed down with three cups of coffee.

As he savored the grease, he watched the international travelers file by, all crusty eyed except for one young woman as alert and crisp as if she had just stepped from a shower. He remembered seeing her on the flight, mysterious in her loose robe and veil. She'd vanished into the tiny airplane lavatory, only to emerge with full makeup, sky blue silk blouse, tight jeans and high heels, ready to party. Not so much a mystery as an enigma, Muslim culture and hypocrisy at its finest.

The bastards had sent him out of Riyadh on Saudi Air, all hot tea and cold water. He eyed the shuttered bar. It was still too early to get a drink. Life had turned vicious. Devon dragged his duffel bag behind him to a soft lounge chair in a deserted corner of the terminal.

An endless line of Boeing 747s mixed with Airbus A300s on the other side of the plate glass windows rolled, one after another, to muted take-offs. Devon bet at least one was heading back to the States, easy connection to Raleigh, but without him. He tossed his bag against the back wall and slumped into a chair, wondering who his contact would be, No use guessing. He closed his eyes to wait.

"Your bag, sir?"

Devon looked up into the face of a stern-faced security guard pointing at his duffle. Devon nodded and pulled the bag into his lap.

"Keep it close by, sir." The guard walked on to be joined by a second, this one a woman, both in sharply creased black pants and shirts and black bullet-proof vests, all color-coordinated with the black sub-machine guns slung across their chests.

Devon stared past them at the fresh-faced woman from his flight as she vanished into a coffee shop. Surely she wasn't his contact.

Devon slid the duffel bag of *souk* clothes to the floor. Well, his contact would just have to find him. He wiggled his toes in his stiff new work boots. He still felt naked without his dog tags. Collected with his ID card by Houston, this was the first time he had traveled without the metal tags around his neck for years. *New clothes, new life.* This spy stuff sucked.

"Mr. Devon." A nasal tone broke into his thoughts. "Nash Devon?"

A man stared down through a pair of tiny eyeglasses at him—three-piece suit and bowler perched on his head, a briefcase in each hand, all at six o'clock in the morning.

"That's me. Who're you?" Devon asked.

"Kilborn is my name. Commission Vice Counsel," Kilborn answered. He smiled for a very brief moment, then sat beside Devon and opened up one of the briefcases. "Let me have your passport, if you please."

Devon stared at Kilborn. *Was this guy for real*? The man acted and sounded like a schoolmaster in an old British movie. Devon just sat there, groggy from the restless fidgeting and thinking that had dominated the all-night flight from Riyadh and the waiting afterward. Then he remembered. Kilborn was the name of the man Houston had said would meet him.

"Come on, old fellow. You have a flight to meet and I must return to Geneva." Kilborn tilted his head toward the woman in the blue blouse standing by the exit, the only person sharing their corner of the lounge. "She is friendly to our service, and will see that no one else will bother us."

Devon fished around in his shirt pocket and handed over the new blue civilian passport provided the evening before by Houston to replace his red official passport.

Kilborn dropped the passport in his briefcase and handed Devon a replacement—this one red again.

"What the hell was wrong with the old one?" Devon asked.

"Had you going the wrong places at the wrong times, old chap."

Devon wondered if Kilborn had picked that line up from the some old movie or if he really spoke that way. Devon opened the new passport. The stats were right—even six feet, black hair, gray eyes. Devon laughed when he flipped over to the photo.

"Is there a problem?" asked Kilborn.

Devon shook his head. "No, no problem." A younger, slimmer him stared back from the photo. This photo was so old his hair was still coal black and even longer than it was now. It must have been taken when he was in grad school. The back pages were filled with smudged entrance and exit stamps, but the face was right, even in the old photo—wide cheekbones, heavy dark eyebrows. Ugly son-of-a-bitch.

"No real spooky stuff? Not changing my name?"

"I don't think a name change would be advisable, Mr. Devon. We didn't want to burden you with too much tradecraft at this stage of the game.

A game?

"Your tickets are in here." Kilborn handed him a worn briefcase. Not brushed aluminum like the one in which Kilborn had thrown Devon's passport, but a scuffed, soft leather case. "Give me your Saudi boarding pass, ticket stubs, anything showing you flew in from Riyadh—including any *riyals*, change or paper."

Kilborn took the handful of change, a wad of wrinkled five-*riyal* notes and the folded Saudi Air boarding pass and tickets vouchers, stuffed them in the aluminum briefcase and snapped it shut. "Now, here's your new history—nothing in writing for you to lose, so listen closely. Last month you returned to New York, were discharged from the military, and accepted a position with UN High Commission for Refugees as an agricultural advisor.

"After a short leave, you flew here from New York en route to Iraq. The tickets and vouchers will confirm your itinerary. From Heathrow, you go to Amman, then by bus to Baghdad. You'll find sufficient pounds sterling in the briefcase to cover your immediate expenses."

"What do I know about being an agricultural advisor? And why a bus?" Devon shook his head at the prospect.

"You really are ignorant about what the High Commission does—and about Iraq—aren't you, Mr. Devon? Your records, on file in the High Commission office in Geneva for all who are nosy enough to read, indicate you're knowledgeable in the basics of farming. I was led to believe that much was accurate."

"Yeah. I grew up on a Carolina tobacco farm. So?" *Where in the devil is this guy going with the farming business?* Devon wondered.

Kilborn continued, "If you've forgotten what you are an expert in, there are some excellent references in the briefcase. As for the bus, in accord with UN directives, all commercial air travel into and out of Iraq is prohibited. I understand the ride from Amman is quite pleasant, about ten hours. And you really should learn something about the country and the political situation." Kilborn shook his head. "But I suppose now is a bit late."

Devon felt the blood climbing up to flush his face. He clenched his teeth, fighting the urge to reach out and grab this Charles Boyer-type by the throat. He leaned over, his face next to Kilborn's. "I'm not a fucking spy, buddy. This is not what I do!"

Kilborn stood, looking down at Devon as he squared his bowler, brim perfectly perpendicular to his stiff back. "Neither am I, Mr. Devon." He gazed at Devon with what appeared to be a hint of sympathy. "But perhaps you should think about what I have said."

Kilborn pushed his glasses high on his nose, still the head master. "I also make the funeral arrangements for our gallant but sometimes ignorant High Commission field workers who meet unfortunate ends. I would rather not see your name in that capacity. A representative will contact you in Irbil. You should not do anything out of the ordinary until then."

Devon bit his cheek to keep from laughing when Kilborn actually tipped his hat. Had this sweetie just threatened him? He needed to brush up on diplomat-speak.

"Good day, Mr. Devon." Kilborn started to turn. He stopped, looked down at Devon's short-sleeved shirt. "It appears to me that you most likely will go back to sleep rather than study the data, so I should warn you. The weather in northern Iraq is still rather chilly this time of the year, especially in the higher elevations. I suggest you spend some of the pounds on something warmer for your travels.

"But you might want to keep the beard—for the warmth, you know. Good luck, old boy." Kilborn tipped his bowler and headed toward the boarding gates without another word.

Devon scratched his day-old growth. Blessed with the dark complexion and hair from his grandma, he was just as confused genetically by the heavy beard inherited from his dad. He could let it grow and use it for a disguise. *The spy kind.* Damn, now he was thinking crazy. But hell, he really was one now. The kind they shot at dawn. He'd really screwed himself into this one. Maybe he should take the old boy's advice.

He checked the ticket and the posted departure times. His flight to Amman, Jordan wasn't due to leave for several hours.

He picked up the briefcase and duffel bag and wandered through the duty-free shops searching for a decent jacket at something less than jet-set tourist prices. In the Harrods shop he found an imitation British commando sweater and something that reminded him of a green canvas bomber jacket, suitably aged.

Crazy. People paid good money for worn looking clothes, like they were either too impatient or too lazy to wear them to that point themselves.

The jacket, heavy socks, a packet of Cavendish pipe tobacco to refill the almost empty pouch, and two plastic bags of underwear joined the clothes from the *souk*. He thought about the desert and picked up two big bottles of water from a concession stand, along with another cup of coffee.

Devon searched out a chair with a bit more padding and plopped down, his duffel and newly awarded briefcase on his lap. Devon glimpsed the flash of a blue blouse and tight jeans mirrored in the plate glass. When he turned to look, the woman hung up a wall phone and quickly strode away. Too bad she was just a watcher. He could use some friendly company.

Someone shook him and he snapped his eyes open. The blue blouse hovered over him, her musky perfume smothering out his sweaty lack of a recent shower.

"Departure time," she said, and once again walked out of his life.

The Royal Jordanian flight was comfortable enough, but there was nothing to drink but orange juice, imitation-tar coffee and his bottled water. Their landing in Amman was delayed by the *sharqi*, the Middle Eastern equivalent of Los Angeles' Santa Ana, blowing sand so thick he couldn't see the city through the haze as they circled.

His bus was one of several vehicles in a convoy. The lead truck sported a machine gun, reminding Devon of the lawless militias enforcing the local version of the law in Somalia. It was after midnight when the convoy left the airport, and he dozed off as they sliced straight across the desert, heading toward Baghdad.

He woke for a moment when the driver blared his horn and swerved the bus across the road. A blur of sand and a wandering camel flashed by in the headlights. For a moment, he thought he was back in Egypt, on the road from the pyramids out to Cairo West airbase. But all too soon he remembered where he was as the bus driver jounced along at breakneck speed, apparently a prerequisite for any Middle Eastern driver.

Devon couldn't get back to sleep as the featureless night flowed by the window, a hint of a camel appearing in the headlights to suddenly whisk away, leaving him to wonder if it had been real or a distant dream.

The bus slowed, pulled off the road and rocked to a stop in the dark. His counterfeit Rolex glowed in the dark. Devon held it up closer to his face. Oh-six-thirty, if it kept accurate time. The handful of passengers stood and shuffled toward the door. Devon pushed himself up and watched them get off. Several wore traditional desert robes. Two in western businessman disguises, but obviously Middle Eastern, followed a couple of real westerners out the door. A tall, slim man got up from behind Devon, leaving him alone on the bus with the driver. The driver, yammering in Arabic, waved for him to get off.

Devon could hardly stand. *Too many hours riding with no exercise.* Hell, his blood had all coagulated in his feet. He had to pry himself out of the seat. And, he had to admit, the bruises from the blanket party had left their mark. He stepped off, shivered in the morning chill and glanced around. Most of other passengers knelt on small prayer rugs, all in a line facing a wall barely visible in the breaking dawn.

He and the handful of infidels stood listening to the prayers while shafts of orange light streaked the deep black sky, broadening to wide bands of pale gray until the overhead stars vanished. On the horizon, a lone star held on, challenging both the dark and the light until the edge of the sun slid up from the horizon and ruthlessly wiped it away.

The faithful rolled up their rugs as the bottom edge of the sun eased over the distant horizon to reveal a concrete block building in the middle of the desert. A smaller building, which, by the smell, housed the latrines, sat further back off the road. A dust-covered military truck, maybe a Soviet *Ural*, appeared abandoned between the two buildings.

After the passengers had all collected their bags, a sleepy-looking soldier herded them inside. Devon, striding along to get his circulation going, found himself at the end of the queue for a table labeled, "Non-Iraqi Citizens" in English and French, along with a scrawl of Arabic script which he assumed said the same thing.

The line, all men, no women, went quickly. The clerk, dressed in the traditional white *thobe*, the Bedouin's flowing ankle-length burnoose, gave each man a glance and their papers a quick slap of a rubber stamp. He took Devon's brand-newest old passport and deliberately thumbed through the stamps in the back. Devon shivered again, this time not from the chill, but wondering where the stamps said he had been.

The building was open to the desert, but the air was already warming from the long slanted rays of the sun glaring in through the doorway. Sweat trickled down the small of his back as he tried to remember if he had noticed any of the entries when Kilborn had given him the passport.

All he had done was admire his picture, too full of himself to pay attention to what was important. What else had he forgotten or ignored? The other passengers' baggage received a cursory examination at the adjacent table while Devon stood and watched the clerk slide his thumb over each page. In the back of the large room, several soldiers leaned against the wall. Their ubiquitous AKs, the Soviet-designed rifles found all across the Arab world, hung across their chests or stood propped against a wall.

The clerk pounded in a new, illegible stamp and handed him his passport, then motioned him on with a nod of his head. Devon started toward the door, following the other passengers.

"You. Stop!" The command was barked from the back of the building.

Four of the soldiers walked toward him. The one in the lead wore an officer's billed cap and a pistol. He was a stubby bastard, a head shorter than Devon. The other two had swung their AKs off their shoulders.

The officer pointed toward the back of the building. "Bring your luggage for inspection."

Devon followed the officer's directions, trying to keep his emotions in check. What the hell had Kilborn done to him? He relaxed his jaw muscles, even tried a slight smile. He decided that was too hard to do as the soldiers gathered around him. The AK barrels seemed to swing a little more in his direction. A sharp reek wafted into his face when the officer stepped close. Devon bit his tongue to keep from wrinkling his nose. The smell was overpowering. Devon figured the officer stunk of everything he had eaten and touched for the past week.

Desert dust covered the officer's uniform, so filthy Devon could barely make out the pips on his epaulets. Devon decided this one should be named Officer Camel Dung, he smelled so bad.

Under the officer's stare, the other two soldiers emptied Devon's bag and briefcase, shaking out every piece of clothing, even ripping open the plastic bags of underwear. The grease from one of the soldier's hands left prints on the new boxer shorts as he ripped open the plastic and held up each piece for inspection. Devon guessed that one doubled as the unit's truck mechanic. He took a deep breath. 'Let the squirrels chatter in the trees,' grandma would have said. 'They'll be supper soon enough.'

"Empty your pockets," barked the officer and pointed toward the table.

Devon laid his billfold and tobacco pouch on the table, the only personal items left from Kilborn's cleansing.

"What is this?" the officer asked, holding up the leather pouch. He opened the zippered pocket and Devon's worn pocketknife fell out. The officer put one hand on his holstered pistol and stared, hard-eyed, at Devon. "A hidden weapon. This is a very serious matter." He waved at the other two to continue the search. "What else do you have concealed?"

Devon shrugged, trying on his I'm-just-an-amateur-spy-nonchalance, wondering if he looked as dumb to the officer as he felt. Then he decided dumb was okay. With these guys, looking smart was the option that would most likely get him in trouble. And keeping his mouth shut was the only way to say the right thing. Especially since the pouch the officer was trying to rip open with his teeth was genuine pigskin. Just what the true believer needed to know.

The officer ripped apart the pouch seams. Bits of tobacco and Devon's battered briar fell to the table. He threw the ruined pouch to the ground.

Devon reached out his hand for the pipe, and one of the soldiers stopped pawing through his clothes to swing his AK, smashing it against Devon's already-bruised cheek. Pain shot though his face. He gritted his teeth, attempting to hold his anger inside. Devon forced his fists to stay clenched by his side and took a step back from the table.

"Just my pipe," he said, his voice too high. *My granddaddy's pipe.* Devon wiggled his fingers, unclenching his fist and pointed at the pouch. "Tobacco. For smoking. I use the knife to clean the pipe."

The officer picked up Devon's pipe and wrenched the stem from the bowl. He peered through the stem as if he expected to find a secret weapon hidden away. One of the other men stirred a filthy finger through the loose pile of tobacco spilled over the table.

"Were you here before, American? When you killed my brother, when the B-52s bombed and the cruise missiles killed the babies?" asked the officer.

Devon had never mastered stoic. "Yeah, I was here when you invaded Kuwait and stole them blind and raped their women." Shit, if he pissed the officer off, maybe they'd send him back to Jordan.

The officer jerked him away from the table, a damn sight more power in his grip than Devon had guessed. His voice screeched in the small building. "You and your damned arrogance. We have our own laws, our own judges." He quickly glanced around the empty room, then almost smiled at Devon. "Sometimes I am my own court of law." He leaned close, his voice soft, and breathing too much rotten-teeth breath into Devon's face. "Perhaps today is my day to judge," he whispered.

One of the solders nudged the officer, eyes wide as he held one of the books open. The officer snatched it from the soldier and held it in front of Devon. "You may take us for fools, but you and your

United Nations cover will not work with me." Spittle splattered into Devon's face.

Devon focused his eyes on the title page. *The World Factbook* blared out from the page with the CIA logo on the bottom of the page. He snapped his head back as the officer slammed the book shut in his face and threw it across the room. His daddy, the old paratrooper, would have said, 'Smack the son-of-a-bitch cross-eyed.' Instead, Devon tried to slide back as the officer stepped close, but a pair of burly soldiers moved up behind to stop him from backing away. No swamp to run through this morning. No tobacco barns to hide in.

The officer barked a command at the soldiers. Two men grabbed Devon by each arm and hauled him through the back door. The soldiers dragged him down into a *wadi* and slammed him against a crumbling mud wall, pocked with fist-sized holes. The air was brisk, the first touch of sun drying the night dew from the ground and bringing only a hint of the day's coming heat.

The mechanic, with the finesse of a pickpocket, stripped off Devon's pseudo-Rolex, then joined the others, AKs at the ready, to form an impromptu line.

Devon leaned back against the dried mud, grinding his head into the dirt, trying to remember what it felt like to run his fingers through the soft Carolina loam, black with leaf mulch and mud washed up from the Lumber River. He shivered, realizing he was standing in a shallow run of cold water, the last of the melt from the distant mountains.

Over the lip of the *wadi*, the roof of the border station poked into the sky, growing lighter by the moment. A crow swooped down, spreading its wings to glide to the peak where it paced back and forth, wings held out from its body, squawking quietly in the morning stillness, then stopping to stare down at Devon.

He had loved to run through the snake-filled sloughs in an old pair of shorts, tanned shoulders almost black from the sun. One day grandma had warned him crows were lookouts for roaming Tuscarora warriors who'd snatch him out of the swamps and burn him at the stake after taking his scalp. He should have listened.

The dry scrape and metallic clacks of rounds being chambered in dirty weapons broke the sudden silence. The sharp smell of sweat enveloped him; the old sweat and dust smell he still associated with death. He breathed deeply, a full chest of desert air.

What was the old tradition? Silence at the stake? Must be some other tribe, not his family. He wanted to scream in rage.

Devon stared back at the line of soldiers, cold sweat running in a trickle down his sides. No eye contact. Each stood, looking at his weapon, except for the officer, a hint of smile underneath his mustache. In the growing light Devon finally could count the pips on his filthy uniform. A lowly captain was the master of his destiny. Hell, he even outranked the foul-smelling bastard.

The captain's smile changed to a frown when the tall man from the bus slid down the sandy bank, splashed across the water and handed him a folded sheet of paper.

The captain ignored the paper and turned back to Devon. "I will speak in English, so you understand your fate." He turned to the line of men and barked, "Get ready."

They jerked their necks back and stared at him like he was insane until he yelled out a command in Arabic. Then each man snapped to his individual form of attention.

The tall man spoke softly, pointing to the paper in the captain's hand. The captain glanced at it with disgust.

"Aim." Again he followed the English with an Arabic command. The soldiers each took aim at Devon.

Devon raised his head so he could see the sky over the lip of the *wadi*. Flimsy clouds streaked with pink gradually dissipated high above. The crow spread its wings and dove out of sight with a squawk. Devon stared across at each shooter. The resolve was there in the eyes of one man, the mechanic. His barrel never wavered; eyes were fixed behind the open sights. Perhaps it wouldn't be too painful. Joe mechanic was going to put one in his heart. The others would be lucky to shoot off a toe and make a bloody mess in the cold water.

The tall man became more insistent. Devon didn't understand the Arabic words, but the authoritative tone was there. The captain thrust the paper back in the tall man's chest, now arguing with a tone of authority, a man who didn't take to being disputed. Even the mechanic's rifle began to waver as the tall man shrugged his shoulders, as if it were all too distasteful. The captain stopped arguing, frowned and looked across the row of soldiers down the *wadi*, then back in the other direction, as if he expected to find someone in the desert.

The Iraqi officer turned back to Devon with a look of disgust, held up Devon's knife, then dropped it into a pocket. "You should be very careful, American. We remember what you have done to Saddam's loyal soldiers, to our mothers, our daughters. We do not forget." He patted the pocket. "Especially for you, no weapons are allowed." Then he splashed through the water and clambered up the bank.

The other soldiers stood for a moment. Devon wondered if they were going to shoot him just for the sport of it to get even for their wet feet. The mechanic lowered his rifle, glanced at his new watch, muttered something to the other three and followed the captain. The others trailed along behind him in a straggly line, not even remembering to clear their rifles.

Devon shivered, then clambered, hand and toe, up the sandy bank, followed by the tall man. When the American reached the top, he closed his eyes and held his face up so the rays of the rising sun warmed his bruised cheekbone. *God, it's good to be alive.*

"Come. The bus will leave without us, Mr. Devon. Or would you rather stay?" the man asked Devon. Slim, pock-faced, but with a smile and not a gun. He led Devon inside to the table and the pile of tobacco, scattered books and clothes.

"Saying thank you seems a little feeble, but thanks." Devon offered his hand. The man hesitated, then finally accepted Devon's hand with an odd grip. "Are you a border official?" asked Devon. "Do you know me?"

"Oh, no. I am not even Iraqi, and I don't recall having met you before. My name is Mohammed Olanti. I am on my way to a new assignment with the Pakistani embassy in Baghdad. It is only by chance I saw them remove you from the building, and I inquired.

Pakistan and the United States have been allies for many years. Members of my family have lived in America. I did not want anything to happen to you, simply because of a misunderstanding." The smile returned. "I suggested to the officer in charge that the CIA was certain to have operatives all around in the desert, watching, if you were a spy. Do you think I was correct?"

Devon had to laugh. "Watching over you, maybe, but not over me. I seem to be on my own this trip." Devon wondered if standing in front of a firing squad, even an interrupted one, made him a full-fledged spy, passing his first search without being executed. *But damn close.*

"Did Kilborn send you?" Devon asked. He scraped the tobacco into a small pile with the heel of his hand. Holding an empty underwear bag like a dustpan, he collected the aromatic flakes and bound them in the bag with a rubber band some hurried traveler had left behind.

"Who?" Olanti frowned, a puzzled look on his face. "I am sorry, but I do not know any Kilborn. Is he someone of importance?" His face was all innocence as he held open Devon's briefcase.

When Devon picked up *The World Factbook*, its spine broken, and dropped it into the bag, he couldn't help but notice Olanti's right hand. He was missing several fingers. "He's one of my bosses. I work for the UN—" Devon had to stop and think, to let the sound of the chambering rounds stop echoing in his head. "—High Commission for Refugees." Devon held up one of the agricultural books. "Farm stuff." He finally remembered Kilborn's narration. "Agricultural advisor."

By the time Devon finished packing everything back in his bags, the building was empty. Outside, the sun had taken control of the morning, drawing long shadows from the distant ridges across the desert. Olanti walked on to the bus while Devon hurried to a latrine for a quick piss. His bladder told him he had to, but nothing would come out.

Heat shimmered from the bus roof as the sun delivered its promise of early summer heat, not a cloud in the sky. The other passengers stared at him from behind the safety of the bus windows. He scanned the faces as he walked by, but no one, nothing, looked out of place. They were probably as surprised as he that he was still alive.

Startled, he dropped the leather briefcase when the bus suddenly backfired, then the diesel grumbled to an idle, sending clouds of black exhaust and fumes into the still air. *A reminder of how close*, he thought, then gathered up his bags and climbed back on the bus. Olanti had taken his seat by a snoring Bedouin whose white *ghutra* had slid down over his forehead, half covering his eyes.

Gears grinding, the bus pulled back onto the asphalt strip. Ahead, the desert stretched toward the rising sun. Devon ignored the scattered passengers and sat back to think. The Iraqis had singled him out for a search. Because he had pissed off the captain? Because he was an American? Or did he have a 'spy' sign around his neck, courtesy of Ron Houston and his DIA friends? Had the captain taken him out back for a good scare, or did he really mean to leave Devon's dead butt out into the desert for the crow to pick over?

Suddenly, his mouth was as dry as the shadow-streaked rocks and sand passing by outside the windows. He slid the briefcase from under his damp boots and pulled out the remaining bottle of water.

What else had kindly Mr. Kilborn socked away in here? Any surprises the soldiers had missed? He lifted the briefcase up and sat it on the empty seat next to him. An old PanAm luggage tag hung from the grip. He turned it over. The tag was imprinted, letters faded, with his name. Devon opened the briefcase.

The first packet of papers in the stack contained a series of press releases. According to the United Nations press officer, the UN High Commission for Refuges was trying to help feed and house a hundred thousand-plus Kurds driven into Iraq by the Turks and Iranians, some in camps and some scattered in villages across the northern mountains of Iraq, and at least one camp in Syria.

Books filled the rest of the briefcase. Fresh, greasy fingerprints tracked their way across the *Iraq Country Study's* white cover, which credited the United States Army as the publisher. Devon flipped through the next book, equally soiled, a thick, tome on soil conservation and irrigation practices. *Good sleeping material.* Next he opened up a worn USDA softcover on seed hybrids.

He blinked at the first page. Familiar—ought to be—his name scrawled on the inside of the cover, in his own hand. He remembered this one, a warning about the loss of ancient, disease-resistant varieties, the dangers of producing new hybrids that could be wiped out by unexpected diseases long dormant in the soil. He scanned the other titles and recognized most of them. So long ago, a different time...where had he seen them last?

He closed his eyes and thought back until he recalled the last time he had seen these specific books. In his mind's eye, they were still on the top shelf in the study—Rachel's study—in Arlington. When Rachel and he were trying to make their marriage work, he had thought about getting out of the Army and going back to Carolina. For a few months, he had seriously studied the pros and cons of farming before he finally realized, or Rachel had told him—he couldn't remember which—their marriage was over.

It suddenly clicked. Rachael worked somewhere in the Defense Intelligence Agency. Houston, like all military attachés, also worked for the DIA. For these books and the old PanAm tag to show up in Heathrow's Terminal Three, carried by a Brit from Geneva, somebody had done a lot of arranging.

Somebody who had set him up. Damnation. Even his ex had gotten in on the act.

Little Miss Susanne from the hospital party was a military intelligence officer who maybe worked for Houston, or Houston's boss, or that guy's boss, which is about where Rachel would show up on the food chain. Whoever it was had played him like a fiddle, right into this godforsaken job.

Which, apparently, was to help scattered tribesmen figure out how to cultivate crops in the saline desert soil of the upper plateau lands. As a sideline, he was supposed to find the nuclear weapons that an entire UNSCOM team couldn't locate before Saddam threw them out of Iraq. He flipped through the texts, mind refusing to accept where he was going and what he was doing.

A flash of reflected sunlight caught Devon's eye. He jerked his head around to stare at the rusted remnants of a vehicle scattered beside the road. In the distance, a sand ridge dominated the highway as they crossed a bridge over a deep *wadi*. More charred wreckage littered the sand floor, the largest chunk recognizable as a giant wheel from a Scud transporter. He packed away the books and rested his head back against the seat, eyes closed. Against the back of his eyelids he could see the flames in the night and the green tracers chewing up the soft limestone boulders, then exploding against the truck. The wide eyes and the soft voice in the ditch, forever to haunt him.

The last leg of his journey across the Tigris River into Baghdad's Karrada district depressed him even more. Piles of rubble interrupted his view of typical concrete and stucco Arab homes, half-hidden behind high walls. No one smiled up at them as the bus slowed to pass a crowd standing by shops and a scattering of goods spread along the side of the road. No shaking fists, but no kids asking for gum either.

At least all the women weren't draped in black like the little moles he had never gotten used to in Riyadh. Many of the men wore western clothes, with an occasional glimpse of a black-and-white checkered *ghutra* and white *thobe*, the Bedouin's personal reminder they were only visiting the city, and that they belonged to the desert. Probably a facade, like America's urban cowboys, but no doubt they believed their myth, as much as the Americans did.

Round columns supporting balconies over the shop fronts graced a section of undamaged street, adding a touch of elegance to the otherwise rubble-strewn look of a war zone.

The bus slowed to let a pack of dented white Datsun pickups scoot by, piled high with produce for the market stalls.

"Bloody awful, eh?" The man across the aisle from him grimaced at the passing view. "Just look at that damned mess." He pointed out a shallow crater just east of the river. "One of your cruise missiles burst a water main." The frustration and irritation were clear on the man's face. "Tell me how missiles will help?"

Devon didn't answer. He just stared out the window at the people in the narrow streets until they reached the High Commission compound where the bus groaned to a stop. The other passengers, even the one who had berated him, seemed just as reluctant to be here as he. Everything was sepia, not a primary color in sight. Clouds formed a solid overcast covering Baghdad, and the temperature had dropped down into the low forties.

Devon shivered and felt even colder with the moist breeze blowing up from the Tigris River carrying with it the stink of dead things and burst sewer lines. Devon grabbed his bags and hurried from the bus into the processing room.

The procedure went so quickly Devon wondered if he was actually on the rolls, or if maybe they didn't want a trace of him left in the office. The *chargé de mission*, a dark-faced Asian who never gave his name, abruptly shook Devon's hand, then hurried back to his office. Apparently the *chargé* just wanted to see his face. Maybe to give a positive ID to Kilborn.

A narrow-faced admin clerk hurried Devon through, no papers to fill out, nothing to sign. All the clerk wanted was to study the illegible stamps in his passport. The clerk—Devon deduced by the garlic aura he must be French—copied out his passport numbers, slapped a badge on the table with his picture already laminated on the card. The photo mimicked the same long-haired dope plastered on his passport.

After Devon stewed on a hard wooden bench for an hour, a voice from the doorway called out his name. Devon spotted the source, an Arab in full tribal garb waving Devon toward him. Devon grabbed his duffel and briefcase and followed the man out to a dusty mini-van. A short ride navigated mainly by horn and the driver pointed him toward a white transport plane, props slowly starting to turn. Not a smidgen of eye contact in the whole affair.

Finé, Baghdad. Where to now? Saddam's nukes?

The *Chargé* knocked on a thin door. *"Monsieur Aragon, l'Américain est parti,"* he announced when it opened.

"*Très bon. Merci,*" Aragon replied and closed the door. He went to the desk and scanned the stack of files.

This Devon, he thought, *is a foolish coward, but perhaps useful in some way*. He picked up the phone and dialed his contact in Islamabad. They were the ones anxious to see Devon, so, the sooner he was on his way, the better. He wondered if this Granwin, the woman described in the commission file, could be of any assistance. *But first, take care of Devon.*

The Echelon duty officer had duly noted the call, added one more name to the Rosemary list and forwarded the transcript over to Russ Allen.

Allen grimaced when he read the report, wondering who this Aragon was, how he was connected.

"What have I gotten Devon into?" Allen muttered. *Will the outcome be worth the cost?* raced though his mind.

CHAPTER 5

Northern Iraqi Safe Haven Zone

The trip to the refugee center at Irbil started on the white Canadian CC-130 full of cargo and one passenger—Devon. He twisted in the net seat alongside strapped-down pallets, as uncomfortable as he had ever been on a parachute operation. Jumping, he had always known what he was supposed to do when he busted his butt on the ground. Here, he wasn't sure.

Yeah, the mission order is to spy out nuclear research facilities, but what's really down there?

He leaned back against the straps and listened to the CC-130's four engines, filtered by foam earplugs shoved in courtesy of the crew chief. After about an hour they landed at a gravel strip, God knew where in Iraq. There he transferred to a white Commission helicopter and sandwiched among piles of boxes for the last leg of his trip, his exile.

The helicopter rocked along at about two thousand feet above the ground, well within the effective range of any stray American Redeye or Russian Grail surface-to-air missiles the Kurds might have bartered from their cross-border neighbors, the Afghanistan *mujahideen*. Devon kept his mind off the rough flight by watching the pilot operate the controls. The French-made Dauphin's instrument panel was different from the familiar Blackhawks, but the controls appeared the same: collective for angle of attack and power, cyclic stick between the pilot's legs, standard rudder pedals and a whole bunch of gauges.

The copilot suddenly began punching buttons and twirling the radio frequency dials. The helicopter climbed for a moment, leveled off, then slowed. Devon shivered when he realized what was happening. The crew was presenting the bird for inspection, probably to a pair of USAF F-15 Strike Eagles or Brit Tornadoes patrolling out of Incirlik, Turkey. It hadn't been too long ago when the Air Force had shot down a UN helicopter in the same area.

Nothing like flying down the middle of a war zone, especially when they were supposed to be at peace. When the helicopter steadied back into normal flight, Devon realized he had been holding his breath.

Daylight was beginning to fade and Devon was more than ready to get off when the pilot dropped the landing gear and made his approach toward a fenced compound perched on the edge of a small plateau. Beyond the compound a broad river twisted though a wide valley that separated foothills leading on each side of the plateau to mountains high enough to still show signs of snow on their peaks.

The Dauphin swayed in the ground effect turbulence while the pilot turtled them sideways as far away as he could get from the flimsy-looking buildings and settled on a circle-marked pad. Gritty dust swirled over and around the helicopter as the blades slowed to a gentle *whick-whick* overhead.

This must be home.

The crew chief slid opened the side door and motioned him out. Devon hopped to the ground and instinctively crouched low, even though the helicopter blades swirled several feet over his head. Everything appeared cold and dirty, like he felt. At least he had made it up-country before the weather had forced him to overnight in Baghdad. The sudden stench of burning shit cans made him wonder for a moment if porcelain toilets might have made it worth staying with his new friend the *Chargé* a little longer. The crew chief handed him his bags and turned back to the helicopter, leaving Devon in a swirl of dust.

"Hey, Chief."

Devon jerked his head around at the sound of a familiar voice. He located the source—a large black man, head above the men carrying boxes hurriedly thrown from the helicopter. Then the voice struck home. It was Bert, Sergeant Wilbert Baker. Instead of the standing tall demolitions NCO in desert cammies, the man in front of him seemed relaxed in a University of Georgia sweatshirt and denims, but still all muscle and tough as the bulldog on the shirt.

Wilbert Baker reached out a big hand and grabbed Devon's shoulder, pulling him out of the way of a stream of wiry men scrambling to unload the boxes from the helicopter.

"Bert, am I glad to see you." Devon stepped back and looked Baker up and down, realizing why he hadn't recognized him at first. Baker had lost his 'geechee' accent somewhere along the way and, in addition to the civvies, one eye was swollen. "Damn, you've changed—especially the shiner."

"Thanks a lot." Baker looked him over in return. "Too many soft staff jobs? You've gone chubby on me. But you look good in work clothes, like you might try to make something of yourself, Nash."

That was the first time Baker had ever used his first name, a reminder Devon was in a different world here. Before it had always been Chief, in deference to his grandmother's Lumbee origins and his inherited dark hair and eyes.

Devon shook Baker's hand, thick with honest work calluses, and nodded his head, agreeing with Baker's assessment of him. He had let himself lose the old edge' physical and mental.

Baker leaned over in the fading light to look closely at Devon's bruised cheek. "And you? Angry husband?" Baker asked.

Devon shrugged. "Close. What's your excuse?"

Baker swung an imaginary bat. "I got a little bored and took up cricket with the Pakistani mechanics in the motor pool. Damn ball skipped off the bat and caught me right under the eye. Found out batting's a bit tricky out here. The ball comes up off the gravel all kind of crazy angles." He laughed. "'Bout like baseball in the cow pasture…lots of hazards. But the Pakistanis are good blokes, as our director would say."

They both turned their backs to the clatter of the helicopter taking off. "Damn, conditions up here must be crap to fly this miserable terrain at night. Maybe I should've hung around Baghdad."

Baker glanced around the horizon with his hands on his hips, head upturned toward the cloud-streaked evening sky, nodding as the last glow of sunlight fading behind the distant mountain peaks. "Maybe you should've." After a moment of silence, he grabbed the briefcase from Devon and guided him toward one of the buildings. "Hungry? We got nothing fancy, but the team director hired an Irishman who thinks he's a chef, so the non-pork version of Spam comes out pretty unusual sometimes. If it comes in a can, Ian can deal with it. If it don't, we ain't got it."

"Sure. It's been a long day," answered Devon. *Or two.* God, he had lost count flying back and forth, riding a bus across a country he once had been at war with. Oh, and yes, standing in front of a firing squad. *Don't forget that one, not quite yet.*

Baker led the way past a treacherous-smelling grease pit to one of the prefab buildings where he shoved open a narrow door. "Bird was a little late today. Regular chow hours are over, but Ian will dig up something for you."

"Is Ian a good enough Irishman to keep a bottle of rye around?"

Baker's reaction was hidden in the shadows as he led the way. Inside, lantern-light flickered over one corner, leaving the rest in shadow. The mess hall was a small, modified steel beam skeleton covered with corrugated metal sheets. No insulation on the walls, no ceiling, just concrete and steel, leaving wide gaps for the wind to whistle through.

The budget for this operation must be minimal. Or maybe the Commissioner down in Baghdad figured they would lose it to somebody else in the next spin of the who-rules-the-mountain-now battle. Devon shivered at the chill that ran up his legs from the bare concrete floor. A hum competing with the wind resonated with the slight trembling of the concrete pad. He finally connected the trembling to the muted roar of a diesel generator, a reminder of his last field assignment to a firing battery command post.

He might be wearing jeans bought at a Saudi *souk*, but this was still mighty close to a military operation.

In the dim light he could make out two rows of rough tables and benches filling three-quarters of the building. A field range and stacks of boxes took up the other quarter. A thin man stood by the range checking the boxes against a list. *Skinny cook, bad sign*, thought Devon. A hissing kerosene lantern hung from a roof beam. Apparently the electricity didn't make it this far down the line.

Baker led him toward the pool of light and the heat. "Ian," Baker called out. His deep voice echoed in what was more of a giant shed than a real building.

The man waved them toward an empty table under the lantern. "Allo, Berty, my boy. Ready for another wicket, are ye?"

Baker shook his head. "Not tonight. A friend came in on the resupply bird." He turned to Devon. "This here is Nash Devon."

Ian stopped to wipe his hand on a dirty dishrag and shake with Devon. "Why, it's me very pleasure, Mr. Devon." He looked at Devon with curiosity plain on his face. "With an English name like Devon you still have the look of a black Irishman on your face. Have you a bit of the Irish in your blood?"

Devon laughed. "Maybe a wee bit. And call me Nash."

Baker sniffed at the huge pot on the open burner. "Got any chow left, Ian?"

"To be sure." He waved toward a table. "Take any seat you like." The Irishman scraped the last of what Devon hoped was thick stew into a bowl, then chopped a chunk of bread from a thick loaf.

Ian peered at the surface of the bread, picking specks from the crust before he set it beside Devon's steaming bowl. "Now don't get too picky. We eat plain 'cause that's all there is and 'specially 'cause we don't want the Kurds to think we livin' on palace rations while they get the scraps. Oh, no, Levison, the Director himself, won't like that a bit, he won't." Ian went back to his list, grumbling under his breath.

Baker waved a hand in the air, dismissing Ian's complaints. "Don't pay him no mind. The locals steal him blind and the staff bitch about the chow all the time. Good thing we got no guns. He'd blow his own brains out."

Devon broke several chunks of bread and dropped them into the stew to soak. He shoveled several mouthfuls down before he stopped to talk. The stew itself was good, hot and thick, but the bread had been stale a day or two ago. "What are you doing here, Bert? Out of the Army or just on a temporary duty thing?" *Or hijacked, like me.* It suddenly struck him. *Was Baker his contact?*

Baker picked up a coffee cup, smelled it, then pushed it away. "After the Gulf War and ROTC duty, I deployed to Bosnia. Nothing but mud, misery and NATO bull shit. Then I lost Clara and retired at twenty so I could take care of my little girl." He grinned, balding forehead glistening in the lamplight. "They made me a deacon in the church, but after Junie started college, there wasn't anything to keep me around Savannah. The GS-8 job out at Hunter Army Air Field wasn't a lot of fun, having to take a bunch of crap from buck sergeants and lieutenants." Baker's grin got bigger. "You know I was never any good at kissing up. Here—" He shrugged his broad shoulders. "Here, I get a little bonus for what I do. For my Junie."

Baker held out a crinkled photo of a smiling young girl, hair in cornrows under a graduation cap.

"She went off to university last fall," Baker continued, putting the photo away, "so I decided to make a little extra to help her along. I started working on my degree when I was on ROTC duty, then finished on the GI Bill. In those days, there was plenty left over for beer. I never thought how damn expensive it would be for a girl nowadays. Tuition and textbooks and upkeep, plus all the extras, my retirement pay sure wasn't enough. And special ops demo guys aren't in big demand in the States, even the ones with degrees in Arabic language and culture."

Devon picked up the heavy coffee mug Ian put in front of him, steaming in the chill air. "Deacon, huh?" Devon asked. He sniffed at the coffee and stirred the contents of the mug. "Well, what do you do here?" He wondered if his question sounded innocent to Baker, or just stupid. Guess it depended on whether he was a card-carrying spy or not.

Before Baker could answer, Ian bent across the table and poured a tall shot from a bottle into Devon's coffee. "Help you sleep. First night's always a bad 'un, wind screaming through the huts and all."

"Thanks, Ian." Devon held the cup up in a toast. He tossed it back and gagged on the raw Irish whiskey. He shook his head and took another sip as Baker laughed at him. "Go on, Bert."

"This whole place is littered with something trying to kill you—mines, unexploded ordinance of all kinds, and once in a while an intentional booby-trap. So, I get to find and disarm 'em all, first come, first served. And, since I speak Arabic, I spend a lot of time going around with different workers to the outlying villages, kind of as a translator-bodyguard."

"Who do we work for out here in the boonies?" asked Devon.

"Team director's named Stanley Levison. He's an old hand Brit." Baker nodded in approval. "He's got a good grip on all this, knows the country and people pretty well.

"Levison? A Jew? How does that go down with the Iraqis?"

Baker glanced over Devon's shoulder. "Ask him."

"Hello, Mr. Devon."

A short, extraordinarily rotund man walked around the table to stand in front of them. Devon had to keep himself from looking under the table to see if the man was on his knees.

"I'm a born and practicing Anglican," Levison explained. "I have nothing against our Jewish friends, but even the stupidest bureaucrat would not put a Jew out here. Iraq once had a very large and influential Jewish population. They are no longer influential. In fact, the lucky are exiled. My understanding is that most are dead. All very unpleasant, I'm sure." He nodded to Baker.

"Has Mr. Baker given you the lay of the land?" Levison stopped, wrinkled his round button of a nose and leaned across the table. A thin layer of fine blond hair barely diffused the reflection of the lanterns from his round pate as he bent over. "I see you've discovered our source of illicit booze."

He waved a pudgy hand at Baker. "Wilbert, please give us a moment to ourselves. I need to apprise Mr. Devon of his duties and responsibilities." He paused for a moment, his moon-face stern, but still the closest Devon had ever seen to the original, yellow smiley-face. "And our camp rules, so he'll understand when he is breaking them."

"Tomorrow, Nash." Baker untangled his long legs from the rough bench and put his coffee cup on a stack of dirty dishes at the end of the table. "Let me know if you need anything."

"Thanks. When I figure it out, I'll ask."

Levison sat across from him, chin just above the tabletop. Devon shoved the empty bowl and coffee cup toward the stack of dishes and waited.

Finally Levison spoke, so softly Devon leaned forward to catch his words.

"We should start out with a clear understanding of our purpose here, Mr. Devon. It is to keep people, especially the children, from starving. Anything else is incidental. We do not get involved in the internal political conversations. We do nothing to draw the attention of the Iraqi authorities, local sheiks or water authority managers." Levison seemed to grow taller as he made his final point. "And most importantly, we do not engage in any activity which could result in our ejection by the Iraqi government, as they have done with the UNSCOM inspectors."

He waved a short arm at the darkness surrounding them. "The people around Irbil know what it is to be afraid. Saddam sent his Army and Special Security Organization across the valley in '93. Those who were left alive do not make many mistakes."

Levison picked up Devon's coffee mug and sipped, made a face and patted his lips with a handkerchief. "You will assist the displaced till the land, as poor as it and they may be. While you are familiarizing yourself with the refugee settlements, their problems and potentials, you will drive the productive members of our team to the various villages. Listen and perhaps you may learn." He pivoted around on the bench and stood, slightly taller than before. "I know why you're here, Mr. Devon. Do not jeopardize *our* mission. If you do, I will personally see to your fate."

Devon didn't know what to say. What did Levison know? More than Devon? Did he have a firing squad standing by?

"Ian." Levison also kept a command voice concealed in his short stature. "Show Mr. Devon to the men's hut. I believe Mr. Baker has arranged sleeping facilities for our new team member." Levison turned back to Devon. "Breakfast is served at six o'clock sharp, Mr. Devon. We have much to do."

Levison spun and walked to the door, his rotund body moving smoothly through the dark, a greased ball bearing.

Devon recovered the mug and walked over to Ian. "Can I trouble you for another?" he asked and held out the cup.

"Sure, mate." Ian slid aside a flour sack, reached behind a row of salt containers, and grinned when he held up a half-full bottle. "Just you remember, the golden is hard to come by."

"Let me figure out what the hell I'm doing here. I'm sure I can be a contributor to your medicine cabinet." Devon drank back the shot without stopping. He wondered when he would get another drink, and what tomorrow would bring.

CHAPTER 6

"New day, Nash. Rise and shine, man."

It was still dark, but he was still alive. The snakes had chased him through the sloughs of his dreams all night long, crows overhead, cawing and mocking.

In the flickering lantern light the men's hut appeared identical to the mess, substituting cots piled with blankets and sleeping bags for tables. Devon dug a shaving kit from his duffel before he stumbled through the maze of cots and footlockers to the end of the building and a row of sinks. He stared at his two-day old stubble in the streaked mirror and thought about letting it grow. *Nope.*

He couldn't see himself going native, plus beards itched. He scrubbed and scraped at his face. The tepid water smelled familiar, the sharp chemical tang that comes with too much chlorine in processed water. Pressure was nonexistent, so he figured it was probably just gravity flow from an outside tank.

"Just wait till winter, Nash. Then it'll really be fun." Baker grinned at him from behind a white mask of shaving cream.

Shave, quick swipe with a wet rag at his armpits, then off to see the wizard. Devon was anxious to start the day and see what kind of havoc Houston had sent him into. Agricultural advisor-cum-spy, exiled to a concentration camp. Which came first? Advising or spying?

He stepped out of the dark building to the landscape of a world under construction. Wisps of hoary mist drifted up from the river to dissipate in the cold air as the *muezzin's* morning call to prayers floated up the hillside. Unlike the raucous blaring of the loudspeakers in Riyadh, each neighborhood mosque vying to be louder than its neighbor, a single voice called across the valley.

And then quiet enveloped Devon. The background murmur of voices and clanking of pans died out as the people of the valley spread their prayer rugs toward Mecca and began their devotions, one of five times of daily prayer shared across the Muslim world. Only the muted drone of the compound generator spoiled the quiet.

Below and to the west, an old town of one- and two-story buildings still lay in shadow. The center of Irbil was an imperfect circle, with roads spiraling from the center like the town had been laid out by a tornado. Between the town and the compound tents the color of the local soil, only varying in shade and size, dotted the valley in a tangled sprawl.

Fed by fires beside the tents and chimneys in the town, short columns of smoke floated up into the waves of haze drifting over both town and tents, slowly rolling in the early morning stillness. A single minaret in the center of the town rose above what appeared to be an old fortress. The inner circle must be old walls, although Devon couldn't be sure from this distance.

Baker stepped out of the sleeping hut. "Better get some chow. We don't have much, and Ian parcels it out till not a crumb's left."

Devon followed him to the mess hall, feeling like an old rag. Around him, the gray morning world waited for the sun to break over the mountains. He was stuck in an old black-and-white Ray Milland movie, hung over and stiff from the taut canvas of the cot, a far cry from the luxuries of Riyadh and a real mattress. Finally the sun finally broke through the mists, drying the high mountain air and bringing a sting to his fresh-shaved face.

Breakfast was typical military—scrambled, reconstituted eggs and toast from the same batch of stale bread of the night before, bolstered with coffee that would start a ten-ton truck, despite Levison's civilian definition of their mission. Not very much food, but plenty of coffee. And no pork sausages.

Baker introduced him to the other dozen or so team members, but their names slid across Devon's mind until they sat down across from one of the women. In profile, her high-bridged nose was a little too pronounced, set between prominent cheekbones in what he supposed others would call a classic Greco-Roman face. She ignored Baker and Devon, continuing her story until Baker spoke up during a pause.

"Nash, this is Renée Granwin." Baker's voice had a distance to it.

She blessed Devon with a brief smile and continued talking, entertaining the others around the table with a story about an Aunt Jeannine, who, she said, still held Granwin in contempt for her Teutonic blond hair. She leaned over the table to explain, in a curious British accent, that in her Aunt Jeannine's eyes, blond hair was proof positive Granwin's father was a German Legionnaire, not the dead Frenchman on her birth papers.

Granwin tossed her blond hair and laughed. "She was right, you know. I'm not really French after all. I'm truly an international." She hauled a big cloth tote bag from under the bench and plopped it down on the table, rummaged around and pulled out a tattered photo album. She smiled triumphantly, showing off an old black-and-white photo of a skinny, towheaded kid. The skirt was the only indication it was a girl. "See. I was a blond from the day I was put on this earth." She waved the photo at Baker and laughed.

Her amusement seemed a little too hollow to Devon. Baker's jaw muscles were knotted, biting down on more than the reconstituted eggs.

"Sleep well, Mr. Devon?" Levison slid onto the bench beside him, his tray stacked with slices of bread slathered with margarine and orange marmalade.

Count on the Brits, always polite, to break the spell. "Well enough," Devon answered and carefully watched his tray while he drank his coffee to see if any of the black specks on his eggs moved.

"Oh, don't be disturbed by the condiments." Levison waved his hand over the table. "The blasted Irishman insists on dousing everything with pepper, just to aggravate my condition, I do believe."

Devon poked at his eggs, turning each lump over to inspect the bottom side.

"You Americans probably will like them." He pointed at Baker's plate. "See, just add catsup and you can imagine you're at one of your McDonald's."

"I think it'll take more than catsup." Devon tasted the eggs, then quickly washed the spicy mass down with a slug of bitter coffee. "When do I start work?" He didn't add he had no idea what he would be doing. He figured Levison would already have something planned out. And how did he address Levison? Somehow, mister didn't seem appropriate. Master might be the right word, but he wasn't going to use it.

"You don't speak Arabic, do you?" asked Levison. He carefully folded a thick slice of bread to capture a spoonful of orange marmalade and took a huge bite.

"No Arabic, but I do speak a little French," Devon answered after swallowing a gritty mass of eggs.

Granwin smiled across the table at him, a crooked grin on her face. "Did you learn to speak French in a bordello like most Americans?"

"Now, now, Miss Granwin. Let Mr. Devon find his own place here, not the one you want to put him in." Levison waved his little wave again, dismissing Granwin's words. He leaned over and smiled at Baker. "Wilbert, will you be so kind as to take Miss Granwin on her tour today?" He tucked another slice of marmalade bread in his tiny mouth.

Devon wasn't sure who had the sourest look at Levison's suggestion, Granwin or Baker. *What in the devil is going on?* He decided the woman was an arrogant bitch, which explained Baker's reaction, but why did she return Baker's scowl? Just her way, he supposed.

Levison patted his mouth, carefully cleaning away the last bit of marmalade. "Mr. Devon, come over to my office and I'll sort out your tasks and find you a place on our team." He beamed at the group, scooted off the bench and roly-polied his way to the door.

Devon finished off the last of his eggs, the group eating in silence until he broke it with a very important question. "Bert, where's the head?"

"Out the door and straight over toward the fence."

Devon nodded to Granwin and got a curt nod in response as he bolted toward the door.

Outside, he followed his nose to the five-holer on the opposite side of the camp. The newspaper-grade toilet paper provided further confirmation of his economic assessment of the camp. After he had finished, he stood outside and took a long look around the compound in the sharp sunlight that had finally begun to warm the air. A reverse osmosis water purification unit—ROWPU, the quartermaster guys called them—with its bloated, rubber bladder sat on the highest elevation inside the fence on the opposite side of the camp. Pipes led to small metal tanks at the end of two of the metal buildings, including the one he had slept in the night before. Next to the ROWPU, a black-painted water tank stood by a small shed.

Devon could see bare legs through the open bottom and water spilling off the concrete pad into a trench. He then recalled another aspect of the Muslim world, cleanliness before prayer. He remembered seeing Arab Coalition soldiers in the Saudi desert dawn, scrubbing their feet and hands with sand before unrolling their prayer rugs.

He shivered, hoping he didn't stink so badly he would have to shower in this chill, not yet. At least he didn't have a God to appease.

The operations hut and the team motor pool were partially out of sight on the down slope, on the other side of the water point. The generator by the water purification unit sent a shimmering column of diesel exhaust into the thin air. Amazingly, he had been here less than twenty-four hours, and already the camp noises faded to the background, unnoticed.

"Nash," Baker called to him from between the operations hut and the motor pool, waving him over.

"What the hell was all that about between you and the Frenchie?" asked Devon when he got to the waiting Baker.

"You'd think the French, of all people, would put race behind them, but she doesn't appreciate my tan." Baker just shook his head and grinned.

Devon guessed he wasn't joking. "I think she must have a hard-on for Americans in general. She didn't cut me much slack today either." He motioned toward the operations hut and the approaching woman. "What are you guys going to do today?"

"I drive her to one of the villages, or maybe one of the nomad camps in the hills. She hands out food and female stuff, and we come back. Sometimes I get to dig up an odd Czech mine, and that's about it." Baker shrugged. "But it puts Junie through school; so I do it." He nodded toward the approaching woman. "I'll even put up with her vitriolic tongue."

Devon had to grin. "You insult with big words for an old sergeant."

Now it was Baker's turn, his wide smile showing his big pearls. "Too much education, not enough work…it's the curse of the wealthy."

Granwin walked by the two men and pointed to a large box in front of operations. "Mr. Baker, please bring the box and come along. We have a great distance to go today." She ignored Devon and continued toward the motor pool.

"See you tonight," Baker said. "Kurds and Rackies willing. We've got some stuff to talk about."

Moments later, Baker drove out the gate with Granwin at his side, both now scowling.

Devon turned to look over the camp as he pulled the tobacco in the underwear bag and hand-worn briar from his pocket. Spy or advisor, he wondered to himself, and slid the cold pipe back into his pocket. Too early to reminisce. Time to go to work.

When Devon entered the operations hut, Levison was standing behind one of the desks.

"Good morning, Mr. Devon. Today will be easy." Levison held out a packet of maps and got right to the point. "Look these over. Get a feel of where we are and our mission. As you can see, I've marked a number of settlements and other, less formal camps on the maps." He pointed out annotations penciled across the first map.

"They're numbered so we have a proper identification for our reports." Levison carefully slicked his sparse hair back over his head with his hand as Devon studied the map. "The people are our cares. Our cares, not our children, as some of the unthinking administrators back in Geneva like to call the wandering Kurds." He shook his round head from side to side, a grimace of frustration across his face.

"The men and women are mostly old. The young men are off fighting, and I don't know where the young women are. Hidden away, I suppose. And too many orphaned children wander the camps and the hills—smart, stupid, lame, wily—but mostly hungry. And they are not ours," he repeated, "but the children of parents poisoned by gases or bombed into the rubble of their homes." Levison paused. An incomprehensible look flashed across his face as he stared at Devon.

Levison leaned back, took up a pencil and began tapping the scarred desktop. "The drum roll begins. Our great performance in the steps of Alexander the Great." Levison pointed at the wad of maps Devon held in his hands. "You know, of course, that Mesopotamia and the mountains between here and to the shores of the Caspian absorbed the remains of Alexander's great army. His greatest victory, the defeat of Darius and the conquest of Persia happened right out there."

Levison pointed out the window with a pudgy finger. "It took place on the plains about fifty miles from here. Greeks slaughtered fleeing Persians all the way to the mountains behind us. But in the end, Alexander fell sick and his armies disappeared, assimilated by the people he had conquered." He pointed the pencil at Devon. "You, young man, are not Alexander. Do not start a new slaughter, whatever your reason for being here."

His schoolmaster lecture over, Levison turned to stare out the window, his thumbs barely touching behind his broad girth. "You should meet some of the support personnel, become acquainted with our local processes." He turned to face Devon, a round silhouette against the brightening sky.

Devon waited. The office was empty, but Levison had nothing to say about spying. If anything, his warning indicated the opposite. Even if Levison wasn't his contact, he sure as hell was in charge. *Young man. Hell, if anything, I'm older than Levison.* He just wasn't in charge of anything. Including his destiny.

"Mr. Otto is our chief of vehicles. Perhaps you can start by assisting him. Breathe the fresh air. Get your hands dirty. A day outside in the mountain air will help you acclimatize." He rocked back and forth, waiting for Devon's response.

Devon nodded. "Got'cha, boss." This he could deal with. Even if Levison wasn't his contact, now he could meet people and get to know what the hell the deal was around here. Earn his boots.

By lunchtime he could hum along with the tinny music coming from the little radio, matching the quavering voices with their lilting vocals, patting his foot to the background beat. And the spy business? He pushed Houston's brief to the back of his mind. Hell, after this morning, he even knew how to change the transmission fluid on a Datsun pickup. Maybe he would find a nuke tomorrow.

Or a way to get out of this mess.

CHAPTER 7

Boots, he had told Houston he wanted, and boots he got. Maybe not issue, but close enough. At least no Class A's with shiny shoes and black tie. The folding cot creaked, almost as loudly as his joints when Devon bent over to lace up the work boots in the morning chill. He sniffed at the shirt and decided it held a bit too much of the *eau du* motor pool, the ever-present bite of brake and transmission fluids, mixed with sturdy thirty-weight oil. He threw the shirt under the cot, on top of his duffel. Across the way, Baker's back disappeared into the latrine.

Baker had said they would talk, but so far it was all mundane rambling about refugees and supplies. But in the close quarters, they hadn't had a chance for any real private discussions. The camp seemed to be full of Pakistanis and Kurds; lots of busy people scurrying around.

"Bert, when're we going to get a day off?" Devon asked.

Baker's cough turned to a laugh. "Not even a full week in the motor pool and you're worn out?" Baker packed his shaving gear back in a footlocker. "Levison has a unique policy. We work Sunday because we're in an Islamic culture and Saturday because we're not Muslims.

"Besides, the Canadian resupply schedule puts the CC-130 in today and Levison made a point that he wanted you there. Guess he wants you ready to fill in for me if I kick up a Valmara 69."

"What the hell is a Valmara 69?" asked Devon.

"The latest and greatest version of the old Bouncing Betty land mine, Italian style. Disturb one of the porcupine probes and it fires up about waist high and rips you apart with a load of ball-bearings." Baker already had his jacket on. "Hurry up. Big bird will land at Bashur in about an hour."

Devon stood and stretched out his stiff back. "No breakfast? How disappointing." He pulled on his jacket. "But it's fantastic to know Levison has such wonderful plans for me."

"Don't complain. You're not the one with the mine probe in his pocket." Baker looked him up and down like a buyer at the goat *souk* down in the valley. "Maybe you'll lose some of that baby fat you came here with."

"Yeah, but I thought I was going to be an agricultural advisor, not a stevedore."

"The Canadian crews won't let any third-countries on their bird anymore since they lost their on-board coffee machine to a work crew. Come on. All we have to do is push pallets to the ramp. Won't kill you."

"Speak for yourself." Devon zipped his jacket to the neck for the short walk to the operations hut. He shivered outside in the biting cold while Baker picked up a set of keys.

Unlike the luxury sports utility vehicles dancing across American TV ads, the Nissan Patrol they climbed into was a bare-bones grunt machine. But Devon had to admit as Baker started the Nissan, it got the job done. Except this one was killing his ears.

"Bert," he yelled over the blatting exhaust. "Can we get the muffler fixed on this damn thing before I go deaf?"

Baker grinned at him. "What you say?" he yelled back and rolled out the gate, waving at a skinny kid standing beside the guard shack.

Below them, the valley had shrunk. Then Devon realized the valley was the same, but the tent city had grown since the day before, creeping another four or five rows across the valley floor. Baker circled the High Commission compound and headed across the plateau. Silty gray dust floated behind them like the wake of a small boat on a peaceful sea. Devon dozed off, lulled by the roar of the motor, until a hard jolt and the realization that he was freezing woke him.

Devon shivered and tried to roll up the window. Despite the calendar, May was late coming. April was still roaring down from *al-Jazira*, the mountains separating Iraq and Turkey. He hammered on the doorframe, but the window wouldn't move. Too late anyway. Baker slid to a dusty stop at the end of a packed dirt runway quickly enough for the Nissan to fill with flying gravel, this time from the deafening prop wash of a Canadian Hercules CC-130 pivoting around the end of the runway after its landing run.

Devon kicked the door open, spit the thick dust from his mouth and joined Baker by the edge of the strip waiting for the aircraft rear clamshell to open.

"Good morning, gentlemen." The loadmaster, harnessed to the intercom system with a trailing wire, waved at them from the ramp control as he let the ramp drop. His shout boomed out as the four turboprops wound down. "A lovely day, what'cha say."

One of the Commission's Mercedes trucks pulled up and spilled a handful of refugees recruited from the valley camp. A Mesopian vision of a Mississippi riverboat and load of cotton bales flashed through Devon's mind.

"You're happy to be in Iraq?" Devon asked the loadmaster.

The loadmaster nodded. "Bloody better than a hot unload, engines running, dodging incoming at Sarajevo International or hauling Kosovo refugees out of Albania." He started disengaging the cargo pallets from the floor tie-downs and pointed at the bags strapped to the wooden pallets. "Looks like all food today. Management must be expecting a bad crop this summer."

He kicked the first pallet, starting it down the rollers toward the men waiting at the rear of the plane. "Or does management have the foggiest?"

Devon nodded noncommittally and started the next pallet on its way…careful to keep his feet clear of the high-piled pallet rolling toward the back ramp. *Levison's flour first. International diplomacy discussions later.*

With the built-in conveyor rollers and the local gang at the bottom of the ramp plucking bags from the pile and transferring them to the truck like ants at a picnic, the plane was unloaded in a matter of minutes. One of the front-end aircrew dropped down the steps from the cockpit as the day hires from the village, under Baker's careful eyes, stacked the bags on the truck.

"Where do you get this stuff?" Devon asked the crew member standing beside him.

"The fig orchard," sang out a lilting contralto voice. "Incirlik, if you want the Turkish translation."

Devon was surprised by the voice coming from the helmet—a woman, a big one from the size of the shoulders stretching the baggy flight suit.

"Off American C-5s," she continued as she unbuckled the remaining pallet from the tie-downs.

Devon had to grin. Probably the same C-5s that brought over the smart bombs to drop on the Iraqi command and control system. What a hell of a place.

She glanced at Devon for a moment. "What's your name?" she asked.

Devon instinctively glanced down, then remembered he hadn't worn a uniform with a nametag for almost a week. "Devon." He had to yell now that the loadmaster had gone outside, and the pilot was starting up the engines, one at a time.

"Here you go, mate." The woman pulled a package from behind the quilted side insulation, thrust it into his hand and, without any further conversation, climbed back up into the flight compartment.

The package weighed and had the heft of a couple of bricks. The box cover said it was a soil moisture content analyzer.

"Going back with us?" the loadmaster yelled at him, palm resting on the ramp button.

Devon shook off his surprise and shoved the package inside his jacket. The plane started to move as he waved at the loadmaster and ran down the ramp. The loadmaster had the ramp closing before he could hop off the end.

Damn, the Canadians really do have an incoming syndrome.

Devon squeezed his eyes shut and covered his ears, putting his back to the flying gravel as the CC-130 started its take-off roll. Soon the roar was gone and the airplane was turning toward the mountains, heading back to Turkey. At the end of the strip, the gang from the tents had almost finished strapping the sacks down on the truck bed. Baker waved him toward the Nissan.

Since Levison's dismissal, Devon had almost forgotten about nukes, false papers and fake travel itineraries. The beginnings of honest calluses on his hands and aches in his back proved he worked with real people during the day. But when night fell and the wail of the desert wind replaced the Pakistani radio, the crow strutted across the rooftop and watched him in the *wadi*.

During the day, he could put the mechanic's grin as he shouldered the AK out of his mind as he waited for whatever or whomever Houston said would contact him. Now, out of the blue, the heavy package inside his shirt was someone's reminder of why Houston had sent him to this God-forsaken place.

"Get what you needed?" Baker's expression was as blank as a Harrah's Smokey Mountain Casino poker dealer up in Cherokee.

"You mean this package." Devon reached under his jacket, surprised Baker had seen the exchange.

"Yeah." Baker shook his head. "A little something I ordered up for you." He held up his hand. "Don't take it out here. You'll need it later when you get around to some of your agricultural responsibilities."

When they got back to the camp, Baker pulled into the motor pool. "You take care of things while I turn in the Nissan and see if I can get my favorite bowler to fix the muffler." Baker called over to one of the Pakistanis in the open shop.

Devon slipped into the sleeping hut and opened the box the woman had passed to him. The nameplate on the rectangular device said it was an Agricultural Grain Moisture Analyzer, Model I-100z. He flipped the power switch and a pair of LED displays lit up, all zeros. He twisted one of several small knobs beside the LEDs and the display changed to numbers.

Okay, he was playing at being an agricultural advisor, so a moisture analyzer kind of made sense.

He turned a second knob labeled 'fine tune' and the numbers jumped through the two hundreds into the three hundreds, very much like UHF radio frequencies, the same band used on tactical satellite transceivers.

He clicked the first knob to the next detent, and the readouts filled with a new set of numbers. If the readout was supposed to be time, it was wrong. His stomach told him it was about noon.

Just my luck, battery's low and clock's running down.

But maybe it indicated UTC, Coordinated Universal Time, the new moniker for Zulu, Greenwich Mean Time. The probes packed in the box also had attachments that looked an awful lot like an earpiece and a microphone.

If he had figured this out right, thanks to Baker, the Canadians had delivered a miniature satcom transceiver with time and location indicators—how neat. Thank God he hadn't had the device in his bag when he crossed the border or old mister crow would have had his bones clean by now.

He turned off the device, shoved it into the bottom of his duffel bag and glanced around to see if anyone else had seen it. Two rows over, one of the mechanics snored, his back to Devon.

Devon kicked the bag under his cot and hurried to the row of sinks. When he saw his reflection in the mirror, his black hair and eyebrows were gray with granite dust, every wrinkle in his skin accented with dirt furrows. He scrubbed off enough dirt to finally get a little satisfaction at seeing his dark face, tanned to an even darker leather brown from the outdoor work. Better than the pasty appearance he had developed in Riyadh, hiding from the sun, only coming out at night when the temperature had dropped below a hundred degrees Fahrenheit.

He wished he had just a few of those hundred degrees with him now as he splashed the tepid tap water over his head. Even more, he wished he knew what he was doing. *Grain moisture analyzer—right!*

"Mr. Devon!"

A rotund silhouette waved at him from the door. Devon grabbed his jacket and followed the director to the his office, marveling at how the man moved, low and round, more like a bowling ball with appendages. Devon stopped to beat his jacket against the siding before he went in.

"My goodness, man. Stop making such a mess. You'll choke us to death with that dust," Granwin said coming up beside him. In the early morning light, her face showed more wrinkles, her hair a little more gray.

He followed Granwin through the door beneath the bilingual sign into the office. Devon didn't have a clue about the Arabic, but the Roman letters spelled out UNHCR-Irbil Operations Center.

This time, Devon took a measured look around the small room. After the beginnings of a career in the Army, Devon had a specific view of what an operations center should be. This wasn't it. A smaller version of the bare buildings scattered across the camp, four desks filled the single room. A lone light bulb dangled from the ceiling. Devon hoped the austere office was an indication Levison didn't tolerate a lot of bureaucratic paper work.

Information overload wasn't going to be a problem. The telephone system consisted of twisted frayed wires leading to a chipped Bakelite set on the director's desk. Based on the breakfast mess hall scuttlebutt of continued US and Brit air attacks on the Iraqi communications network, Devon wasn't surprised the phone hadn't rung while he was in the building. Maybe it never had.

Otto, Levison's motor pool manager, sat at the desk in front of a board covered with hooks and a tangle of vehicle keys. The days Devon had spent with Otto and his team of Pakistani mechanics had been almost fun. Otto liked to grin under his Germanic face, and the Pakistanis were good guys who seemed to be glad to be earning good Swiss francs.

Otto was already covered in grease, sipping from the ubiquitous plastic bottle of water. Like almost every other country in the world beside the United States, no one drank from the tap, or in the camp's case, the ROWPU. Devon wondered which polluted creek provided the water for the bottling entrepreneur.

Granwin stood beside one of the other desks, speaking in Arabic to a woman pinning a large map to the wall. The woman paused and smiled at Devon. Black hair in sharp contrast to her white scarf tucked under her rounded chin, the woman exuded sensuality. Devon couldn't help but return her smile. She pushed back a strand of glossy hair, her brown eyes reminding him of his monastic existence for months now, especially since Susanne didn't count.

Even the woman's half-hidden ear lobes were rounded, in stark contrast to Granwin's sharp angles. Just to look at her was exciting, as the tip of her tongue flicked the corner of her lips. She was a complete contrast to Granwin's aura of dryness, as if she had spent her life in the desert.

Beside her a boy sprawled on the floor, reading. His book was in Roman script, not Arabic.

"Are you a competent driver, Mr. Devon?" Levison settled behind his desk.

Devon hesitated. "I don't know anything about your big Mercedes trucks, but anything smaller you got out there, yeah, I suppose I can deal with it. Another few days bumming around the motor pool and I'll be ready to drive the big ones."

Granwin looked at him with a grimace. "Please, Monsieur Levison, not an amateur. I would rather have the African-American drive me. This savage will drive me off a cliff."

"Mr. Devon needs to learn more of the countryside and our operations in the distant villages, Miss Granwin. I'm sure he will be an able chauffeur." Levison smiled, apparently enjoying Granwin's discomfort. "And he speaks French. I'm sure you'll develop a wonderful rapport."

"But—"

Levison waved away her objections, stood and turned to look at a big map on the wall behind his desk. "It will be dark soon and you wanted to get out to K-11. Please, Miss Granwin. I'm very busy today with our other new arrival." He motioned toward the dark-haired woman standing by the map. "I must brief Mrs. Qasim on our normal procedures." He nodded toward Otto and the rack of keys. "Mr. Devon, draw a vehicle and take Miss Granwin wherever she directs."

Damn. Levison spoke and they all jumped.

Otto pulled a set of keys for the board. "The Nissan parked by the motor pool gate is best for you...the one you greased Saturday. It is gassed and ready to go."

Devon tried to remember the interior of the vehicle, but all he could picture was the caked gray dust on its underside. "Does it have all its windows?"

Otto frowned and tossed the keys to Devon. "You look. If it doesn't, you can fix it yourself when you get back."

This Nissan had all its windows, plus a muffler that muffled. Devon waved at the black-haired kid who had laid down his book and followed them out to stand at attention by the gate. *Playing soldier.* Too young, too soon, just like Devon remembered his own childhood. How great, he had thought, when his dad took him to Fort Bragg and he got to see the paratroopers jumping, streams of camouflage parachutes spilling from the rear of the silver C-130s. How he had wanted to be like the jumpers, fearless and brave. And where had it gotten him? Mechanic in a refugee camp, for God's sake.

"Drive carefully, Mr. Devon," Granwin said. "There are many dangers out in the hills."

Granwin didn't have to remind him—the spy who didn't know what he was looking for.

CHAPTER 8

Shadows covered the tree-covered lower slopes of the Zagros Mountains ahead of them. They had been on the road to Rawanduz, still in Iraq, but close to the Iranian border, for two hours. For Iraqi backcountry, Devon found the going wasn't too bad, but the frequent stops to let tribesmen with their scrawny goatherds straggle across the road wore on Devon's patience.

They topped a steep ridge and Devon shook his head in disgust.

A military convoy labored over the crest of the hill, blocking the way. The line of trucks forced them to slow to a crawl for over half an hour while fine gray dust rolled back over the Nissan. Finally the convoy pulled to the side of the road.

Devon accelerated up the line of vehicles, only to slow again as he passed a Russian *Kub* transporter with a trio of SAMs—surface-to-air missiles—pulling into a setback from the road, half-hidden in the shadows of the trees. The soldiers around the vehicles brandished their rifles, yelling at Devon and Granwin.

Granwin clutched Devon's shoulder as he slowed to get a better look at the missiles, trying to discover anything new or unusual. Finally, a chance to do what he thought he was here for, a bit of spying.

Granwin hissed, "Keep going!" and gripped his shoulder even tighter. The violent undertone of her whisper too demanding to ignore, Devon turned his eyes straight ahead and downshifted.

Horn blaring, a dusty *Ural* six-by-six truck nosed out from the convoy, crowding the Nissan toward the edge and a long tumble to the valley floor below. Devon fought the steering wheel, fishtailing the Nissan back into the *Ural*'s path. The Nissan slammed into the side of the *Ural*'s fender and they bounced closer to the edge. Devon floored the gas and slid back to the middle of the road, forcing a waving soldier to leap for his life. When Devon glanced back in the mirror the soldier stood in the middle of the road, watching them speed away and around a sweeping curve cut into the side of the mountain.

Devon kept his eyes on the road ahead, afraid they would run into another element of the convoy. He wasn't sure how much communications the Iraqis had up here, but he wanted to stay away from the guy waving the rifle, or any of his friends.

"Are you all right?" he asked Granwin, suddenly silent beside him.

"Yes. Just slow down, please. I want to live a few more hours." Her voice returned to her normal tone, calm, like he was a kid and they had just passed an interesting zoo.

They had only gone a couple of miles when Granwin yelled, "Turn here!"

Devon jerked the steering wheel at her sudden shriek. She pointed off to the right, bracing herself as the Nissan canted, threatening to tip when he slammed on the brakes.

"God dammit to hell, tell me where I'm going. Don't just yell and point!" Devon gripped the steering wheel to keep from pointing his finger in her face. His legs trembled as he held the stiff brake and clutch pedals to the floor and waited for her answer.

Granwin stared back with a frown. No, more the look he'd have expected if he'd passed gas. Devon recognized his frustration, fear, and all the reasons why he shouldn't be here simmering in his mind, trying to break out in his words.

He took a couple of deep breaths and tucked away his anger. No sense taking it out on the woman. "Look, lady, I just want to know where I'm going so I can pick the best way across this hill."

"Then kindly do not use such profanity. I do not say it and don't want to hear it. Just drive, please."

Devon craned over the steering wheel and found a faint trail leading between the trees. The Nissan lurched from side to side as he followed Granwin's pointing finger over the heavy roots, slowly winding his way between the dark trunks.

"The village is in a depression on the far side of those rocks." She pointed again, this time at an outcropping where a stream splashed its way down the slope.

"I don't see any village." He started the Nissan forward, nervous at the increasing angle of the incline. The Nissan tipped up as he bounced over a rock and Granwin slid down against him.

She quickly pulled herself back across the seat, as far from him as she could get, and clung to the doorframe. "I know this place, and these people, much better than you. So do what I say. And I say drive more carefully. The village is just ahead."

She was right, at least about the village. On the other side of the boulders a cluster of tents filled a shallow depression, just enough level ground to keep them from sliding through the trees to the riverbed at the bottom of the slope.

"Unload the boxes for me, please, Mr. Devon." She hopped out and marched immediately to the largest tent, the wind whipping at the black shawl Granwin had kept wrapped around her head since she had left the compound.

At least she can ride in the front seat beside me, Devon thought. In Riyadh, she would have had to sit in the back seat, away from any possible contact. Not that he wanted any. Her bony fame bouncing against him was about as romantic as being kicked by one of the wild-eyed goats wandering around the tents.

When he ducked under the tent flap with a box under each arm, she was standing in front of an old man, talking ninety miles an hour. Arguing better described the exchange, judging from the old man's growl. In contrast to the sharp tone she had used with Devon, Granwin kept her voice low as she spoke to the elder. But Devon could tell she was having a hard time controlling the look on her face. *Too much French in her for a bluff.*

Before he could decide if he should interrupt or not, she bowed to the old man, spun on her heel and marched out of the tent, keeping her head lowered as would any woman in this part of the world.

"Old ingrate. Bring the boxes back to the vehicle," she hissed as she stomped by the old man.

Devon smiled at the old man and followed her out. A gaggle of women swarmed around Granwin, all talking at once, hands flying in the thin air. They were covered, but with a mixture of white and flowered scarves, not the heavy black shawls of the desert or Riyadh.

He nudged one of the boxes open with his chin. Cans of food, five-pound bags of flour, and a string sack of oranges weighed down the box. Arms already starting to ache, he walked back to the Nissan. The rapidity of the words and the volume went up as he passed the women, fingers jabbing toward him, or rather toward the boxes, the really important part of why he was there. When he looked directly at the women, they whipped their scarves up over the lower half of their faces, dark eyes staring back at him.

Devon paused when the old man threw back the tent flap and waved his arms at Granwin. Devon set the boxes on the tailgate, sat down beside them and gazed across at the next ridge, dark with trees, ignoring Granwin and the old man's arguments reverberating across the valley. He pulled out his pipe and filled it with tobacco, picking out bits of lint, disregarding the glint of desert sand in the dark Cavendish, carefully snapping the rubber band back around his dwindling supply.

Far below, the riverbed dropped away sharply, leading back to the Great Zab, the river that ran past Irbil and eventually merged into the Tigris. The snow melt from the lower mountains was almost completed, the narrow stream by the boulders probably the reason the nomadic Kurds camped at this location. He sniffed the air. The wind had picked up. The only smells he could catch was a combination of fresh goat dung and burning goat dung.

Devon had to shade his eyes against the dropping sun as he inspected the road leading back out. The days were getting longer, but the evening wind still carried a bite as it sang through the trees. He opened a bottle of water to wash the dust from his throat. From what he remembered, this wasn't the part of the world to be driving around after dark with the rival Kurd factions, the Patriotic Union of Kurdistan, the PKK, and—what was the other bunch?—the KDP, the Saddam-backed Kurdish Democratic Party, killing each other, all stirred up by the *Mukabarat*, the Iraqi secret police.

Baker had warned him that the biggest danger in the mountains was enterprising young bandits. Every man on the mountain except him had a gun. Hellfire, he didn't even have a pocketknife any more. And sure as the devil he didn't want to run into the Iraqi soldier he had left standing in the middle of the road.

Loud voices sliced the thin air. By the tent, the old man raised his long rifle over his head and shook it as he yelled at Granwin.

"Ah, shit," muttered Devon. He froze to the tailgate, unsure if he should run in Granwin's defense or in the other direction.

She turned away from the old man, pulled back the shawl and spat a long stream of spittle out across the slope. No one spoke. Suddenly, the old man threw up his hands and marched back into the tent. Granwin waved the women toward the Nissan. Devon scrambled out of their way as they emptied the boxes and disappeared into the surrounding tents, never acknowledging his presence.

"Take me home, Mr. Devon." Granwin slipped into the Nissan.

He knocked out the burning ash, slid the hot pipe in his jacket pocket, slammed the tailgate shut, and joined her.

He glanced over as he started the Nissan. "Everything all right?"

"Perfectly fine, thank you."

He expected a smile, a frown, or some show of having won whatever the argument was about. But she rewrapped the shawl and clutched the grab bar, ready to go without further word. He backed and turned the Nissan in the narrow flat. When he drove back across the stream, a man, dark burnoose whipping around his legs, stood on top of the boulder pile. Not the old man with his ancient long gun.

This one sported a flowing mustache and a bolt-action rifle held across his body. Devon started to wave, but decided he didn't know what the hell was going on with Granwin and these people.

She pointed at a towering tree by the trail leading back to the main road. "Just past the big tree, turn toward your left. The way is a bit rougher, but we can avoid the bastards who tried to stop us coming up."

Devon glanced out of the side of his eye at Granwin but refused to rise to her profanity, especially since he agreed with her. He turned and leaned forward in the seat, searching for the almost invisible trail she wanted him to follow.

Driving as fast as he felt he could without tipping over, he made his way around the tree and followed the meandering goat trails, squinting as the golden ball of the sun glared directly into his eyes.

Lurching from side to side beside him, Granwin didn't remark on their gun-toting watcher on the rock nor explain the transaction.

The silence was a relief, letting Devon concentrate on the narrow track winding around the side of the mountains and the river valley. Devon pounded his foot down on the accelerator when a series of shots rang out, close enough to be distinctive through the closed windows and grinding of the gears. The reports had the soft crump of an AK-47 assault rifle's 7.62 mm bullet, not the sharp crack of the M-16's NATO 5.56 mm round. But technical analysis wasn't appropriate here. He wrestled with the wheel, teeth chattering as they skittered across a washboard section of road.

"Slow down, you fool. They are not shooting at us!" She squeezed the handgrip with both hands, arms braced out in front of her.

"How do you know?" Devon asked. He careened around a corner, tires sliding toward the edge and a sheer drop down to the river, now close enough he could see the setting sun glistening on the water.

"They never shoot at me." Her voice rose at least an octave. "Now slow down before you kill us."

Devon had slowed to negotiate a loose pile of rocks when a man, an Iraqi soldier by the uniform, stepped out from the tall cliffs bordering the road ahead. Granwin stopped talking when the soldier motioned them to stop with one hand while, with the other, he shifted an AK to point directly at them. Past the cliff, the road funneled through a narrow cut through the rock-strewn mountainside, dipped into a ravine and climbed up a steep incline to cross another of the endless ridges. Devon downshifted and weighed their chances, his foot poised to jam the accelerator to the floorboard.

If the soldier wanted to shoot, the Nissan would be in the open, grinding across the ravine and up the grade, far longer than it would take to empty the magazine into the thin roof over their heads.

The soldier moved to block the path, rifle up and leveled at the windshield. Devon jammed on the brakes and bounced along the loose rocks to a stop. Granwin sat back against the seat, hands folded in her lap.

The soldier yelled at them, motioning with the barrel of the rifle. Devon turned off the motor and stepped out, wondering if this was the same soldier he had almost run over coming up the mountain. When he got a better look, he decided not. This man was fat to the point his belly hid his belt.

Damn her. Granwin, the magnificent, couldn't stay put. She slammed the door behind her and immediately started on the soldier with a stream of Arabic so rapid Devon wondered if the soldier could even follow her. She stopped when the soldier yelled at her, loose jowls flapping as he motioned them away from the Nissan with a wave of his head.

"What does he want?" Devon asked Granwin.

"He asked what we're doing here, but I think he just wants to rob us." Her voice was steady, steadier than he felt, watching the gun barrel wave back and forth between them.

"If I wanted to steal, you would already be dead." The soldier shocked Devon with his reply in English. "Speak to me with respect. I am Senior Sergeant Dalantish, not just some bandit. Now, again, I demand. What are you doing here?" The soldier ignored Granwin and stepped nose-to-nose with Devon. "You bring the blond *houri* to the mountains to break the laws of Islam?"

Devon stared into the man's beady eyes, wondering if he should simply take the AK away from him and shove it up his ass. Not knowing what kind of back up the jerk had, he decided to try to talk his way out of it. "She's my wife. We bring food to the refugees." Devon pointed at the block letters, 'UN,' side-by side with smaller Arabic letters on the side of the Nissan, barely decipherable under the dust on the hood.

The soldier laughed at Devon's reply. This time Granwin kept her tongue, simply nodded and cast her head down.

"I know of your ways, American. You sin and make sinners of all your women. You think all Iraqis, all Muslims, are beneath you." He spat on the ground. "She is not your wife. I have seen her in the mountains before with the African. She is but a *houri* for anyone who wants her." He stepped back and leveled the rifle at Devon. "You, liar, come with me."

Once again, Devon figured he had made a wrong choice.

The soldier motioned toward a narrow path leading around a large boulder beside the track. "Later I may teach her the penalty for being such a sinner." He prodded Devon around the corner, out of sight of the Nissan and Granwin.

"Wait." Granwin's voice had too much plea in it for Devon, echoing around the rocky walls bordering the path.

He willed Granwin to stay with the Nissan, not to follow, as he tried to negotiate. "Maybe we can make some sort of business arrangement, Sergeant Dalantish." Even if Dalantish had the rifle, maybe he was smart enough to believe there was more money in not killing. Perhaps all this was just an opportunity for a deal, out of earshot of Granwin...man's business. And a few pokes with the rifle just to keep it interesting—he hoped.

Ahead of Devon, a narrow path snaked alongside a rocky ledge overlooking a deep ravine, curving around the rock formation towering between him and Granwin. He scanned the sides of the wall for anything he could use. He should be able, somehow, to take one man with a rifle. Devon stopped when a second man in uniform stepped out from the sheer rock wall to block the path.

"I believe you will have me to thank a second time, Major Devon, for saving your life."

Closer, Devon recognized the lean, pocked face of Olanti, the Pakistani from the border crossing, garbed in the dirty brown fatigues worn by most of the world's armies, with the addition of officer epaulets. He was a major if Pakistanis counted pips the same way most ex-Empire countries did.

Devon's heart thumped. Well, he started talking. Might as well keep trying. "It seems we're destined to meet in odd places."

"Oh, no. Quite on purpose, Major." Olanti turned so Devon could see the heavy revolver dangling from his hand. "My colonel was becoming agitated over your whereabouts. You see, my initial mission was to insure your safe arrival in Iraq. Now I must see that you complete your journey. Come with me." He waved the pistol toward the path behind him.

"What about the woman?" Devon looked back at the fat sergeant. "Surely, you aren't going to leave her out here in the mountains." The look Olanti passed to Dalantish carried a message Devon didn't want to hear. He suspected a night in the mountains was the least of Granwin's worries.

"I will take very good care of the *houri*." Dalantish poked his rifle into Devon's kidney, deep enough to bring a ragged pain. His sneer implied he already had a plan in mind.

"I'm sure the sergeant will determine the fate of the woman in accordance with our laws, never fear." Olanti waved the Iraqi back. "You Westerners might be welcomed by the Kurds, but the Iraqis are not as happy. You should welcome the opportunity to live a bit longer." He stepped closer, the pistol pointed toward Devon's gut.

"The captain at the border recognized you for what you are, an American soldier, but with the help of the documents provided to me by the *Mukabarat*, he fortunately allowed you to enter Iraq. Now it is time to continue your journey." He waved the barrel of his pistol. "Come. No more delays. I tire of these mountains and long to see the minarets of Islamabad." He reached out, grabbed Devon and pulled him down the path.

Devon could understand being shot by the Iraqis, but he still didn't understand what Olanti was doing here. Or what the Pakistani had in mind for him. But it was too easy to see what Dalantish had in mind for Granwin. Devon jerked free.

Olanti backed against the stone wall, carefully raised the pistol to eye level and levered back the hammer. The lead bullet noses glistened in the revolver cylinder as it clicked in place. "You are an important man, Major Devon. I am told you have some special knowledge. But my brothers will understand if I must shoot you in the leg, or some other dispensable body part. All they require is that I drag you to them, capable of talking. I can accomplish this task with a great deal of pain on your part, if you insist."

Devon searched the ground around them, moving only his eyes, head lowered, as Olanti spoke. Even against the two, listening and waiting wasn't the right tactic, Devon decided. If he went along, Granwin would probably die during the night, either by the Iraqi's or her own hand. He brushed his fingers against his pants leg. His folding Case was long gone, now residing in the border captain's pocket. Olanti held the pistol in his left hand. Olanti's right hand was shy several fingers.

Devon shrugged his shoulders. "This way?" he asked, looking down the path, at this point a narrow ledge clinging to the side of a ravine, so deep the shadows hid the bottom.

"Lead the way. Hurry. It will become dark soon." Olanti stepped back, giving way and motioning down the path with his head.

As he stepped past Olanti, Devon reached up to keep his balance. He ran his hand along the green moss growing on the overhanging rock, shuffling along the edge of the path inches away from a long drop down into the ravine. He felt for loose slivers of rock as his eyes searched for an escape. He glanced behind him to see Olanti look away, toward the other soldier. Thinking this could be his best—maybe his only opportunity—Devon clenched his fist and swung his arm down toward the gun.

Dalantish yelled a warning. Quick as a cat, Olanti grunted as he blocked Devon's blow with his right arm and snatched the gun back, out of Devon's reach.

Devon shoved his shoulder into Olanti's chest, forcing him back against the rock face. The pistol fired, a deafening blast that burned his cheek and a sudden sear of the bullet along his forearm. He grabbed the pistol with both hands and twisted the barrel away from his body, forcing it back against Olanti's stomach, driving the Pakistani back against the rock.

Devon half fell as Olanti twisted and landed a soccer player's heel kick to the back of Devon's knee, buckling Devon's leg. He teetered on the edge of the path for a moment, then used his momentum to spin Olanti around. He levered all his weight, forcing Olanti between him and Dalantish.

The rough granite scrubbed the back of Devon's head as they grunted in the confines of the path, so close Olanti's pungent breath washed over Devon.

Olanti worked his knee up between them, prying Devon away.

So slowly, Devon twisted the pistol, shielding it with his body so Olanti couldn't get his other hand to it, crushing Olanti's fingers around the pistol until he felt and heard a pop, and Olanti's arm suddenly gave way. He slammed the gun and Olanti's hand against the rock wall. The pistol discharged again, the crack and twang of the bullet ricocheting all around Devon's head. He searched Olanti's face, hoping this bullet had struck, but all he saw was Olanti's lips curled back in a determined snarl. He squeezed harder and felt a bone in Olanti's hand crack. Olanti jerked back in pain.

"Dalantish, shoot him," Olanti shouted and twisted Devon around, his back to the soldier.

A gunshot exploded in the narrow ravine, this one louder than the pistol, so close the burning powder fragments stung the back of Devon's neck and the burnt gunpowder smell swirled around his head. He glanced over his shoulder to see Dalantish slam the AK charging lever with the heel of his hand.

Olanti jerked back. "Shoot him, not me, you fool!" He staggered against the rock face, almost losing his balance.

Devon grabbed the pistol barrel, the hot metal searing his hand. He jerked and twisted, forced the barrel back toward the Pakistani. Behind him, loose rock clattered. A muffled, tiny bang sounded and the pistol bucked against his chest. Olanti unexpectedly relaxed his grip, and the pistol clattered to the path under their feet.

Devon spun to see Dalantish lunge toward him with the rifle. He swung the butt up from the ground, catching Devon in the chest. Devon felt the pipe in his jacket pocket crack—or hoped it was his pipe and not a rib. He sensed the return of the wooden stock, this time toward his face. Devon ducked away as Dalantish thrust the butt end toward him, missing to crash into the granite overhang.

They both stumbled over Olanti, underfoot in the narrow path. Dalantish lunged again, relentless and desperate. Devon twisted away and backed against the wall, trapped, as Dalantish grunted and brought the butt up to graze his cheek. The fat man was slowing, his aim less sure as the rifle slammed against the rock beside Devon's ear, splattering more sharp fragments across his face.

Devon swung an uppercut into Dalantish's fat belly. The soldier stumbled back, a mixture of surprise and hate in his eyes. Devon felt behind him for a rock, anything. The fat man was wearing him down. If one of those slaps with the rifle butt connected, he'd go down and might not get up. The path was empty. Their struggle had swept away any loose rock, any possible weapon. He reached into his jacket, closed his hand around the bowl of his pipe, pulled it out and stepped from under the overhang toward the soldier. Dalantish hesitated, then laughed when he saw what Devon held in his hand.

Devon looked down at the pipe. The remains of the stem glittered in the afternoon sun. Only a sliver of Lucite poked out from the briar, shaped like a tiny flint point. reminded him of the ones his grandma had showed him how to chip from the riverbed flint and craft the arrows. those he used to shoot fish in the slow-moving swamp water. Bigger game today. Smaller shard. Through narrowed eyes, he watched Dalantish sidestep like a big fat fish, then move to a threatening crouch, coiled like a swollen cottonmouth, ready to strike. Devon had killed snakes before, too. You just had to be quicker, strike before they could strike, and not toy with them like you could the little crawdaddies or bluegills swimming lazy in the pools.

Dalantish stepped back, re-gripped his rifle by the barrel and began a long, underhand swing, the trajectory planned to launch Devon out and into the ravine. Devon slid inside the arc and plunged the pipe shard toward Dalantish's throat in a short jab. The rifle slammed against the rock and bounced down against his shoulders. Dalantish grabbed Devon's hand with both of his, eyes bulging. Devon pushed with every bit of remaining strength until a gurgling sound rose from somewhere around the clenched fingers.

The pipe, slick with blood, slipped from Devon's grip as Dalantish stumbled back, clutched at his throat and rolled to the narrow ledge. His legs twitched for a moment, then stilled. Far below them Dalantish's rifle clattered down the steep rock wall. Devon leaned back against the cool granite, took a deep breath, and squinted up at the sky, a deep blue, high clouds hinting toward pink in the late afternoon. A buzzard soared and swooped down toward him, already drawn to the carcasses.

"Devon." Granwin's sharp cry brought him back to the moment.

He bent down and yanked what was left of his pipe from Dalantish's throat. He struggled with the bloody broken stem, finally worked it free from the shank and pitched it down the slope to bounce out of sight in the rocks. He took one more deep breath, then shoved Dalantish's body over the edge to follow his rifle and the pipe stem.

Olanti laid still, one hand dangling out over the ledge, staring up at the sky. Devon stepped over him and looked down at his own blood-spattered hands and the remains of the pipe. As he stood, breathing hard, big, green-eyed flies buzzed over Olanti's chest, growing to a swarm over the puddled blood. Devon reached up and scrubbed the pipe and his fingers on the thin moss, finally finishing his cleaning with a handful of sand from the path. Just like prayer time.

"Devon." Granwin's cry was a little closer this time.

He pushed his sleeve up. The bullet had left a raw mark, like a rope burn, across his forearm.

"Be right there," he called out. "Sergeant Dalantish and I have reached a settlement."

He took several deep breaths, pausing to inspect the pipe. These damned people were taking everything he had ever owned—his grandpa's pipe, his life as a soldier. He looked down at the Pakistani and had to resist the urge to throw the bowl after the stem. Instead, he dropped the sand-scratched pipe remnants into his pocket. He leaned back against the cool rock for leverage and shoved the body over the edge with his foot, then walked back around the boulder.

Granwin stood by the Nissan, clenched fists crossed over her chest, shoulders hunched. "I heard shots, but was afraid to come, afraid you were dead, and I would be next."

"Oh, no. You know the Iraqis, they like to scare." Devon glanced down at his hands, raw from the scrubbing. "Dalantish was just upping the ante." He waved Granwin back into the Nissan. "He finally agreed on mutually acceptable terms and left. Let's go." He turned the key, listening to the starter grind, pumping the accelerator. *Flooded.*

Devon wanted to get away from the bodies, to hide the trembling of his scoured hands. He held the accelerator down, the smell of gas in his head. Finally, the engine caught. He jammed the lever up into first gear, spinning the tires as he gunned the Nissan over the incline and down toward a distant road. Out of the corner of his eye he caught a glimpse of a brown vehicle parked between a gap in the rocks. He watched the mirror, but the vehicle didn't burst out after them, and no one waved a rifle to stop—or shoot.

Devon suddenly realized Granwin had spoken to him and was waiting for his reply. "Sorry. What?" he asked.

"Your jacket?" Granwin motioned toward his dirt-stained sleeve where the bullet had ripped its way through.

"Snagged it on a rock." He tried to smile at her, but felt like a clown with a painted-on grin. "You sew?" His arm itched where the bullet had grazed him.

Granwin's curiosity seemed to evaporate. Whatever she heard or saw, she had returned to her own world. She started talking, to the point where he began to wish she would shut up. According to the litany of Saint Renée Granwin, the Patriotic Union of Kurdistan seemed to be winning the war against the Saddam-backed Kurdish Democratic Party, if winning could be defined as who slaughtered the most old men and women last week.

But when he drove through the pathetic settlements—some tents, some old stone huts, some just shelters of rusty tin and cardboard—as far as he could tell the road to peace was no straighter, just strewn with kids, begging or just sitting by the wayside. Big, brown eyes asked why he was going back to the safety of his compound when they had to stay out in the dark and cold.

Granwin talked to him as if she had found out everything in Devon's dossier, if one existed, and his vulnerabilities—children, religion and everything French. Bouncing over the rough roads between villages, she kept prying, asking.

"Mr. Devon, are you agnostic? Or are you devoid of all belief, a soulless vacuum?" Her eyes rolled up toward the sky as she quizzed him.

Devon didn't reply. Maybe he was just a simple heathen, believing in the rocks and sky of his Lumbee Indian grandmother? Truth was, he had tried to be a good Lumbee, a descendant of the Lost

Colony and Croatans, a believer in assimilation, despite his mother's Presbyterian teachings. Like the Buddhist, he had been willing to accept anything righteous, even Christianity, the mostly Baptist kind, from his father, but willing to let the Pope have his say.

That was one reason he had stuck with the Army all those years. Most Army Protestant chaplains were noncommittal, preaching a bland religion that stayed in the background, ready to wield the sword of Gideon for Jew, Catholic or Protestant if the shit hit the fan. Even for a Muslim, if he didn't get too anti-Christ. But that one night of death in the desert, the boy dying in his arms and his mother dead in the ditch, had convinced Devon that God was in some other universe, and piss-ant humans were on their own, especially the children.

Venus was up, surrounded by a host of brilliant stars by the time they crawled back up the slope to the compound. Otto waved them into the motor pool, looking relieved Devon had brought his Nissan back in one piece. Apparently, minor body damage was par for the course. When Devon had finished checking and servicing the vehicle to Otto's satisfaction, Levison appeared out of the operations hut.

"Miss Granwin reports you were an adequate driver." Levison nodded as if Devon had earned perfect grades on his exam, perhaps enough to warrant a treat. "Please report to her in the morning and see she gets to her destinations, and back." Levison patted his hands together in a mimic of applause. "I'm so glad you have found a place on our team, Mr. Devon. I was worried about you."

"I'm just fine," said Devon, longing for a few minutes of peace and quiet.

Levison looked at him, a smile on his face, and then just walked away.

Exhaustion nagging at Devon, pain keeping the exhaustion at bay. All his thinking about the dead soldiers, mixed with Granwin's talk about children and God made Devon's head hurt. He skipped the night's mystery stew. Instead, he wandered back to Ian's kitchen retreat and smiled him out of a water glass filled to the brim with his terrible Irish whisky. Devon sat alone on a bench with his thoughts, wishing he had his pipe, sipping from the glass. Overhead, a cloud of smoke rose from the other smokers in the hut. At least the anti-smokers hadn't yet taken over this corner of the world. *Don't they realize we need the cancer to keep us from living so long?*

"Hard day, mate?" Ian held the remnants of a bottle in his hand. When Devon nodded, Ian upended the bottle until the last drop drained into Devon's glass. The glass trembled, the rye whisky rippling in little waves back and forth in the glass, an ocean of turmoil in his very grip.

With each sip, he wondered what he was doing here. What he wasn't doing. What was he going to do? Why hadn't Granwin said something to Levison about Dalantish stopping them? Why hadn't he? And for the first time, the question crossed his mind. Why had Olanti come to take him—where? On whose orders?

Devon jerked his head up as a plate shattered on the concrete floor, dropped by one of the refugee hires. Who else out there was after him? Baker had mentioned Pakistani workers in the camp, but not a word of warning.

Devon rummaged around Ian's supplies until he found a cheap bamboo-handled fork. He slipped the tines between two boxes and snapped the bamboo from the tines. He worried the remaining metal shaft out of the joint, then whittled and shaved away at the hollow bamboo with a paring knife until the bamboo fit into the old briar. Finally, he carved a grip for his teeth. He held the remodeled pipe up to the light.

Looked stupid.

He packed a load of Cavendish into the pipe and sucked through the makeshift stem. The bitter taste of smoked tobacco popped into his mouth. He spat the bit of old tobacco out onto the concrete floor. Was the blood taste real or his imagination? *To hell with it.* Now he had a pipe that had taken *coup*.

No, *coup* meant striking without killing, and getting away to boast about it. Wasn't quite what happened. What would Grandma and his Lumbee cousins think about killing with a pipe? He re-lit the tobacco and sat alone with the canned goods, puffing dreams into the smoke cloud and sipping raw whiskey.

For a moment, he thought he had gotten into Ian's private stuff and was going blind, then realized someone was blowing out the lanterns, one by one. When he looked up, Granwin stood in front of him. When he stood the lights whirled around and around the deserted building.

"Here, let me help." Devon tried to reach the nearest lantern, but staggered instead into Granwin's arms. He looked down at her. Was he that drunk? Her eyes were emerald green, shiny as the finest polished beryl. When he tried to smile at her, she stiffened in his arms. Her head jerked back and she wrinkled her nose. Those emerald eyes seemed to sadden when his breath hit her face.

"Are you a drunken atheist also?" She shoved him away.

Devon tried to joke back. "My dear, it's just sacramental wine." He stifled his laugh as the rage on her face registered, along with the silhouette of one of Ian's heavy pans high over her head.

He awoke to the gray light of dawn and the smells of cooking, head throbbing like one giant toothache. He tried to move his arms, finally gripping the rough boards of a bench enough to lift up his head. He was still in the mess hut. When everything stopped swimming, he finally focused on Granwin, sitting across from him, smiling like an angel.

"Lie still, laddie," she said. "You've a bit of a bump across your noggin."

Damned woman. In addition to her ability to understand many languages, apparently she was an adept mimic. This morning she was a bit of a lassie for his benefit. How in hell could he be angry with her when she pushed back her gray-streaked blond hair and smiled down at him? He wondered which she had intended for him—salvation or sacrifice?

God knows he needed looking after, even if there was no God.

CHAPTER 9

Sara Qasim's son Arif opened the door and stared out toward the distant mountains. Sara shivered and frowned when the cold wind whipped by her feet. A fresh topping of late spring snow sparkled, brilliant where the early morning shafts of sunlight sliced through the clouds.

"Come back in, boy, and shut the door. The air is too cold for my old bones, especially first thing in the morning."

Arif slammed the door at Director Levison's rebuke and glanced back at his mother, eyes wide.

"Return to your studies, Arif." Sara frowned at her son. They could not afford to irritate the director. Arif's future, their very lives, depended on her job with the foreigners.

Her son sat on the floor behind her desk with the book in his lap. He leaned his head back and stared at the ceiling. "I want to go outside, Mother." He smiled, so like his father. "I saw a dog out by the trucks. May I go play with him? I'm the only boy in the camp, I think. I want to find a friend."

"Stay inside, Arif. We are new here. I do not want to cause problems." Oh, the boy was all too much like his father, too impatient to learn, always had to be doing, going. Now his father was gone forever. She would have to live whatever life was necessary for her son. She flipped through the pages of documents. It would take her days to learn the Commission administrative procedures.

"Mother." Arif stood by her arm until she looked up at him. "I finished reading the book." He held up the tattered copy of *Gulliver's Travels* Director Levison had loaned him. "When Mr. Otto comes, may I go out to the truck park?"

Director Levison stood. "Desk work is tiring, is it not, Arif?" He put on his jacket and started for the door. "If the telephone should decide to work, Mrs. Qasim, take a message." He studied the grease-penciled schedule on the wall next to the map. "I will be at the municipal center until noon prayer time."

After the director left, Sara gave in and shooed Arif out into the compound. She picked up the phone and listened. No tone, no sound at all. She tapped the post only to hear a dry click.

The door suddenly opened She slammed the phone to its cradle. It was only the Frenchwoman. "*Kayf haaluk*, how are you, Miss Granwin?" Sara took another breath to slow her racing pulse. "May I help you?"

"I'm fine, thank you. Where is Mr. Otto? I must get a vehicle," Granwin replied in faultless Arabic. She swirled her shawl around her head, hiding the short blond hair, the talk of the handful of women in the compound. Before Sara could answer, a man burst through the open door and smiled over Granwin's shoulder. This must be was Mister Devon, the American the officer had told her about. He was broad across the shoulders, but not very handsome with his unruly black hair.

"Going to introduce us, Granwin?" Devon stepped from behind the Frenchwoman.

Granwin seemed exasperated with the man. "You had your entertainment last night, laddie. We have no time for social affairs. Ready the vehicle."

Devon turned his smile toward Sara. His smile was obviously for the capture of loose women, but Sara smiled back in return anyway. She still did not know what the military expected of her. She tried to keep her smile in place when the man picked out a key from Otto's board.

She had heard the cooks laughing, but hadn't believed the gossip. Apparently it was true; the man had a dark lump on his forehead.

Granwin nodded at Sara. "Mrs. Qasim, this is Mr. Devon, our new American agricultural advisor." Granwin turned to Devon. "Mr. Devon, this is *Mrs.* Sara Qasim."

Sara was glad Granwin had emphasized the "Mrs."

"Director Levison told me that Mrs. Qasim is newly arrived as our Iraqi liaison. She will take care of all local administrative matters for him." Granwin looked at the American for a moment, her face hard. "Not your personal needs." Granwin turned toward the door. "Enough talk. We have a long distance to travel and it is already afternoon."

Sara smiled at their backs as the two left the office. That much bickering. They must either be good friends or adversaries in some matter. Perhaps of the heart.

With the two out of sight she picked up the phone. The line hummed back. A bit of an echo responded when she tapped the instrument. After a moment, a voice came on speaking Arabic. Sara responded in the same language, asking for the number she had been given by the officer in the jail. Her smile left her.

"Yes." The voice was distant, indistinct.

"My name is Sara Qasim. I was told to report to this number." Her hand began trembling and she closed her eyes for a moment, waiting.

"Yes, go ahead. Give me your report." The voice sounded impatient.

What was she supposed to say? The voice frightened her, reminding her of those last hours with her husband, after the explosion in the nuclear research facility. She must keep her wits. "The American, Devon, is in the camp."

"Did anyone come with him?"

Sara thought for a moment. They could be watching, testing her. *Had anyone else come?* She could not remember any other new faces. "He arrived before I did. I have not seen anyone else new since I arrived."

"Has he contacted anyone outside the camp?"

"He has not called out on the telephone, but he now drives one of the relief workers to the villages."

The voice turned angry. "You are not providing the assistance we expected and demand. You must get to know him, to learn exactly what he is doing."

"How can I do those things?" Sara tried to control her voice, but it rose and cracked, like a schoolgirl's.

"Take him to bed. Do whatever is necessary, I don't care. Give him your son if that is what he likes. Results—or you and your son will be removed from the camp and dealt with according to law, as the wife and son of a traitor."

The voice was now very quiet as she pressed the receiver to her ear with both hands, tears streaming from her eyes.

"Do you understand? You now owe your life to *Ahad* in a debt that will remain forever." Very slowly he repeated, "Do you understand me?"

Her own voice surprised even her, now calm. "Yes, I understand."

The connection broke and the line went silent again, not even a faint hum. Sara put the phone in the cradle and wiped her tears with the corner of her sleeve, then walked over, knees weak, to stand by the window. *Where was Arif?*

She felt a wave of relief when she saw her son beside Devon pumping gas into a can. She was not a *houri*, but she knew she would do anything for Arif. She had lost her husband. She would not lose her son, whatever the price.

"What are you doing?" Arif asked.

"Dipping my Zippo and filling it with gasoline." No more land of the PX—regular old gasoline or nothing for the old Zippo until he could figure how to get out of here. Devon held the battered chrome lighter up to dry, thankful the lighter had been deep in a jacket pocket at the border crossing or it would be with his knife in the captain's pocket now.

"To start a fire?"

The kid was full of questions. "Just to light my pipe." Devon shook off the excess gas, dropped the lighter into his jacket pocket and watched the boy grunt under the weight of the five-gallon can. Arif grimaced, but never asked for help, and carefully poured the gas into the Nissan.

"Can you drive, kid?"

So the kid's mom was the liaison to Saddam's government. Probably an informant like most of the Iraqis, Pakistanis, and Kurds in the compound. Here Iraqis had all the desk jobs—the positions with titles, the Pakistanis did the real office and shop work, and the Kurds had what was left over like cleaning out the latrine or pulling KP for Ian. And he bet each layer had its own networks, its own secrets.

Arif put down the empty can and grinned at him. "Sure, Chief."

"What's this 'chief' stuff?" Devon screwed the cap back on the tank.

"Mr. Baker says you are a real American Indian, and I must be careful or you will scalp me. I read a book one time about Apaches. Are you Apache? Do you smoke a peace pipe?"

The boy stayed right by Devon's side, watching his every move. Devon had to step around him to get to the front of the Nissan.

"Well, Baker's right, so don't cross me. I'm Injun, and it's a war pipe." He reached across and tugged at the kid's hair. Arif jerked back with a giggle.

Devon popped the hood and searched for the oil dipstick in the dusty engine compartment. Otto might be efficient, but he didn't worry about a little grease and grime on the in-line six. No shiny chrome under any of his hoods. Arif handed him a scrap of rag to wipe the stick. The kid was smart about vehicles.

"And for you, my name is Mr. Chief. Doesn't your mom teach you manners?" *Kid probably has read more books than me.* "How old are you?"

"I have ten years," Arif answered. "And I have manners."

"How in the world did you learn to speak English?"

Arif stood up with his chest puffed out, his grin stretching ear-to-ear. "My mother and father worked in a very important place with many books in English. My father told me I must learn English to be smart, to be an engineer as he was. Do I speak goodly?"

"Better than most." Devon handed him the rag. "But say 'I speak English well,' not 'goodly.'"

Arif frowned at the rebuke.

"You going to be my assistant, you got to speak perfect English," Devon added.

A grin Arif's replaced frown. "Official assistant?" he asked.

"Very official," Devon answered, his face straight.

"Mr. Devon?" Granwin called from the office. "Please fetch the other box."

Devon winked at Arif. "Here comes the wicked witch of the north."

The boy frowned at the reference.

"Haven't read *Wizard of Oz?*" asked Devon.

"No. Is it a story of evil?" Arif carefully folded the rag and stuffed it in a back pocket.

"Not really." Devon set the empty can in the rack by the fence and nodded toward the motor pool gate where Granwin strode toward them, a small cardboard box under one arm and water bottle under the other, shawl trailing in the dirt. "I'll explain later. I expect Mademoiselle la Granwin wants to leave—right now."

Devon trotted to the operations hut, picked up a second box and loaded it with the other in the back of the Nissan.

He climbed into the Nissan to an unusual silence. Granwin was already in her place, staring straight ahead, hands folded in her lap. No comments about the soldier or the frying pan incident. He was surprised Granwin hadn't complained to Levison and gotten Baker to drive her after their battle in the mess hall. But it seems they were just out for a ride.

Devon started the Nissan moving and waved at Arif as the boy trotted alongside the truck with a mangy dog yapping at his heels. "See you later, kid," he yelled.

The boy and the dog ran ahead to the gate where Arif stood at attention, waving a half-salute when Devon drove out.

Granwin sat quietly beside him for the first few miles, breaking the silence only to give directions. Was she his contact, for God's sake? Or on the other side?

Devon remembered the few letters from Vietnam he had peeked at when his mother left them on the bedside table, about how his dad never knew who was good and who was bad, and worried about little girls with grenades. He wondered what Granwin carried in her big handbag?

But as they worked their way into the foothills, Devon discovered that whatever side she was on, making up after a fight, for Granwin, meant a lot of talking. For Devon that meant a lot of listening. And listening and listening. After the third village as her handy man and faithful listener, he decided it was a punishment, not a reprieve. But there was one thing she hadn't explained.

"Why, Granwin?" He interrupted her comparison of the Bible and the Koran for a more earthly question.

She frowned, not understanding his question. "Why what?"

"Why do we come out to these villages? The villagers have lived here for years, been poor for years."

Granwin nodded. "Yes, some. Many are from the towns, driven out by poison gas raids and sweeps by Qusay's Special Security Organization, his solution for the Kurds, God help them all." She stared up through the windshield and shivered as clouds streaked across a deep cobalt sky stretching up from the snow-tipped mountains rising in front of them.

"Who's Qusay?" Houston had made some reference to the name, but Devon had lost the connection.

"Saddam's son. An exceptionally evil man, so they say." She braced back against the seat at a long, belly-dropping lurch across a wash. "Like most men who wear uniforms."

"I'm a soldier, just not in uniform."

"But you don't kill children."

He had no answer, no quick retort to tell her how wrong she was. She didn't seem to notice. She just kept talking.

"My father was a soldier, too. He really *was* a Frenchman, despite Aunt Jeannine's accusations. Father had warned me there was danger. The Algerian uprising had begun, but I didn't understand any of the politics. I only wanted some sweets. He was such a good father. He took me to the Tripoli *souk*.

"I remember the day so clearly. He was in uniform, with his shiny, leather holster and pistol. I thought no one could hurt me if my father was with me. I stepped into a sweets shop and he stayed outside to watch. Then the bomb went off in the alley." She sighed. "He was a soldier, so I never cried."

She turned and looked at him. "But I still believe God will save us all." She leaned forward to look into his eyes. "Don't you?"

Devon shook his head in disagreement. "God is just a symbol for the weak to pray to. The ones with power don't need God. They just use His name as they see fit." He waved at the craggy hillside and the sky above it. "My grandmother told me that if there was a God, he lived in the ground and the stars and all the plants and animals of the swamps."

Devon glanced over at Granwin's somber face and tried to lighten the mood. "But then grandma smoked a pipe and dipped snuff. Maybe she was growing stuff in the edge of Hog Swamp I didn't know about."

"You should treat your grandmother's memory with more respect." Granwin held tightly to the handle as he bounced them around a curve. "You asked why I come to the villages. My grandfather is one reason why, as much as the food for the children and the little babies." She stretched her chin up, pulled a small gold cross on a chain from under her blouse, and held it out toward him. "Grandpère told me about an old superstition among the Syrian Christians. It was about an icon, or something to do with a cross either lost or hidden in the mountains. He called it the Image of Christ. So I ask about it among the villages and the traveling merchants." Her smile was apologetic, as if she knew the search was foolish.

"An icon is one of those little Russian pictures. All gold, aren't they?" Devon shook his head. "Nobody's going to give their treasure up to you."

She shrugged her shoulders. "Icons can be many things—pictures, crosses. Perhaps the legend is about a fragment of the real Cross of Jesus. Perhaps only God knows. Anyway, I ask." Her look was a little defiant. "For Grandpère." She returned her cross to hiding, teasing Devon with a hint of pale flesh.

He shook any thought of her as a woman from his head. The throb the motion restarted in his head should be enough warning. The story of the icon was enough of a mystery. He didn't need to ponder this strange woman, but he couldn't resist one more question. "Why do you believe such old tales?"

"Grandpère told me, so I believe."

"My grandma told me the old stories about the spirits of the swamps. She mixed up hand-me-down Indian tales from her grandmother, some Cherokee, some Tuscarora. Sometimes I think they were just scary stories to keep me awake at night. Sure made understanding Sunday school hard with her telling me Jesus was just the white man's God. But the Lumbee's god was all around us in the sky, in the earth, in every living thing, especially the birds and the snakes."

He glanced over and realized she was staring at his face, frowning at his words. "Don't get all high and mighty on me. I listened to my grandma, like you listened to an old man. Why do you believe this Image of Christ thing?"

"After my father died, my mother and I lived with my grandfather for many years. He was an archeologist at Palmyra. Damascus and the Bekáa Valley were beautiful then, many of the people Arab Christians. When I was only a school girl, Syrian soldiers came to our home." Her voice dropped so Devon had to strain to catch her words over the growl of the laboring engine.

"They tied me to a bed and made me watch. Grandpère worked for an American university as the director of a major archeological site. He was a Frenchman, but still a respected elder in the community. That day the soldiers called him an infidel and a sinner, a spy for the Americans. They used the wine they found in his cellar as an excuse." She paused.

When Devon glanced over she was looking up in the sky, blinking.

"They drank his wine and beat him. They all passed out, but Grandpère was too hurt to untie me. He wept and begged me to search for the Image of Christ if he were to die. When the soldiers woke, they slit his throat."

Tiny tears on her cheeks glittered in the afternoon sun. She finally stopped talking.

We all have our dreams, Devon thought, *and our quests*.

He slowed to maneuver through a cluster of small sheds—pieces of tin and canvas held together with piles of rocks. He jerked the wheel when a blur of yellow and white flashed across in front of him. The blur slowed to a child running along beside the Nissan, yelling and waving at Granwin.

"Stop!" Granwin snapped and rolled down her window.

A little girl stood at the edge of the road, dressed in a dusty white dress patterned with yellow flowers. Granwin reached back, pulled a can from the box on the back seat and handed it to the girl. The girl turned and dashed back down the road without a word, can clenched to her chest, to stop in front of one of the huts. An old woman joined the child and they stood together in the roadway, small in the mirror Nissan's side mirror. Without a word, Granwin rolled up the window. Another satisfied recipient.

Intrigued by the pair in the mirror, the wheel twisted in his hands as Devon bounced over a scattering of rocks. Granwin muttered something under her breath, and a sudden look—anger or irritation—he wasn't sure which, flashed across her face. Devon wondered if she was still mad at him from the night before or if his driving was really so irritating. Then he saw she was glaring at a man sitting in the sunshine.

In uniform, like half the men in this country, he leaned into a thin column of smoke rising from an open fire to stir the contents of a smudged pot and peer back at them. A camouflage net draped from the top of the ravine shielded a Soviet Straight Flush fire control antenna from overhead observation. The bullet burn on Devon's forearm suddenly itched, and the knot on his head seemed to swell. Faded and flaked paint and dented support struts marked the age and disrepair of the radar, a match for the man's dusty uniform.

A *Kub* transporter crouched behind the radar dish loaded with a trio of missiles, a reminder his and Granwin's jobs were as different as night and day. He was the missile expert, slipped into Iraq to uncover any sign of Iraqi doomsday weapons hidden in the mountains around Irbil. Her job was to keep as many kids from starving as possible. Devon suspected her task was harder than his, but at least she could find the kids. Still, he wondered why she had reacted so angrily toward the soldier, she with her love-them-all-with-Jesus attitude.

Complex woman.

He mentally added the site to his catalog of surface-to-air radars and gun emplacements he'd spotted on their various outings. Certainly not interesting enough to risk putting down on paper for some zealous soldier to find while he was out in the field. But he would add this site to the notebook when he got back to the compound.

Suddenly, a roar erupted from the trail behind them. Devon leaned out the window to watch a white cloud of smoke shoot up from the missile emplacement, arrowing into the sky toward an intersection with a pair of vapor trails. Devon slowed the Nissan to watch the vapor trails split, one curving away, the other sweeping in a wide arc, suddenly straightening, coming their way.

"Damn it!" Devon jammed the Nissan into first and spun the tires, accelerating away from the missile site.

"What was that?" asked Granwin.

"SAM launch. One of the planes is coming back this way. Hang on." He had the accelerator as far down as he dared on the tricky path, dodging around boulders and steadily climbing. "Hope they're using HARMs—anti-radiation missiles that track down the radar beam to the antenna. If so we should be clear."

A glint in the sky prompted Devon to whip into a gap in the rocks just wide enough to hold the vehicle. He locked the brakes. The

Nissan hopped across the rocky surface, finally skidding to a halt. Devon looked up. Rock walls encased them on three sides by. All he could see was a bit of blue sky directly above.

"Did they hit the aircraft?" Granwin asked the unexpected question.

"Can't tell, but unlikely. I don't think the Coalition Forces have lost a bird up here yet."

She looked relieved, and then asked the obvious, the answer written across her face. "Are the planes going to bomb us?"

Before he could answer, an explosion flung the Nissan forward. The hood crumpled like tinfoil where it slammed into the rock face in front of them. Devon glanced up to see an F-16, turbofan screaming as it flashed directly overhead.

He jammed the Nissan into reverse and started backing out of their hiding place when they bucked into the air and he jerked forward, slamming his head against the steering wheel. Granwin screamed, then the concussion pounded his ears, blocking out Granwin's yells. He looked over. Her mouth was open, but he couldn't hear a word.

Another blast rocked the Nissan to the limits of its springs, throwing Devon up into the air, then down against the seat. Dust filled the air all around them, hiding the mountain and the trail behind a heavy gray pall. He was wrong about the HARMs. The F-16 was flinging iron bombs all over the mountain.

Devon jerked back against the seat when a shard of twisted metal bounced off the hood, followed by a barrage of debris rattling down out of the sky onto the Nissan, some with dull, fleshy thumps too descriptive for Devon's imagination. The boulder beside Devon's open window splintered with a report like a rifle shot. Broken rock lurched up out of the ground toward them, then teetered overhead like a pouting lip. Devon floored the accelerator, banging the front right fender against the splintered boulder. Just as the Nissan cleared the opening, the fractured boulder toppled down in another thunderous eruption of rock, dust and noise.

"Holy Mother of God." Granwin crossed herself with one hand and held on to the handgrip with the other.

Damn. He could hear again. Devon turned back onto the track and deliberately drove out of the settling dust cloud as his heart slowed to closer to its regular beat.

Granwin craned her head around under the windshield, searching overhead. "Will the planes return?" She shook a cloud of gray dust from her shawl and rubbed her ears with the palms of her hands.

"Pray they don't, lady. A truck climbing up the mountain would make a fine target. And pray they aren't spoiling to use a Maverick missile, or we're cooked."

He slowed when they came to a sloping pasture. The trail emerged from the high boulders, running naked across the mountain-side to vanish on the other side of the slope. He bent forward and scanned the sky. No vapor trails, nothing in sight. "Try rubbing your cross, or whatever makes good things happen. Here we go."

Granwin closed her eyes as Devon started across the open slope.

"Home free," he muttered when they reached the far side, the five-minute drive taking forever in his mind.

Granwin nodded, granting him a slight smile. She gestured up a steep incline between two outcroppings of rock, toward another collection of stone huts in the distance. "This is our final stop today."

Devon drove toward the small village huddled against the side of the mountain, slowing to weave through a herd of grazing goats. Beside the trail, another sullen-faced man in baggy, striped brown-and-white pants and shirt watched them pass.

Granwin waved at the man, but he didn't wave back. She pointed toward a gap between the huts. "This is a good place. Park here, please."

He pulled in beside the first of the houses—piles of rocks loosely mortared with crumbling mud and bits of straw sticking out like a week-old beard from the mortar. She turned to look at him, and then reached out to touch his forehead. When the bombs hit, he had banged the knot on his head smack against the steering wheel.

"The bruise has turned purple. That means it's healing, so the sisters always told me." She didn't hide her grin. "I truly am sorry about last night, but your drunken raving was more than I could bear. Like today, there is much to fear without fearing each other." She paused, a sad look returned to her face as she composed a truce. "We should be friends. Please call me René." She reached over to pat his shoulder, like a doting aunt. "And I shall call you Nash." She smiled and placed a condition on her grant. "When we are alone."

He killed the engine. Granwin got out, still shaking dust from her clothes, and started sorting through the boxes. Devon spread the tourist map Houston had given him over the steering wheel and looked out across the valley. Unlike the Zagros Mountains on the other side of the river, this ridge bared layers of multicolored rock, probably exposed by Noah's flood. Stripped of its trees by nature, man and goats, a thin layer of close-cropped grass held the soil to the slope. Here and there a sprig of buckhorn thorn waved with a hint of a small yellow flower on the tips of the bristly limbs.

The UNHCR camp was a smudge on the far side of the Great Zab River. Probably fifteen miles away by road, maybe ten straight across. The first mile was down a steep, winding goat trail, then across the open slope and past the missile site. He had taken half an hour to negotiate their way up the final pitch after the bomb attack, grinding along in first gear most of the way.

As he watched, their camp across the valley vanished, obscured by a long shadow cast by the mountain peak jutting toward the sky behind him. He stared back along the trail. Rocks, dirt, and another hole in the side of the mountain where the bombs had struck…another pinprick in history.

He followed the map's contour lines, locating where he thought the radar and SAM had been before the bombs hit. The map didn't show a road or even a trail, just a bare mountainside. He quickly jotted down a set of coordinates and what he had seen in an abbreviated code along the margin of the map. He still had no idea what he was going to do with the information. The details on the map faded away with the failing sunlight, along with the bit of warmth the sun had brought to the mountainside.

Damn. It would be pitch dark before they could get down out of the foothills. He recalled the ambush the day before. 'Not shooting at us,' she had said. *Was it all an act?* Had she expected Olanti to come back around the boulder instead of Devon? He called out to Granwin, digging through the boxes. "I think we're too far out to get back to camp tonight." His concern must have shown on his face.

"Don't worry, atheist. I will keep you safe out here with the rest of the heathens—and the true-believers." She picked several large cans and a bottle of water from the boxes behind the seat, dropped them in her tote and turned to a welcome from a straggle of dark robed-women with a handful of children.

Granwin passed out the cans, scooped up one of the children, apparently a young boy from the cropped hair and pants long enough that they weren't supposed to be shorts, but so short they barely met the top of an old pair of rubber boots. She spun him around, laughing, and carried him on her hip toward the center of the hovels. Suddenly, Devon couldn't tell her dark dress from the other women, all laughing in the falling light.

He secured the Nissan and walked through the village looking for Granwin as the first stars climbed above the ridge towering over the small village.

She wasn't hard to find. In this country, laughter was an oddity, especially coming from a somber pile of rocks that he hesitated to call a house, perched on the bare hillside. Her laughter, for some reason, really got under Devon's skin. Hers was different—loud, pealing, like she was not afraid of anything and had nothing to hide.

The bits of history Granwin had parceled out along the way had only made Devon more curious about her. After the cruelties she must have seen in these hills, she should have been a step or two to the hard side, the side away from the heart, the side away from God and children. But no, she was a devout, bead-carrying Catholic.

Laughter filtered through the chinks between the rocks, refusing to be held in by the cold stones. When Devon pushed open the heavy wooden door, Granwin had a whole family gathered around her, wide grins on the adults' faces, children's eyes sparkling in the light of the smoky fire. She was parceling out slices of mandarin orange from a can, talking ninety miles an hour as she carefully laid an orange section on each person's spoon.

What she was saying escaped him. He wasn't even sure what language they were speaking…another thing that irritated him about the woman. She seemed to be able to grasp anything anyone said, no matter in which rocky valley they found themselves lost and wandering. She had mentioned a doctorate from the American University in Beirut in languages. Not "a" language—apparently all of them.

The boy she had plucked from the ground sat in her lap, eyes intent on Granwin's face, blinking as smoke from the fire rolled under the low sill.

Devon backed out and shut the door. This was not his place. He wandered back to the Nissan and prepared for a cold, lonely night.

CHAPTER 10

Devon woke to a loud explosion, followed by an impact into the Nissan's windshield that left a giant spider-web pattern in the glass. He kicked the passenger-side door open and tried to crawl out. His leg snagged in the gearshift handle. He jerked loose and slithered to the ground, head on a swivel searching for the source of the incoming.

The chill mountain air was silent for a moment before a shriek cut the silence, followed by screams and the bawling of an animal. Devon scrambled to his feet and ran between the houses toward the source of the noise. As he passed, women and children peeked from doorways, half-seen blurs.

He expected this was nothing new for them. Death and destruction walked all around them, every day, every night. He glanced up into the sky where the blue just starting to push out the gray from the dawn. High, overhead white streaks marked the daily flight of British Jaguars or American Strike Eagles out of Incirlik, keeping the peace—at twenty thousand feet. Devon wondered if some fool Iraqi had set up a SAM site just the other side of this village. If the Iraqis had, and turned the radar on, they all would die.

Devon stumbled across the loose rocks by the side of the narrow road, finally hitting his stride in the trail rutted by years of goats going and coming from the higher pastures. A few more steps and more frightened faces, then suddenly he could smell the gore. He stopped in the middle of the trail leading from the village up into the mountains. An eerie vista stretched before him, gray smoke rising from churned-up ground, scant bits of dew-damp grass, and an occasional patch of high pasture in the distance.

The screams came from Granwin, restrained by several other women to keep her from darting across to a child teetering on a flat slab of rock. Mangled remains lay scattered between Granwin and the child.

Devon took a deep breath. At first, he had thought the blotchy white and brown chunks of flesh were the remains of a herder or one of the children, but, as reason focused his eyes, he decided the victim was a goat, bloody bits still steaming in the chill morning air.

Granwin's scream took form as her voice broke. "Taj."

The name was all Devon could understand. The rest was a stream of Kurdish directed toward the child, the small boy Granwin had carried on her hip the evening before, now perched on a rock about twenty yards from the main trail. Even this far away Devon could see him shiver, skinny arms clutched tight against his chest, elbows clasped in the palm of each hand, shoulders hunched. Thin rivulets of blood streamed down his bare arms.

But his eyes were wild, darting from Granwin to the remains of the goat and back to Granwin, head never moving, just the eyes, huge with an unspoken plea. Devon started toward the boy, arms held out.

"Stop, stop," Granwin screamed at him.

Devon turned to her.

"Mines. The goat was killed by a land mine." Granwin slid from the women's grasp to her knees. "There may be more." She waved toward the valley below. "Fetch Baker and his machines." Her waves became frantic. "Hurry, before Taj falls from the rock."

Devon scanned the short expanse. The ground appeared even, no sign of digging or a trap. But the goat and the disturbed turf was proof enough. He turned and ran to the Nissan. In moments, he was roaring down the mountain, bouncing from gulch to gully, hands straining to hold the wheel steady as he slammed the brakes, skidding sideways along the path past the scattered remnants of the missile battery.

Bombs had obliterated the cluster of houses—not a living soul in sight. If he hadn't seen the woman, the waving kid, the day before, he wouldn't have believed any of it existed.

The steering wheel twisted in his grip and the Nissan skidded off the track. He pushed the thoughts of the bombing out of his mind and focused on the dash down to the valley road and across the river. Horn blaring, he sped past a slow-moving truck, then slammed on the brakes to miss a man prodding a small herd of goats, only to skid off the road. He gunned the motor, flinging mud onto the bleating goats as he regained the road. Devon accelerated from second through the gears to fifth, running the Nissan flat-out, speedometer pegged at some unknown number the last five miles to the camp.

Otto jumped clear of the compound entrance and the careening Nissan as Devon slid to a stop. The gray dust settled over the freshly washed white vehicles in the compound as Devon leaped from the Nissan in front of the startled man.

"What sort of reckless driving have you been doing to my truck?" Otto frowned and pointed at the crazed star on the windshield and the crumpled hood.

Devon ignored him and jerked open the door to the ops hut. Sara Qasim looked up with surprise.

"What is the matter, Mr. Chief?" asked Arif as he jumped up and ran to the doorway.

Devon pushed the boy aside. "Mrs. Qasim, is the helicopter coming today?"

"Yes." She glanced at the schedule on the wall. "It will come today, Wednesday, if the weather is good."

"Come here." He picked up a grease pencil. "When they come, tell the pilot a kid has been hurt...about there." Devon followed the ridgeline up to where someone had penciled in 'K-15' and circled a spot on the map. "Tell them to come pick up an injured child."

Her eyes registered concern. Arif made a face when she clutched him close against her hip.

"Understand?" he asked.

"Yes, I will tell them." She looked across the valley at the distant mountainside. "What happened?"

"A mine exploded."

She squeezed Arif even closer until the boy squirmed in her grip.

He picked up the phone. *Dead!* He threw it back to the desk. Who the hell was he going to call? 911? Too much talking... He had to do something. This boy, this Taj, was not going to die if he could help it. "Where's Baker?"

She started to speak when Arif interrupted. "I think Mr. Baker is in the men's hut."

"Thanks." Devon burst out of operations and ran to the sleeping hut. Baker wasn't in his bunk. The cold building was deserted. What time was it, and where was everyone? Devon sprinted across the compound to the mess hall. He stopped inside the door, nauseated by the sudden smell of greasy food. The hut was half-full, but he easily spotted Baker's graying hair. Devon barged his way through the rows of tables, knocking a tray to the floor.

Baker grinned when he saw Devon.

"Slow down and have some eggs, Nash." Baker waved him over, forked a mound of scrambled eggs into his mouth and chewed. "Ian's out of pepper and they're tolerable this morning. Glad to see you, man. Heard the booms yesterday and wondered if you were scattered around in little pieces up there." He put down his fork when he saw Devon's face.

"Come with me. Now," Devon said.

Baker's smile turned to a frown. "What the hell's wrong? Is Granwin hurt?"

Devon took a breath, leaning on the table. "A kid in a minefield. On the other side of the river and up the mountain. Get your stuff."

Baker moved quickly for a big man, past Devon before he could turn. "You got a truck?" he yelled back.

"Nissan. Waiting at the gate." Devon ran back to the truck. He dumped a can of gas into the tank, impatiently waiting for Baker. He opened the back and shoved the half-empty boxes against the seat back, clearing room for Baker to throw in an armload of gear—a long-handled mine detector, a bundle of marker flags and a clatter of loose tools. As they raced back across the valley and started back up the goat trail, Devon explained what he had seen.

"What kind of sound, a bam or a boom?" Baker asked.

"It woke me up, Bert. I'm not sure." Devon pumped the accelerator and ground the transmission as he missed second. He jammed the transmission into third gear, accelerated up a smooth stretch of the trail, then braked to swerve around a boulder and dip down and across a creek bed, then a quick downshift to first gear as he pointed the Nissan back up the slope. The heat gauge needle quivered in the red. Devon ignored the gauge and slid around a massive boulder.

"Think, man! Did the explosion have a crack to it, or a black powder slow roll?" Baker's voice rose as the Nissan pitched him against the doorframe.

Devon hesitated, playing the explosion back in his head. "More of a crack than a boom."

Baker nodded, glanced back at the equipment. "Most likely a plastic foot popper. If the goat had triggered a Valmara, the kid would've been cut down on the spot."

Devon knew about foot-poppers without asking. His dad's letters had mentioned the old French mines left behind in Vietnam. *Small, plastic, hard to detect, just enough to blow off a heel.* He jerked his mind back to driving when he realized a soldier was standing in the road, blocking the way with a deer-in-the-headlights look on his face. *Ah, shit, not again.* He jammed the accelerator to the floor and swerved around the man.

"Jesus Christ Almighty," roared Baker. "How 'bout I live long enough to get killed, Chief."

They flashed by the soldier. Devon kept the pedal to the floor, spewing dirt and rocks behind them as they climbed toward the village.

Baker leaned over to peer into the side mirror. "Was that a missile site up the ravine?"

Devon up-shifted as the trail leveled off for a few hundred yards. "Yeah, looked like air defense missile, a SA-6 setup. I only got a glimpse of the missiles, but the radar was definitely a Straight Flush." Devon sped across the open stretch. "That's what the bombs were after yesterday."

"Looks like they took out a village instead," Baker said. "You get the transceiver okay?"

Devon glanced over at Baker. "Yeah. You knew about that the device, didn't you?"

Baker nodded, both hands on the grip. "You watch the damn road."

Devon let his foot up from the accelerator as a hovel flashed by and a goat scrambled out of the track.

"I ordered it up. Cowboying around in these hills, you're going to need it. Something big is going on and one of us is going to find it pretty soon. And I 'spect you're the only one that'll recognize it. Levison will have you all over the area now that Granwin has picked you for her driver. Pretty soon we'll figure out an excuse to get you out to a new site you need to look at."

Before Devon could ask anything else, he had to pound on the brakes and skid to a stop beside a waving Granwin.

"Hurry," she cried as he jumped out of the Nissan.

The boy was still standing out on the hillside. "Tell me what to do," Devon said. He felt helpless while Baker dragged his gear out of the truck.

"You bring up stuff if I call for it." Baker had a pair of binoculars to his eyes, sweeping over the ground between him and the boy, still frozen to the boulder.

Granwin joined them. Tear tracks streaked the dust on her face. Her blond hair stood in spikes, tousled, uncombed.

"Ah, shit." Baker handed Devon the glasses.

"What do you see?" Granwin grabbed Devon's hand, intent on Baker's face. "Please, Taj has been there over an hour. Can't you just go out and get him?"

"Bits of blue plastic all over the ground around the goat parts. Probably a popper, maybe even one of ours, an M25 Elsie. This dude just picks up metallic mines—" Baker tossed the metal detector back into the Nissan. "—and we haven't been able to get hold of the new radar jobs." Baker pointed at the rocky ground. "Anyway, they say the new detectors pick up every rock in the ground, probably just slow me down."

He grinned at Devon. "What the hell, huh?" He stuck a handful of tiny flags on pieces of stiff wire in his back pocket, picked up a slim wooden stake and walked up the trail to the closest point to Taj.

Baker dropped to his knees at the edge of the trail. "Just have to do it the old-fashioned way." He began gently prodding the ground at an angle with the stake, inching forward on his knees.

He moved with the hasty deliberation of someone who knew what was at risk. Every yard or so, Baker marked the cleared path with one of the flags.

Devon pried Granwin's grip from his fingers. She was trembling under his touch. He put his arm around her shoulders and pulled her close. "Who's the boy?"

"His name is Taj. He's an orphan. When the Republican Guards swept through Irbil, they killed or drove out many of the Kurds. His parents were killed by the *Mukabarat* and these people took him in." Granwin discreetly motioned toward a young man in the striped brown shirt and pants standing at the far edge of the group. "He worked on *Ain Kawa* Street with Taj's parents. He brought Taj to this village where I found him, starving."

Devon stared, long enough for the man to turn and walk away. One ear was missing. Devon shrugged his shoulders. "So? Should the address mean something to me? I've never been to greater downtown *Ain Kawa* Street."

"Of course you haven't. That was the American CIA headquarters in Irbil. Saddam's forces obliterated it, and most of the people who worked there. The Americans deserted the rebels—and vanished." She glanced up at Devon as if he might do the same. "Taj is one reason I come here and, of course, to help the others as best I can."

She shrugged off his arm and walked ever so carefully up the trail, one foot in front of the other, behind Baker. He looked back at her, then at Devon, shook his head and continued probing, stopping only to brush away the swarm of flies attracted to the scattered bits of goat. She began speaking in what Devon guessed to be Kurdish to the boy. Taj replied and unfolded his arms, a hint of a timid smile on his face.

He stood for a moment, then shooed at the flies buzzing around his head. Baker and Granwin were only about five yards from Taj when the boy suddenly tottered, waving his pale hands around his head. He arched his back, fighting for balance. He lost it, arms and legs flailing as he tumbled from the rock toward the ground.

"Taj," Granwin screamed, followed by a stream of Kurdish. When she bolted toward the boy, Baker grabbed her around her waist and swept her off her feet. He turned and carefully carried her back to Devon, one slow step at a time. Granwin screamed over Baker's shoulder at Taj, now lying motionless on the ground.

Baker stood Granwin on her feet beside Devon. "Hold onto her before she blows both our butts off."

Baker called out to the people from the village. The women and children huddled behind Granwin. The men watched from the far side of the trail with what Devon perceived as more curiosity than fear or sympathy. No one moved in response to Baker's shouts.

The big man waved his big hands, pointed at Devon and roared a string of Arabic at the men. Granwin added to his shout, this time in shrill Kurdish. Suddenly, several of them ran toward the goat pen, a corral in the rocks with a gate made of scraps of corrugated metal and wood nailed together. Granwin turned and called out to Taj. He buried his face in the ground and covered his head with his arms.

"What's Baker doing? What'd he say?" asked Devon.

"He told the men to send the goats out to the boy, to explode any mines that might be left. They refused until I told them you would pay for any goats killed, even the one already dead." Granwin's voice was hoarse.

Shooed by a pair of laughing men, the goats wandered out toward the boy, grazing in the sparse grass, oblivious to the shouts and gestures of the crowd lining the trail. A black and white nanny and her tiny kid walked up to Taj, motionless on the ground. The nanny sniffed at the prone boy for a moment, then nibbled and tugged on his shirt. Granwin slumped against Devon as the boy peeped up and, with a grin, shooed the goats away.

"He's alright," whispered Granwin. "Nash, he's alright," she repeated, almost a laugh.

Baker walked out to Taj, slowing to stare intently at the ground before each step after he passed the last flag. He picked up Taj and turned back, the boy now grinning from ear to ear as he perched in the big man's arms. Just as he had gone out, Baker's return was methodical, each step in the faint print of an outgoing step.

Still clutching Devon tight with one hand, Granwin wiped her cheek with the tail of her shawl.

"Okay now?" Devon asked.

Her smile vanished when the second mine exploded.

CHAPTER 11

Devon froze for an instant. Finally instincts took command. He reached out, ears ringing, shoved Granwin to the ground and pulled her head under his shoulder.

Her fists pounded on his back as he sprawled over her in the middle of the road, dirt and rock fragments showering down on them.

"Get off!" she screamed, batting at the falling debris.

Devon rolled off of Granwin, shaking the dirt from his hair. She shoved him away, climbed to her feet and staggered toward the field.

"Stay here!" he tried to yell at her, not sure if anything had come out of his mouth, or if she could even hear. He reached out, grabbed her by an arm and pulled her down to her knees.

A moment earlier, he had been watching his friend rescue a boy under a brilliant blue sky. Now he didn't know what he saw. A wisp of smoke rose from around the crumpled heap that was Baker and Taj. His heart skipped several beats, and then began pounding, rushing blood to his head. Granwin's screaming started again, and his legs moved without any command without any thought of what else was left for him to step on, if he were to be the next. He dashed to where the two lay, picked up the boy and carried him, limp and motionless, the few steps back to Granwin, now silent as she reached out for Taj. Her face was pale as she took the boy.

Devon spun and ran back to Baker.

Baker raised up on one elbow, moaning. The trail of flags that ran partway out to Baker were trampled, half of them smashed flat to the ground. Devon walked back, more deliberate than he wanted, to the last flag.

Baker groaned, muttering under his breath as he contorted his big frame, trying to see his feet.

Devon swallowed the dust in his throat and took three long steps across the bloody ground to stand beside Baker. He tried to keep his knees from quivering, but they wouldn't stop. His baggy denim jeans, stretched out at his knees, visibly quivered as he stared down at Baker and the ground around him, searching for hints of blue plastic, thin metal whisker triggers.

"Is it gone?" Baker asked. He turned his face to the sky, eyes closed with a grimace. "Nash, I can't feel anything."

"What do you mean? Of course it's gone. The damn mine exploded. It ain't coming back."

"No, stupid. My leg! Is it gone?"

Devon dropped to his knees beside Baker. Baker's pants legs were tattered and blood was splattered from head to foot. "Can you can feel your leg?" he asked.

"Don't feel nothin'." Baker pressed his forearm to his eyes. "Come on, man, what's left?"

Devon ran his hand down Baker's bloody pants leg. The left leg seemed intact.

"Ahaaa..." Baker's fingers clutched his elbow when Devon ran his hand down the other leg.

The right calf was a mess. Devon stripped away the shredded denim—all that was left of Baker's pant leg. He picked his way gingerly along ragged flesh. "Your leg, all of you, is here." Devon could see both feet, still at the correct angles at the end of the shredded pants. One boot was half gone, toes sticking out, but there. "Both feet, too. You have steel inserts in your soles?"

Baker nodded, then interrupted with another loud groan as Devon ran his hand over a large knot just above his ankle.

"Feels like at least one bad break, maybe more, and a lot of cuts." The villagers lined the edge of the road, watching like a pack of dogs along one of those invisible electrified fences. Granwin had disappeared with the boy. "What now, Mister Mine Expert. Any instructions?"

"Well, we came out here. We gotta go back." Baker grabbed Devon's arm and squeezed with the pain. "No more magic. We just get up and go back to the road, or we don't. Hell, you've done it once already. Follow the flags."

Now that he had time to think, Devon began to breathe deeply, then had to stop and shake his head to clear away the dizzy spots.

Hyperventilating—just stop and hold my breath for a moment, let my heart slow down, he thought, eyes squeezed shut. The smell of blood and sweat and goat guts filled his nostrils when he finally took a deep breath, snuffling to blow the pesky flies out of his face.

"Chief, you gonna be some help and get me out of here or not?" Baker's deep baritone rose to a falsetto.

"Just checking to see if my knees still worked." Devon slipped one arm under Baker's and the other around his back and eyed the gap, littered with goat parts, between them and the row of tiny flags.

"Whoa, man, what'cha doing?"

"I'm going to carry your ass out of here," Devon replied. He squatted and breathed deeply, then picked Baker up with a grunt.

Baker tried to grin, but it came out a twisted grimace. "Pretty strong for a white kid."

Devon turned toward the road. All he could say was, "Adrenaline. Gonna drop you on your butt soon's it wears off." He stood for a moment, Baker dead weight in his arms. No sign of footprints, his or Baker's, just the goat remains splattered between him and the road. "Ready?"

"Let's go. I'm startin' to hurt bad."

Ten terrifying steps later, Devon was at the trail. His arms ached by the time he lumbered down the trail to the Nissan. He stopped in front of the rear doors. "Tell somebody to open this thing up for me."

Baker yelled at the crowd and one of the men ran over and opened up the back of the Nissan, all the while earnestly yammering at Baker.

"Mighty nice of them, worried about you so much." Devon slid Baker into the back of the truck.

This time Baker forced a laugh. "Akmed over there just wants to know when you're going to pay for the goat."

Devon pulled the first aid kit from the clutter in the back of the truck and took out the bandage scissors. "I'm going to cut away some of this trash flapping around your legs to see what I can find." Devon cut the laces to Baker's boots and then worked them off his feet. "Good thing it tore up your boot. Foot's swelling so much I couldn't get it off otherwise."

Bake didn't seem to appreciate his attempt at humor.

Granwin appeared by their side. "How are you, Mr. Baker?" she asked.

"I'll make it, Miss Granwin. How's the boy? Up high like I was holding him, he should be okay once the scare wears off."

"He's still unconscious." Her tone was somber.

Devon paused. Granwin's face was even paler than before. Devon opened his mouth to say he hadn't seen anything wrong with the kid, but stopped when he thought back. He barely remembered snatching the boy up, much less his condition. He finally asked, "What's wrong?"

"He has a big bruise on his head, perhaps from the explosion. I don't know." Granwin leaned against the side of the truck. "The women are watching him." Her face had visibly aged since she had smiled down at him on the bench and called him her laddie. Her rapid-fire dialogue had slowed to a crawl. "He's breathing, but barely."

Devon sawed away with the scissors, leaving Baker with a ragged pair of shorts.

"Thank you for going out after him, Mr. Baker." She started to turn away. "I'm sorry I have been so unkind toward you."

"Miss Granwin." Baker's words were strained as Devon wiped a clump of disinfectant ointment across a deep laceration running down the inside of Baker's left leg. "Tell me. Why don't you like me?"

She stood for a moment, then took his hand in hers. "You shouldn't address me as miss." She turned his hand over and ran her fingers over his palm. "I was married once. His name was Ralph, Ralph Albert. His fingers were long and black like yours." She smiled. "I never had enough time to truly become Mrs. Albert before he went off to war. Ralph was a lieutenant in the RAF, like his father."

Granwin kept stroking Baker's long fingers. "Mr. Albert, senior, had stayed on in South Africa after *his* war to fly the bush. He and my Albert's mum met after a crash. She was a sister in the hospital. And she was colored." She smiled up at Baker. "That's what they say in Africa—and England—colored, a British father and an African mother. My Albert was a lovely man, kind as could be, colored or white."

A faint rumble reached down from the sky and she looked up at a pair of faint vapor trails. "Flew one of those, a RAF Tornado. The Iraqis shot him down during the Gulf War." She took a deep breath, her shoulders moving up and down. "He wouldn't let me have a child."

Her words ate at Devon.

"Albert said he didn't want to raise any coloreds to be ridiculed." She looked up at Baker, then at Devon. "He died before I could convince him otherwise. So perhaps Taj is my recompense." The muscles around her jaw tightened. "Despite your heathen beliefs, Mr. Devon, God does reward those who are charitable." She took a deep breath. "I'm sorry both of you have risked your lives for Taj. You should be the ones receiving rewards. You especially, Mr. Baker, for your injuries."

She pulled the gold chain from under her blouse and over her head and unsnapped a small medallion dangling from the chain beside the cross. She placed it in Baker's palm, a pale blue oval of jasperware set in silver, with a raised black figure in the center.

Baker turned the medallion, took a deep breath and read the raised letters around the top half. "Am I not a man and a brother." He held the piece out. "You ever seen one of these, Nash?"

Devon stopped his ministrations and inspected the oval in Baker's trembling palm.

"Pretty, but no."

Baker's eyes closed as he held the brooch out toward Granwin.

She shook her head and again closed his fingers around the broach. "It is yours now." She stepped back. "I must go and see about Taj. Thank you."

Neither of the men said a word as she walked away.

Baker broke the silence. "Granwin's hurting as bad as the baby." He held out the brooch. "This is too valuable for her to give away on a whim. Here. Give it back to her when she can think straight."

Devon noticed Baker was beginning to shiver. He dropped the bit of jewelry into his pocket and pulled a blanket from the back seat and over Baker's shoulders.

"Just another orphan kid," said Devon. "I keep telling Granwin all her God-fearing talk doesn't mean anything. We're only what we are, or what other people make us. Around here, we made a lot of them orphans."

"Yeah, just another snotty-nosed kid. Like the one back in the desert." Baker shivered violently. "You don't know what the kid said when he died in your arms, do you, Nash?"

Devon didn't answer, wishing he had never come out here, had never seen the little boy who reminded him of another child. And now Baker, in his delirium, had to drive the memory through his heart like one of his wooden stakes.

"He said, 'We'll meet in heaven with Allah,' while looking up at you." Baker paused, took a deep breath. "He died with his faith in God. And family. That's all we really got, Nash—family and God." Baker's eyes were beginning to show a lot of white. "The boy's last word was *walidak*, father, in Arabic. He believed he was in his father's arms."

Devon couldn't meet Baker's eyes. The words burned his ears.

Baker reached out to grip his arm. "You think they put me out here just to step on mines?" His hand trembled. "I'm the one who asked for you. I know you, better than you think. I knew you'd come up with a way to find the nukes."

Baker's grin faded back to a grimace when Devon began wrapping a long spiral of gauze around his leg, avoiding the protruding knot. "So quit messing around and get on with the search. I was gonna go with you, but now I can't. Bad things are out there, man. You gotta find them."

"Later, Deacon. Take care of yourself and don't worry about that other shit. I'll take care of it after we see you and the kid safe." *Take care of what?* Like he knew what the hell was going on. Like he took care of Granwin and Taj. Devon pushed all the thoughts about children and nuclear weapons from his mind, and focused on bandaging Baker's leg. "You're not bleeding too bad. This'll stop most of it and at least keep the trash out until you get to a doctor."

"Man, I ain't looking forward to that ride." Baker's head dropped back with a grunt of pain when Devon butterflyed the end of the gauze.

"Maybe you won't have to ride—at least with me." He pointed across the valley. Dark clouds covered the sky and the wind had started to whine through the rocky outcrops supporting the houses. A dot grew larger until he could make out the partial silhouette of a white helicopter slide-slipping and buffeting against the winds.

Baker turned his head and watched, then barked out a short laugh, cut short by a grimace. "Way that baby's bouncing around, let them take the kid and I'll ride with you." Baker reached out and grabbed Devon's hand. "Chief, we've got friends in the mountains. I was supposed to put you in contact, but it ain't gonna work out. Listen to the old man." Baker closed his eyes with a grimace.

A hell of a time to confirm what he had suspected. Baker was his contact. *Now what? Who is the old man he was supposed to listen to?* Devon trotted to the other side of the houses where the ruts crossed a short stretch of level ground, took his position and stood in the middle of the road with his arms up, palms facing up, and waited for the pilot to pick him up.

The helicopter flared, then slowed and extended its tricycle landing gear. Devon could see the copilot lean forward and point in his direction, and the pilot helmet's answering bob. He began motioning the bird forward, palms up and over his shoulders, then dropping them by his sides and toward the ground, motioning them down. The pilot followed his directions until the helicopter, a white-painted UN High Commission Dauphin, settled in the middle of the road. Devon crouched and ran under the turning blades to a man crouched in the open side door.

"Speak English?" he yelled.

"Better than you, Nash," the man yelled back.

"What?" Devon stared at the man, unsure what he had heard over the whine of the turbines.

The man took off his headset and hopped off the bird as the twin turbines whirled to a stop. Devon grabbed him, a full head shorter than Devon, but wide across the shoulders, to keep him from stepping out of the roadway. "Watch out—mines. Stay on the road." Devon pulled him to the side of the helicopter as recognition hit. Heavy mustache, powerful arms under rolled-up uniform sleeves, but the scar across his chin convinced Devon he wasn't seeing a ghost. "Pancho?"

"That's Colonel Panchaman Khan to you." Khan's smile beamed from under a pair of mirrored aviator sunglasses.

"Bullshit, Pancho, what the hell are you doing here?" Devon pounded him on the arms, relieved to see his old friend.

Khan turned to motion for the crew chief to join them, pointing at a litter strapped to the floor. "Let's get the injured on board while we talk." He leaned inside the helicopter and relayed the warning about mines over the low growl of the turbines, now almost down to an idle. Both the pilot and copilot nodded in acknowledgement. Then he turned to follow Devon and the crewman to the truck and Baker.

"When was the last time we saw each other, Pancho? How in hell did you get out here?" Devon hadn't so much as thought of Khan since Devon and Khan were still captains, and Panchaman Khan was a Pakistani Army exchange student at the Fort Sill Artillery and Missile Center where his stocky figure and belligerent attitude had inevitably gained him the Mexican revolutionary's nickname.

"It's been a very long time since we parted, my friend. A lifetime ago, for both of us."

Khan and the crewman began easing Baker onto the litter.

Baker motioned Devon closer. "The mountains," Baker whispered.

Devon bent closer, not comprehending.

Baker pulled him closer. "Go to the mountains. And don't throw away the box."

Devon barely understood the words over the building whine of the helicopter turbine. But he still didn't comprehend where he should go in the mountains.

Khan and the crewman picked up the litter and started for the Dauphin.

"What do you mean?" Devon yelled.

Baker's eyes closed, and he didn't seem to hear.

Granwin walked up and stood beside the truck with her arms folded over her chest. Her shawl was wrapped around her head and face like one of the village women, hiding all but her eyes.

"Where's the boy? We can take him down to a doctor."

"You may depart." All the luster was gone from her eyes. "There is no reason to wait."

CHAPTER 12

Devon took Granwin by the shoulders. "What?"

"Taj is dead."

She had scrubbed her face, smudging the tear streaks furrowing her pale cheeks. She silently leaned her head against his chest. Behind her, Khan and the crewman waited by the truck and the litter with Baker.

Devon waved them toward the helicopter. "Pancho, go ahead and get Bert out of here," he shouted over the whine as the helicopter blades began to wind back up.

"The child?" asked Khan.

Devon shook his head.

"We'll talk when you get back to the compound," Khan yelled over his shoulder, and he and the crewman hoisted Baker into the side of the helicopter.

Devon turned to shield Granwin from the blowing dirt and dust as the helicopter lifted and turned into the wind. The helicopter slowly climbed away from the mountain, then clattered down toward the valley, leaving them with the growing moans of the afternoon winds, building toward the shrieks that would come in the dark of night.

Granwin shrugged off his hands and walked away.

Devon didn't stop her. He had no words to bring back the boy. Instead, he busied himself gathering Baker's tools and piling them in the back of the Nissan, partially covering Baker's bloodstains on the floor.

Devon's stomach rumbled, and he suddenly remembered he hadn't eaten all day. Shadows stretched across the valley behind him. Everything had happened too fast. He rummaged around in the back seat and came up with a bottle of water and two brown plastic packets—MREs—Meals, Ready to Eat. He stuffed the MREs in his pockets and looked around for Granwin. The village reminded Devon of a deserted cemetery, somber gray rock piles, with homes instead of tombs. The road was empty. Everyone had disappeared.

The call to prayer echoed up from the valley, carried up the mountainside by the winds. The people had returned to the routine of the Islamic world, leaving him to deal with his own fears.

Devon walked down the ruts looking for Granwin and her irritating chatter, her booming laughter.

The reality was as stark as the cold rocks of the hovel. He found Granwin kneeling on the dirt floor, all her laughter gone. Her breath formed white clouds over a bundle of thin blankets laid across the empty cardboard boxes in the center of the stone hut, a pathetic excuse for a bier. The only light was the last bit of sun, a sliver of pale pink light coming through the open door along with the growing chill of the mountain night.

A puff of breath, then the cloud dissipated, another puff, another cloud, all in silence. But the clouds were all from Granwin. Taj lay still, his face frosty white, no sign of breath, warm or cold. The bruise on his forehead had turned black.

"What difference does it make if I'm an angel or a sinner?" Granwin rocked on her knees. "I, we, none of us could do a damn thing for poor Taj. Even when he died, he has no one to mourn for him but me, no one to bury him, no one to wail his soul to heaven."

Devon knelt down beside her and pulled her to his chest. "You came to help, Renée. You tried. Look, you cry for him and his soul."

Her tears soaked through his shirt, her sobs muffled when she buried her face under his open jacket, her breath warm against his chest. She looked up at him, her face splotched with dust mixed in with her tears. "Pour me some of your whisky. A big drink. One to last all day, all year, forever, until I can get out of this God-forsaken country."

She suddenly pushed herself back from him, mouth turned ugly in a grimace. "No. That's not right."

"You said it, not me." Devon reached out toward her, but she stood and backed away.

"Forgive me, Lord. I know God's will and His way does have meaning. I just can't understand at times." She backed against the wall, her hands out in front of her body, shielding herself from him.

"Going Arab on me?" He stood, suddenly exhausted, and took a deep breath.

"Not predestination, not *Inshallah.* God's plan for us must be real or my life is not." Granwin blinked her tears from her eyes, jaw clenched. "Damn you, you can't take my belief from me, from any of these people. They have little enough. Would you do that, just to prove life is cruel while you hide in a bottle?" She reached out and grabbed his arm. "Faith is all that keeps these people from killing their children the instant they are born." She slid to the floor and curled her arms over her head, shaking.

Devon squatted, slipped his arms under her and picked her up.

She let her head fall against his chest as he carried her over to a wooden frame that passed as a bed, shoved up next to the bare stone of the mountain that served as a wall.

"Oh, Nash. Why do we live in such a mean world?" she whispered.

"Because you care, Renée." He thought about the boy in the desert, the children he and Granwin never had, then Taj. "Because we both care." He eased her down on a thin mattress. "Now sleep."

She straightened with a long groan when he pulled the last of the threadbare blankets over her.

"You don't need any whisky. You just need to rest." He tried to smile, thinking he was the one who needed a drink. "Lots of kids need you. Tomorrow, next week. For years and years. Just rest tonight."

She shivered under the blanket and closed her eyes.

He started a small fire on the rock hearth. The smoke gathered, swirled, then rose up and out a wide chink between the top of the door and the sill, sooty black from years of greasy smoke. It carried the same smell he remembered from the night in the desert so many years ago—what he would always remember as the smell of death.

He pulled out his pipe, tamped the bowl with black tobacco and thumbed the flint on his lighter. A sudden glow of pink washed across the child's cheeks. He stopped himself from reaching out to the child. It was just the reflection of the flame from his lighter. Devon shivered as he took off his jacket and covered the still body.

The children. Why is it dead ones turn into demons? Devon blew out the lantern and sat down in the cold dark, gnawing on the bamboo pipe stem and letting the dead children run amok across his sleepless dreams. The Cavendish aroma diluted the other smells, bringing back a hint of family, happiness, all those things he remembered as a boy. Smelling the smoke his grandpa would silently blow in the air while his grandma chanted in the background, too low to understand even if he had known the old words.

The moaning wind brought its own chant to the hovel. He would never admit it to anyone, but in his mind, he suspected that smoking his pipe was part of what his grandma had taught him, a way to be closer to something, if not God. Tonight, he needed to be closer to something greater than himself. He sat on a stone platform next to Granwin, his hand resting lightly on the blanket covering her arm so he could feel her rhythmic breathing. He leaned back, closed his eyes and let himself drift into dreams, soaring high above the mountain peaks with the hawk, gliding free out over the valley.

Suddenly awake, he lay still. A suffocating odor filled his sinuses and clogged his throat. When he opened his eyes, a stinging, gray mist floated around his face, an ephemeral reminder of the grieving woman and the dead child sharing the dark room. Devon shivered. He was cold or— He cut off the macabre images of death to replace them with a reminder he was cold because he was in his shirtsleeves. When he raised himself up on his elbows, a loose rock poked a gnawing ache into his buttock, reinforcing reality.

Cloying smoke hung in the closed stone hut, bringing tears down his face. He stumbled to the door and pulled it open. Colder air rushed in to swirl the smoke and acrid smells out into the morning. He scrubbed his eyes on his shirtsleeves and peered back through the dissipating vapors into the hut. Granwin and Taj were gone.

When he walked between the ruts, soft morning sounds of the village floated on the heavy air along with the sour smell of the goat pen. He searched the trail, then up the slope behind the huts. Small groups of goats grazed over the rocky ground, seeking out every surviving blade and leaf, moving toward the top of the ridge. The one-eared man stopped and stared at him for a moment, then turned and followed the goats. All concern for mines seemed to have disappeared with the smoke from the fires, just floated up into the sky. *Inshallah* at its finest.

Devon searched the mountainside. In the distance, a woman knelt by a low stone cairn. Devon scanned the slope around her. These people and their goats had walked here for years without stepping on a mine. Just as they had triggered two yesterday. He shook his head and walked up the path and across the bare ground to Granwin, her head bowed.

She spoke after he had stood silently by her side for several minutes. "Taj was too young to understand all the death, all the suffering." She placed one more rock on the pile and wiped the dirt from her hands.

Devon walked over to a rocky outcropping and picked up a large stone in each hand. He knelt beside her and placed them on the cairn, covering the last vestiges of his jacket.

Granwin put her hand on his shoulder and pushed herself to her feet. Devon stood and watched while she fished a rosary from a bottom corner of her tote, then let the beads slide through her fingers, dropping down through the rocks. "He was taught to pray with Islamic prayer beads." She shook her head. "I know my rosary isn't the same." She held her chin up, a challenge to for him to argue with her logic. "But the prayers go to the same God."

Devon only nodded, then put his arm around her shoulder and helped her down the path to the Nissan. Taj's death had transformed her from a strong woman to a frail shape buried beneath her shawl and dark dress, leaning on his arm for support. The drive down the steep trail was silent. Devon slowed at the rubble where the bombs had dropped. A flutter of white and yellow rags blew across the trail, a reminder of children lost. The clouds held back the sun, then finally let a fine drizzle float to the ground about the time they crossed the Great Zab and slowly drove up the slope and back into the compound.

Panchaman Khan stood in the dark operations hut watching Devon drive in. He spoke into the Bakelite phone. "Yes, Commissioner Aragon. Devon is here. I will see that he arrives at his destination soon."

CHAPTER 13

"Nash."

Devon looked up from his plate. "Hi, Pancho. You still here? Figured you left with the helicopter and Baker." His voice sounded tired, even to his own ears.

He put another spoonful in his mouth. The carrots he could identify by color, but the white stuff was either turnips or potatoes, or some other nameless root. He supposed the meat was lamb, out of deference to the Muslims. He couldn't tell by taste. He had thrown the MREs back into the Nissan, unopened, and he had driven a silent Granwin down the trail through the rising river mists and into the compound. Ian had reheated a plate of the noon meal for him. Now all he wanted to do was blunt his hunger.

"Oh, I think you'll see plenty of me." Khan swirled a cup of coffee under his heavy mustache.

Devon raised his eyebrows as he chewed on a chunk of stale bread. He remembered Khan as a tenacious student at the Field Artillery Center and School. Never left the instructors in peace, always nose-to-nose, willing to challenge the 'school solution.' And he often had a better solution. Even his scar had grown bigger. He wondered if Khan really had been wounded in a Kashmir border skirmish as he had boasted.

Or had it been a woman—or the woman's husband? Khan had always had the Middle Eastern inclination for intrigue, or at least played the game.

Devon reached up to rub the tender bruise on his forehead…all that remained of his encounter with Granwin. His intrigues weren't as romantic as Khan's.

"I know the news will please you." Khan leaned back and sat up straight. "In a minor way, I will be your supervisor. Geneva has assigned me as the deputy team director."

He laughed when Devon paused with his spoon halfway to his mouth, then laughed so hard he sloshed his coffee on the table. "Don't worry, I won't lord it over you. I said only 'in a way.' I expect you work directly for Director Levison and—" He shrugged his shoulders. "Anyway, I know nothing about farming."

Ian dropped a rag at Khan's elbow, scowling at the top of the Pakistani's head. Khan wiped away the spilled coffee and continued talking to Devon, ignoring Ian's presence.

"I am surprised you do—know anything about farming—that is. I believed you were a city person as I," Khan said. He stared at Devon with eyebrows raised.

Devon put down the spoon and blinked through the crust in the corners of his eyes, ignoring the question. "Seeing you is great, Pancho, but I'm too addled to talk. We'll have a good get-together later, and I'll tell you all about my adventures down on the farm."

After I dream about dying and killing and kids and God for a few hours, Devon thought as he walked out into the damp drizzle and half-stumbled toward his bunk.

"Mother. Someone is coming." Arif's voice grew more insistent. "It is Mr. Devon. He is coming this way. Hurry."

Sara Qasim shoved the bag back under the bunk and scurried out the back entrance. She grabbed Arif's hand and pulled him away from the door, leaving it partially open as they had found it.

"Mother, I was afraid while you were inside. What if someone should find you in the men's hut?" Arif asked.

"You are right to be afraid. What I did was too dangerous, and I will not do it again." She held Arif close. "You know why I do such things, don't you?"

He nodded. "Are they here? Men of *Ahad?*"

She squeezed him closer and stopped at the line of buildings. "Yes."

It was noon prayer time and no one was about. "Quickly, now." She pulled him across the open space to the operations hut door. "The man on the phone told me I am to obey the colonel, the one who came on the helicopter that took away Mr. Baker."

Arif's brown eyes, so like his father's, were full of questions when she pushed him into the empty office building.

"We must do these things to survive."

"Are they right in the eyes of Allah?"

"I don't know, my son. Fetch the rugs, and we will pray and ask for forgiveness and guidance."

She watched Arif retrieve their thin prayer rugs from behind the desk and unroll them on the bare concrete floor. He was so smart. Sometimes he seemed to understand what they were doing better than she. Soon she would be following his lead, but for now she must guide him.

She sat back on her heels and waited for Arif to begin his prayers before she joined him, forehead to the ground. She forced the doubts from her mind as she repeated the ritual words, and added a plea for her son's safety and escape from the evil ones. Those who pursued them, who wished death upon the world, who would have her dishonor the memory of her dear husband Nadav, now watching, waiting with Allah.

When the door clicked shut, she opened her eyes and saw the face of evil—Colonel Khan.

"Sara Qasim, time for prayer is past. Boy, put away the rugs and go outside. I have private things to discuss with your mother," Khan said.

She shivered when he reached out for her son and shoved him toward the door.

Sara stood to face the colonel. Her entire body felt numb as her son sidled out the door, shying away from the evil touch. The colonel stepped over to her and held out his hand after the door had shut behind Arif. "What do you have for me?" Sara reached deep in her skirt pocket and pulled out the small notebook she had slipped from Devon's bag. She had never stolen anything before in her life. Not that she had any affection for the American, but she still felt as if she was betraying a trust.

Khan flipped through the lined pages, shook his head and handed them back. "Radars, missile sites. There is nothing of importance here. Was this all?"

"I'm not sure. It was dark and I did not want to light a lantern." She watched his face, trying to read his emotions, and gauge what she should say. "It was the men's sleeping hut after all."

His face wrinkled around hard eyes. Anger, irritation, she couldn't tell.

He sat in the director's chair and rocked back and forth. "Time is growing short for our program. The Hindus cannot be left to think they have the upper hand." He pointed to her desk. "Sit down, Sara Qasim." No anger sounded in his voice, just a sullen evenness that unnerved her even more than a fit of rage.

She walked to her desk and sat. She pressed her trembling knees together, but held her face calm, waiting. She hoped he could not see her heart pounding in her chest. He sat silent for a few moments, going back through the notebook. Outside, she could hear Arif's voice in the motor park, calling to the cur. She would be strong for her son. Her knees stilled.

Khan stared at her. He finally stood, pointing at the map on the wall. "A small town named Sinjar lies about a hundred kilometers on the other side of Mosul." He pounded the map with his knuckle. "The High Commission has sent down orders for Devon to help the farmers in the region with their irrigation system."

He came over to her desk, placed both hands on it and leaned toward her. "I have a much more important mission for Devon, so we cannot let him leave the camp without me." He straightened, a slight smile showing under his dark mustache. "You must gain his confidence. You are an attractive woman for your age. I'm sure you will have no trouble with the American. They all are easily swayed by women." He smiled. "And their women by strong men."

He leaned back in the director's chair. "You and I must work as a team, and we will both benefit." He suddenly lurched forward in the chair, his face dark. "Understood?"

She hesitated, then took a deep breath. "I am not a woman of loose character." She forced the defiant words from her trembling lips.

Khan slammed his fist down on the desk. "Damn you and your morality. You forsook any possibility of salvation at the hands of your Iraqi friends when you and your husband acted so traitorously at the research facility. Woman, don't you realize you have been spared your husband's fate by the very hand of Qusay? And we both know you will continue to live only as long as Qusay believes your life represents some value."

His voice dropped. "Now prove this value, or I will proceed without you." He straightened up and smiled at her, a gesture empty of humor. "Without you, and your son." He turned his back to her to look out the window.

Her throat suddenly so tight she felt she could not speak, she looked over his shoulder. Arif galloped in a circle around Mr. Otto, the mongrel dog yapping at his heels. Qusay may have spared her and her son. But, just as surely, the same evil beast had ordered her dear Nadav's death. She understood Khan's price, but she had no idea what to do. "What are my instructions?" she asked, her voice tight in her throat.

He turned back, the smile returning to his face. "The commissioner has instructed me to accompany Devon to Sinjar to oversee his activities there. But, on the chance my plans do not complete themselves as I wish, you must become his friend. His very good friend.

Tell me everything he does, everyplace he goes, everyone he contacts," Khan demanded.

Again she nodded. She jumped back against her desk when the door burst open.

Levison fairly skipped through the door, thin hair flying all around his round head. "Well, Colonel Khan, I see you've met my intrepid Mrs. Qasim." When Levison unzipped his blue parka, Sara had the sudden vision of an overripe grape bursting from its hull.

Khan was all smiles. "Please, Director Levison, not colonel, just plain Panchaman Khan. I'm not here as a representative of the Pakistani government, but as just another humble employee of the High Commission."

Levison swept around to his desk, strewing an armload of papers across the already cluttered desktop. "I know, I know. Very modest of you, I must say." His head bobbed as he plopped down in the chair and began sorting through the papers. "But we'll see." Levison smiled at Sara. "I dare say, the others might claim I am a bit of a task master, behind my back, of course. Eh, Mrs. Qasim?"

Sara tried to return his smile, but held back from answering, not knowing if he was being humorous or sarcastic, wondering if she had a smile on her face or not.

Levison glanced around the office. "Hmm... It appears we've filled our modest facilities." He pointed a stubby finger at the remaining empty desk. "Your office, Mr. Khan, awaits." He bounded up from his desk, gathered up a fistful of papers and dropped them down in the middle of Khan's. "Here, these are all for you anyway. I must remember to share some of our most important work with you."

He turned back to Sara. "I will show Mr. Khan our amenities, the exciting parts like the ROWPU, then he can return and you can fill him in on the administrative aspects of our operations." He zipped up his jacket. "Come Mr. Deputy Director Panchaman Khan, and I'll introduce you to our staff before you tackle the paper monster that consumes us." He stopped his whirling around the office to face Sara.

"And, oh, yes, Mrs. Qasim, please tell Mr. Devon to see me when he is recovered from his ordeal." Levison shook his head. "Poor child, such a pity" he muttered. "And Mr. Baker, such a brave soul. But the commission doctors will take good care of him in Baghdad." Levison shuffled through the stack of papers on his desk. "Wouldn't you agree, Mr. Deputy Director?"

Before Khan could reply, Levison continued, with a hint of a smile toward Khan, waving a sheet of paper he had retrieved from his desk, "One of the directives our new deputy brought with him asks us to assist the township of Sinjar with their irrigation system. A little out of our territory, but part of our agricultural advisor's mandate. However, I am concerned Devon may have a problem getting by the Iraqi roadblocks around Mosul." He spun back to face Sara.

She was almost dizzy from keeping up with him.

"Mrs. Qasim, do you have any suggestions as to how we should approach the Iraqi Army for permission to pass?" Levison asked.

Sara avoided Khan's eyes. "I could telephone the district headquarters and apply for a travel permit."

Levison shook his head, sending his hair flying. "No. I don't want to set a precedent of UN teams asking for travel permits. We have the mandated right to free access north of the 36th parallel. All I want is some guarantee of Devon's safe passage to Sinjar."

"I should travel with him," suggested Khan. "If you're speaking of Nash Devon, he's an old friend of mine." He held one of the papers from the desk up. "It appears that is Commissioner Aragon's instructions.

Levison stood in thought, wiping his head with one hand, the other on his hip as he stood in front of the map, looking all in the world like a teapot. "No, no. I have many things here for you to do." He held his hand up, forestalling Khan's protest. "Unfortunately, your presence on the trip might be even more provoking. I'm afraid the Commissioner, in his exalted position in Baghdad, does not appreciate the finesse we must work here afield.

"Despite your modesty, the Iraqis will not overlook the fact you're a military officer, and may suspect your intentions, paired with an American."

Sara realized both men's eyes were on her, waiting for her comments. Khan raised his eyebrows, a slight suggestion, then frowned with an almost imperceptible shake of the head as she hesitated.

Sara took the initiative with a deep breath. "I can travel with Mr. Devon. I can represent the government's authority with the commission. I will conduct him to Sinjar and introduce him to the town council and the water management authorities."

She felt a blush rise up from the back of her neck at the deception she was about to propose. "Perhaps Mrs. Granwin could accompany us. I must follow the *Shariah*, the law of Allah, and it would be inappropriate for me to go alone with another man. But with her, a European woman, and her facility with languages, I am sure the authorities in Mosul would grant us passage."

She looked down at her desk, afraid to face Khan's reaction to her proposal.

Levison nodded in agreement. "Of course. You are correct, Mrs. Qasim. And it will do well for Mrs. Granwin to be out and about after the tragedy. I do believe she has taken the loss of the child very close to heart." He drummed his fingers on his desk. "Good. It is decided. Please leave as soon as possible, perhaps tomorrow. The people of Sinjar are probably anxious to resolve their water problem before the planting season ends."

He turned to Khan. "Now, come along, Deputy Director Khan. I have much to explain." The director stepped out of the door. "Come now."

Khan hesitated and turned back to Sara. His face was impossible for her to read as he zipped up his jacket. So low Levison could not hear, Khan said, "I'll see to it the telephone at Sinjar is operational. Return the notebook, then report to me at least once a day." He turned and followed the director.

Sara walked to the window. She watched Khan follow Levison toward the motor park. Beyond them, Arif skipped by Devon's side, showing the American an archer's bow the boy had constructed from a stick and a piece of string. Her heart seemed to slow and skip a beat when the colonel gripped Devon by the hand, then embraced him with the greeting of an old friend.

She willed Arif to move away from the men, to escape from the presence of evil, but her son remained beside Devon, studying the colonel. She clenched her jaw. She didn't understand any of it, but she would do as he directed. Arif, forever on the move, turned from the men and bounded around the motor park, chasing after the scrawny dog that Mr. Otto kept, supposedly, as a watchdog. Now she had her own watchdog, one with a bite that could be deadly.

CHAPTER 14

"Watch it, kid," Devon hollered.

The glowing tobacco sputtered from a random droplet kicked up by the boy and the dog. Devon re-lit his pipe, stepped back from the stream's edge and watched the boy and dog splash and frolic in the cold, fresh melt from high on the peaks of the distant mountains. The river spread out across the valley in front of him, broad and shallow at the edges with a deeper channel in the center, deceptively fast as it moved toward the Tigris and eventually the Persian Gulf. He took a deep breath, inhaling the smells of the river flats and maybe a hint of sewage from the refugee settlements. Better than the smell of death that had followed him from the mountain village.

He shrugged his shoulders under the heavy wool sweater. Still a chill in the air, but the light breeze on his face felt good. He squatted down and pulled on the pipe. Makeshift bamboo stem, dirty Cavendish and all, the burning tobacco brought him back some of his granddad's calm as he smoked the old pipe and let the memories of the dead children slide deeper in his mind.

Devon grinned as he watched the boy dart around the Nissan in a big circle. Life as a kid sometimes could be a big game. Today, Devon's memories of the good ones overwhelmed the others, like the nights sitting around the old tobacco barn with grandma telling tales of the swamp animals while her youngest son, his Uncle Lemuel, fed pine slabs into the old-style ovens to cure the green tobacco leaves. The curling smoke from Devon's pipe was reminiscent of the heavy aroma leaching from barn-cured tobacco as it gradually cooked to a golden yellow. Life had been simple then, as it was now for Arif. Or so the dream went.

Still, a flat rock to skip and a dog were plenty of fun. Water to splash, even cold water, was a bonus. The kid whistled a piercing blast that turned heads across the sand flats. The dog came flying around the Nissan, and they took off again, perpetual motion.

Arif had insisted, as part of his new official assistant duties, that he to come with Devon to translate. Like Granwin, Arif also spoke the local Kurdish dialect. Arif was also a shrewd negotiator, bargaining the two serious-faced men from the refugee camp down from some higher demand Devon didn't understand to a final announced price of one thousand *dinars* to wash the Nissan. An extravagant amount, Arif had reported, drawing out the word "extravagant," but reasonable, he added.

Sand flew up from Arif's feet as he raced by with a burst of speed, jerked open the driver's door and jumped into the Nissan a micron ahead of the dog. Mottled slick-coated gray, tail curled over its back, the dog shared the boy's enthusiasm, bounding up to window level, barking at Arif, ignoring the two men sloshing away the mountain dust. The boy's head barely made it to the top of the steering wheel, shoulders sliding from side to side as he pretended to drive.

As he watched Arif, Devon laughed silently, remembering the blistering he had gotten when he had played the same trick with his granddad's tractor, only to have it roll, ever so gently, into the irrigation pond down past the pack house, Devon screaming bloody murder all the way.

"Chief!" Arif's scream broke through his reverie.

He watched, not believing his eyes, then sprang to his feet and sprinted toward the Nissan. It was rolling down the slight incline toward the river. The two men stood with their bucket of water and rags watching it gathering speed.

"Brakes, put on the brakes!" Devon yelled between strides.

The dog joined in, barking and bounding up beside the window, keeping pace with Arif's ride toward the river. The big tires crunched over the packed river sand, leaving a faint trail leading toward the sluggish eddies. Devon's boots sank into the river sand just as he was about to reach Arif. The Nissan eased away from him. The dog circled back, yapping and nipping at Devon's heels, then spurted ahead to bounce, stiff-legged, by the open window. Devon stumbled, almost fell in a soft patch of sand. He struggled to his feet and sprinted after Arif.

As the front tires neared the water's edge, Devon snatched the door open. He clutched at the emergency brake handle, wrapped his fingers around it and yanked back. Before he could let go, the Nissan, still moving, dragged him across the damp sand. With a lurch, the front tires dropped over the river's edge where the slow moving water had cut away the bank.

The Nissan finally stopped. The front wheels rested on the river bottom, barely awash, leaving the front bumper to barely kiss the slow moving river.

Devon pushed himself back from the lip, climbed to his feet and leaned against the top of the Nissan with both hands to catch his breath. Game over, the dog sat in the sand by his feet and began chewing an itchy place back toward his rear end. Arif sat frozen, his hands still locked in a death-grip on the steering wheel. Devon worked his tongue around and spat out a granule of sand. He brushed the grit from his face and clothes.

"Listen here, kid." Devon was still having trouble getting his breath.

Arif looked up at him, with a look Devon suspected resembled his very own when Uncle Lemuel had finally made it to the pond from the pack house.

"You've got to understand. If you're going to drive across the river, you got to back way up, get a good start and go like the devil." He patted the boy's trembling shoulder. "Or you'll never make it all the way across."

Arif blinked back what Devon suspected might have been the start of a tear, so Devon looked away, studied the broad flat expanse of the river toward the rise of mountains on the other side, and Taj's cairn. "Want to try it again?"

Arif shook his head, still not ready to talk about it.

Devon pulled his sweater over his head, shook out the sand and threw it into the back seat.

"Okay. Move over and I'll back it out and show you how to change gears."

The boy maneuvered his legs around the floor-mounted shift and slid over to the passenger seat.

In a moment, Devon had the Nissan started and shifted to four-wheel, low range. Slowly, the eased out the clutch and backed up to the hard-pack washed down by the spring thaws. As he made a wide turn in the sand, one of the men waved them down, Devon's pipe in his hand. Devon stopped long enough to exchange the sand-coated pipe for a thousand-*dinar* note.

"*Shukran, shukran*," he repeated. 'Thank you' was one of the few Arabic phrases in his vocabulary. Understood or not, the bill was accepted with a grin. Devon waved a goodbye to the two men and drove along the riverbed until he could ease up on to the roadway.

As he turned the steering wheel to angle up on the road he glanced over. "Hey, Arif."

The boy cleared his throat, then answered, "Yes, Mr. Chief."

"I'd rather you didn't tell your mother about your trip to the river." He nodded back toward the water. "She might think I wasn't being careful enough around you." He glanced back at Arif. The boy's averted his face, watching Devon's hands and feet working the shift and pedals. "Deal?" Devon asked, and held his hand out for a formal shake.

Arif timidly smiled, a touch of color returning to his face. "Deal," he replied, and they shook.

Devon could sense the load lift from Arif's shoulders. He glanced back in the mirror. The curly-tailed dog trotted along off to the side, smart enough to stay out of the gray cloud of dust kicked up by their passage. *Our own carriage dog,* thought Devon. It reminded him of the Dalmatian in the beer ads on TV back home. *Boy, would a beer taste good.* But not to be. *Focus on here and now, not wherever and maybes.* Beside him, Arif was still intent on watching his feet.

"See, I start off in first gear—that's when you go real slow—then mash down the clutch with your left foot and move the gear shift lever to second, then do it again for third." Devon pointed out the numbers engraved on the shift knob. "When you slow down and press the brake pedal, make sure you push the clutch in."

When they got back to the compound, he switched with Arif and let him cautiously drive the Nissan forward, then back, forward, then back, until the boy had a feel for the clutch.

A lot better feel than I ever had for the tractor.

Perched on the edge of the seat, the boy's feet barely made it to the pedals, but he worked at them and the gearshift with his tongue firmly in the corner of his mouth. His foot slipped off the clutch, grinding the gears with a shrill rattle. Arif stomped down on the pedal, both hands on the wheel.

"That's okay. Your leg's getting tired. Enough for today." Devon reached over, turned off the ignition and returned Arif's grin. "Just don't tell on me, about the river thing. I don't want to get in trouble with your mom."

"Me, either, Chief."

"Okay kid, out. I gotta get ready to go."

Arif and the dog disappeared around the side of the operations hut. After a final check of the Nissan, Devon walked through the compound to the sleeping hut and his bags. He pulled the leather briefcase from under the cot and spread the books across the blanket.

Most weren't applicable, Devon realized as he sorted them into two stacks. The meager stack of four having to do with crop soil moisture measurement, irrigation and salinity, he put to one side, along with the infamous CIA fact book. At least it had maps. He balanced the box labeled Agricultural Grain Moisture Analyzer, Model I-100z on top of the short stack.

His flannel shirt had a slightly fishy smell that Devon decided was from the river sand. He stripped it and the T-shirt off and pulled on clean ones from his bag. Levison had indicated he might be gone as long as a week, so Devon stuffed his last clean shirt, a couple of changes of underwear and socks and his shaving kit in the old leather briefcase with the books, all on top of the moisture analyzer. He paused, ran his hand inside, then all around the duffel bag. It was too dark in the windowless building to see clearly in the folds of the bag, but he could have sworn he had hidden his notebook inside a pair of dirty shorts.

Devon took a deep breath of relief when his fingers finally touched the spiral binding. *Stupid even* having *something as incriminating as this around really.* He needed to throw it away and stop recording that kind of common knowledge.

The book was a passport to an Iraqi cell—or worse. Baker had tried to remind Devon his mission was much more important than finding a few radar sites or SAMs. Devon stuffed the notebook in his shirt pocket, to be disposed of at the first opportunity.

When he got to the Nissan, Sara Qasim and Granwin sat in the back seat, both staring straight ahead. He began to wonder if he needed a chauffeur's—or maybe a trucker's—license. Arif stood by the front passenger's door, bouncing from one foot to the other.

Levison had told Devon he was going to Sinjar to advise on a water shortage problem, but not that he was taking this crew. In fact, the last words he'd heard as he left breakfast to ready the vehicle were Khan's, arguing he should accompany Devon, and Levison insisting that Mrs. Qasim accompany Devon. Levison had rebuffed Khan in his British schoolmaster way, telling Khan that his deputy director duties in the camp were much more important than some agricultural advisory task.

Devon checked the back of the Nissan. He really should have cleared out Baker's tools and the rest of the junk from their trip to the village. With the added suitcases, the back cargo compartment barely had enough room left for Devon's bag and the two five-gallon gas cans he had pumped after he and Arif returned from the river

Devon threw his bag on top of the pile of luggage and walked up to the open driver's side window. He bent down to look across at Arif, his hand on the open door. Devon waggled his eyebrows at Arif. Arif grinned back. He glanced from Granwin to Mrs. Qasim in the back seat.

"What the devil are you doing in the vehicle?" he asked Granwin.

Mrs. Qasim leaned forward. "Director Levison instructed us to accompany you."

"All of you?" Devon asked.

"Yes, Mr. Devon, all of us. Now I'm tired of waiting. Let us go, please," snapped Granwin.

Devon wished Khan hadn't lost the argument. Now he was stuck driving a load of women and a kid. At least Granwin had returned to her regular, sour self. Devon surveyed his group. His newly trained assistant driver danced around by the open door. "Arif, you need to go to the toilet?"

Arif immediately stopped hopping from one foot to the other, slid into the Nissan and slammed the door. "No, Chief. I'm ready to go."

An hour down the road Devon felt a touch of chagrin when he realized he was muttering a tiny prayer—thanks that the misery of the death of the child was dimming with time and that Baker was in the hands of a real doctor. Mostly that Granwin had decided to cease her incessant talking. For a moment, he felt a twinge of guilt, then rejected it. Over the past couple of years he had firmly held to the theory of 'don't worry about what you can't control.' Taj's death and Baker's injuries had been out of his control, and he had shouldered plenty of remorse over the one child's death he *had* caused.

So let this one go, he kept telling himself. But the image of Granwin kneeling over Taj's cairn washed across his mind each time they passed a shawled woman trudging along the road.

He found something else to occupy his mind when they crossed the bridge over the Great Zab River. Marking the halfway point between Irbil and the fortified city of Mosul, a gaggle of solders with AKs guarded the east end of the bridge.

The west end was different. A dusty T-72 tank squatted on the right side, blocking the road, the 125mm main gun's muzzle aligned with the roadway. The muzzle opening grew bigger and bigger as they approached. Two soldiers leveled their AKs at the Nissan and a third, an officer, stepped over to block the remaining lane leading off the bridge.

Devon relaxed his grip on the wheel and slowed. *I'm just another UN worker*, he thought. *Not anything else. Never killed an Iraqi soldier, nothing crazy like that. Must have been somebody else.*

He stopped at the officer's signal. Devon stared straight ahead down the pot-holed road, wondering what the city of Mosul looked like and if he would ever see the Tigris River somewhere out of sight to the west.

The officer spoke to him in Arabic. Before Devon could answer, Mrs. Qasim responded, also in Arabic, and handed the officer a packet of papers. Arif nudged Devon, motioning for him to turn off the ignition. They sat for a long moment while the officer studied the papers.

In the rearview mirror, Devon could see both women had wrapped their shawls around their faces in the traditional manner, leaving only their eyes showing.

The officer paused in his scrutiny of the documents to ask a question. This time Arif answered and the soldier laughed.

Devon stared straight ahead, wondering what Arif could have said that was so funny. The notepad in his shirt pocket seemed to grow hot as Devon sat, waiting. Why in hell hadn't he thrown the list of missile sites in a burn barrel back at the camp? He jumped in his seat when the soldier suddenly pounded the top of the Nissan with his fist.

"Go now," whispered Arif.

Devon glanced at the boy and reached for the ignition key, eyebrows raised. Arif nodded an affirmative. Devon started the Nissan and deliberately drove off the bridge, winding around the concrete anti-tank barriers. After a few moments' silence, he asked Arif. "What did you tell the soldier?"

Arif smiled. "I told him you didn't speak Arabic...that you were an Indian."

"You must not speak like that again, Arif. All of the soldiers are not fools," said Mrs. Qasim.

Devon glanced up in the rearview mirror to see Mrs. Qasim frowning at her son.

"But I spoke the truth, Mother." Arif poked Devon. "Tell her, Chief, that I spoke the truth." He pointed to Devon. "And look. Your hair is black, your eyes brown, like the men from Bangladesh who work in the compound. They are Indians." He popped a dried date in his mouth and grinned at Devon, his cheek distended.

"It was a truth the next soldier might not find funny, Arif. Just let your mother do the talking, okay?" *Now the kid believes he's a comedian.*

Arif suddenly pointed out the window. "Look, Mother. Is this the place where we lived?" Arif asked. He gestured past the radar dishes and missiles of an air defense site—carefully hidden from aerial view by the flat roof of a covered market—toward a second tank and another line of concrete barriers blocking access to a smaller bridge leading back across the Tigris.

"Quiet, Arif," was his mother's sharp answer.

Mrs. Qasim's image was stiff in the mirror, staring straight over Arif's head at the road ahead.

"Mother is sad. This is the place is where Father died." Arif spoke softly.

"Enough, son. Learn to hold your tongue before you speak of things you should not." She tapped him on the top of his head with a knuckle. She popped open a can and held it over the back of the seat. "Now eat some almonds and be quiet."

Devon glanced over. Arif's gaze was straight ahead, like his mother's, devoid of any reaction as he held the can. *Never teach this kid to play poker.* But he had stirred Devon's curiosity.

"Mrs. Qasim, where does that road lead?" Devon asked. He wondered if she was going to thump him on the head. Or end up cutting his throat?

After a pause, she answered, "It is the road to Saad Sixteen, the research facility where my husband and I worked until his death last year."

That was all. No explanation, no tears. So Devon let it pass.

Over the next few kilometers, they passed a series of roadblocks and checkpoints. Devon slowed at each one, but the soldiers waved them on with nothing more than stares at the women in the back, as if he were an invisible chauffeur. Once into Mosul, no one seemed to notice them in the traffic, despite the dusty white paint with the UN markings on the sides.

It was approaching noon when they left the town and a soldier waved them to a stop at another checkpoint. Devon sat silently, while the officer in charge talked to a distant authority on a telephone. Once again, for the umpteenth time in his life, Devon wished he could say more than *Inshallah* and *shukran*, understand a bit of the conversation, and have some idea what was going on.

Neither of the women spoke a word, and Arif, after his mother's admonishment, just sat and fidgeted, rolling the window up and down, sliding back and forth on the seat until Devon caught his eye.

"Bored?" Devon asked.

"No, only tired of sitting so long." Arif took a deep breath, leaned back and leisurely selected almonds from the can, examining each one for imperfections, then crunching it between his teeth and chewing, savoring each nut before he ate the next.

Devon had almost dozed off when suddenly the wailing from a distant minaret loud speaker broke the silence.

Mrs. Qasim spoke. "Come, Arif. Put away the almonds."

Devon turned to see Mrs. Qasim carefully pour a splash of bottled water over Arif's hands and feet and then her own. She gathered up two rolled prayer rugs under her arms and led Arif to a guardhouse by the road. She spoke to one of the soldiers standing by the barrier control, who pointed off to the south, toward Mecca. She nodded to him, and took Arif around the side of the house, out of sight.

On the other side of the road, far in the distance, oil-drilling scaffolds poked up into the sky.

"What's going on, Renée?" Devon asked. The officer was taking too long, and now half of Devon's entourage had disappeared. And Devon still had the incriminating notebook burning a hole in his pocket.

"Mrs. Qasim asked about *qibla*, the direction toward Mecca, for prayer," Granwin replied. She paused for a moment. "I think I will pray also." Her face relaxed and the shawl slid down to her shoulders. As she relaxed, her head tilted back, leaving her chin out-thrust, defiant even as she rested. Her blond hair glowed in the backlight from the whitewashed walls of the guardhouse. The reflected desert sun created a halo effect, enhanced by the glitter of her tousled silver streaks.

The creases still lined her face, etched, he supposed, by the desert wind and all the death she had witnessed, burned into permanence by the relentless sun. Devon hoped she had finally left Taj's death high in the mountains, buried under the cairn of jagged rocks. He wanted to reach back and run his fingers over her cheekbones, to let her know he did care. *His own fallen angel, resting with the mortals and their evil ways.*

Devon wished he could as easily purge all his demons. He closed his eyes and tried, but is teemed everything was totally out of his control. Had been and would continue to be as long as he was in this country and with these people.

"You are Mr. Devon?"

Devon practically jumped out of his seat at the question. The officer had walked around and leaned down stuck his head in the passenger window. Devon nodded and cleared the dust from his throat. "Yes, that's me." He started to ask if the officer wanted to see his identification card, then decided to let the soldier remain in control, just flow with the questions, the good old agricultural advisor at work.

The officer leaned over to look directly into Granwin's face, at the very least an Arabic insult to her status. "And you?" he asked.

Granwin responded in Arabic, again leaving Devon frustrated in his ignorance of the language. She had pulled the shawl back over her head, hiding her gray-streaked yellow crown.

The officer stood back and opened the passenger door when Arif bounded up, then opened the rear door for Mrs. Qasim. She nodded to him, her face hidden behind her shawl, replaced their rugs and settled in her seat.

"Mr. Devon." The officer handed him their papers, then pointed down the road where the road snaked to the west across the fields, a hint of green showing where the spring grain had burst up from the ground. "When you cross the large oil pipeline, the road divides. Take the left fork to reach Sinjar. Have a safe journey."

"*Shukran.* Thank you." Devon turned the ignition. The starter turned the engine over, a grinding sound like it had ingested all the dust from the road between there and Irbil. Devon smiled up at the officer. "Probably just a little water in the gas." God, he hoped so.

Eventually, he knew he was going to run out of checkpoint luck. Devon turned the key again and the engine sputtered, then caught, and they were on their way, a long way from their camp, and getting further away by the kilometer.

Mrs. Qasim handed Arif a box of dates, a creamy orangish ball and a small bottle of water over the seat. "Would you like something to eat, Mr. Devon? Mr. Hillsom prepared some food for our journey. I have *labneh* and bread to share." In the mirror, he could see her holding up one of the balls.

"Who's Hillsom?" he asked. Next to him, Arif crumbled his ball, releasing a sour smell.

"Mr. Hillsom is your bartender, Ian," responded Granwin. "And *labneh* is dried yogurt cheese, very healthy."

Devon shook his head. "No, thanks."

Arif opened a paper box and worried a dried date from the gooey mass.

"Can I have one of those, kid?" He held out his hand and Arif dug out a second date. Devon popped the date in his mouth, chewed the flesh and sucked on the pit. He could feel the jolt of sugar work through his system.

"Another date, please?" Devon asked. He wiped his hand on his pants leg and held it out. A lone desert hare dashed across the road in front of them as he slid the date into his mouth, the only wild animal he had seen the entire trip.

In the distance, an old man rode a dun camel, colored so much like the desert that the old man looked as if he were floating along the sand. A plodding line of loaded donkeys followed the magical man across the barren Iraqi landscape toward a distant range of mountains. He never looked Devon's way, preferring the open desert to the pavement.

In the distance, the Sinjar Mountains rose gently out of the plains. *Why am I here?* he wondered. Did anyone really care about these people and their water? Was this trip Levison's idea, Kilborn's or did it belong to someone somewhere else?

All questions, no answers.

CHAPTER 15

Arif pointed at a road sign, the Arabic script half obscured by yellow dust blowing in from the dry fields. "Sinjar," he announced, squirming in his seat. "The sign says Sinjar is the next town. I am very glad. This trip is too long."

Devon peered ahead through the dust, expecting to see a village of huts straddling the highway leading to Syria, a hundred kilometers to the west. Three eighteen-wheelers turned across in front of the Nissan, blocking the road ahead and oblivious to any Western sense of right-of-way. Devon slowed to let the trucks clear and their dust cloud settle.

Mrs. Qasim tapped him on the shoulder. "Turn and follow where the trucks go." She pointed over his shoulder at the side road heading north toward a range of low mountains.

Devon downshifted, steered around the potholes and onto the smaller road. A chill ran over his neck as the dust cleared and a huge gun barrel emerged from the cloud. Another T-72 tank crouched half-hidden behind a high berm, its gun barrel pointed toward the main highway. A dirt-covered soldier sat on top of the turret in the mid-afternoon sun, lazily tracking them with a heavy machine gun. Devon slowed to let the trucks pull away. The paved road crumbled into potholes, then into desert hard pack marred by deep ruts left by the trucks. The rolling brown cloud gradually settled over a low row of buildings on their right.

Mrs. Qasim spoke from the rear. "Follow the signs to the center of the town."

"What'd she say?" Devon asked Arif as they bounced across the ruts.

Arif pointed toward a faded sign, 'Centre,' a vestige of the long-past British influence in the area that directed them down a narrow alley. At least the road was too narrow for the trucks. Or the tank. Arif slid forward to the edge of his seat and navigated them through a maze of roadside stalls and shops. Wash hung from the upper balconies over the shops, despite the brown grit in the air. Each passing block had a theme of similar shops in the traditional Middle

Eastern fashion. Rug merchants filled one block, brass pot makers the next, apparently kitchen fixtures from all the porcelain and pipes, the next. Sinjar was much more of a town than Devon had expected. Money from somewhere, but he hadn't seen an oil exploration derrick or pump rig since Mosul.

Mrs. Qasim leaned over the seat and thumped Devon on the shoulder. "Stop here." She pointed to a modern building—modern in that it appeared more 1940s European concrete than the 1800s Bedouin clay of the rest of the town. "The administrative center. I expect this is where Suleiman Murshid will meet us." She readjusted her black shawl across her face. "Wait for me, please."

"May I come, Mother?" asked Arif. He was out the door and around by her side before she could answer. Arif took his mother's hand and walked by her side up three wide stone steps and through a heavy wooden door.

Devon shivered. The heater had kept them warm through the day, but as the sun dropped behind the low buildings, the Nissan cooled rapidly. He turned to Granwin. She was watching the people wandering down the street.

"No one seems to be in a hurry," Devon said. He waited for Granwin's reply but, for a change, she was silent. He followed her gaze to the building. 'British Colonial Office—Sinjar' was carved in stone across a front arch. Brits, French, Turks, Caesar's legions, back to Alexander and before. Everybody had had a piece of the Mesopotamian action at one time or the other. He got out of the Nissan and stretched in the sun.

Arif reappeared, bounding down the steps and beckoning them.

Devon opened the door for Granwin. When he stared into her eyes, the sparkle of their first meeting, the sarcastic greeting, was missing. The shawl covered the rest of her face, but the eyes were dark. He followed her inside, wondering where her jazz had gone.

"Welcome, Mr. Devon, Madam Granwin, to Sinjar." A tall man in a threadbare black suit and white shirt buttoned to his protruding Adam's apple stood on the top step. He bowed. "I am Daris Fagham, Chief Engineer for the Sinjar Water District."

He seemed to draw himself up even a little taller, his hair a thick mass of silver brushed back in a mane down the back of his neck. He spoke in precise English. "Sheik Murshid was not able to be here this afternoon. He asked me to apologize for his absence and assured me he would more than make it up to you this evening. Also, be assured you have my personal gratitude for coming to our assistance." He bent at the waist to peer back toward the vehicle.

Devon saw a frown wash across Fagham's face, so quickly Devon wasn't sure he had seen it. "Ah, Mister Baker did not accompany you?" Fagham asked, or commented, Devon wasn't sure which. Apparently, Mister Fagham had expected Mister Baker.

Fagham led them midway down the entrance hall into a small office.

Devon tried to relate Fagham's position in the local hierarchy from the location and size of his office relative to the other bureaucrats Devon had glimpsed as he passed the open doors. He smiled and nodded in response to the stares of the curious occupants. He gathered the chief engineer had some unexpected element of authority in this larger-than-expected town, far more than Devon had expected. His impression was reinforced when two young men brought in extra chairs and arranged them around a delicate oak desk. After cursory bows they left, closing the door behind them.

After every one had settled, Fagham sat in his desk chair, arms folded across the uncluttered top. "Would you like tea?"

Devon realized the question was rhetorical as one of the young men returned with a traditional brass pot, a tray of small glasses and a heaping bowl of sugar cubes. A unique aspect of Iraqi culture, in contrast to Saudi, was that the men had no hesitation in serving the two women. A Saudi man would as soon walk naked down the hall.

For once, Devon was glad for the custom of tea. It washed down some of the travel grit and, with the sugar, seemed to revive him from the long trip. He half-tuned out the exchange of travel and weather conditions, the polite conversation that always preceded any Middle Eastern business conversation.

"When Suleiman Murshid approved my suggestion to request assistance from Baghdad, I expected perhaps a letter explaining why the water had been diverted from the Tigris irrigation canals, nothing more, other than perhaps a vague promise that the flow would someday be restored. I am overwhelmed by your presence. And pleased."

Fagham leaned forward as Devon sipped the last of his tea. "I know you are all tired from your travels, and wish to soon retire to your rest, but if you like, Mr. Devon, I can summarize the issue." He pointed to a map on the wall. "It is a quite simple problem and I know how you Americans like to tackle issues without delay."

Devon nodded and stood as Fagham stepped over to the map. *Very self-assured,* Devon thought. *Not just a local bureaucrat.* Fagham apparently considered himself a man of the world.

"May I?" asked Devon, pointing to the map.

Fagham nodded.

Devon recognized the general area by the contour lines, waterways and the political boundary of Syria to the west. The scale was too large to include the Tigris to the north or the Euphrates to the south, the general boundaries of the Mesopotamian valley. All the notations were in Arabic, but the purpose was clearly to follow the water flow from the mountains to the reservoirs. The town of Sinjar seemed to be off the path of the water flows except for one meandering riverbed out of the nearby mountains.

"I am pleased that Mr. Devon, an American agricultural advisor, has come to our assistance, and I understand Madam Qasim's position with our government, but why are you here, Madam Granwin?" asked Fagham.

Devon continued to scan the map, surprised Fagham would ask the question. He had wondered the same. He wondered what Granwin's reaction to the blunt question would be.

A hint of the old Granwin returned with her smile. "Mrs. Qasim and I are both widows, and I am here to serve as a chaperon of sorts for Mrs. Qasim, in the Islamic sense of the word." Granwin laughed, a soft hint of the humor Devon had seen at the village with Taj in her lap.

"But, in truth, I suspect it is as much for my feelings. A young child I cared for recently died, and our kind director sent me here to keep my mind busy. I am sure young Master Qasim here will more than take care of his mother." Granwin paused, then smiled, a shy look Devon had never seen before. "Perhaps you could introduce me to the abbot of your monastery before we depart."

"Ah, you know of the Sinjar monastery?" Fagham asked. His sun-burnished face paled.

Or was the flickering of the single bulb above them playing tricks on Devon's eyes?

Granwin nodded. "Mr. Baker said I might find some interesting information there."

The color seemed to return to Fagham's face. "Ah, yes, Mr. Baker would know of such things. Certainly, when we have the opportunity, perhaps tomorrow?"

Granwin and her icon. Baker and his mysteries. If he were here for a reason other than water, Devon wished someone would tell him. He resisted the urge to tap his foot, anxious to get on with the meeting, to get to why he was really here.

Fagham turned back to the map and pointed at a narrow blue line coming out of the mountains. "Mr. Devon, as you can see, the mountains shield us from the direct flow of the water from the lowlands just over the border in Syria. Our principal source of water is the snow melt from *Jebal Sinjar*, the mountains to our north. We received an especially reduced amount this year."

"What's the impact in the fields? I need to know more about the crops, to get the feel of the dirt in my hands." Devon surprised himself this time, the sharp memories of what farming is about overwhelming the spy business.

"Do you also taste the dirt, Mr. Devon?" Fagham had a hint of a smile on his face.

"Actually, yes." Devon could still remember the loamy taste of good riverbed soil, tart with the leached tannic acid from the trees, but with a fresh organic richness so different from the silica blandness of the desert grit he had tasted in recent years. "If there are no mules grazing around to foul the ground."

Fagham laughed. "Good. I have been told tasting the dirt is a trait of a true farmer. People from the universities stare as if you are crazy if one says things of such a nature." He twirled his finger beside his temple. "But every successful farmer I know tastes and smells, his own laboratory inside himself." He stood, straightening his jacket. "Perhaps we can best address the problem out in the fields."

He turned to the women. "As I told Madam Qasim, Suleiman Murshid, our community leader, will be your host tonight. I will ask one of the clerks to take you to the sheik's home so you can rest while we men examine the problem." He rubbed his hands together as he stood. "Are those arrangements satisfactory for everyone?"

Arif sprang from his chair where he had been sitting with his hands folded in his lap. "Mother, may I go with Mr. Devon?"

Mrs. Qasim glanced over at Devon with a question in her raised eyebrows.

Arif's head bobbed from side to side as he waited for Devon's approval, his grin about to pop off his face. Devon nodded, remembering the days on the farm with his grandfather patiently explaining the mysteries of nematodes and the wonders of an emerging butterfly.

She agreed. "You may go, but you must do exactly as Mr. Devon instructs."

Fagham spoke to one of the older ladies in the hallway, who smiled and engaged Granwin and Mrs. Qasim in conversation as she led them down the hall. Fagham turned back to Devon. "Come. The women are in good hands. We will see them again at the evening meal."

He led the way out to the Nissan where Arif waited in the back seat, sitting tall under the stares of several local children all dressed in their Sunday best. As he started the vehicle Devon remembered that children in this part of the world didn't dress for Sunday. The Islamic day of worship is Friday. In fact, now that he was paying closer attention, it looked like everyone on the street appeared well to do. He had gotten so used to the ragged, mismatched garb of the mountain Kurds that the Sinjar children and adults seemed from another world.

"Is something special going on today, Mr. Fagham?" Devon asked.

"Pardon me." Fagham looked at him, gray, bushy eyebrows raised in question.

Devon wondered if this were some show to impress him for some reason. The Datsun pickups even looked newer with less rust and dents than the Baghdad fleet. But why in the hell would anyone want to impress him?

"Is today a local holiday?" Devon motioned toward a couple crossing the street. "Forgive me…I don't mean this to be insulting or disrespectful, but everyone seems to be all dressed up. Maybe I've spent too much time around the refugee camps."

Fagham's smile faded. "There are many things for us to discuss when we reach the fields." Fagham looked back at Arif, then straightened in his seat.

Curious but silent, Devon followed another convoy of trucks up a slight incline as Fagham pointed the way along the road leading toward the mountain range. A series of short poles alongside the road, topped with crossed beams and old-style glass insulators, supported a pair of wires leading toward the mountains. In places, the wires almost touched the dry ground, barren of even a weed to keep the winds from stripping the topsoil.

Fagham pointed down a side road. Devon slowed to maneuver under the sagging wires, then turned left to drive alongside an irrigation canal cutting across a barren field.

"Stop here, please," directed Fagham, pointing at a hard-packed widening of the farm road. "Come around to this side of the vehicle, if you would."

Fagham climbed out and waited until Devon joined him beside a rusting red farm tractor. The tractor, abandoned with one tire flat to the ground, leaned precariously toward the canal bed.

Devon tried to read the rusty lettering on the side, but couldn't make it out.

"A Belarus, produced by the Belarus Tractor Works in Minsk." Fagham patted the rusty hulk. "The Soviet Union produced many able machines, very sturdy. But they have left us Iraqis on our own.

Left us with Saddam Hussein and rusty tractors that do not operate because there are no spare parts." He shrugged his sloped shoulders. "They have no more Union, and we have no more tractors."

Together they watched Arif sprint along the road, then skid to a stop and squat down by the side of the canal to watch some tiny something stirring the surface of a dirty pool of water. "He is a fine boy." Again noticeably pale, Fagham scanned the bare fields around them and led Devon back to the truck. He leaned back against the Nissan and paused, as if to catch his breath.

Devon got the impression Fagham was wrestling with an internal decision. Probably who to trust.

Fagham finally pointed toward the dust plume stirred up by a row of trucks heading toward the mountains. "We once grew some of the finest barley in all of Mesopotamia. Then the water stopped coming down from our mountains. Like the others, at first I didn't care. None of us cared. We once had nothing, then we had plenty. For poor farmers, plenty is sometimes too much. A poor man can lose his reason very quickly."

Devon tired of listening to the old man tell of hard times. He had farmed. He still remembered how a farmer relishes the few good years—the years without hail, without drought, without tobacco worms, without nematodes in the seedling beds. The sun dropped down toward the edge of the low ridge curving around to the west. It had been a long drive, just stand out in the chill air to see a dry ditch.

"Mr. Fagham, I'm sorry, but I don't understand. I'm familiar with the implications of soil alkalinity and salinity and moisture content, all the technical parameters of agriculture. I have tools to analyze these things, and perhaps I could make some suggestions for treatment. But if the water was diverted upstream, why am I here?" he asked.

"You are here because I sent for you." Fagham's voice was suddenly harsh. He pointed toward the mountains, his finger trembling. "I, with many others of the villages and the farms, worked in the facility up there. Perhaps because I had too much education I realized what we were doing and refused. There is something there you must stop." His voice became angry. "Didn't Wilbert tell you what was happening here?"

Wilbert? Devon shook his head. He scanned the mountains to the north. There were no buildings, no sign of industrial plumes or the roar of power conversion where the sun painted an orange glow across the tops of the low peaks.

Devon thought back to what Baker had said as he lay in the back of the Nissan, covered with blood. Devon had let the explosions and the death of the child mute Baker's message. He didn't remember the exact phrase, only that Baker had urged caution, but insisted Devon press the search.

"Bad things out there," Devon muttered, finally remembering Baker's words, and something about—what? "—listen to the old man," was all he could remember. Was this the old man?

Fagham frowned at Devon. "*Wallachi*, great God, I had hoped they would not send a fool."

Devon had to smile at Fagham's loss of patience, so out of character for this part of the world. The old man must have spent a lot of time with Westerners to express his impatience so openly. That kind of free expression usually was saved for family. Devon wondered what the expression on the old man face represented. Irritation, resignation, or just exasperation?

Fagham waved toward the mountains. "Yes, there is danger. My brother-in law is the only reason I was not executed immediately. When they find out I have been talking with you—" He paused and took a deep breath. "Tomorrow you must take Madam Granwin to the old monastery. There you will see for yourself the danger.

"Now we must return to Suleiman Murshid's pavilion. I am sure he will want to meet you." Fagham shook his head. "But do not speak of any of this to him or anyone. I may be the only one who understands. All the others only live to spend the German marks and the Swiss francs brought over the borders by the truckers. Especially Suleiman Murshid." He opened the Nissan's door.

Devon whistled at Arif as he tried to think his way through the puzzle. "If Sheik Murshid is part of the problem, why are we going to his pavilion?" he asked as Arif, all knees and elbows, ran up, kicked the dirt from his shoes and bounced into the back seat.

Fagham folded his tall frame to accommodate the doorframe and climbed back into the Nissan. A smile returned to Fagham's creased face. "Suleiman is the sheik, our leader. A traitor. And my brother-in-law."

CHAPTER 16

Fagham guided them along a confusing lattice of roads following the hatch-work pattern of the irrigation ditches around the bare fields. After the warning, Fagham had not spoken, letting his bony finger point the way. Devon was left to drive and wonder at the hints of intrigue, Fagham's references to Baker implying an old friendship.

Water—the sole focus of life in the desert. But was water truly the issue here in Sinjar? "Bad things out there." Now that Devon remembered, he couldn't get Baker's words out of his mind.

The vehicle lights swept over a large white tent.

"Park there, by the fountain." Fagham pointed to a standpipe at the end of the road. "This is Sheik Murshid's pavilion."

Enough water gurgled from the open spout to fill a shallow depression and nourish the low grass by the fountain. A faint hum of an engine floated from behind the tent. Devon guessed the engine drove a generator for the lights. *Murshid must be a man of means, even if he lives in a tent out here in the middle of nowhere.*

The edge of the moon rose over the tent, visible after Devon had turned off the headlights, as a faint thin sliver floating up into the darker sky high above the tent.

"Yow!"

Devon spun at Arif's cry. His heart pounded and he took a deep breath, then chuckled as a flock of doves fluttered over the tent and into the gathering night, the beating of their wings lost in the groans of the desert wind.

The tent glowed from the lights inside, silhouetted shadows swaying with the movement of the canvas. Behind the tent, faint lines of a mud wall stretched to both right and left, fading into the night.

As they washed at the old pipe stand, Devon's mouth watered with the smells floating from the tent. Blunted by years of MREs and mess hall eating, he struggled to catalog the odors, to sort the garlic from the curry.

"Come, and let us join Sheik Murshid and his family," Fagham said. He took Devon's sleeve and led them into the tent. "He enjoys his meals very much. Let us not keep him waiting."

Devon had been a big reader on the farm, one way for a kid to travel the world with just a trip to the school library. He vaguely remembered an old book, *Arabian Nights* expunged for Southern Methodist school children, but left with pen and ink sketches of voluptuous women in swirling pantaloons and veils and barely hidden breasts. Tonight he walked into his dream.

For a moment, Devon expected Scheherazade to come dancing across the sand floor, bells on her fingers. Instead, a short, heavy man with a thick beard rose from a pillow in the middle of the tent, brightly lit by a dozen or more bare light bulbs strung on wires between the tent poles. On one side, Sara Qasim, wearing a subtly patterned dress, leaned over a platter of food, her wide skirt demurely covering her feet.

"Welcome, my friends." Their host held his arms wide then, with a sweeping gesture, ushered them toward the center. He moved with a lumbering gait, favoring his right leg. "You must be Mr. Devon. Welcome to my humble home. I am Suleiman Murshid and this—" He waved an arm around the tent to include two other women and one young girl carrying large platters of food. "—is my family." Murshid turned to Fagham and embraced him in the desert custom with a touch of lips on Fagham's cheeks.

The older women, dressed in traditional pastel gowns, but without the veils Devon expected, placed the steaming platters on a low table while the girl poured an iced drink into tall glasses.

"Steria—" An old, wrinkled woman in a pale red robe flashed a smile at Devon. "—is my first wife," Murshid explained. The second woman, in an eggshell blue robe, held her face down out of view. "This is my second wife, Mairia," he added.

Murshid turned to Arif, standing at the entrance to the tent, eyes wide as he took in the pile of food. "Join us, boy." Murshid followed with a string of Arabic, and Arif raced to his mother's side.

"Thank you for your hospitality, Sheik Murshid." Devon answered as he bent his head, the hint of a bow the people of the Middle East use to show their acceptance of hospitality.

"You are most welcome, sir. Come, my boy." Murshid motioned to Arif. "You will sit on my left, between your mother and me."

Over the whispers of the evening wind the distant wail of the muezzin penetrated the canvas walls with the Islamic loudspeakered call to prayer. Devon smiled at Sara, wondering where the prayer rugs were stashed. He caught Arif cutting a glance at his mother, unsure of what to do. She took his hand and pulled the boy next to her, patting his clasped hand with her other. Devon guessed the infinitesimal pat was to reassure the boy that Allah would allow them this compensation.

Murshid also saw the exchange, smiled and nodded, at first at Sara, then at Devon as Murshid sat, pulling the boy down beside him by his elbow. "Mr. Devon, you are not Muslim, so don't be concerned for us. In Sinjar, we have our own traditions, not bound totally by the Shariah as dictated by the imams in Baghdad. As you may know, Shariah literally means 'the way to the water,' interpreted as the pathway to righteousness. I believe there are many paths. I choose my own.

He motioned Devon to sit down beside him, on the opposite side from Arif. "Tonight, the women and children will join us for a feast honoring your visit. It is a Western tradition for families to gather together, is it not?" He patted Arif's knee. "I most welcome Mrs. Qasim and her son. The voice of a young boy is very appreciated in my home."

He reached over and caught the girl gently by her arm as she placed a dish on the table. She kept her head down as Murshid presented her to the visitors. "This is my daughter, Anna. She is a wonderful daughter. But she is not a son."

Anna was a miniature of her mother, complete with the fine gold bangle bracelets and loops of gold coins chained around her neck over a bright print dress, the traditional Bedouin display of wealth.

Across the tent, Marina's smile seemed a little forced as she whispered to Fagham. She was tall and stoop-shouldered with a hawk nose that mirrored Fagham's. Devon looked around the tent and wondered where Granwin had hidden away. He was surprised to realize he missed her.

Murshid brought his attention back into the tent as they sat by the mounds of food, trays of sliced tomatoes and cucumbers, a large platter of rice full of unidentifiable bits. Devon's mouth began to water as the women laid out platters of cold cuts, raw vegetables and steaming trays of gummy rice.

"Our people are of the Yezidis. Do you know of the Yezidis?" Murshid wagged his finger at Sara's obvious disapproval. "Yes, Mrs. Qasim, around Sinjar live those who pray to the Devil to wish ill upon their enemies." He shook his head, flinging bits of food from his beard. "But we also pray to Allah."

He waved Mairia over and plucked a marinated olive from her tray. "A part of the ancient Kurdish empire, we Yezidis have taken the best of all: Jesus and Mohammed. We recognize all of the great

Prophets as guides to Paradise following many paths, just as we accept Satan as the sinner's guide to Hell."

He nodded his head as he popped the olive in his mouth, chewed and took another. "Please, try one," he said to Devon. Murshid examined his olive carefully, then offered it to Arif, smiling as the boy nibbled at the fruit. "But we reject no stray path, unlike our militant friends of the mosques and monasteries. Not so bound by rules, no rushing away from a good meal to pray, compelled by the rising of the sun and the moon." He spit the olive seed onto the ground and held up another green globe, waiting for Devon to take one from the tray.

Devon cautiously slid an olive into his mouth. He had learned the hard way that Middle Eastern hospitality and exotic foods could extract a price even higher than Ian's peppers. The olive skin was smooth and hard—flavor tinged with unknown spices, but savory, not fiery. The women all smiled at him, sitting there like an idiot with the olive popped out in one cheek. Devon felt the flush rise up from his neck. Next his folded legs would cramp, and he would make a complete fool of himself.

Arif spit a seed onto the sand, mimicking their host, and grinned at Devon's embarrassment. "One time mother showed me a picture of an African monkey collecting tree fruit in its cheeks," he said.

"Arif, be polite to Mr. Devon." Sara Qasim frowned at her son.

Murshid's laughter rumbled up from his belly to his beard. "Let the boy enjoy himself, Mrs. Qasim."

Devon quickly chewed the olive away from its seed and followed Murshid and Arif's example by spitting the seed onto the ground, then laughed along with Murshid.

Murshid turned back to Devon. "You savor the olive? It is one of my favorites before the meal. But it saddens me." He held up a glistening green orb. "The olive is the fruit of the female blossom. Did you know that, Mr. Devon?" Murshid took Arif's head in his hand and turned the boy's face toward him.

Arif blinked in the glare of the lights. Devon glanced from the boy to his mother sitting beside him, both on the other side of Murshid. Her eyes stayed fixed on Murshid, her face emotionless.

Not just the son. Don't play poker with either of those two.

Murshid stroked Arif's hair. "I have longed for a son, but like the male olive flower, I cannot. At first, I blamed Steria. But my dear wife was not at fault. After my brother was murdered by the Turks in the mountains, I took his widow, Mairia, and her daughter into my home, but still could not conceive a child."

Murshid patted Arif's cheek and turned back to Devon. "As a man, I know you understand my pain, in here." Murshid beat his closed fist onto his chest. "The doctors tell me I suffered many bad wounds in the mountains, fighting the damned Turks. So I humbly accept the will of Allah in the matter of my manhood. But I do not surrender."

He turned back to Arif and smiled. "I'll find a son of my own. And teach him to fight the Turks."

"Were you a soldier of the Kurdish army?" asked Devon.

"Oh, no," interrupted Fagham, as he sat down across the low table from Devon and the others. "We both were loyal members of the Iraqi army, many years ago, before the rise of Saddam Hussein. Sheik Murshid and I first met as soldiers."

Murshid nodded and spit out a seed. "We did well, my good friend Daris Fagham and I. We served with honor. The government was in the process of taking over the assets of IPC, the foreign oil concession, and sent us both off to school so we could be part of the new Iraqi management. For Daris, because he was smart. For me, because I was a good soldier and had suffered much."

He smiled and pointed toward his burnoose. "I remain proud of my Bedouin father and my Kurdish mother, but I also have a civil engineering degree from the University of Manchester." He leaned back on a padded leather-covered box and grimaced as he straightened out one leg. "But enough about me. Daris tells me you are here to help with our water problem."

Murshid dropped his smile as he stared across the table at his brother-in-law. "I'm surprised he has asked for help. Daris Fagham is himself an expert in water management."

Fagham quickly spoke up. "I am concerned that the source of our problem may lie over the border, in the marshes of Al Qaminishli. The Syrians continue to expand their oil fields at the expense of the water table. Very short-sighted, I believe. They would rather have oil than water.

"Mr. Devon is both an expert in the matter and a representative of the United Nations. If the Syrians are involved, perhaps he can help us." Fagham picked up a sliver of chicken from the bed of rice and placed it in his mouth, escaping the need to continue his explanations.

It was hard to tell under Fagham's weathered face, but Devon sensed a bit of fluster, a hint of a flush. Was Fagham's discomfort from Murshid's comments?

Renée Granwin's entrance interrupted the questions. Granwin's plain white blouse, tucked into a dark brown loose skirt, offered an unexpected contrast to the colorful gowns of the other women.

"Good evening, gentlemen," she greeted the men. She made a slight bow to the wives with the traditional Arabic greeting, "*As salaam alaykum*."

Her words brought smiles and a murmured response from Steria and Marina.

Granwin leaned on Devon's shoulder and gracefully folded her legs under her full skirt to sit next to him. She leaned forward to smile and nod to Sara and Arif. Her hand was warm resting on his shoulder, comfortable.

Devon put his hand over hers wishing, for a moment, they could be having this meal in some quiet, safe place. Not where he was afraid to speak, that he would betray someone. Especially since he wasn't sure whom he would be betraying.

Mairia knelt beside Fagham and placed a small brass tray of rolled green leaves in front of Granwin. "*Eprakh?*" she asked.

With an out-of-character shy smile, Granwin drew her hand away from Devon's shoulder, took a green leaf from the tray and unrolled it for him to see, freeing a burst of aromas. "Rice, mutton, tomatoes, all bound in a marinated grape leaf. Try one," She rolled hers back up and slipped it into her mouth.

The spicy smells included garlic and onion, but other than that Devon couldn't tell as he tried to interpret Granwin's sudden demureness. He leaned over and took one of the rolled leaves from the tray. Cold, the leaf lent a little crunchiness to the soft mass of rice and tender bits of meat as he chewed, watching Granwin pluck a slice of cucumber from a tray and nibble the green skin away from the fleshy core. She had a drawn look about her eyes. Granwin really did need a diversion, to get away from the memories of Taj.

Watching her eat, Devon suddenly realized how hungry he was and scooped up a mass of hot rice and chicken. Beside him, Murshid turned to Arif and his mother and spoke to them in either Arabic or Kurdish, indecipherable to Devon.

Fagham leaned toward Granwin across the pile of food. "Madam Granwin, do I understand correctly you are interested in old Christian artifacts?"

Granwin's head popped up at Fagham's question. She answered with a silent nod as she swallowed the remainder of the cucumber slice.

Devon tasted his drink as he watched, wondering how far Murshid strayed from the Islamic law. Not far enough. Only lemonade, very sweet lemonade, but it soothed the spices from his palate.

"Tomorrow, I intend to take Mr. Devon to the spring head that feeds our small river. The Sinjar monastery shares the spring, and has many interesting relics, some dating back to the Crusades." Fagham chewed and swallowed another bit of chicken.

Granwin sat across from him, her hands in her lap, eyes focused on Fagham.

"Would you care to join us?" he asked.

"Of course," she replied. Her wide smile returned for the first time since Taj's death, the face-splitting smile that had irritated Devon so when he first met her. Silver streaks glittered in her blond hair, almost hypnotic as the lights swayed with the wind.

In the light of the bare bulbs, the truth struck Devon like a tobacco stick across the butt. He was smitten. *Like a schoolboy.* By a woman who despised him enough to smack him with a frying pan.

Devon leaned back against a pillow watching Granwin move around the table to sit between Fagham and Steria. Fagham explained the history of the old monastery, something about the Crusades. Granwin became so animated she actually laughed, low, but a bit more of the old Granwin.

Devon sensed an unusual hesitancy in Sara as Sheik Murshid reached out and tousled her boy's hair. In contrast to the other women, she sat with a sad look on her face as she listened to Murshid spin out an exaggerated story. Arif giggled with Anna at something the sheik said to his mother. Sara answered with a slight smile.

"Thousands, all around us," Murshid cried, arms waving. Murshid nodded to Devon with a conspiratorial smile then continued with his tale about fighting the Turks in the mountains to the north. He interspersed enough English so that Devon could follow the gist of Murshid's boasts and the children's laughter.

Mairia was the only one who seemed to remember Devon was still in the tent as she refilled his glass and took away the empty dishes.

At the far end of the tent, Steria pulled a flap back exposing the flames flickering in the outside darkness and vanished into the night. She returned carrying a tray of steaming sweet tea in small, clear glass cups. Uncertain whether she spoke English, Devon waved his hands and smiled, hoping the tea wasn't some ritual he was offending. Then he decided neither Fagham nor Murshid would care. And Granwin was too occupied with Fagham to notice.

Devon pried himself from the pillows and walked out to the fire. He pulled out his pipe, filled it with tobacco, and flicked his lighter. The flint sparked in the night, the lighter apparently out of gas. He squatted by the low flames and picked up a thin reed to light his pipe, then quickly threw the reed back as the flame raced up to singe his fingertips. He licked his scorched finger, then, a little more carefully, searched the fire and picked out a piece of glowing hardwood. He waved the stick until the glow was cherry-bright, then placed the ember to his pipe and drew, savoring the taste and smell of the burning tobacco and oak wood.

The Cavendish tobacco had dried like a shriveled mouse, unprotected from the dry high desert air in the makeshift pouch. When he drew too hard there was a distinctive bite, but, with a slow, easy draw, the crackling tobacco reminded him of the popping pinesap oozing from the slabs feeding Grandpa's tobacco barn ovens. And his desire to be done with this place, Baker's worries and Fagham's mysteries.

He bent closer to the fire and examined the stick in his hand. The wood was smooth and tight-grained, shaped like a small barrel stave and polished to a hard, slick finish except for a series of impressions along one side. In the flickering light, Devon squinted to make out a faint imprint of Chinese characters. He tossed the glowing stick back into the fire and turned to a small pile of staves by the tent. He picked up several, turning and studying them in the firelight before he began fitting them together like a puzzle.

He had seen the staves like these at a Defense Intelligence Agency 'museum,' for lack of a better description, a place where they showed off the fruits of years of espionage and countries' going-out-of business sales. An old MiG-15, Chinese anti-aircraft weapons from Vietnam, even a Soviet tank had interested most of his tour group.

Of all the material displayed in the museum, the clever use by the Chinese of ordinary oak staves to cap their nuclear ballistic missile re-entry vehicles most intrigued Devon. The Americans and Soviets used exotic ablative heat shields, perfected from modern ceramic and carbon fiber materials, to protect the sensitive electronics and weapon assemblies from the blast-furnace heat of warhead reentry. The Chinese, in their crude but effective way, used simple oak staves for the same purpose.

Devon imagined a little old man sitting at a table, sanding block in hand, fitting each stave to the next to form a perfect shield over the re-entry vehicle nose cone. And the shields apparently worked as well as the exotics, an intelligence analyst-guide had told him in the cold fluorescent light of a warehouse.

What in hell was Murshid doing with Chinese nuclear warhead components? He tossed the oak staves back onto the pile. *Bad things out there*, Baker had said. He must be getting close.

Devon noticed the murmur of voices had stopped. Party must be over. He didn't even have a date to take home.

CHAPTER 17

Devon returned to the tent to find Fagham helping Murshid to his feet. The women and children had already left. Murshid embraced his brother-in-law and motioned both men toward a flap in the tent. "Come, Mr. Devon, and I'll show you to your bed."

Fagham inclined his head. "Good night, Mr. Devon. Rest well. Remember, we have much to see and do tomorrow." His eyes held Devon's with not a hint of a smile.

"Yes, tomorrow," Devon replied. Fagham's earlier warning resonated in the wind whistling through the tent. "I'll remember, thank you."

Devon followed Fagham through the flap in the tent and an arched opening in the wall, waited while Murshid secured a heavy wooden door behind them, and then followed Fagham's example, taking off his boots after he stepped into a hallway. Devon expected to enter another tent, some sort of a camp out, a rich-scouts-in-the-woods-with-servants affair. Instead he found himself in a palace. Italian marble, smooth to his stocking feet, glistened on the floor beneath plastered walls inset with small patterned tiles, each a piece of fine art.

"Come with me, please." Murshid motioned Devon to follow one way as Fagham disappeared in the opposite direction.

A screech filled the hallway.

"What the devil was that?" asked Devon.

Through an arched opening, the leaves of a small tree set in a huge oriental urn wavered in the starlight filtered down through a paned skylight. A pair of golden eyes stared at him, irises huge as they reflected the stars. The eyes disappeared when a series of fluorescent tubes flickered on, filling the enclosed courtyard with light.

Murshid laughed at Devon's surprise. "Anna's pet lemur feasts on the small insects that venture out at night. We all have a part to give in this world, wouldn't you agree, Mr. Devon, even the smallest of us?" Murshid waved for Devon to follow him across the courtyard. They paused by a large fountain. "Ah, my leg begins to stiffen in the night."

He dipped one hand into the water as it splashed down the fountain and into a shallow pool. The water around his fingers flickered with the golden undulations of a school of koi. "We are simple desert people, Mr. Devon, but we have learned how to use our resources well. The water, the mountains, all has their value, to the right buyer. Don't let Daris Fagham's concerns burden you. My friend Daris worries, but you can see the people of my *ashore* are wealthy in many ways. *Sahara*, your people would say tribe, like in the cowboy movies."

Murshid smiled, crooked teeth gleaming in the light. "I listen to Arif and his talk about Indians. He's a very intelligent boy. He speaks very well of you, Mr. Devon." Murshid's gaze seemed to settle on the skylight. "I like him very much." He stopped and pointed to a doorway. "There's your room. Please rest as my guest. Sleep well with Allah as your guardian from Satan."

"And you, Sheik Suleiman Murshid." Devon caught himself in the middle of a small bow. *Eating with my fingers, bowing...I've been here too damn long. Houston would be proud of me, acting like a real spy.*

Inside, the room was as pretentious as the rest of what he had seen. Finely woven rugs were scattered over a marble floor. Porcelain fixtures, hot water, clean sheets on a soft bed...Devon couldn't help but agree Murshid had done much better than his Kurdish cousins in the camps surrounding Irbil. *But at what price?*

He showered, turned out the light, then paused to stare at the stars through a double-paned window, tiny flecks in a glowing sky. He walked to the window, shivering as the water dried on his bare. The sky over the Sinjar Mountains reflected a glow of lights from the ground, reminding him of the radiance in the sky over Vegas as seen from Edwards Air Force Base. *What was in these mountains that called for so much light?* As he watched, the lights died, leaving nothing but the stars overhead.

The wind whistled through a tiny crack in the window casement. Fagham and Baker? Somehow they had schemed to get him to Sinjar. *But for what purpose?* He stood and listened. The villa was quiet, thick walls keeping the hum of the generator at bay with all the other evils. And Murshid's Satan.

Devon hoped. He slid under the cool sheet and wondered if he had misread the staves.

It all must be a dream.

In the middle of the night, his dream became real with the soft slide of silky cloth over his bare chest, the heat of another body over his. He let the fantasy lead the way. Slowly, the heat engulfed him. A gentle warmth moved over him—slow, tantalizing touches leading to a full weight on his body, pressing from his chest to his feet with a heat greater than the desert sun. Warm breath washed over his ear.

He began to move his body in synchrony with hers, allowing himself to be drawn further and further in, until they were fully coupled. Her fingers gripped Devon's shoulders as he slid his hands over her body, caressing the smoothness under the soft material of her gown, His urgency grew, and he closed his arms around her, pulling her close, regulating her movements to match his own. She began to breathe in short gasps, matching his rhythm with her own until they met at the end.

Devon continued moving inside her, reveling in the sensation even as he shrank. She lay still on his heaving chest until he stopped, their only movement the swelling of their chests as they breathed, his long and slow, hers still rapid, as if she were afraid.

Until now, Devon had kept Granwin from even his dreams, and now she was with him, her body as burning hot as he knew it would be.

Her whispered words floated through his dream. "I give you my soul in return for Arif's."

The words became clearer as he pulled his mind into reality. He slid his hands over her soft buttocks, up across her back, heart pounding at what he had heard. Heavy hair covered her shoulders, tangled in his fingers as he stroked her warm skin.

His eyes snapped open. In the dim moonlight, Sara's soft face hovered over his. Her long, black hair fell down over his face. Devon started to push her away.

"No, wait," Sara commanded. She imprisoned his body against the bed. "I have sinned, but for my son. Now let me sin for myself." She began moving forward and back, sliding ever so gently over him, her wetness teasing him to grow and swell until once again they were fully together.

This time she took control and moved at her own pace, lazily at first, then with focused deliberation. Devon thrust upward, giving Sara all of his body as she took him, then collapsed back as they both finished, together again.

Devon rolled them over to their sides, disconnecting their bodies. He brushed back her coal-black hair to search for her eyes.

They were wide open, luminescent in the moonlight. "You must become Arif's father," she said in a soft whisper.

Devon's heart raced at her words. He was speechless; all he could do was listen, still not believing the softness in his arms.

"Nadav Qasim died to save many from Saddam's bombs. He was Arif's father, my husband. I do not ask for you to love me, or even take me away from this place. But you must remove Arif from this country and these people. I give myself to you in exchange for Arif, and Nadav's memory."

She hurried through the rest of her speech before he could respond. "Last night, Sheik Suleiman Murshid asked me to become his wife. In an Islamic world, even the world of the Kurds, this is an honorable thing—to take a widow and her children into a family." She pressed her fingers over Devon's lips as he started to speak. "But I fear for Arif's future. You must promise. You are Arif's only hope. There is only one answer." She smiled at him. "And you have already given it."

She pulled away from him and was gone, leaving behind a heavy scent of sandalwood and sex.

CHAPTER 18

The smell of coffee woke him. Or was it a sense of guilt? Whichever, he hurriedly washed, shaved and dressed, appreciative of the steaming hot water. When he opened the bedroom door, a cinnamon aroma reinforced the smell of brewing coffee. Granwin sat at one of the tables in the central court, picking the raisins out of a pastry and examining each one before she ate it. A swaying tree limb gave away the lemur, silently watching her eat the pastry.

"Good morning," Devon said with the best smile he could muster.

Granwin didn't speak.

A faint sandalwood scent filled Devon's nose, masking the coffee and cinnamon. Was it real, or his inner psyche's way of punishing him? Granwin's blue eyes were as cold as the desert sky.

Over Granwin's shoulder, the lemur peeked from the branches of the potted tree. Granwin's nostrils seemed to flare as Devon sat across from her. *Could she smell the musk of the night before*? Granwin and the lemur silently stared at him as he poured a cup of coffee, tar-black in a clear glass cup.

"Where is everyone?" Devon asked after he scoured the desert dryness from his throat with a sip of the dark liquid.

Granwin shrugged. "Sheik Murshid has not arisen. Mrs. Qasim is in the sheik's office, phoning back to her masters, whoever they are. I hoped you would drive Daris Fagham and me to the monastery." Her eyes seem to regain their sparkle when she mentioned the monastery. "He says the monks there have many old relics from the Crusades."

Devon nodded in reply, his mouth full of raisin-and-cinnamon pastry.

Granwin stood. "I will be ready in a moment. Mr. Fagham said he would meet us at the vehicle." Granwin stood by the table, waiting for his response.

Or for him to beg for forgiveness? Damn woman!

Devon washed down the pastry with a tall glass of fresh orange juice. "Okay. I'll top off the gas and meet you outside." He picked up his cup, poured himself one more serving of coffee and watched Granwin's stiff back as she stalked out. What a mess.

The old telephone cord was as frayed as Sara Qasim's nerves. A distant instrument rang, the bell-like thrumming overriding the humming and crackles of static. Sara stood by the table watching Arif sidestep in front of a low bookcase from one book to the next, reading the titles, hands clasped behind his back like an old man. *I make him grow up too soon*, she thought as she waited for Satan to speak.

The telephone base rested on a marble-topped Italian carved wood side table. Ancient rugs covered the plastered walls. A dark, polished wood desk dominated the center of the office. She realized Murshid must be a very important man, someone linked closely with power to have a telephone in this far region. Had she made a terrible mistake? Should she let Murshid be her master, the father of Arif?

Too late. She had made her decision last night, and begun the end of her life. No, not really. Her life had really ended when Nadav died a martyr at Saad Sixteen, leaving her alone with their son. These were just the closing days.

Beyond the heavy glass of a large window, the low range of the Sinjar Mountains dominated the view. The cold light from the high blue sky did nothing to make her smile.

"This is Colonel Khan," blurted from the handset.

Sara jumped at the sudden words. *Satan speaks.*

She covered the gap between her mouth and the telephone with her hand to keep her answer from Arif and the others in the house. "I have acted as you directed. We are in Sinjar, at the home of Sheik Suleiman Murshid, and I have gained Mr. Devon's confidence." She had practiced her words after morning prayers, hoping they would be adequate.

Across the room Arif smiled over at her. No, her life was not over. Not until Arif was safe.

"What are his plans?" asked Khan over the scratchy phone connection. "Is Devon going into the mountains?"

"He is driving Mrs. Granwin to the monastery this morning."

"You must go with them and report what he sees." Khan's angry tone overrode the static on the old lines.

"I cannot go with them. They have already left, and I am at Suleiman Murshid's home, in his office. I supposed it was important that I contact you, to tell you where Mr. Devon was." *But not all of what we did*, Sara thought.

"Damn you, woman. Is your life so cheap you would ignore my commands?" Khan's pitch rose. "Have you forgotten the boy?"

How could she forget with Arif standing there in front of her? Before she could answer, the distant phone crashed down, leaving a muted buzz on the line.

The engine staggered as Devon nursed the Nissan up a sharp incline. With a jolt, the transmission popped out of gear, slapping the lever against his thigh. Devon forced the transmission back into low range and held the lever back with his hand as the Nissan labored up the narrow road cut into the side of the mountain. Higher up and ahead of them a thin cloud, torn by the wind, partially covered the jagged peaks of the ridge. The gusts tugged at the Nissan as they climbed up the side of the gorge. Devon couldn't help but glance out his window at the sharp granite outcrops that occasionally obscured the riverbed below.

"Renée, if you want to pray, ask your God to keep us on the road."

She shook her head. "Driving is your task. God doesn't have time to keep you from killing yourself, and us with you," Granwin replied. She clutched the handgrip firmly and slid all the way up against the door, the farthest she could get away from the drop-off and Devon.

Fagham chuckled at their exchange. "It is only a little further. You will see when we come to the top of this climb."

As Fagham predicted, when Devon eased over the crest, the road leveled out. Even better, it opened to a small plateau cut into the side of the mountain, just wide enough to relieve the feeling they were going to crash down the mountainside.

"Ahh...Thank you for bringing us to this wonderful place." Granwin leaned forward and squinted against the glare of the sun rising over an old stone fortress.

Devon followed her gaze to the crumbling parapets topping the ancient walls, the gaps resembling rotten teeth. As soon as Devon stopped, Granwin got out, her face alternating between a serious frown and a smile that kept dancing across her lips. She wore a white shawl over her head, glowing in the morning light in an aura of optimism. She hurried over to a small door recessed in the massive walls, then turned, waiting for Fagham.

Devon wondered who or what would greet them. Twenty or so feet above them, a face watched from one of four small openings spaced across the otherwise blank wall. A glitter where the morning sun reached one of the openings betrayed the presence of glass, out of place in the primeval walls.

Fagham stopped by Devon's rolled-down window. "You may wait here for me. I will see that Mrs. Granwin is welcomed by the monks. Then you and I will discuss the water issue."

Fagham walked over and waited with Granwin by a deep recess in the old wall. The face vanished from the window and, after a couple of minutes, Granwin stooped and disappeared through a shoulder-height door set deep into the recess.

Devon got out of the Nissan, walked out to the edge, and looked down. Could there be an answer here? He stuffed his hands in his pockets as the wind cut through the loose knit of his wool sweater. Grandma had always said eagles embodied the spirit of goodness, followed closely by the hawk. He hoped this one was a hawk, not the crow, friend of the snake, or worse the buzzard, friend of the dead.

I've been in this God-forsaken country, what, a week, and I've been lined up to be shot, killed two men, seen a child die and friend mangled, Devon thought. Across the narrow gorge, a bird swept by riding the wind. "Not to mention I broke grandpa's pipe," he muttered to the bird.

Fagham joined him at the precipice. A puzzled look crossed his face at Devon's words. He turned his weather-beaten face up to the sun, arms behind his back.

"What's Granwin doing inside?" asked Devon.

"Mrs. Granwin is meeting with the rector. I believe, from what Mr. Baker told me, she hopes to find a lost icon here, as unlikely a place as this may be." Fagham waved a hand back over his shoulder at the monastery, an enigma of Christian peace and violence set into the cliff wall. "Only Allah and perhaps the Pope truly know what is hidden behind those walls."

Devon scanned the sheer rock battlement, searching for hidden faces, guns. Hell, he wouldn't be surprised to see a green dragon rear up from the parapets.

The bird dipped and disappeared around a ledge, only to reappear soaring over the monastery walls. A hawk.

"You and Bert must have been good friends?" Devon let it come out as a question, wondering where Baker had crossed paths with the old man. They watched the hawk, body weaving as it fought to hold position in the gusts.

"Merely acquaintances. Wilbert and I met in Athens," Fagham answered.

Devon was confused. "Athens? Is there an Athens in Mesopotamia, or is Greece part of Mesopotamia? I never heard Bert talk about Athens."

Fagham laughed. "Oh, no. Athens, Georgia. Mr. Baker and I were both students there. I told you the government sent both Suleiman Murshid and myself to university—Suleiman to Manchester to be an administrator, and me to the University of Georgia to learn about—" He stopped, looking around the gorge. "Enough history. We must focus on today."

The problem, whatever it is, must be burning inside him for a man of his culture to want to hurry directly to the subject. Or had Fagham absorbed more of the UGA Bulldog than expected? Devon prodded him on. "What's this place got to do with the water issue?"

Fagham swept his hand to encompass the valley and the snow covered mountain peaks above them. "The peaks of the Sinjar Mountains are a little more than fifteen hundred meters above sea level, perhaps eight hundred meters higher than Sinjar, and covered with melting snow." He hesitated. "But come, I can show better than explain the crucial problem."

Fagham led Devon around the corner of the fortress wall to a torrent of water gushing from a fissure in the mountain. The crystal-clear stream splashed and swirled around a small, walled pool, then cascaded out into space. "The water flow is not as great as some remember, but there is some, certainly enough for the monastery and the few fields we have around Sinjar. But for this monstrosity." He pointed down into the narrow chasm.

Devon carefully leaned over the edge. From his days as a paratrooper, he quickly judged the drop to be about two hundred feet. It was far below the minimum for a safe parachute opening, but too far to jump sans wings.

Loose shale, bordered by a staggered row of withered trees, marked what had once been a wide streambed. Along the near edge of the riverbed, a scraggly hedge, pale green with new leaf, marked a trickle of water flowing toward the valley. Shadows from the morning sun helped him trace a faint line along the far wall. The glitter of glass insulators perched out on the end of wooden posts marked the supports for what must be the telephone line from the valley.

He stepped back from the edge as three eighteen-wheelers rolled alongside the riverbed, unheard over the roar of the water. Devon couldn't read the truck markings—too dusty and too much of an angle. Belching black smoke, the trucks pulled out of sight around a bend in the gorge, grinding up the incline.

"Where are they heading? Does this road lead to a pass over the mountains?" asked Devon. "And what monstrosity are you talking about?"

"They're off to the seed repository. Come. I'll show you," Fagham answered. He climbed up on the wall surrounding the pool and sidestepped to his right along the top of the damp rock. Each step deliberate and careful, Fagham kept his back pressed to the rough granite.

Water gushed from the rock just over his head, floating a fine spray into Devon's face.

"Be careful," Devon called after him.

Fagham smiled and shouted back at him. "Sheik Suleiman Murshid tells the great stories, but I was actually the better soldier when we fought in the mountains. Join me." Fagham slid his feet along the wall until he reached the corner, then beckoned for Devon to follow.

"Where the hell are you going, Fagham?" Devon asked. He leaned over the wall holding back the water and peered around the cliff edge. All he could see was the road leading further up the gorge.

"To show you why Wilbert sent you to Sinjar." Fagham smiled and inched his way around the jutting rock.

Wilbert sent? Devon watched Fagham move out of sight around the corner as he processed the news, surprised the older man would take such a risk. Nothing else to do, Devon hopped up and followed. The low wall paralleled the road at first, quickly turned into a narrow ledge jutting out from the sheer rock cliff. He sidestepped, following Fagham's footsteps to the corner of the cliff overlooking the road, shoulder blades scraping against the sheer rock. Devon shivered in the fine icy spray and stepped, very carefully, around a sharp corner.

Buffeted by the wind, he stood on the edge of a sheer cliff, facing the mountain peaks.

"Stop." Fagham's voice seemed like a whisper. As he slid along the damp rock, Devon realized Fagham was shouting to be heard over the rush of the water.

Devon bumped into Fagham, teetered for a moment, then regained his balance. Heels pressed against the rock, his scuffed work boot toes projected out into empty air. Once he had turned the corner the ledge had narrowed to mere inches; he barely felt the edge beneath the balls of his feet. Devon leaned his head back against the cool rock and turned to look at Fagham. "Enough. Why we are edging across the mountain like we're goat hunting? Surely there's an easier way to figure out where the water's going."

Fagham's silver hair glistened with the fine droplets of water that gathered and ran down his face to drip from his nose and chin.

"The water is important, but only a minor part of the problem. Look below."

Devon glanced down, then quickly pressed back against the rock. He took a deep breath. The hawk, hanging on the updraft, wheeled out where the gorge opened up in front of them. Below, the water fell into a basin, walled with rock like the pool above. Devon was puzzled. The pool's only visible outlet was a narrow stream running to the left, alongside the road. *Where did the rest go?*

Further up the gorge toward the mountain peaks, two men dragged a gate shut behind the last truck. The gate was the only opening in a high chain link fence topped with tangled coils of wire. Beyond the fence, the gorge widened, then as suddenly, ended at the side of the mountain.

The wind whipped the mist from the falling water across the rock face. Devon inched farther along the ledge for a better view of the disappearing trucks. He sensed the slickness under his feet and the smallness of the trucks below.

The hawk hung in the air level with them. The bird seemed to study the two men perched high above the rocky floor. Devon flinched as a loud bang echoed across the rocky wall. Beside him, Fagham clutched at Devon's sleeve. The soaring hawk veered and dodged. Wings widespread, it swept by, seemingly only an arm's reach out from the ledge and pierced the air with a loud keen.

"Backfire." Fagham relaxed his grip and pointed toward a cloud of black exhaust floating up from the last of the three trucks. Devon leaned forward just enough to peer around the corner of the rock wall, back past the monastery. The roadway back to the valley was empty.

"Where the devil are the trucks going?" asked Devon.

Fagham pointed toward the end of the cul-de-sac. "Look closely and you will see a great door in the rock. Beneath the overhang."

"Nobody knows about this place?" Devon teetered forward, but still couldn't see any opening in the wall. To his right, past Fagham, the ledge continued, then widened to a shelf broad enough to sit.

"Contrarily, many know of the presence of the cavern. Several years ago, the government declared the presence of a grain repository to store seed grain against the threat of blight and disease. The weapons inspectors have even been here. In Sinjar, the people call this place The Facility. Your friend Baker called it the Hell Hole after I told him the work actually accomplished inside.

"You see, I once worked in The Facility, one of approximately three hundred technical workers." Fagham stared down at the men in uniform. "Also about thirty soldiers are on duty at one time, plus the detachment at the highway ready to defend the valley." He cocked his head with a show of pride. "Hydraulic engineering is my engineering specialty."

He paused, long frown lines replacing the prideful smile as he watched the hawk pirouette around a wing tip in the clear morning air. "Inside the hidden doors lies Saddam's Nuclear Weapons Research Facility Number Seven." Fagham motioned toward the mountain rising opposite their perch. "The water is diverted from the ice melt to the facility inside the mountain. It circulates through a nuclear reactor until the vapor is released, to vent through the top of the mountain and blend with the mountain mists."

Suddenly, the hawk swerved away and dove toward the ground. A sharp report filled Devon's right ear, like the crack of a bat when you hit a baseball wrong against the grain. He searched the gorge. The trucks were gone.

Fagham clutched Devon's arm, a stricken look on his face. A dark stain spread across Fagham's white shirt. Devon leaned back into the wall, trying to hold Fagham erect.

"Go. Quickly." Fagham's voice rasped. His knees buckled slightly, the wall bloody behind his shoulders as he slid from Devon's grip.

Devon reached across with his other hand, grabbed Fagham's flapping jacket and pulled the old man's lanky body closer. Fagham's chest rattled, mint-scented breath flowing over Devon as Fagham choked. Devon held on, pressed back against the cliff wall as the old man convulsed.

"Do not delay." Fagham tried to escape his grip, levering his long arms between their bodies. "Return to Granwin and the boy. They need you."

"Let me get you around the cor—" The smack of a bullet into the rock above his head cut Devon's plea short.

Fagham put both hands against the wall. "I will soon know if Allah has listened to my prayers." He pushed away from Devon. He fell, a slow tumble of long legs and arms. No cry, barely the whistle of wind through his clothes. Then a thump echoed back from the rock walls.

Tiny in the distance, one of the guards pointed a rifle in Devon's direction. As he stood, frozen against the cliff face, the muzzle flashed. The impact of the bullet between him and the corner galvanized Devon into an agonizingly slow shuffle back to his left along the ledge. A second shot—the bullet cracked into the rock below his feet. His legs were trembling by the time he edged back around the sharp rock out of sight of the rifleman. He shuffled as fast as he dared under the waterfall, hopped down and ran toward the Nissan.

Granwin stood by the vehicle. She held her tote bag with both arms crossed over her chest, shoulders hunched like a mother carrying a baby through the rain.

He waved at her as he ran. "Get in!" he yelled, and stumbled as he searched through his pockets for the ignition keys.

"Where's Mr. Fagham?" Granwin asked, a puzzled look on her face. She opened the door on her side as he started the engine.

"Get in the damned vehicle!" he shouted, and spun the Nissan around so fast her door slammed shut as she sprawled across the seat.

"Nash, what happened to Daris Fagham?" Granwin shouted over the wind roaring through Devon's open window and the rattle of loose rock thrown up against the undercarriage as they raced down the mountainside.

Devon skidded along the left wall, knocking off the outside mirror, grinding away at the metalwork. Granwin screamed and pressed back against the seat.

He held the Nissan in second, fighting to control their descent. "He's dead, damn it—"

Granwin bounced against him and clutched his shoulder. "What happened?"

Devon waited until the road straightened out for the final drop down to the riverbed to answer. "He took me to see an Iraqi facility hidden back in the end of the gorge. Somebody...one of the guards, started shooting."

"Are you sure? Shouldn't we go back and check?"

"Renée, I'm sure." He speed-shifted through fourth into fifth, accelerator smashed to the floor. "We've got to get out of here. This gorge is a death trap. We need to get out to the fields. With the four-wheel drive, I can get us away from them. Across the ditches, if I have to."

"From whom, Nash?" she asked.

"Whoever shot Fagham." He glanced over at her. "Did you know the Iraqis had a research facility back there?"

She clutched her tote to her chest with one hand and held on to the grip bar with the other. "Facility? What do you mean?"

They dropped down into a pothole, bounced out and into the air, left side tilted up away from the ground, twisting sideways. When the tires hammered back to the ground, Devon sawed the wheel back and forth just enough to keep the skid from turning into an uncontrolled fishtail. He let up on the gas. Below them, the road twisted away from the gorge wall, dipping down and up to cross the riverbed, sloped like the lip of a ski jump. When they came up over the riverbed, all four wheels left the ground.

The Nissan began a slow turn in the air. Devon held on, helpless. They hit, tipping sideways, then slid across the road into a patch of sand that slowed them. For a moment, Devon thought he had regained control. The Nissan seemed to be going where he was steering. A roar thundered through the Nissan, a sure sign he had left the muffler back in the sand. Ahead of them, the road spilled out across the flat fields surrounding the dried-up river.

He glanced over at Granwin. "What did Fagham tell you?" he yelled.

"Only about the monastery—" Granwin paused. "Look out!"

Devon jerked his head forward to see an oncoming car in the middle of the narrow road. He slammed on the brakes and jerked the wheel at the last moment. The Nissan slowly tipped as they careened off the road and back into the riverbed, this time with the right side wheels tilted up in the air. He turned into the roll and gunned the engine.

The Nissan responded by digging its big tires into the loose gravel, spinning them around in a big donut. The engine backfired, stalled and they rocked to a stop. Devon looked over at Granwin, eyes closed.

"Thank God," whispered Granwin. "Perhaps it would be better to die some other way."

CHAPTER 19

"Nash!" A familiar voice called out from a cloud of chalky dust around the Nissan.

As the dust settled, Devon recognized Khan, striding down the riverbank. Well, Khan certainly had been unexpected when he showed up to pick up Baker, and for damn sure he was a welcome sight here. One of the few times Devon was pleased to see the cavalry to the rescue. He grinned at Granwin. "He's an old friend, Renée."

"Who is he? Do all of your friends carry pistols?" Granwin asked.

"You met him back at camp. The new deputy director." And sure enough, Khan was waving at them with a heavy revolver in his hand. Devon laughed. "In this instance, I won't complain. Come on. He'll get us out of here." Devon shoved his door with his shoulder, but it didn't budge. His brush against the granite mountainside had crumpled the frame like a weird origami animal. "Go ahead and get out. I've got to slide your way. My door's jammed."

"Welcome to Research Facility Number Seven, Major Devon," Khan called out. He motioned them toward a big silver Mercedes E-class station wagon. "Come. We don't want to keep the director waiting."

"Levison?" asked Devon, as he slogged across the sandy riverbed.

"No, not that fat fool. A real director," replied Khan with a smirk

Ah, shit. Why did the pistol suddenly look so threatening? Devon took Granwin's arm and together they climbed over the round gravel and up the bank. "Maybe you were right again. I believed he was here to help. Sounds like he's playing Lakota scout to our Geronimo," he muttered to Granwin.

Granwin looked at him with the forced calmness Devon remembered from the time Dalantish stopped them in the mountains.

"Who is Geronimo?" she asked.

"Old chief of the Apache tribe. He'd convinced himself that his friends, the Lakota reservation police, had come to protect him. Somehow, he died that day." Devon struggled up the scree marking the edge of the riverbed, pulling Granwin along by her hand. "What the hell's going on, Pancho?"

"Get in the car. You'll know, soon enough." Khan jerked the side door open. "Get out, old man. Out," Khan commanded.

Sheik Suleiman Murshid peered at them from the driver's seat before he climbed out of the car.

Kahn spoke again. "Take the boy with you and wait by the other vehicle. I'll see you get back to your villa when my friends and I finish our business."

Sara Qasim slid across the seat and pulled Arif with her to stand beside Murshid, her arms clasped around the boy.

Khan jerked Arif from Sara's grasp and shoved him toward Murshid. "Go."

"*Min fadlac*, please." The plea showed in Sara's face as much as her voice.

Khan pushed her back into the car. "We have other business. When we succeed you will see your son in time for evening prayers. Now get in." He waved her into the back seat, finally prodding her with the barrel of the pistol. "You." He pointed at Granwin. "I haven't yet understood your part in this, so for now you'll accompany us. Get in the back with Mrs. Qasim."

Now the pistol waved Devon's way. "And you, Nash, behind the wheel. Drive." His tone demanded compliance.

Devon hesitated, looked at the frightened women in the back seat, then slid behind the wheel. His stomach churned as he started the car and drove back in the direction of the waterfall, past Arif standing with Murshid's arm on his shoulder, close enough to see the questions on the boy's face. Devon felt those little, cold points high in his cheeks where the nerves seemed to freeze when he was trapped and couldn't find a way out. He swallowed to rid himself of the sensation and some of the dust clogging his throat.

His voice sounded like a croak when he spoke. "Pancho, are we going the right way? The guards up this road shot at me, and killed the man who led me up here in the first place."

Droplets ran down the dusty windshield and through the open window as Devon drove them past the falling water glinting in the waterfall's mist and toward the gate. High above, the monastery's parapet disappeared in the glare of the morning sun.

"You should have asked me to bring you to the facility. With me would not have been so dangerous," Khan said.

A soldier in green fatigues with a rifle slung over his shoulder and a dusty slouch cap rolled open the gate in the chain link fence ahead of them.

"See. If you call ahead, it is very easy to enter here."

Devon searched for an entrance in the walls. Where were the trucks he had seen from above? The noon sun left the sheer wall in shadow, but as he drove, Devon began to make out the faint outlines of a rectangular opening underneath a massive rock overhang.

As they approached the end of the gorge, a door rolled up into the rock, large enough to swallow the big transport trucks. Inside, a handful of bare bulbs in metal reflectors dangling from the ceiling cast dim shadows across the cavern where a group of men unloaded boxes from the transport trucks. 'Silop Trucking' was painted across the side of the nearest truck, with 'Dairy Products' in large block letters below the name, all in English, with Arabic letters below.

Khan pointed toward the lights. "Park beside the trucks, my good friend."

Devon followed Khan's orders and pulled the car to a stop beside the truck.

"Now. Everyone get out." Khan smiled and holstered his pistol when Devon walked around the Mercedes. "Nash, I'm so glad we're finally together for such important work. I was not sure the commissioner was correct in sending you here." The smile quickly vanished when Khan turned to show a set of papers to one of the guards.

Friends, huh. So the pistol was just show. And Fagham's death was just routine security. What bullshit!

"We have much to discuss. I promised the commissioner and Dr. Kee you would be able to help with our problem. We all have greatly anticipated your visit."

Who is we, and Dr. Kee? All good friends, Devon thought. He had nothing but questions, and it didn't seem Khan was going to him the answers he wanted, not with the fake smile and big revolver he had on his belt.

Two more guards watched them from the loading dock—maybe not such good friends—with rifles casually slung to point at them.

Why had Khan betrayed him? What did he want? Devon searched his memory for anything he had that Khan could want. Olanti's comment flashed through his mind. *—he was important to somebody.* Or maybe it was one of the women? And who the hell was this commissioner who had sent him here?

Devon glanced back at the trucks nestled up to the loading dock, now barely visible with the big door rumbling down, shutting out the sun. *No damn way out.* He shook his head, jaw clenched in frustration. It suddenly struck him. Khan had taken Baker away in the helicopter. And Devon hadn't heard a word back from his friend.

Devon quickly caught up with Khan. "Pancho!" He spun Khan around. "Where did you take Bert?"

On the loading dock, one of the guards racked back the bolt of his AK and slapped it forward, stripping a bullet from its magazine and slamming it home.

Khan shrugged off Devon's hand. "Don't antagonize the soldiers. They do not know me. They only respect the authority of my papers. They certainly do not know you. The guards' standing orders are to kill anyone threatening the facility. You're an old soldier, Nash. You know how the young, poorly trained sometime overreact. Don't worry about your friend. The last time I saw Baker he was on the helicopter. I presume heading to Baghdad."

Devon hoped he could believe Khan. He glanced overhead as he followed Khan across the rock floor, trailed by the two women. It was too dark to see the top of the cavern, but the echo of their footsteps and the murmur of the laborers' voices as they unloaded and stacked a small pile of boxes suggested the place was bigger than he had expected.

Behind him, the grinding of the outer door mechanism fell silent, shutting out the last sliver of daylight. Khan led them to one end of the loading dock, where another of the bare bulbs illuminated rough steps cut into the stone and, at the top of the steps, a door built into an inner concrete block wall. Everything was raw, primitive, hewn stone, unpainted concrete and dim lights.

Neither woman had spoken since Khan had ordered them into the car. Somebody here was definitely not on the side of good. Surely not his blond angel? And after last night he couldn't believe Sara would betray him, with Arif at risk. *Unless she got a better offer?* He had never been right about women before, so why be surprised now.

Ahead of them, Khan knocked on the inner door. The uniformed guards spaced along the loading dock continued to track their progress with the muzzles of their rifles, the ubiquitous AKs that seemed to rule this world. Devon stopped beside Granwin on the bottom step. When their shoulders touched, he could feel her trembling. Or was it he? She slid her hand into his. Her fingers were cold as she clutched his for a brief moment.

At the top of the steps Devon caught a glimpse of Sara Qasim's face under one of the bare bulbs. She had replaced her smile with a wide-eyed solemnity, an intense stare flicking from Granwin to Devon.

"Follow me," commanded Khan, and led them in to an unfinished chamber crudely carved from the mountain's black granite. Inside, a single bulb left the far corners of the room in darkness. Khan greeted a frail, pale-skinned man who rose from a desk, then exchanged the customary kisses to the cheeks. Rows of shelves stretched behind the man into the darkness.

Khan turned back to Devon and waved his hands toward the shelves. "Nash, have you been told about the seed repository? Our friends, the Iraqis, do not deceive in this regard. They have collected seed grain from many varieties to store here—abandoned grain from the fields, old cemeteries and courtyards of ancient ruins, even the crumbling monasteries built by the marauding Crusaders to hide their plunder.

"Like many things in our world, the old things are often the best. Technology may serve us, but often in the cruelest of way. Mr. Meheena, the curator of this collection, is a brother of the new *Ahad*, as am I. One of many true believers who have sacrificed their own needs to follow the words of Allah, the Compassionate, the Merciful, as brought to us by Muhammad, the one true Prophet."

Khan turned to Sara Qasim. "Are not those the true facts, Mrs. Qasim?"

Sara seemed to wilt under his smile.

"Mrs. Qasim lost her husband to technology. He knew too much and refused to share with *Ahad* and all true believers. I hope she has not let that lesson go unlearned."

He motioned the curator to lead them down a corridor between the shelves. "Unfortunately, the brotherhood, indeed, the entire Islamic world must do what we can to survive, not just the grain blights, but the continued trampling of our countries. First it was the Europeans, jealous of the Moorish victories in the far past, then the Jewish threat, supported by the British and Americans.

"Now we Pakistanis must contend with the desire of the Hindus to destroy every Muslim. Indeed, they all conspire to wipe out all Islamic influence in their distorted version of the British Empire. So, you must understand the necessity of *Ahad*—a unity of all true believers, regardless of birth—to unite."

Was this all some gigantic act of revenge? Did Khan know about Olanti's death? Devon's arm suddenly itched again. *Ahad.* Ancient history—a secret society of the early twentieth century that sought to unite Muslims across the warring tribes and sultanates in the name of Allah, only to disintegrate in the face of European manipulation and the personal greed of the Arabic leaders.

Khan continued his harangue. "All Islam must bind our nations even closer together to destroy these combined threats. The future of Islam lies behind these walls."

Meheena vanished between the shelves of seeds, his solemn voice echoing through the hallway. "Follow me, please."

Sara Qasim and Granwin followed Khan down the narrow corridor. Devon trailed after them, but he had no idea how he would escape. Or how he could get the two women out. Or if he wanted to. He followed the others to the far end of the corridor where Meheena struggled to push open a heavy door, gradually exposing a wedge of bright light. The end of the tunnel? Or the train? Devon followed the others through. The door slammed behind him, the metallic clang of the lock very final.

Devon blinked. Unlike the dark repository, rows of fluorescent lights glowed from the ceiling. The rock floor vibrated to the beat of a distant generator. When he saw the open vault door, breakfast's cinnamon pastry made a couple of loops around his inner gut. The white enamel-painted walls and sudden rush of cold air reminded him of the entrance to Site R, the Joint Chiefs of Staff's Alternate National Military Command Center buried in the mountains of Pennsylvania. For all the ANMCC's sophistication, this Iraqi chamber inside a cold mountain, with the glare of florescent lights and vibrating with the hum of powerful equipment, had a feel of similarity about it.

Even the guards standing outside the massive door resembled the serious-faced military police guards at Site R. Unlike the militia types out on the loading dock, these wore berets, strange green and mustard-brown cammies, and carried shiny machine pistols. No cheap, Chinese, knock-off AKs for these guys. Each guard cradled a shiny Heckler & Koch MP5, the ten-millimeter submachine gun made famous by the West German border police.

"Who are these guys?" Devon whispered to Sara Qasim as they waited for one of the guards to study Khan's papers.

"*Amn al Khas*," she replied. She didn't bother to whisper, and her voice reverberated in the narrow corridor. "The Special Security Service."

Khan spoke over his shoulder. "Qusay followed his father's directives very well in setting up a special protective service for the research facilities. Republican Guards outside. Adequate soldiers, maybe better than the run-of-mill Iraqi soldier, but not elite. Inside, the *Amn al Khas* are much better for security. Even though I've been here before, they carefully inspect my papers. Rather like your old

SAC command center, isn't it?" Khan strutted down the corridor, leading them deeper into the maze.

Devon clenched his jaw, remembering the dog and pony show the Strategic Air Command had performed for the foreign students a whole life ago. SAC had changed names since then. Devon hadn't even kept up with their reorganizations. But once upon a time, long ago, he had been one of the tour leaders from the Artillery Center at Fort Sill, impressing the foreign officers with the massive nuclear might of America.

Before Devon had a chance to study the door, two of the guards hustled them inside, MP5 held as if they really did know how they worked. Devon's ears popped as the vault door oozed shut behind them and the air repressurized.

Inside, a long hall reached back into the cavern, pocked with a row of small doors and large plate glass windows on each side. Khan led the way down the hall. The two guards' hob-nailed boots clacked on the concrete floor and echoed from the bare walls behind them as the women and Devon trailed along behind Khan.

The Facility—Baker's Hell Hole, like Site R and Cheyenne Mountain—appeared to be a gigantic concrete box inside a massive cavern. Inside the rooms on the right side personnel in white smocks scurried around rows of workbenches in an assembly areas of sorts. The rooms on the left side were relatively empty. Only a few technicians, most in protective suits, worked at a slower and more deliberate pace.

Devon felt like a tourist walking through Nuclear Research Facility Number Seven, the reason so many new Datsuns roamed the streets of Sinjar and the children dressed so well. And why Murshid had marble floors.

Khan paused to let a group of men push a huge round metal container down the hall on a large dolly, grunting as they rolled it through a wide door. He turned to Devon. "Their research is impressive, wouldn't you agree, Nash?"

Devon pointed at the twenty-foot diameter donut-shaped apparatus as the door shut behind it and the men. "Pancho, was that really a calutron?"

Khan's delivered his answer with a sneer. "Very good, Nash. You haven't forgotten how to make an effective atomic bomb. I'm encouraged my suggestion to bring you here was correct. The warhead developers will add the additional calutron to a cascade sequence, key to the Iraqi uranium enrichment program.

"Mrs. Qasim can tell you all about their progress in nuclear refinement. She and her husband were researchers in the program before he decided to betray his country."

Devon glanced over at Sara Qasim who acknowledged the indictment with a very slight nod.

One of the laborers from the loading dock rolled a cart past them. The wooden crate was unmarked except for the words 'Hamamatsu Photonics—Medical Research Materiel.' Khan tapped the crate as it rolled by. "Another important function of the *Amn al Khas*. Saddam directed the organization set up a series of false companies to purchase embargoed goods. If I remember correctly, this is a high speed streak camera, part of the fission research project."

Khan's scar stretched with his smile. "Doctor Kee's Chinese associates purchased it in Japan for delivery to Shanghai. The importers then sent the camera by train through North Korea to Nampo, where they transferred it to a small freighter for shipment to Istanbul. There the shipping agents, our Silop friends, loaded it on one of the tanker trucks. Each truck only carries a few crates across Turkey so no one looks at them."

He shrugged his shoulders. "Everyone knows Silop Trucking carries illegal gasoline back from Iraq, so no one cares what they bring in. The Turkish officials make money, the truck drivers make money." He pointed to a small box with the words 'California Technologies' stenciled across the wood in small print. "Even American companies participate, either through greed or ignorance." Khan chuckled. "Western corruption is so good to see."

He gestured at two workers prying open a massive wooden crate marked *Moissonneuse - Matériel Agricole – Aragon Systèmes Internationaux.* "We have special friends among the French, as well as the Russians. The French are especially eager to profit."

A large, stainless steel vessel appeared from the packing. Not an agricultural harvester as the French lettering promised. Another calutron.

Khan stopped at the door to the last room at the end of the corridor as he continued his lecture tour. "The important cargo, so the customs inspectors at the Silop border crossing believe, is the embargoed, processed gasoline carried back to Turkey in the hidden tanks. They are paid nothing for the trucks coming into Iraq, but accept *baksheesh* from the oil merchants for the trucks going out, so the inspectors are deceived to believe the money marks the important transaction."

A guard opened the door and Devon followed Khan inside. Much smaller than the assembly areas, a single large worktable cluttered with circuit boards and missile re-entry cone dominated the room. Three men clustered behind a computer station, staring at the screen. One of them rapped the monitor with a wooden pointer. He spoke Arabic, but much too loudly for the small room. All must not be well. A bank of television monitors along the wall was blank and quiet. No cartoons today.

Khan called to the *Amn al Khas* guards, standing with the women in the corridor. They shoved Granwin and Qasim into the room behind Devon and Khan.

Khan led Devon around the table to the three men and the computer. Scattered blue prints and manuals marked with Chinese ideograms covered the worktable. The loud man with the pointer stepped back from the computer screen and came to meet them. The other two looked up at the approaching group and Devon realized they were women.

"Dr. Kee, it is good to see you again. This is my associate, Mr. Devon." Khan presented himself with a slight bow to the doctor and a wave toward Devon. "Nash, this is the director of research at this facility who I mentioned earlier. May I present Dr. Kee?"

Khan's associate?

Khan beamed at the two men. "Mr. Devon is an expert in the field of missile guidance. I've worked very closely with the *Mukabarat* for the past few weeks to arrange his visit. I'm sure he will quickly solve your dilemma."

Dr. Kee stared at Devon through thick glasses. Devon suddenly thought of Levison, the round Englishman who wanted nothing more than to save a few children. Kee was probably trying to figure out how to kill a few thousand of the children Levison was trying to save.

"Good morning, Colonel Kahn. I expected you—and your Mr. Devon—several days ago." His tone demonstrated his impatience, even louder now than when they first came in. The closer they stood, the louder Kee spoke, an ugly man with stained teeth and a pock-marked face.

Devon followed Kee's gaze to a wall clock beside the row of blank monitors.

"I am no longer certain it is morning, or even which day it is. I have not been outside for a long time, and I am not certain of the clock in here. And, of course, your expert would understand our reluctance to wear personal watches, especially with radium faces around all the radioactive material." Kee waved toward a radiation detector mounted high on the wall.

Devon looked around, but didn't see anything that seemed dangerous. The doctor must be referring to the disturbing effect tiny bits of radium had on radiation monitors in nuclear research facilities, even at low levels.

Kee spoke even louder. "Don't be concerned, Mr. Devon. Weapon production is undertaken in the adjacent area, in the reactor facility. We only do design work in this room."

The two women stared back at him, neither showing a sign of sympathy for Granwin nor Sara.

Kee swept back his white scientist smock as part of a slight bow of welcome. "At the moment, we concentrate on the accurate delivery of the warheads. An area in which I was told you have some expertise?"

Cantonese intonations so colored the doctor's English Devon had to listen carefully to understand. The rising inflection, Devon figured, meant he was supposed to prove Kee's hypothesis. Was this the point of the whole fiasco? Khan's stay at Fort Sill had coincided with Devon's heated and public arguments with his commander over the terminal homing guidance components for the Pershing II, once developed as the Army's intermediate range nuclear tipped missile.

Devon's terminal guidance recommendations had helped drive the theoretical CEP—circular error of probability, the military term for how accurate a missile was, down to ten meters—the probability fifty percent of the impacts would be within ten meters of the target. Tied with a small nuke warhead, the Pershing II became a precision weapon of destruction.

Devon discovered later, with inner relief, that the missile eventually became the perfect sacrifice to the Soviets, bartered in exchange for them to back off their mobile missile deployments in Eastern Europe. *Just a pawn, not even a knight in the scheme of things.*

But here, today? Had the Pakistani brought him here to build a Pershing for the Iraqis?

CHAPTER 20

Perversely, Devon understood the Iraqi and Pakistani desire to develop a small accurate nuclear missile capability similar to the improved Pershing. Maybe, in the contorted logic of nuclear war, the two Islamic nations wanted to limit their own countries' potential damage in view of their proximity to each other. A practical matter also prevailed. Each country had only had a limited amount of enriched uranium or plutonium, whichever they had decided to use, and smaller warheads could be thrown further.

Everyone knew Pakistan had the warheads. Underground blasts had confirmed the dangerous truth.

Effectiveness was limited with inaccurate missiles—other than the simple fear factor of a nuclear weapon exploding somewhere on your side of the world—but accuracy could make it a personal issue.

Voila.

With a ten-meter CEP, the Pakistanis could take out an Indian regiment assembling on the Jammu-Kashmir border. A nice little five kiloton warhead plopped in a high valley north of Kargil would be detected by one of the orbiting Defense Support Program sensors, which sensed and identified missile launches and nuclear explosions, and reported to the National Command Authority by the Missile Warning Center team locked deep in Cheyenne Mountain.

The first public confirmation for the teeming Hindu population of India could be when the water flowing down from the Indus River started killing people. Then the Indians, alerted by the Russians, would spin up one of their splotch-colored *Prithvi* short range ballistic missiles. The nuclear exchange would begin. The rest of the world would know, whether the Americans told them or not, when the radioactive rain began to fall. It would be just a small tactical nuclear war, like Americans once thought they could survive.

Sweat popped out on the palms of Devon's hands at the memory. The parable of the four horsemen of the Apocalypse ran through his mind as he imagined Israel's response to an Iraqi nuke falling on Tel Aviv. How did it go?

How did it go? *A whirlwind came out of the north, a great cloud, and a fire infolding itself, and a brightness was about it, and out of the midst thereof as the color of amber, out of the midst of the fire...*

His memory gave out on him and his focus returned to the laboratory, Dr. Kee and Khan. They were waiting for him to speak.

"Dr. Kee will tell you where they are in their research, and you'll tell them what they need to know to finish the task. Very simple really."

Khan shook his head. "Nash, your face reads like one of your cowboy and Indian stories, silent brave until the death. Remember, I also lived in Oklahoma. I understand the legendary bravery of the American Indian." His voice rose. "Do you not think we of the Muslim faith have suffered enough? The Jews take our lands, displacing the Palestinians on the west. The Hindus have allied with the Sikhs to persecute us on the east, and conspire with the Russians to the north. The Saudis, with all their piety, sell oil and go to France to womanize. Bahrainis, Kuwaitis, the others all bow before the euro and dollar.

"We are isolated, in a *jihad* not only for our lives, but for Islam, the one true religion, praise be to Allah. I am but one of many, the new *Mujahideen al Ahad*, warriors of the true God, not your three-headed sacrilege."

Khan pulled his pistol from his holster and waved the guard to bring the two women forward. "I'm not the fool you think I am. That's why the *houri* was allowed to live this long."

Devon wanted to reach out and grab Sara, to pull her behind him. She wasn't to blame. He was. Sara had entrusted Arif, and herself, to his care. Baker had told him to watch for the evil, and Fagham had tried to warn him. Now he and the women were trapped!

"Sara!"

Her head jerked around toward Devon at his hoarse plea.

"You're Muslim. Tell Pancho he's wrong."

Khan stepped between them. "Quiet, Nash. Leave the woman alone. She has a great debt to pay." He turned to the women, still standing by the door with the guard, and spoke in Arabic.

Devon figured from the look the two women exchanged that whatever Khan said wasn't going to cause happiness. He glanced around the room. The heroes always had a trick up their sleeve. Hell, once upon a time he'd even had a killer pipe. Now it all seemed like a fairy tale.

A gasp from Granwin brought him back to the here and now. One guard had grabbed her by her short blond hair and forced her down to her knees on the floor in front of Khan, her ever-present tote bag clutched as a shield against her chest. The other guard had his eyes and MP5 trained on Devon.

"You have too much of the Englishman's chivalry in your blood, not enough cruelty of the *Amn al Khas* or even your famous desert Apache, to let harm fall to the woman. Am I not right, Nash?" Khan waved Devon to an empty chair and turned to Dr. Kee. "Inform Mr. Devon of what you need. I'm sure he will help."

When the guard pulled Granwin to her feet, a small wooden box fell from her tote bag. She jerked away from the guard, snatched the box up and stuffed in back into her bag.

"What do you have, woman?" Khan roared.

Devon sat back in the chair and forced his clenched fists to relax as Khan ripped the bag from Granwin's grip. He had to be careful. These guards weren't just dumb kids with guns, no over-the-hill Senior Sergeant Dalantish with a rusty AK. No trickery would get them out of here. *Patience,* he told himself. A commodity he never had much use for. See—do, he had always believed. *Now, for at least a minute or two, just watch and listen.*

Khan dumped the bag's content on the table. A wooden box bounced on the metal top. Khan picked it up and stared at the ornate decorations as he turned it from side to side, rage growing in his face. He turned and waved the box for Devon to see. "She found her icon, Nash. Inlaid with a gold cross and Greek gibberish, truly symbolic of your materialistic sacrilege." His voice had worked up to a shout, echoing in the small room.

He shook his head and sneered at Granwin. "Christians and Hindus…neither understand Allah is the one God and Mohammed was his messenger." He held the box in Devon's face. "See, here, before your eyes, your icon, your cross." Khan's spittle sprayed the box and Devon's face as Khan waved the box.

Devon blinked and tried to keep his breathing under control.

"Nothing to this box but the sinful idolatry to a lesser god, all forbidden by the word of Allah."

He turned to shake the box at Granwin. "Your insistence that a mere man, a prophet I agree, is a god, equal to the one Allah—" He threw the box to the floor where it burst apart. "Christians are only Jews who have lost their reason."

Granwin silently dropped to her knees, hands clasped in front of her like a schoolgirl at prayer.

Khan pointed at the fragments. "There is your Jesus and his cross, broken on the floor. He died, as all of us will. His body rotted in the ground, and perhaps his soul lives in Heaven, if it is Allah's will." He kicked the fragments away and shook his finger at Devon. His face wore a mask of rage. "But not because you or your church in Rome say it is so. Only if it is Allah's will."

Granwin moaned when the guard pulled her to her feet and shoved her toward the door. Sara Qasim's face was almost as pale as Granwin's as she stood silently through Khan's rampage, her eyes never leaving Devon's face as she shook her head from side to side.

What is Sara trying to tell me? Devon wondered. *Say it woman, or we'll all die in this damned place!*

But she silently followed Granwin and Khan, her reply as unspoken as his request.

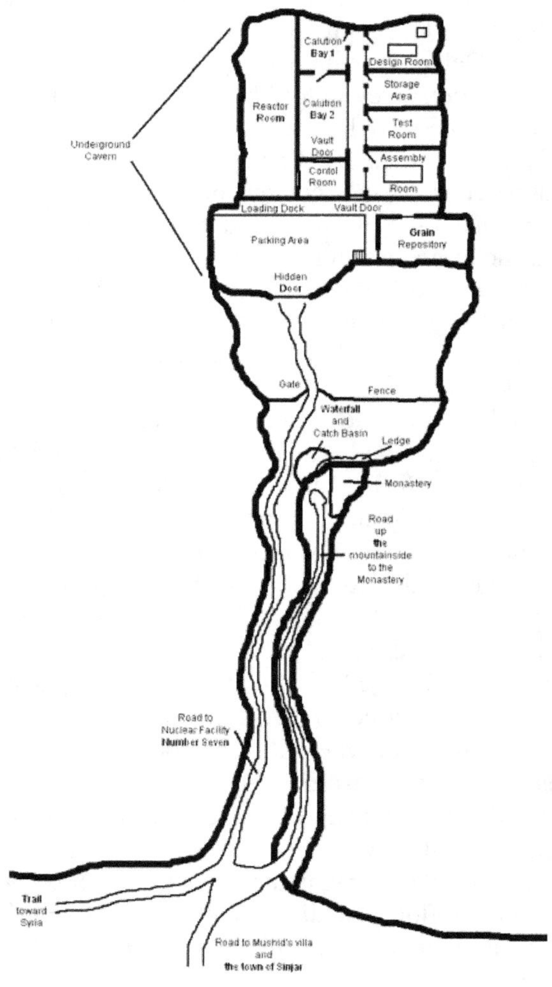

CHAPTER 21

"Our problem is basic. I'm sure you will grasp the simplicity of the dilemma, and the complexity of the resolution." Dr. Kee pulled a chair up beside Devon.

"Our Russian and German colleagues at *Jurf al Sakhar* produced a usable atom bomb, similar to the one detonated over Hiroshima." Kee smiled, his crooked teeth front teeth distorting his lips. "However, their new bomb, like your Big Boy, weighs much more than a ton. Effective for driving to the target in a large lorry, but not what my employer wants." He motioned toward the door. "Across the corridor, our host's enriched uranium program has allowed the manufacture of a smaller weapon, a warhead mated to a missile that can now reach as far as London."

Devon glanced at the door. "I don't know anything about warhead design. I'm a missile man."

Khan had followed the women out, but one guard had remained with Kee and Devon.

"Exactly, Mr. Devon. Thanks to the assistance of a man who once worked in the Soviet government, my Iraqi colleagues built an enriched uranium gun-trigger device based on the Soviet suitcase bomb." He smiled at Devon, small mouth more in a pucker than a grin. "Similar, but smaller and even less sophisticated than the primitive American W-54 warhead used in your obsolete Small Atomic Demolition Munition."

He pointed at a pair of large, old-fashioned leather suitcases on the table. "Our colleagues assembled several cleverly disguised portable bombs for the *jihad*, light and sufficiently compact for a dedicated *mujahideen* to carry. But, even so small a weapon exploded by a martyr is very dirty. A ground level atomic explosion generates a great amount of radioactive dust. Prevailing winds can carry the fallout to neighboring nations, perhaps. The results of air bursts from small, accurate missiles are much better for precision warfare, yes?"

One of the television monitors flickered on. Devon leaned forward, squinting, as the image resolved into Granwin, seated in a chair. He relaxed, grateful he wasn't seeing her being tortured. The image of Granwin tied to a bed and watching her grandfather killed flicked through his mind.

"What can I do?" Devon asked.

"The employment practices of the Iraqi officials are very unique for the modern world." Dr. Kee was no longer smiling. The frown lines turned his scarred face into an evil mask. "Success is highly rewarded. Failure, and one disappears. As I, you may now consider yourself in the hire of the Government of Iraq and its benevolent president."

He opened a brushed aluminum briefcase on the table and pulled out a stack of drawings. "Our team has developed a suitable guidance package. Not as sophisticated as the American ICBM stellar correction or the cruise missile terrain following systems. They have developed a crude, but effective, inflight and terminal guidance designs. Here is the applicable set of drawings." He selected a thick, folded sheet from the stack and slid it over the table to Devon.

Devon smoothed down the sheet of paper covered with engineering drawings, penciled Chinese characters on the left side and Arabic annotations down the right side. He glanced at the other pieces of hardware spread across the table as he unfolded the sheet. A Russian carbon fiber nose cone fitted with an electro-optical seeker stared up through a heavy crystal window at the ceiling. *No need for Chinese oak staves.* What else had they improved upon?

"Launch with preset latitude and longitude?" he asked Kee.

Kee nodded. "That technique is very simple now, thanks to the American global positioning system. And we have solved the inflight guidance problems to our satisfaction."

Devon followed Kee's pudgy finger along the drawing that described V-2 vintage point-and-shoot followed by inflight and terminal phase guidance systems. *Almost too simple.* Correctly integrated inflight and terminal data would do the job they needed. Devon shuffled the papers under Kee's silent gaze. The new warhead design, tipped with the Russian electro-optical scanner that separated from the final stage in flight was a critical step to achieve a ten-meter CEP. *Hell of an improvement over the old Scuds.*

Devon wondered what key development made this design work when other approaches apparently had failed. Then he found part of the answer. A pair of laser ring gyros were embedded in the final stage electronics package. Even if the damn motor sputtered and danced, the gyros would feed in exact positioning corrections fast enough for guidance corrections. So why did they need him? He still didn't understand. *Unless they haven't sorted out the terminal homing package.*

The Pershing II utilized radar, a design almost twenty years old. Today, an American Patriot, or probably one of the better Russian SAMs, could track up the radar beam and destroy the warhead, causing a premature explosion, releasing just a dab of radioactivity. Not much more than Kee's glowing radium dots on a watch. Devon scanned the drawing, searching for the answer. Better yet, a way to get them out of this mess. Alive.

Kee interrupted. "I admire a man who is able to focus under duress. But perhaps you are not fully aware of your circumstances." He pointed to the monitor. "The woman is across the corridor in what our employers call the 'oven,' where German technicians and a Russian professor conduct radiation experiments. I understand the radiation dosage is usually very low." Kee's thin lips turned up in a slight smile. "Does your expertise include the effects of radiation on living subjects?"

Devon took a deep breath and looked up at the monitor. One of the guards jerked at a strap binding Granwin to the chair. A calutron pulsed in the background, lights alternating back and forth on a control panel. He closed his eyes for a moment, wishing what he saw would go away. When he opened them, Granwin's lips moved silently on the monitor screen.

Devon turned back to the drawings. Now was not the time to let loose the bear. "It looks like you have the missile design nearly complete." He couldn't resist the urge to glance back up at the monitor, Granwin, eyes closed, strapped a chair that closely resembled an old fashioned electric chair. Suddenly the scab on his arm itched like a stream of fire ants gnawing on his arm.

"Almost." Kee's answer brought Devon back to the task. Kee's pudgy finger left a greasy splotch as he pressed it against a detail of the warhead assembly. "The terminal guidance is based upon infrared mapping. We have obtained access to the latest Russian satellite infra red spectrum imagery. Theoretically, the data can be processed, much like your cruise missiles use digital mapping, to find and correlate the final target position." He tapped a satellite image. "But a design for this process has not been completed. Yet."

Devon studied the image, still not understanding their design problem. He bent closer to the grainy reproduction. When he realized he was looking at an IR image, it began to make sense. The river, bridges, even the hot spot marking the power plant between the Pentagon and Fourteenth Street—all led his eyes across the old railroad bridge over the Potomac to the distinct outline of the Pentagon. He was able to trace out the Treasury Building and Pennsylvania Avenue. Even the sidewalks and tiny center point marking the Washington Monument were obvious when he oriented the image in his mind.

Kee interrupted Devon's analysis. "Of course, the Iraqi missile does not range across the Atlantic, but I like to reference this image to remind me I should not limit my goals. It also serves to remind me of the price of failure. The Russian who sold the Iraqis the database failed to supply the technology for interpreting the imagery. He is no longer on the program." Kee frowned. "He is no longer anywhere."

Devon shivered. The dry air pumped through the overhead ventilation system chilled his skin, almost as cold as his thoughts. *Hell!* He had fought, killed, and been stood in a firing line. Surely he could bamboozle this so-called doctor and Khan until he could figure a way out of Research Facility Number Seven. He needed just a little time. Every situation had an alternative. Didn't it?

Kee slapped two more photos on the table—one a naval base, another a complex of runways on a peninsular protruding into a bay, all to remind Devon why they were staring at a mass of papers. "Even with sufficient resolution to visually identify these targets, we have not been able to use the infrared images for terminal guidance."

Devon began to see the pattern. Rocket motor, weapon assembly, inflight and terminal guidance, everything was there except the final sensor array and logic to use the digital data, the electronic replacement for the human staring at the image.

The solution stared back at him, brilliant by its absence from the drawings. Apparently Kee and his female assistants hadn't seen it yet.

"Looks like you and your girlfriends are shit out of luck." Devon grinned back at the doctor. No hint of truth serum, or any of that other spy crap, or even the more practical items like thumbscrews on the table. Maybe he, Sara and Granwin could get out of this alive. All he had to do was come up with some plausible scheme that didn't work, but close enough to save their lives. Just how smart was this Kee?

Kee stared at him for a moment as if he understood Devon's mind, then pointed at the wall opposite the monitors, at a small camera. "Not only can your good friend, Colonel Khan, see us, but he can also hear as we speak. I wonder if he knows you well enough to understand you have no intent to help us."

As Kee spoke, a second monitor flickered to life. This one displayed a single vertical indicator. "The gauge is calibrated in millirads per hour detected in the oven." Kee leaned forward to better see the numbers. "The levels appear to be rising. If the woman is of any interest to you, I would suggest we hasten to a resolution."

"What are you talking about?" Devon asked. He stared up at the two monitors.

"She looks very peaceful and calm, doesn't she?" Kee pointed at the second monitor. "From what I have seen of the radiation experiments, the subject does not initially realize there is any damage." He stretched up on his toes to point out a dark line on the indicator with his pointer. "Skin begins sloughing off as the reading reaches about here.

"Extended radiation exposure, measured in minutes, at lower levels will result in certain death, but only after several days of great pain and disfigurement." He shook his head, eyes sad as he implored Devon. "I have no wish to see the woman suffer. Please assist me. None of us may live through these troubled times, but I, for one, do not care to sit in that chair."

Granwin's image sat alone on the first small screen, unmoving. In the second monitor, the radiation indicator perceptibly moved toward the line where Kee's pointer had tapped. What were the alternatives? Devon didn't see any. His decision was easy.

Devon picked up the master drawing and sketched in a rough, three-dimensional representation of a phased array receptor and a series of logic steps. Kee leaned over his shoulder, staring at the diagram. Devon glanced back at the remaining guard, even as he resisted the urge to reach up and grab Kee's fat throat and smash his ugly face against the table.

Give the wolf something better to eat, as long as he could. He added a hatched box to the sketch. "Use a quantum well-phased array detector as your charged-couple device." He circled the added components with his pencil. "With the array integrated in a multi-layered systolic architecture with your current optics, you end up with a wide view charged couple device with extremely fast processing times and low power requirements."

One of the women shook her head. "Efficient IR phased arrays are constructed of indium gallium arsenide and require cryogenic cooling systems."

The other shook her head even more vigorously. "Don't waste our time on foolish things."

The women understood English and microtechnology. Devon closed his eyes for a minute. This would have to done carefully. The design in his head would actually work. Could he convince this

Communist technocrat and his assistants that his design was plausible? Like the old days back at Fort Sill, do the hard sell for his proposal.

"Yes, of course, but open cycle solid cryogen systems will work—hell, they're as simple as a block of carbon dioxide vented to the CCD chamber—and work great in space applications." He stared at the piece of paper for a moment. "Basic cryogenic dewar design has been around for years. The warhead is still in space vacuum when separation occurs. Dewar kicks in and cools the array through reentry and target acquisition. Perfect, simple and small.

"You can buy a mega-pixels array in a one- inch camera format with a built-in thermoelectric cooler off the shelf, over the Internet." He scratched a crude dewar system into the warhead drawing, nestled beside the focal plane array. "See how it can all be shaped to the available space. The entire terminal guidance package is so small it'll fit in the existing design cavities. Components are all commercially available. Your Chinese buddies probably use them on your Long March payloads."

Sara and a guard stood on the other side of the plate glass. She had a desperate look on her face.

Devon had run out of arguments, had talked too long, already given them too much.

Devon decided it was time to take control. "Here, let me show you." He walked over to the leather suitcase containing the portable nuclear device. He flipped off a gray metal cover searching for anything he could use as a weapon. HA chill ran down his back when he found it. He disconnected the wires from a heavy polished steel cylinder, then twisted the cylinder loose from its fasteners.

Kee frantically twiddled his fingers toward Devon. "Do not meddle with what you do not know," he screamed. "The weapon is armed." He pointed with both hands at the cylinder. "You are holding an enriched uranium warhead."

The guard waved his weapon back and forth, shouting at Kee in Arabic.

Kee yelled back, then directed his tirade at Devon. "Stop, you fool. If the guard fires and you drop the warhead, we will all die."

And if he didn't act, God knows what would happen. Devon threw the cylinder at the guard. He dove to one side, the guard to the other. The warhead cylinder thudded against the plate glass, splitting into two polished sections when it hit the concrete floor. The technicians screamed in unison as Kee dove under the table.

An ear-splitting radiation alarm shrilled through the door. Orange lights flashed in the corridor.

Was Kee right? Had he had just killed them all, spewing radioactivity from the warhead sections slowly spinning across the floor? *Holy God, have mercy!*

The sound of a long burst of automatic weapons fire overrode the alarm. Through the open door he caught a glimpse of Sara with a submachine gun in her hand and a determined look on her face. The guard on the floor rolled to face Sara. The guard triggered a burst from his gun.

Devon covered the space to the prone guard in four strides and a final, desperate dive. He drove his elbow into the back of the guard's head, slamming his face into the stone floor before he could fire again, and snatched the guard's weapon from the floor. Devon spun to face the two technicians, the unfamiliar MP5 hot in his hands. One of the women had drawn a pistol. Devon cut her down with a short burst, the MP5 stuttering in his hands. The other woman dropped to the floor, hit or frightened.

Ears still ringing from the gunfire, Devon realized the alarm was still sounding, deep somewhere in the building. Kee's eyes stared out from under the table, large and round like the rest of his face. Devon ignored him and dashed out into the corridor after Sara.

CHAPTER 22

Devon expected a hail of gunfire from the guards at the vault entrance. Instead, screaming workers filled the corridor, shedding their smocks like garments of shame as they raced and pushed their way from the assembly rooms. The steady ringing of the alarm could barely be heard over their shrieks. At the vault entrance, workers fought to get through the narrow opening, panic clear on their faces. At least they understood the seriousness of the alarm.

Where were Granwin and Sara?

The plate glass in front of him rattled. Devon ducked when he saw Khan on the other side of the glass, spraying the window with a long burst from a submachine gun. Devon raised back up when he realized the heavy plate glass had absorbed the impacts.

"Run!" Sara's voice rose over the reports. Down the corridor, Sara stood at an open door firing short bursts, trapping Khan inside.

"You promised!" she yelled at Devon. "Save my son. Save Arif. My son must live!"

Devon sprinted to her side. "Go, Sara. Get out! I'll take care of Khan." He stuck the MP5 around the doorframe and sprayed a burst across the room.

Sara grabbed Devon by the arm and pulled him back. Her eyes were big, round with fear. Her lips trembled. "No, no. You must leave now. I have let the Devil have his way too long. I can no longer live with honor. Nadav died for his belief that Hussein should not have nuclear weapons. I must respect my husband's memory. Now I can—now that you have promised." She triggered a short burst into the room, answering a rain of bullets ringing against the steel door. "I leave Arif's life in your hands."

"Jesus, Sara." Devon cringed when a bullet ricocheted over his head. "Where's Renée?"

"She is inside somewhere with the colonel." Sara glanced at Devon. "You have seen the evil of this place. My husband died trying to stop this madness at Saad Sixteen. This is what I wanted you to know. If we must all die to destroy Khan and the bombs, then I will lead the way before Allah for His judgment." She fired through the doorway, empty shell casing clattering to the concrete floor until the magazine emptied. "We cannot let the colonel escape to continue his wicked work."

She struggled to load her last magazine. "If I can reach the control room, this mountain will be no more. I must stop the colonel. If not, he will find an escape, we will all be dead, and his *Ahad* will be the victor. Please go. Hurry."

The door jerked open with the shrill clang and whine of metal-jacketed bullets slamming into the heavy metal, spinning Sara back against Devon. She smiled up into his face. "*Min fadlac*."

She gasped and fell back against the doorframe. Her white blouse bloomed with a row of bloody dots.

"Arif." The boy's name was spoken again, very softly but clearly, over the rattle of bullets on the other side of the wall. She pushed away Devon's hand. "Tell him to never forget his father—to know my Nadav was a martyr, not a traitor." Sara's feet slid out from under her, trailing blood across the concrete floor.

"I understand," Devon whispered. He saw the dying look in her eyes as he helped ease her to the floor, holding her head. Her eyes told the story of old women who knew their time had come, wandering into the deep swamp to die in peace. He understood all too well the death of a mother and son.

"Arif will be safe—I promise you—forever." Devon took a deep breath, inhaling Sara's faint sandalwood fragrance. "Forever."

She closed her eyes, the pain beginning to show on her face. "Oh, but I failed to stop the evil. The colonel escaped."

The firing stopped. Devon eased the door open with the heel of his hand. He quickly glanced inside the room. No one moved. Submachine gun held ready in one hand, he leaned around the doorframe into the room. Khan was gone, the room deserted.

Sara gripped his hand, pulling his face back toward hers. "What do I do?" he asked.

He knelt and held her in his arms. Her voice was almost too soft to comprehend. "The control room. Door inside here. More important than even my dear Arif. Destroy. Levers to advance the uran—" Her breaths were short in the final struggle for life.

"Initiate runaway in the core. Is that what you mean?" He bent closer to her, ear by her mouth.

She tried to speak, but instead a staccato series of sharp breaths blew over his face, cinnamon and clove, then stillness. Devon looked into her eyes. Her soul was no longer inside.

"I promise that also. The facility will be destroyed, dear Sara. We will stop *Ahad*."

Devon rolled away at the flash of a reflection in her eyes, a vague image of a white smock. He dove back and crashed into a stubby pair of legs. Kee swayed over him, briefcase in one hand, the Russian nose cone in the other. He swung the nose cone in a great arc toward Devon. The synthetic crystal seeker window clanged as the nose cone glanced off the rock wall, then brought stars to Devon's eyes as the heavy carbon fiber shell connected with the back of his head. Devon kicked out for Kee's legs. The two of them tumbled into a tangled pile on the floor.

"Get away from me. Let me out!" screamed Kee. He lashed out with his feet and scrambled away from Devon, briefcase clutched to his chest.

Devon knelt on all fours, shaking his head, trying to clear away the bright flashes. By the time he was able to focus, Kee had staggered to his feet and was running toward the deserted guard point, briefcase clutched under his arm.

Kee stumbled down the corridor.

Devon shook his head, trying to think despite the pain shooting though his head. Kee had listened to Devon's description of the terminal homing system, watched him sketch out the array and logic. With the Chinese doctor alive and the scribbled notes, Devon knew he couldn't keep his last promise to Sara.

Devon struggled to his feet, shaking off the dizziness. When he regained his balance, he sprinted down the hall after Kee. Devon was gaining as Kee turned to the right, out of sight. Devon caromed off the wall and out the vault door. He caught sight of the fat man churning to his left through a wide doorway.

Devon skidded to a halt. The large cargo door opened to the cavern. A diesel engine bellowed and one of the trucks pulled out of the loading area into the bright afternoon sun.

When he burst through the door, the remaining truck belched a stream of black diesel fumes and followed the others out of the cavern and into the open gorge. The truck swayed, people clinging to the back like ants on a sweet roll. Devon squinted against the light of the open doorway, finally spotting a man in a white smock running across the parking area toward the Mercedes station wagon.

It had to be Kee. Devon jumped off the loading ramp and followed. "Stop, you son of a bitch!" he yelled.

Startled, Kee stared back for a moment, threw the briefcase through an open window and jerked open the car door. It took him two tries before he could jam his fat belly behind the wheel.

Devon ran toward the Mercedes as he watched Kee stuff himself into the front seat. The Mercedes moved, jerking forward by fits and starts. Kee apparently had not mastered the art of shifting. Suddenly, the station wagon's long nose swerved around and accelerated, coming back through the cavern toward the loading ramp.

Kee pointed the Mercedes' hood ornament directly at him, the triangular peace symbol aimed like a gun sight as the station wagon accelerated, tires squealing and echoing in the rocky chamber. Devon leaped toward the loading dock. The station wagon's front fender slammed into his buttock, spinning him along the wall, threatening to crush him between the rock and the heavy Mercedes.

Metal screamed and sparks lit up the cavern as the Mercedes slammed into the rock, inches away, and rebounded. Face-to-face for a moment, Kee grinned at him, gunned the engine, and the Mercedes wobbled toward the light and out of the cavern.

Devon pulled himself up onto the loading dock, trying to ignore the throbbing pain in his thigh. He crawled on his hands and knees to a guard lying at the entrance into the labs and snatched up a discarded MP5. Devon flicked the butterfly lever, pulled the stock extension back and swung the submachine gun up until the Mercedes filled the sight. Kee was pulling away. He would have just one shot. Devon squeezed the trigger.

The trigger held firm. "God damn it." Devon glanced down at the lever. A white *S*, red *E*, and a red *A*.

German gun, the lever was on *S*, safety. He wanted "*Ein*," one, single shot. He thumbed the lever to the middle position. The Mercedes was almost to the gate, out of reasonable submachine gun range, along with Kee and the guidance solution.

Racing ahead of Kee toward the gate, a careening truck slammed into a post. Shrill screams pierced the thrumming of the alarm bell, then were overwhelmed by a crash. The bed of the truck fishtailed, knocked down a handful of people like a scythe, dragging pieces of the gate and fence down the road. Kee veered to miss a body tumbling from the truck. The Mercedes spun out of control, almost toppled over, then slid to a stop facing Devon.

Maybe it isn't over. The Mercedes' engine backfired and seemed to stall. The engine re-fired and the Mercedes jerked forward. Kee accelerated, sweeping in a wide turn back toward the gate.

Devon pulled the bolt back. An unfired round flipped out of the chamber and over his shoulder. He flipped the lever to auto and pulled the trigger. The MP5 spit a stream of bullets across the ground, ricocheting into the side of the car. Devon centered the impacts on the driver side door and held the trigger down until the magazine emptied.

The Mercedes slowly rolled to a stop. Kee's head slumped against the steering wheel. Somehow the angle suggested he wasn't just resting.

Around Devon, no one else moved. The alarm bells continue to ring, to remind him he had yet to find Granwin. And Khan.

He threw down the empty gun and hobbled back into the facility. He searched each room as he ran by the plate glass windows, stretching his bruised muscles with each stride. He stumbled to a stop by Sara's body. Her open eyes gazed far into the distance. He pulled her body clear of the door and ran into the room, searching for Granwin and the reactor controls.

He twisted his head back and forth, watching for Khan as he ran. In the first room a row of calutrons gleamed in the overhead lights. Sweat popped out on his forehead as intense heat radiated from the stainless steel vessels.

He tried the next door, similar to a submarine hatch but bigger, heavy with a round locking mechanism. He spun the wheel and pulled. The damn thing didn't budge. Two welded handles were spaced far enough apart so two people could get leverage on the massive hatch. Devon put a foot on the wall and hauled back the handle farthest away from the hinges, pulling until his shoulder joints popped with the effort. The hinges groaned, then suddenly released, flinging Devon across the floor. He scrambled to his feet and edged through the half-opened hatch. His heart skipped as he ran into the room and saw Granwin, motionless, still strapped to the chair.

"Please help me, Nash. I can't get free," she cried out to him. Her wrists were bloody under the leather straps. "Why is the alarm sounding? Where is everyone? Why is it so hot? Can we get out of here?" She shook her head, flinging her shawl down around her neck.

Breathless, Devon worked at the buckles. His fingers, the leather straps and metal buckles all were slick with his sweat and Granwin's blood. The heat was even more intense in this room, too hot to talk. He didn't even try to answer her questions. When he finally freed her arms, he pulled her from the chair and, to his surprise, she threw her arms around his neck.

"I thought I would never see you again. Thank you, Nash. Thank the Lord." She clung to him like a drowning person to a life ring. "Can we get out?"

"Stay with me, Renée." As if she would turn him loose.

Suddenly, the alarm stopped and a gush of cold air whooshed through the room. Deep inside the facility, Devon could hear, feel, the sudden surge of air turbines. *Probably the emergency cooling system, if they had such a thing.* Maybe they weren't going to cook.

"I was afraid I had lost you, too, Renée." He pried her fingers loose. "But I still don't know where Khan is, and I've got one more thing to do before we leave." He pulled her through the hatch-like door and shoved her toward the corridor. "Go out the door and to the right, then to the loading ramp. I don't think there's anyone else left to stop you."

"Dear God. Is that Sara?" She stumbled toward the corridor, then stopped, staring at the bloody body on the floor.

"Go on. I promised Sara I would finish this for her." Devon searched around for the reactor controls. No international radiation signs, not a hint. *Just another seed repository.* He pointed at the Arabic signs over a series of doors. "Do any of those say control room?" he asked.

Granwin mouthed the words as she read the signs, shook her head. "It's all technical words. I'm not sure." She looked back and forth before she pointed at the far one. "The sign over the last door says reacting room, or something like that."

Devon started for the door. "Get out of here. Find Arif. Make sure he's okay." He ran to the door and pulled it open, chilled by a sudden blast of frigid air.

"Devon, this place is full of death. Come with me," Granwin screamed at his back.

He waved her on. "Leave before the radiation cooks you, damn it. I'll be right behind." He turned back to a room full of meters and dials and control panels labeled in German. "And watch out for Khan," he yelled over his shoulder as he searched for the reactor controls.

A series of sliding levers on the sloped control panel looked serious, marked in percentage increments. Bright red warnings started at the sixty percent marks and continuing to the top of the bar, marked with an optimistic one hundred and fifty. He slammed each lever all the way forward, deep into the red, sidestepping down the control panel as fast as he could move the levers. He had made it halfway down the line when a loud hum began to fill the room. The hair on the back of his neck stood on end as the sound grew louder and climbed in pitch. On the wall in front of the panel several large dials quivered, then gradually moved toward their maximum readings, also marked in red.

Devon raced, a half-stumbling gait, to the loading bay, searching for Granwin and watching for Khan. Devon squinted out the big doorway into the glare of sunlight. Kee's white-clad body lolled in the open, but the Mercedes was missing. Granwin was nowhere to be seen. Had she taken it? He looked back at the empty corridor, wondering how much time was left.

"God, woman, you need a saint to watch over you, and all you've got is me," he muttered and ran back inside, scanning each of the windows as he ran down the empty corridor.

A low-pitched wail began, then built to a warbling scream, deafening in the narrow corridor. The last time Devon had heard anything like that was the night he flew into Riyadh during the Gulf War and the sirens were sounding a Scud alert.

Devon skidded to a stop when Granwin popped up on the other side of the glass in the room where he had drawn the plans with Kee. Her face was as white as the plaster walls. He ran inside. One of the technicians lay sprawled across the floor, blood pooling beside her. The guard and the other woman were gone, along with one of the leather cases. The shiny pieces of warhead still lay on the floor.

He ran the length of the table. The drawings and his scribbled notes were missing, along with the briefcase he had last seen with Kee. He squatted, searching as the damn reactor prepared to blow a passage straight to Murshid's Satan.

"Jesus!" He found Granwin on her knees under the table, picking up pieces of rock and throwing them into her old tote. "Renée, please!" he screamed, hardly heard over the warbling of the siren.

Devon grabbed her by the collar and dragged her out from under the table. Wind shrilled down the corridor, the temperature gone again from chill to blast furnace. Sweat ran down his face and soaked his shirt. Beside them the plate glass window shattered and a rack of test equipment crashed against the wall.

Devon shoved Granwin out into the hall, ahead of him toward the loading dock, stepping over bits of the control board, red numbered aluminum panels wrinkled like notepaper.

"What's happening?" she yelled in his ear.

"Come on, woman. The whole place is going to explode!" He slid down from the dock and turned to help Granwin. He half-dragged her toward sunlight and the distant fence. "What in hell were you doing in there?" He was hoarse with the heat and yelling.

She clasped her bag to her chest, holding on to him with the other. "For Grandpère, I must save the icon. I have come too far, lost too much, for it to be left behind."

Devon nodded. "You've got your icon, so hurry!" He felt a rumble build up under his feet. "This place is going to blow damn soon."

Granwin stumbled against him. "Is it over, Nash? Are we going to die here?"

The rumble built and the floor began to heave. A slab of rock cracked away from the entrance opening, then toppled toward them with a crash. Devon pulled Granwin with him through the rock dust toward the opening, the wind building to a fiery exhaust behind their backs. Deep behind them, the mountain grumbled louder. Suddenly, the siren stopped.

Together they ran, bursting out of the cavern and into the gorge. Bodies, a few still in their white smocks, littered the ground between them and the fence. Off to the left, Fagham's lanky body rested at the base of the cliff.

A flock of buzzards danced along the ground, picking out choice scraps from the debris left by the panicky evacuation. Devon had never asked grandma about the buzzards, but figured they must be pretty close to the eagle, taking care of all the mess man made. One stood on top of a dusty pile, wings spread, ugly head arched in defiance, guarding its pick of the crop. Devon wondered which enterprising survivor had taken the Mercedes.

Granwin suddenly slowed to a walk, then stopped. Devon grabbed her arm. "Don't stop. The whole mountain is going to blow up."

"It will be a nuclear reaction, *oui?*" She shrugged her shoulders, clutching the box close to her heart. "There is no need to run." She motioned with her chin at the narrow roadway leading out to the valley. "The walls are very tall and close. We will not escape whatever happens inside. Perhaps it is time to pray." She grinned her crooked grin at him. "Perhaps just say *Inshallah*, and trust our souls to the Lord?"

Overhead, the sun had already dropped behind the edge of the cliff, slicing sharp beams of light through the dust. Uncertain, the buzzards whirled overhead in the hot wind, in and out of the light, swooping back down to the carrion, then soaring up toward the top of the cliffs.

Which spiritual metaphor should he concentrate on, Devon wondered. A pacifist Lumbee lashed to the bonfire stake while the painted

Tuscarora warriors hopped and spun in a victory dance? Or join Granwin's line of thought and be Squire Jean d'Aulon to Granwin's Joan of Arc. He put both arms around Granwin. Squire Jean it would be.

A shrill cry echoed from the rocky walls. Overhead a hawk swooped low over their heads, then wheeled through the formation of buzzards, heading down the gorge toward the valley to vanish into a boil of dust rising from the dry riverbed. Devon squinted down the track. A white car raced toward them, skidding back and forth in the loose shale, driver-less so far as he could tell.

No, not a car.

As it swerved around the debris blocking the gate, Devon saw the remains of the blue UN letters on the scarred side of the Nissan. The driver's head bobbed up from behind the steering wheel, then disappeared from sight as the Nissan turned toward them. Brakes locked, the Nissan bore down on them, smoke boiling up from the heavy tires as it slid across the smooth rock, fishtailed, then broke free into a four-wheel slide.

Devon pulled Granwin with him, backing away from the out-of-control Nissan sliding broadside toward them. It finally stopped, inches away, surrounding them with a cloud of acrid tire smoke that at least masked all the other carnage smells. Devon shoved Granwin toward the back seat and jerked open the passenger door.

He had barely spoken, "In the back," when Arif scrambled over the seat and tumbled down beside Granwin. Devon ground the Nissan into gear, dodged around the bodies and sped down the Sinjar road away from Facility Number Seven.

"Where's my mother?" Arif screamed to be heard over the raw exhaust echoing back from the narrow walls.

Devon shook his head.

"My mother is dead."

Devon met Arif's eyes in the mirror. He recognized the quavering tone, more of a statement than a question. Just checking for confirmation.

He remembered his grandpa coming out to meet the school bus. Grandpa had never met him at the road before, and the look on his weathered face had told Devon more than he wanted to know, but you have to be sure when you're a kid. Sometimes grownups confuse things, and make it hard to understand. It was the only time ever he had seen his grandpa cry. Grandpa had sat on the broken-down fence and stuffed the old pipe, wiping his eyes with a faded blue bandanna before he could reply.

Yes, grandpa had said, a phone call from Western Union, a telegram from the Department of Defense. His dad was killed, heroically, the telegram had said, leading his platoon up some hill in the highlands of Vietnam. Devon never could remember the hill's number, but he remembered exactly how many times his grandpa had folded his bandanna—six times one way, then twice across, nice and neat, white lines all parallel on the faded blue background

Devon nodded. "When we stop, I'll tell you. Everything." He jammed his foot on the gas. *God, I never want to stop.*

CHAPTER 23

Devon held the accelerator to the floor, more guiding the Nissan down the road than steering. He wanted to roll up the window to block out the dust and noise, but was afraid to take his hands off the wheel. He slid past the point where they had met Khan this morning—a lifetime ago—and suddenly the valley spread out in front of him. Murshid's villa sat to the left about a mile down the road. Further away, the low silhouette of Sinjar nestled close to the ground, barely visible through a dusty haze blowing in from the southern deserts.

"Chief, look," Arif blurted in his ear. His thin arm stretched by Devon's face, pointing toward the villa. A helicopter rose up into the gray sky, then dipped its nose, heading directly toward them. "The colonel, the one Mother called 'the evil one,' came to the villa in a helicopter, same as that one."

"Khan?" asked Devon. "In a UN helicopter?"

"Yes. The man who made me stay with Sheik Murshid."

Devon slammed on the brakes and spun the wheel to the right, sliding the Nissan on to a track running beside the dry canal. They flashed by the abandoned Belarus tractor, down and up the canal bed, then followed a single rut, more of a goat trail, around the side of the mountain. "Is the helicopter still following us?"

Arif grabbed a handful of Devon's shirt, twisting around to look back out the window. "The helicopter is almost beside us, Chief." He jerked on Devon's shirt. "Look! Look out of the window."

Devon glanced to his left. The white Dauphin's side door opened, and the helicopter slid sideways, close enough Devon could see the man in the open door pointing a gun.

The Nissan almost got away from him as they bounded across a shallow cut in the slope. The rear wheels bounced up in the air, over-revving the engine. Devon hung on to the steering wheel and pulled his chin down to keep Arif's frantic grip around his neck from cutting off his wind. Granwin's scream cut through the bellowing exhaust as they slammed back to the ground.

The helicopter maneuvered just ahead, meters away, a sure shot for the gunner.

Devon cut away from the goat track, ducking underneath the helicopter. The rotor blades dipped down, flashing in front of the windshield, so close Devon could hear the whap-whap of the blades clawing at the air.

The pilot jerked the aircraft up and away as the Nissan bounded up in the air toward the blades.

Devon cringed when the rip of a submachine gun burst cut through the cacophony swirling around him. He steered toward a pile of boulders. "Where's the helicopter now?" he yelled.

"Over on the other side, up high." Arif's answer was deafening, right in Devon's ear. "Look, look. *Haboob, haboob.*" Arif pointed toward the plain south of them. A wall of brown dirt climbed up from the ground toward the setting sun's pink glow, driven by a massive wind rushing in from the deserts.

Devon leaned forward and peered up through the windshield. The Dauphin had rolled back around, this time in front of them, but in a steep climb. Devon searched the boulder field coming up, looking for any kind of cover. A hundred meters from the boulders, the Nissan began to pitch and yaw like a sailboat in the middle of a category five hurricane. The Dauphin abruptly gained altitude, spun, almost swapping tail for nose, then dived toward the ground, coming directly toward them. Devon's stomach heaved when the vehicle wheels left the ground, the steering wheel useless in his hands, rising to meet the helicopter.

He slammed the brake pedal to the floor and yelled a warning. "Hang on. We're going to roll." The Nissan crashed all four wheels back down on the ground and slewed around, but stayed upright.

They had almost come to a stop when the world erupted around them, slamming Devon down in his seat, pounding his head against the steering wheel. The slope buckled up in a wave, moving like a tsunami toward them, dislodging huge boulders from the mountain-side. A giant rock tumbled past the hood and snowballed down the slope. As the tremor passed underneath, the Nissan tipped up, nose-high, then surfed over the crest and fell back to the ground.

Devon heard his neck snap and squeezed his eyes shut as they slammed back to the ground the same time the dust cloud hit, obscuring the sky, the slope, the front end of the vehicle, everything. Rocks and dust pelted the Nissan and swirled through the open window. The engine barked one more time, then stopped.

Then, just as suddenly as it all started, everything was quiet. Devon listened, then decided the noises were only echoes in his head. Arif finally released his grip, and Devon took a deep breath and blinked open his grit-filled eyes. The sun glowed, gray-brown and feeble through the dust.

"Arif. You're bleeding!" Granwin cried out.

Devon spat dirt from his mouth and spun around in the seat at Granwin's cry. She dabbed at Arif's head with a rag.

Arif squirmed free from Granwin. "I'm not hurt, Chief. I held on to you—just a little bump, on the top." He rubbed the top of his head and looked down, grimacing at the blood and grit on his fingers.

"Come here to me." Granwin pulled Arif over to her side.

On the opposite side of the globe, Air Force Lieutenant Jessy Hicks felt a sudden urge to pee when a large-screen display over the attack and early warning console flashed an ominous warning triggered by the Defense Satellite Program downlink. She flipped open her notebook, ran her finger down the acetate-covered page to the computer-prompted script some anonymous staff officer had prepared for just this contingency.

When her trembling finger stopped on the correct entry, she waved over Major Dennison, the Deputy Duty Officer, while she punched up a detailed map of the alert area with her other hand. She glanced up and Dennison nodded a silent approval. Hicks began reading the scripted entry in the controlled tone she had practiced for weeks, settling for the Midwest neutral resonance of a weather forecaster. She followed the words under her finger like a first-grader, precisely reading each word, then glancing up to fill in the estimated yield numbers from the console display.

She hadn't wanted to be known as the 21st Space Wing's 'squeaky' desk officer, or worse, when the shit hit the fan. And this indication was very real, passed all the decision gates. She carefully pronounced each number of the latitude and longitude into the telephone mouthpiece at the same time the warning system computer automatically transmitted the sequence to the North American Aerospace Defense Command Cheyenne Mountain complex.

Locked down in the mountain, the NORAD watch officer, a Canadian Brigadier General, watched the computer-generated input scroll across the huge wall screen. He picked up a second phone while he listened to Hicks' voice confirmation. The second phone was a hot line to the Pentagon NMCC sub-basement command center.

With Hicks' voice still coming in one ear, the watch officer started his report with an authentication code to confirm his identity.

"National Military Command Center, this is General Alston at the North American Aerospace Defense Command Center authenticating alpha three zero mike."

He glanced at the other screens, searching for conflicting information, anything to point to a computer glitch, an errant simulation like the false alarm that had caused a panic in the '80s. "I have correlated the Defense Support Program IR indication with AFTAC seismic reports and confirm a nuclear event inside Iraq, vicinity the Turkish, Iraq, Syrian border convergence. Coordinates transmitted separately.

"There is no, I repeat, no indication of missile launch. Surface and seismic readings indicate a near-surface underground event. Detonation size estimated less than ten kilotons, indicating possible premature detonation or reactor accident. NORAD standing by for further indications at this time." He scanned all the other screens one more time and finished his report. "We have no indications of a computer malfunction or technical reporting error. Please acknowledge."

In the Pentagon, Les Fowler watched the scramble around him as NORAD's call blared out on the speakers. He checked his standing operating procedure manual to confirm he had nothing official to do, then leaned back and picked up his direct line to the NSA operations center. "Allen, got news."

He glanced down to make sure the red LEDs indicated the phone was locked in secure mode. "Remember the Rosemary call you passed to us last week?" Fowler nodded at the response. "No, this isn't grief for you. Don't be so damn sensitive. Just the opposite, man. Alert call just came in from NORAD. Defense Support Program and Air Force Technical Applications Center indications suggest an underground nuclear explosion somewhere close to Rosemary's last known location. My man must've struck uranium. You heard anything from him?"

Fowler grimaced and shook his head at Allen's negative answer.

"Damnation. Let me know if you hear anything. I'm praying he wasn't in the middle when it went down." Fowler hung up the phone and waited for the shit storm to stop.

Arif twisted out of Granwin's clutch to look out the windows. "Where is the helicopter? Did it crash? What happened? Was that an earthquake?"

Lines furrowed Granwin's dirty brow. "Did the mountain explode?"

Overhead, the sky faded from the strange pink glow to a muddy darkness.

Devon stared at the dark sky. "Something big happened. My guess is the reactor cut loose. Sara wanted me to start a meltdown, and I did my best." *Maybe too good.*

The swirling dust began to coat the windshield and everything around them. "Come on, we need to get under some cover. I don't know if the reaction was contained, if this dirt is radioactive or just desert dust from Arif's *haboob.*"

He slid to the passenger side and kicked at the door. It didn't budge. When he tried the window, the crank spun uselessly. Otto was really going to have his ass this time. He slid back to the driver's side, put the gearshift into neutral and tried to start the engine. The solenoid didn't even click.

Arif hung over the seat, a strip torn from Granwin's shawl tied around his head, assistant driver on the job. "I think the battery cable is loose," he suggested.

Devon glanced up at the rear view mirror. It was missing. He turned to grin at Arif. "Bud, you been hanging around Otto too much."

Arif frowned at him. "Why?"

"Just joking, kid." Devon wormed out the window and scanned the sky, the brown desert dust gradually being replaced by a darker gray mist. "And what's a *haboob?* If that was one, I don't want to see another."

No helicopter anywhere in the sky or on the ground, and even more importantly, no towering fireball over the mountain back toward Facility Number Seven. But he did have an eerie feeling about the fine grit beginning to cover the Nissan and himself with a gray layer that matched the sky.

"*Haboob* is what the Bedouins call the terrible sandstorms. A loose translation is 'worse possible combination of things.'" Granwin explained. She rolled her window up as the gray grit continued to accumulate.

Not far down the slope, a cluster of rocky huts straddled the goat path. Devon stood back and surveyed the Nissan. Both tires on this side were flat. He guessed the same on the other side.

Arif stuck his head out the driver's window. "Want me to help, Chief?" Before Devon could answer, Granwin hauled Arif back into the Nissan by his pants.

"No, you stay inside with Renée, out of the dust," Devon replied. "Get behind the wheel and guide the Nissan toward those huts down below us when I push. It's going to be real hard to steer, so don't try to turn too sharp, just let it roll in a wide sweep down the slope, all the way to those huts."

Devon put his shoulder to the back of the Nissan and shoved, rocking it back and forth until it gradually began moving across the slope. Even with the shredded rubber flapping around the tire rims, the Nissan gathered speed quicker than he expected. "Jesus." He tried to run and discovered his bruised leg didn't want to gallop, just maybe lope a little. He jogged along, then realized the gap between him and the Nissan, bouncing back and forth from side to side on the ragged flaps of rubber left for tires, was growing.

"Long way to the river, Arif," he yelled, voice ragged in his dust-coated throat. "Turn against the slope and let it slow down."

Granwin stared back through the dirty glass.

"Yeah, you're right, too, Renée. I'm nuts," Devon gasped.

He cut across the curving arc left by the rims and finally chased down the Nissan, fumbled with the latch for a moment, then dropped the tailgate down. He flopped on the tailgate, along for the ride, all the way to the river if Arif could handle it.

The Nissan gradually wobbled to a bumpy stop. Arif had done all right. The kid, or the grace of God, stopped the Nissan with its nose poked between two huts.

"Come on, Arif." Granwin crawled over the back of the seat and past Devon. "Nash, get the food box and take it inside. Hurry." She gathered up the water bottles and inspected the first hut, then scurried to the next. "In here," she called out. "This one has a solid roof."

Devon could feel the heavy dust gathering on his arms. The brown dust was just desert dirt. But the fine gray grit settling from the sky could be all that remained of the mountain and the nuclear reactor. It even smelled different. He scooped up an armload of gear, piled it on top of a box of canned goods, uncaring what he had, just gathering for survival. "Come on, buddy."

Arif had shot back over the seat and was gathering up odd items. Devon shoved Arif out the back of the Nissan and followed him into the hut. Outside, a sharp crack of lightning arced across the sky, skipping from mountaintop to mountaintop. Large rain drops—one, two—splattered in the dust, then a torrent pelted the ground outside the door.

The ground rumbled under their feet, answering the thunder with a long, rolling grunt.

"Oh, Lord." Granwin grabbed Devon's arm, swaying.

Arif stumbled to his side, hanging on while the ground under them rolled.

A secondary explosion, or the beginning of the big one? Devon dropped the box and tangled gear to the floor, put his arms around Granwin and Arif and drew them back against the wall farthest from the door. Overhead, the old timbers holding the rock slabs and sod rocked back and forth as the oscillations built, then as quickly stopped.

The timbers held, and soon the rocks and sod settled back to await the next catastrophe. Chunks of dirt dribbled out, followed by tiny feathers left by some nesting bird. Rivulets of rainwater trickled through the gaps in the rocks and flowed along the timbers toward the front wall, out the doorway and down the slope.

They stood, waiting. Devon could feel three hearts beating until Granwin wormed out from under his arm and picked up one of the water bottles from the ground.

"Take off your shirt and sweater," Granwin directed as she screwed off the bottle top.

Devon stared at Granwin, not comprehending. Now they were safe, he felt dehydrated, starved, exhausted, all at once. A tremble started up his legs.

"Come on, Nash. Stand here beside me." She sat the bottle on a ledge. "You're covered with the gray dust. What if it's contaminated?"

It finally registered on him what she was trying to do. He took a deep breath and started stripping. Devon glanced at Arif and threw the filthy sweater out the door into the rain.

Granwin unbuttoned his shirt and pulled it off. "Bend over and close your eyes. And hold your nose," she added.

Devon shivered, cold water running over his back, his hair. He had never been baptized. Was this how it felt? Cleansed of all his sins by Saint Renée?

She splashed his back and shoulders, pushing his head down toward his knees so the water ran off his head to the ground. "Arif, stay away from the door. The rain might be contaminated also."

Devon closed his eyes and let the cool water run down the back of his neck and through his hair. Granwin had taken charge. Fine with him.

"Enough for you." She gave Devon the tail of her shawl to wipe his eyes and motioned Arif over. "Nash, you and I would have died this afternoon but for Arif." She sloshed the remaining water on to the other end of her shawl and used it to carefully clean the small gash on the boy's head, then wipe Arif's face and hands, then finally her own.

"Now we will sit here, in this dry place, and pray to God that he lets us live another day."

Devon slipped his damp shirt back on and dug through the food box, hungry to feed their mortal bodies now that Granwin had satisfied their souls. Arif watched him toss a dust-caked cheese ball out the door, hunger evident in his eyes. The boy continued to stare out into the black rain, but now with something of a more thoughtful look on his face.

Devon wondered if he had seen the bloody sweater, or realized the source of the stains. He had a lot to tell the kid. *In a minute, food first.* Any excuse to wait. He handed Arif the can of salted almonds left over from the start of the trip, so long ago.

Arif popped off the plastic lid, fished out the remaining nuts and offered a share to Devon and Granwin.

Devon shook his head. "You eat them, bud."

Arif put one in his mouth and chewed for a moment, swallowed, then ate a second. As he chewed, he looked at the can, as if it had reminded him of something. "You are correct, Mrs. Granwin. It is prayer time." Arif pulled his shoulders back, granting Devon a reprieve. "I must remember on my own now." He picked his rug up by one end and let it unroll. "Which direction is Mecca?" he asked.

Granwin looked from Arif to Devon. Devon took his cue from the slope of the dirt floor and pointed toward the rock wall on the downside of the slope. "To the south, across the valley toward the desert." He watched as the boy smoothed the rug, then knelt.

He hoped Allah was listening to the boy's low murmur, a far cry from Devon's failed attempts at religion. Miss a meal to pray? Not likely, then or now. He hadn't even been very good at memorizing the memory verse in Sunday school, never even tried serious praying on his knees.

Devon dug through the box and pulled out three MRE envelopes left in the Nissan from their trip to the mountain. He tossed one to Granwin.

"Rinse off the dust before you open the bag. And don't open the foil bags yet. The main dishes need heat before you can digest them." Devon pulled one of the Department of Agriculture handbooks from his briefcase and began tearing out pages, wadding the sheets into a tight ball and packing them into the corner of a crude hearth. "You guys cold?"

"Is the food plastic?" Granwin asked.

"Kinda. But better than radioactive cheese and dates."

"Only a spoon to eat with. Not very civilized." The plastic spoon quivered in the air as Granwin held it between her thumb and forefinger like she had found a cockroach in the bag.

Devon flicked the wheel on his Zippo. It sparked, but no flame. He had neglected to refill the lighter. Outside, rain still beat against the rock walls, washing the dust from the sky. Now was not a good time to go out to look for gas. What else had he neglected? He dug a pack of matches from the accessory pack. When he struck the match, yellow letters across the box in the bottom of the old briefcase he had so carefully packed for a trip to the mountains caught his attention. He dropped the match onto the wad of paper, then pulled the box into the flickering light and read the words to himself, "Agricultural Grain Moisture Analyzer, Model I-100z."

"Quit talking to yourself and help." Granwin's face twisted in a grimace as she tried to tear open the inner foil envelope. "How can you eat when you cannot open the package?"

Devon slid the satellite transceiver back into the briefcase. *No sense getting excited. Batteries probably dead, atmospherics, all the excuses the comm guys used when the satellite communications systems went bust, damn thing probably wouldn't work anyway.* And it was raining too hard to go out where he could get a clear line-of-sight to the satellite.

"Here." Arif held out a black-handled folding knife to Granwin.

"Where'd you get the knife, Arif?" Devon took the knife and flicked the thumb button. A wicked-looking blade sprang out from between lightweight magnesium handles and locked in place.

"In the back of the truck, with Mr. Baker's things."

Devon poked at the pile of gear on the dirt floor. Most of it was Baker's tools, left in the Nissan from their quick trip up the mountain to save Granwin's Taj. Devon glanced over at Arif, reminded again of his promise to Sara. This boy would live.

"Beef stew." Arif read aloud the label on his MRE. He screwed his face up at the effort as he pulled at the flaps, finally tearing open the sealed pouch.

"Not as good as the old C-Ration canned ham and scrambled eggs my dad used to bring home, but a damn sight better than the smelly cans of pork and lima beans."

Arif made a face at the mention of pork and lima beans.

"Here, bud." Devon tossed Arif a brightly colored bag of candy. "Spoil your supper with these. Save the toilet paper and go easy on the hot sauce." He dropped a tightly wrapped wad of tissue into his pants pocket for later, along with the matches. As he remembered, with

MREs there always was a later, sometimes sooner, especially any dish with beans.

Granwin wrapped Arif's prayer rug around the boy's shoulders while they waited for the food to heat. "It is time to speak to the boy, as you promised." She left Devon no excuse.

Devon fumbled with the wicked-looking knife. Arif needed to understand his mother had not died in vain. "Your mother was very brave, Arif. She died to destroy an evil thing." Devon forced himself to look Arif straight in the face as he flicked the blade open and locked, then found the release and eased it closed.

From the calm look on his face, Arif seemed to know more about what went on than Devon. "Does the door in the mountain, where all the dead people were, lead to a nuclear place where they make bombs and things? A place like Saad Sixteen?"

Devon nodded, remembering Arif had been raised by two nuclear researchers. "Yes. Your mother saved my life. She told me how to start the reactor into an overload, a runaway of some sort." Devon shrugged his shoulders. "I don't know enough about nuclear reactors to understand what exactly happened, but we destroyed it. She and I."

Arif bit his lip, but not a tear fell. "Mother probably withdrew the dampening rods from the core."

Devon shook his head in admiration. The kid understood at least the fundamentals of nuclear reactors, and probably knew a lot more than Devon suspected. His dark eyes hinted at the tears, the grieving to come.

Devon remembered when his time finally caught up to him at his father's funeral. The paratrooper, dress green jacket covered in decorations, pants bloused in glistening jump boots, had carefully folded the flag, bright blue with the white stars glistening in the Carolina sunshine, and handed it to his mother. Grandpa had stood stoically beside her, faded bandanna safely folded in a pocket. The rifles fired, rocking Devon back on his heels. Then, when the bugle began *Taps*, he hadn't been able to hold back his tears, watching his mother stroke the flag, all they had left of his dad.

Devon swallowed, trying to think of what to say that would help Arif.

Arif pulled the prayer rug tighter around his small shoulders. "What will happen to me?" he asked.

Devon forced his grin to return. "I promised." Her eyes had made his promise more real than any oath he had ever sworn. "I promised Sara I would watch after you."

"Will you be my father now?"

Arif's eyes fixed on his. Devon could feel their souls connect. He knew what he did at this moment—what he said—could stay with the boy forever, perhaps shape his life. Or Devon could be just another Jason, a faint and fading memory.

Several years after his dad's death, Jason occasionally visited, kind to his mother, but only a distant friend to Devon. After Devon started to college, his mom moved in with Jason, leaving grandma and Uncle Lem on the farm. Jason was a pretty good guy, but not his dad. A good dad could never be replaced, not really. Jason was comfort for his mom, not quite an uncle to him.

Certainly not a dad. Nor would Devon be Arif's father. *But more than a Jason.*

Devon thumbed out the blade, razor sharp with a partially serrated edge. "Your father was a brave man. You don't have to replace him. Or your mother," Devon said.

When Devon got home from the cemetery grandma met him at the steps, mud splattered on her skinny legs. While Devon, his mom and grandfather endured his father's funeral, grandma had trudged deep into the swamp to wail alone and ask her gods for a peaceful flight to the sky for her son. Grandma assured Devon that all would be well, she had spoken to the earth and the trees, and they would take care of Dad's soul.

Maybe grandma's gods had helped Sara on her trip to join Arif's father. Maybe they would help Arif.

"You and I will be blood brothers. You will have the blood of a brave." He took Arif's hand in his own. "Know what that means?" Devon asked.

Very solemnly, Arif shook his head from side to side. His small hand trembled in Devon's light grasp.

Devon held the knife up in the flickering light, ran his thumb across the edge. "Indian warriors were called braves by the European settlers when they came to America. Sometimes the Indians and the new settlers traded. Horses, a few cows, blankets, but when the settlers plowed up their land or built houses in the middle of the Indian hunting grounds, they fought. The Indian tribes already had a long history of fighting each other."

Devon leaned closer to Arif. "Even though a warrior might be wounded in battle—tortured—the warrior never cried out, or even let his enemy know he was afraid. So the English called them 'braves.'" Devon nicked his thumb with the point. A bead of dark blood welled out, a tiny star in the dying firelight. "Are you ready to become a brave, take my blood into you, give your blood to me, become my blood brother?"

"'Brave.' Same as *mujahideen*, a warrior for Allah, one who fights for goodness?"

"That's it, scout."

Arif's hand became very still, not a tremor. He nodded. "Yes, then I am ready. Will I have any special powers?"

"The powers are inside your own soul." Devon tapped Arif on his chest with his finger, wishing he could tap his own chest and make good things come out. "Deep inside there. But ready to come out." Devon raised the knife.

"Wait. Are there secret words to say?" Arif asked.

For a moment Devon thought a hint of a smile played across Arif's face. Who was humoring whom here? Or was it just the light?

Devon nodded. "I think there are, but my grandmother never taught them to me. So you'll have to make up your own. Maybe a pledge to honor your mother. Not of revenge," he cautioned. "Something blessed in the eyes of Allah."

Arif closed his eyes for a moment, then opened them. "I'm ready."

Granwin watched all this from across the fire, silent, probably amazed that Devon would bring Allah into the heathen ritual.

Devon carefully mashed his bloody thumb against Arif's.

Arif turned to Granwin. "Will you become my blood sister?"

Granwin shook her head. "I have no Indian blood. I doubt it would work for me."

"Well, will you marry Chief, so we can be a family?"

Devon stared at Granwin.

Granwin paused for a moment, then shook her head. "Mr. Devon and I are just friends, Arif. But don't you worry a bit. You will have a family again, we both promise." She smiled at Devon. Maybe more than a smile. "Isn't that correct, Mr. Devon?"

"Betcha," was the only reply Devon could think of, numbed by Arif's comment. *A family—*

"Now eat," Granwin said.

They each spooned the sparse meals from the foil, discovering the treats in the various bags. Renée spread some of her strawberry jam over a dry cracker, and Arif devoured it, along with Devon's packet of candy.

"Now I think I will go to sleep." Arif twisted the rug higher around his shoulders and leaned back against Devon. In just a few moments his breathing was slow and regular, his chest rising and falling against Devon's arm.

"Nash." Granwin's voice was low, barely heard over the crackle of the burning paper. A tiny flame raced along the edge of the last page. Granwin picked up several small pieces of wood from the ground and fed them to the fire. "It was a nice legend you made up, much better than the true origins of the word 'brave' in the English language."

He wasn't sure if he was being rebuked or educated. Whichever, he was about to find out.

"It comes from the Latin, 'barbarous.'" The smoke from the burning sheets of paper drifted between them, obscuring her eyes. "Perhaps the Europeans were simply remarking on the native's savage ways." Her voice became quieter. "But, for the boy's sake, I will accept your definition. For him. But for you, perhaps 'barbarous' is more appropriate. Blood brothers. Huh." Her grunt signaled her disapproval.

But Devon really did believe. "You have your faith, your cross, your icons." Devon couldn't help but argue, at least a token. "Sharing blood is a token, no more, no less—a pledge of the heart."

Granwin smiled, relenting. "Yes. My icon." She dug deep into her tote bag, carefully laid the splintered pieces of inlaid wood aside and removed several pieces of rock. "You must help me with some words."

The rock glistened in the flickering light, a marble tablet broken into several large pieces. Granwin slid the pieces around, changing their positions, trying to fit them all back together like a jigsaw puzzle.

"Where did the tablet come from?" Devon asked. Faint marks, angular engravings, marched across the fragments in neat lines.

"It was in the box." She turned a piece of the tablet from side to side, peering at it from different angles. "The letters are Greek, as are the ones inlaid on the cover of the box, but I can't decipher the words."

"Do you read Greek?" He realized how stupid the question was as it left his lips.

"Of course I read Greek." She picked up the inlaid wood, what was left of the box's lid, and bent toward the failing light. "K...H...R...I...S...T...O...S." She read the letters off, sounding out each letter with reverence. "*Khristos* is Greek for Christ. And look." She held the fragment up into the flickering light. "The same letters are lightly scratched by hand, over the engraved letters on the tablet."

"How old is the box and the tablet?" Devon shook his head, trying to be attentive. He realized this was important to Granwin, but Arif's slow breathing was pulling him down into a restful oblivion.

"Very old. The tablet reminds me of the engravings I saw in Rome, pieces left by the early Christians soon after the time of Jesus. Cryptic engravings left to mark their burial plots, recognizable by other Christians, but only gibberish to the Roman officials. Cryptic—cryptology—the word came from the Greeks. So it must—"

Devon interrupted her. "Caesar used a simple substitution code invented by the Greeks." He yawned, talking, but barely hearing. "Substitute one letter for the other, easy to break if you know the language.

"In English the letter 'e' occurs so often you can pick out common word combinations such as 'the,' 'them,' and so on. Identify a few key words, fit the rest together and pretty soon you've got the whole thing. Arabic scholars in Baghdad broke the Roman substitution codes about that quickly."

Granwin smiled at him in the dim light. "Do you have anything upon which I can write?"

Devon fished out the notebook and pen and handed them to her.

Granwin carefully placed the fragments of the tablet on the ledge in front of her. She moved them back and forth, sliding the pieces around until they fit back into a rectangle. "May I?" she asked and held up the book from which he had been tearing pages for the fire.

Devon nodded. His breathing had synchronized with Arif's, their chests rising and falling together.

Granwin dropped a wadded handful of paper on the fire and bent close to the box lid as the flames momentarily brightened the room. She transcribed letters from the box to the notebook, then turned to the letters on the marble, pressing a pair of fragments together to make out the letters crossing their juncture. She looked over at him, her crooked grin back in place.

Blow up a mountain. See good people die. Kill some bad ones; solve a puzzle.

He held his hands up in the yellow firelight, wondering if his skin would soon begin to slough off like a snake changing skin. If the warhead had spewed its radiation over the lab floor, both he and Granwin were not long for this earth.

He shivered at the thought and flexed his fingers. The skin stayed put. For the moment. He had to figure out where they were, how to get away from the *Amn al Khas*, Khan and the Commissioner who Khan said had sent him.

Soon. He drifted off to sleep.

CHAPTER 24

Devon pried his crusty eyes open. The damp hut stank from the paper fire, still smoldering between the rocks of the crude hearth. A yellow spark ran through the blackness, popped into flame and disappeared. As he watched, a second spark flared up, flamed for a moment, then died away. Except for the tiny flames, it was pitch black in the hut. Moonlight painted the rocky floor and the ground outside.

Arif twitched in his sleep, curled over Devon's right arm, and Granwin lay against his left shoulder, both covered with thin prayer rugs. Devon worked his arm from under Arif, eased the boy's head down to a corner of the rug and leaned forward, peering out the doorway. Where was the Nissan?

Granwin's eyes popped open as he lifted her head from his shoulder. "What time is it?" she asked, her voice soft, almost a whisper as she pulled Arif over to her side.

"Still the middle of the night." As his eyes grew accustomed to the darkness, moonlight crept into the hut, giving form to the bags and boxes they had hurriedly dragged in from the Nissan.

Granwin pulled the rug back up to Arif's chin after Devon extricated himself. "Yes, I can see that. But what time is it?"

Granwin's head shimmered in the silver moonlight. He stroked her short hair and smoothed it back from her eyes. The furrows on her forehead were gone, leaving behind a crust of dirt. Dirt was fine; it'd wash off. They were going to be okay. "I'll look. You go back to sleep," he told her.

Devon rummaged through his bag until he found the small cardboard box. He took out the moisture analyzer and set the box on the hearth, squatting beside it. "Ahhhh." A low groan escaped before he could stop it. His bruised hip had stiffened in the chill.

"Are you all right?" Granwin asked.

"Sure, just a little sore." God, he hurt. Every tendon from his calf to his butt threatened to pop loose from the bone when he bent down. He stretched and decided today he was just going to hurt.

"Do you have any way to measure radiation? Can you tell if it is safe to go outside?" Granwin asked.

"No way to tell. The rain should've washed everything down." *Right.* What the hell did he know? He had pulled a bunch of levers, finished off what Sara had intended to do. Had he gone too far? Had the whole of Mesopotamia been more devastated by his actions than all of Alexander's army had done?

Devon unpacked the 'analyzer.' Once he had the probes plugged in, he bent low at the stone doorway, torquing another set of muscles he didn't realize he had. This time he let the groan escape unfettered into the night. Overhead the stars overhead sparkled in the rain-cleansed air, as bright as he had ever seen them. So close he felt he should reach out and touch it, the lunar sunrise line sliced across the half moon, shadows clearly delineating the craters and plains. A streak flashed across his view. Comet, or more likely a meteor, perhaps a dying satellite. Not a sound disturbed him. Not a howl or a screech. No sign of any habitation, wild or domesticated, friend or enemy.

Devon squatted and placed the analyzer on a flat rock, twisting around the flat plate until what Devon presumed to be the antenna surface had an open aspect toward the equatorial sky. He flipped on the power switch and the red LEDs flickered to life. The first row of numbers read 0-1-2-3, 01:23 hours Zulu—04:23 local—if the batteries were right and he had made a correct assumption about UMC time. *That's stupid. If the batteries had drained the readout would be blank. Come on, man, get your head on straight.*

Now for communications. He flipped the knob to set the uplink and downlink frequencies.

He squatted there, staring at the numbers glowing back at him. He had no idea what frequencies to set, or how to set them. Had Baker given him any hint? Devon cursed himself for not paying attention to Baker's words. Baker had known, or at least suspected, the existence of the research facility and probably arranged for Fagham to ask for help. And Baker had warned Devon he was getting into deep shit, if only he'd had the sense to pay attention.

Devon stood, searched the down slope. The Nissan was gone, vanished into the darkness along with all the other equipment. The rain had even washed away the tracks. Light flickered from inside the hut. He needed to ask Granwin. Perhaps Baker had told her something useful. He stifled a grunt as he stood and turned back to the hut and the tiny fire.

"Nash, it's cold. Please get something else to burn…another of your books, perhaps." Granwin squatted beside the fire, carefully tearing the analyzer box into pieces and feeding it into the flames.

"Stop!" Devon hissed. He snatched a cardboard fragment from the fire, singeing the hair from his hand.

"What's the matter? Is someone outside?" Granwin threw down the remainder of the box and reached out to Arif, fear cracking her voice.

"No, nobody's out there, Renée." He collected the remaining pieces of cardboard. At least half of the box was gone, ash and smoke. "I just remembered. Baker told me to keep the box. Maybe it has something useful written on it." He laid the box fragments aside, tore a handful of pages from the *CIA World Factbook* and fed them into the fire. So far he had burned his way through from Afghanistan to Mali, and Malta was next. "It's still dark, only about four-thirty. You go back to sleep."

"I can't go back to sleep. I'm sorry about burning your box. Was it something important?"

"I don't know."

"My mind is full of what I found out last night. I know the way, now, Nash. I know the way."

"Good. Glad one of us knows where they are going."

"Not figuratively…literally!" Granwin's voice echoed in the rocky hut. She took a deep breath and continued, more softly. "I know the way to salvation."

"Renée, you can take me to church every day, mass even, once we get out of this. But leave me alone until we find our way out."

Granwin shook her head. "Poor man. Faith is the only way out."

"Okay, okay. You win." He picked up the cardboard fragments, one by one, and held them in the light of the fire, turning each piece from side to side, inspecting them in the flickering light. He held the charred end flap closer to his eyes. Two rows of numbers were penciled across the inside surface. Three numbers, a dot, then two more numbers. The bottom row was the same, except the last two digits after the dot were burned away, charred ash. Devon clenched his fist and shook it toward the low ceiling in celebration. He would fly with the hawks tonight. "Renée, you're right. You gotta believe. Now I do."

Outside, he squatted back down beside the device, whatever the hell it was? Transceiver? Analyzer? A device. He plugged in the false probes—the miniature microphone and earpiece. What if this was all a crock, and the damn thing was just a moisture analyzer and his imagination had made up the rest? He stuck the speaker in his ear. A satisfying rush of static tickled the inside of his head.

Devon dialed in the first set of numbers, neat little red LEDs shining in the night. He shifted on his haunches. Now he'd found the frequencies, his bruises weren't as painful. But which frequency was transmit, which was receive?

He thought back to the hot nights in the desert with Baker, but couldn't remember which frequency was usually higher, or if there was a set pattern. Why was he worrying? The damn thing didn't come with instructions, 'For Spies Only.' He didn't know which knob was which, so none of the techno crap mattered. Just play monkey at the typewriter and see if he could get Hamlet to come out.

He dialed in the first digits, then began the process of elimination, starting with zero-zero for the missing digits. He held the probe he suspected was a microphone to his lips and clucked. Did this contraption have a push-to-talk switch? Had to. The biggest knob—the one that selected between time and lat/long—traveled about a quarter of an inch when he pushed down on it. He clucked into the microphone again, this time holding down the knob.

Nothing. He turned what he hoped was the frequency knob ninety degrees. The numbers changed from zeros to twenty-five. He clucked again. If the original owners of these huts had left any chickens, he was soon going to be surrounded by a bunch of hungry birds. He tried both combinations, knob down and knob up. *Damnation.* He had talked over satellite transceivers a million times—in the desert, jungles, on the rooftops of dizzying high-rises. Why didn't he know how to do this?

To confirm satellite signal lock, transmit a sharp tone, he remembered, a cluck of the tongue. With the quarter of a second or so time delay for the signal to travel the twenty-two thousand miles up to the satellite in geosynchronous orbit and back, the operator can distinctly hear his cluck come back to earth as a tinny click. Except Devon's clucks were going out into space and nothing was coming back. He fumbled for the black knob. He cycled through the frequency band until he was back to zeros.

He stood, breathing slowly. He looked back inside the hut, where yellow light from the fire danced over Granwin's face as she watched him exercise his lack of patience.

I'm one hell of a stoic brave.

The moon edged down into the haze of the western horizon. To the east, a faint glow hinted at the coming day. Devon squatted again and spun the knobs, reversing the frequency setting by putting the complete frequency in the top window and moving the incomplete frequency to the bottom window. Was their time running out?

His hands were beginning to shake and his hip screamed at him. He stood, stretched, took a deep breath, and stared up at the sky. It reached forever, full of millions of stars, each dimming as the sky grew noticeably paler. Devon wondered if his target satellite was one of the pinpoints of light overhead.

The hillside around him was silent but for the drip of water from a corner of the hut. Since the rain had stopped not a breath of wind had blown past. No dogs barked in the distance, no whispering of doves, just the drip, drip from the hut's roof. Far down the slope and across the parched fields, a set of headlights knifed into the darkness, moving from right to left—a traveler coming from Syria. Devon listened, but the lights were too far away to hear the engine. The silent lights cut through the pre-dawn and vanished around the slope.

They were in the middle of nowhere or, more exactly, in Iraq close to the Turkey and Syrian borders. *Worse than nowhere.* If he were by himself, he could just say to hell with it. Bad leg and all, he'd hoof over the mountains toward Silop, a mere hundred miles, skirting the Syrian border up to the tip of Turkey that stabbed down into the top of Iraq. He'd slip across the border and tell them he'd come to Turkey to sell black market gasoline. Or trek across the Syrian swamps, fifty or sixty miles across to the Turkish border. *Nope, not to be.*

Time to call a taxi.

He eased the knob around until the number changed. A five and a zero stared back at him. Devon clucked his tongue, listened for a moment, then turned the knob to seventy-five. A faint click tickled his ear as he turned the knob. He pulled the earpiece out, ran the tip of his finger around his ear and stuck the earpiece back in and clucked. *Nothing.* He turned back to fifty and tried again with the knob up. Nada. He pushed down the knob.

"Cluck."

"Click." The echo boomed in his ear.

"Hot damn!" Devon grinned at the glowing horizon and mashed the knob down.

"Any station, any station, mayday, mayday, mayday." What else was he going to say? 'Spy number one checking in,' had a nice ring to it.

He listened for a reply. No answer.

"Any station, any station."

He waited. Maybe hoofing it to Silop was going to be the way out for all of them, unless Granwin had some friends around here she hadn't told him about. Ones that hadn't been cooked in the mountain with Number Seven's eruption.

The hair on his neck stood up when the rushing noise stopped followed by a burst of tone, then the words, faint but distinct, "Calling station, standby."

Real words whispered in his ear. Somebody, somewhere. He waited until he began to wonder if he had imagined the words.

"Calling station. Verify the words around the man in chains." The transceiver hissed, waiting for his reply.

What? Now wasn't the time for fancy codes and passwords he didn't understand. Just send a damned helicopter for them.

"Say again?" he blurted out, not sure what he had heard.

The voice sounded far away, but clear and steady. "Verify the words around the medallion, the man in chains."

Medallion!

Devon patted his pockets. Front right, the lump. He reached past the matches and toilet tissue until his fingers closed on the forgotten piece of Wedgwood. He pulled the medallion out, but couldn't make out the tiny black letters around the edges. What did it say? Someone expected him to remember, and his mind had gone blank. He reached back into his pocket for a MRE matchbook, folded out a single match and struck it, one-handed against the abrasive strip. He ignored the flame gnawing at his thumb and held the match close to the medallion until he could read the words around the outer border. He threw down the matchbook and smashed down the knob.

"Am I not a man and a brother!" he shouted into the microphone.

He let the knob up and paused a moment, listening. The hissing continued. No reply. He tried again, slower this time, pausing between each word in the phrase. "I say again. Am...I...not...a...man...and...a...brother."

A click and a terse "Stand by" replaced the hissing."

Devon squatted by the transceiver, finger on the transmit knob, waiting. The eastern horizon hinted at a subtle pink, the sun not far behind.

A voice replaced the click and the hissing. "Chief. You up?"

Devon mashed down the spring-loaded knob. "Roger. Deacon?" The voice sounded electronic, every bit of nuance filtered out by the digital transponders, but Baker was the only person Devon could imagine calling him Chief or knowing about the medallion.

"It's me, man. I'm reading your location and have Defense Support Program reports from Cheyenne. What's your status?"

Baker wasn't wasting time on long-winded radio procedure, just listening for the squelch to start talking.

"Frenchie and the kid are with me. His mother's dead, lots of others. Are we in trouble with fallout? Can you get us out of here?

"Remotes show normal radiation levels, but our info is all from high sensors. Trust your own judgment on the radiation levels—" Words were muttered in the background while Baker held down his transmit switch. "Was the reaction caused or accident?"

Devon didn't like Baker's pause, the failure to answer the second part of his question. If all Baker knew came from satellites, he wasn't anywhere close by. So ask. "Deacon, where are you?"

"I'm not in-country, not your country. I'm sitting close to the Mercedes factory, down the *bahn* from where we had a beer or seven—"

Devon had drunk too many big bottles of *Stuttgarter* and the rest of the Oktoberfest night was a blur, but he still remembered the big neon Mercedes symbol over the autobahn just outside the gate to Patch Barracks. Patch was headquarters for the United States European Command, located on the outskirts of Stuttgart. EUCOM ran Northern Watch, the strike aircraft that had almost obliterated them on the mountainside two days ago. Or was it three?

The transmission continued. "The bosses here have stopped overflights until they know the extent of contamination. I see where you are and will work on extraction. Any hostiles in the area? Give me a quick summary of what you found."

"Hostiles tracked us yesterday using Commission helicopters, armed with automatic weapons."

"The same kind of bird that medevaced me out?"

"Affirmative. Khan took us inside the mountain at gunpoint. Missile and warhead research facility in the mountain. Khan killed Sara. Big, fucking explosion, probably took out the facility, but we were out of sight when it went."

"Say again hostile name!"

Devon understood the question in Baker's demand even after the radio signal's trip all the way up and back down the satellite hop. Devon held down the knob. "Khan, the Pak colonel."

He released the knob, wondering what kind of help was coming from EUCOM. Maybe one of those Pavehawk search and rescue birds from Incirlik like the Search and Rescue guys flew into Yugoslavia to snatch out the downed Stealth pilot.

As he watched, the LEDs flickered and the hissing in his ear abruptly stopped. He flipped the on-off switch several times. No lights, no hiss. *Dead. So much for technology. So much for rescue.*

"Colonel."

A light stung Khan's eyes. He clenched both fists as he jerked himself awake. One hand clasped the grips of the briefcase and the other found the worn grips of his pistol lying across his chest. Khan rolled up from the hard bunk, and squinted for a moment until his eyes acclimated to the light. "Prayer time?" he asked the Iraqi sergeant standing at attention by the door.

"No, Colonel. Call for *Fajr* will come soon, but the commander asked that I bring you to the operations center for an urgent meeting. I will be outside." The soldier stepped back out the door.

Khan touched the rough stone wall with his hands, brushed them across his face and spoke the words declaring *Tayammum*, the symbolic ablution, then began his prayers with, "*Allaahu Akbar*." Completing the ritual, he looked over his right shoulder toward the angel recording his good deeds, then the left toward the angel recording his wrongful deeds, saying each time "*As Salaamu 'alaikum wa rahmatulaah*."

Khan stood and took a deep breath knowing he now was blessed by Allah's words. He pulled on his tunic, securing the Webley revolver in his holster. The pistol was his single most prized possession, taken from a British officer murdered by Khan's father's own hand. Following in his father's footsteps, Khan had worked very hard to detach himself from his Bengali heritage, dedicating himself to Allah and proving his allegiance to Islam and Pakistan every moment of his life.

He picked up the brushed aluminum briefcase he had managed to snatch off the facility floor in the confusion of the radiation alarm. The notes with the improved warhead and terminal system design secure in the briefcase would prove his loyalty to the true leaders of Pakistan and the *Mujahideen al Ahad*. Or so he prayed, trusting in the wisdom of Allah.

The only problem was the sketches added by Devon. *Damn the man!* Khan had no idea what they meant, no time to ask Kee in the panic. He must find someone else to decipher their meaning. He stared at the large leather suitcase at the foot of the cot he had lugged out of the nuclear facility with the smaller aluminum case. Too bulky to carry with him, he would have to temporarily leave it in the care of the Iraqis.

He silently followed the Iraqi soldier across the floodlit compound. In the distance, the quavering voice of the eldest muezzin hailed the men of Mosul to *Fajr* from his minaret in the center of town. Then another caller echoed across the river and into the small valley, followed closely by an indistinguishable mingling of voices, each crying out across the Tigris summoning the faithful to begin their day in a holy way.

Perimeter lights flickered out, one by one down the long fence line, until the gray dawn glow cast long shadows over the squat buildings. Sturdy concrete, the new buildings replaced the Condor II missile research facility leveled by the American bombs. The faithless still persisted, unleashing their bombers whenever the Iraqis were foolish enough to turn on their radar or fire a missile.

Khan glanced skyward past the guard towers. No contrails, no other sign of air activity: Iraqi or American. The reactor incident had frightened them all from the sky. He detoured around a crater, one of many scattered throughout Saad Sixteen, *al Kindi* as the Iraqis had renamed the research facility. The craters provided constant reminders of the bombs from above and the continuing harassment from the Americans and the damned Brits who still pretended Iraq and Pakistan were colonies, not free and independent Islamic nations. Still worse, every crater was an embarrassment, a reminder of his own government's support of the Americans and the British.

He added a personal thought to his prayers as he walked to the buried operations bunker. *May Allah bring fearsome destruction to the Americans, the English, all the infidels, and those traitorous scum among our own.*

He stumbled through concrete fragments and rusted rebar, deep in his thoughts. One should not have fear of their own sky—the sky of the faithful—but everything in this backward country operated in fear, of the Americans and their Cruise missiles, of the *Amn al Khas* and of Saddam. But as long as Saddam controlled the faithful of Iraqi, especially the *Amn al Khas*, fear was beneficial to survival.

Khan saw the proof when he stepped into the operations center. Trepidation glistened from the eyes of the officer who saluted him as he stepped into the brightly lit room…fright Khan might report them for some breach of orders, fear he might have some unexpected power over their lives. He cared not if they lived or died, and they knew it. Therefore the fear.

"Colonel Khan, my apologies for waking you so early," the officer said, stiff at attention.

"Proceed, Captain. I'm sure the issue is significant. Don't be disturbed. I have completed my prayers." Khan stifled a yawn as he willed the captain to get on with his report.

Devon was dead, Facility Number Seven destroyed, and Devon's notes and the portable weapon in his possession. Now he could return to Islamabad, away from these *Amn al Khas*, Saddam's personal assassins. No one would blame Khan for the destruction of the Iraqi facility.

Khan brushed at his mustache with his fingers. To the Iraqi people, the *Amn al Khas* held life or death. But the nuclear incident at Research Facility Number Seven had reminded the cruel guards of their own tenuous existence with the threat from the sky above and, equally dangerous, the researchers below ground. The nuclear weapon in the leather case was a perfect trump card for whatever the day might bring.

"Sir, a flash report from our intercept facilities at *al Rashedia* mentions you by name. I thought it best you see it as soon as possible."

"What?" Khan snatched up the message, a verbatim transcription of a satellite communication in English.

Chief. That had to be Devon. *The bastard should be dead.*

Deacon? Possibly Devon's African-American accomplice? Didn't matter. What did matter was that Devon was alive and a serious embarrassment.

Now Khan began to truly understand the Iraqi officer's fear. Death by contamination. With him.

Khan had made a serious mistake by not ensuring Devon's death. The reactor explosion he could blame on the Iraqis, or the Germans, or the Chinese. Yes, Kee would be a perfect explanation for the explosion. But Devon's unexpected escape was his problem.

"Captain." Khan carefully folded the message and secured it in his pocket. "Do you have the status of my helicopter?"

The Iraqi nodded. "Your crew has had difficulty repairing the damage. We do not have the required tools here. The repairs are taking longer than expected."

Khan clenched his jaw, stifling back a bark at the captain.

The captain hurried on. "I anticipated your need and already have alerted my own helicopter crew. I also called out the reaction force at Sinjar and told them to move toward the mountain. The report I gave you includes approximate coordinates. The signals appear to have come from the south slope of the Sinjar Mountains."

"American air activity?" Khan asked.

"Our radar systems indicate no activity. With the explosion at Facility Number Seven, apparently the Americans have halted their overflights. You should be able to fly without harm, at least for the moment. The report is also marked with the radio contact frequency and codes to contact the reaction force. They are driving from Sinjar and should arrive at the source of the transmissions in about thirty minutes…about the same amount of time it will take you to fly. When your crew repairs the Dauphin, I will instruct them as to where you can be found."

"Good. I thank you. You have been very efficient." *And quick to be rid of me.* "I ask one more task of you. I have left a container in the room, with the appearance of a large leather suitcase. It contains radioactive material and is very dangerous. Please inform your men they will likely not survive if they open it. Do you understand?"

Now a distinct look of fear returned to the Iraqi's face. "Certainly, sir. After the explosion at Facility Number Seven, everyone is concerned about the radioactivity."

"As well they should be." Khan spun on his heel and burst from the underground bunker. At least one Iraqi had his wits about him.

Khan waited impatiently for the dawn, and the crew to finish their hasty prayers. Today, prayers could wait. He fingered the Webley at his belt. Today he had Allah's will to convey.

Major Les Fowler jerked his head up from reading the EUCOM report a second time when the alert bell rang. The NSA Echelon message scrolled down his computer screen, confirming the summation report on his desk. He reached out, put his hand on the secure phone receiver and started counting. At three, the set rang.

As soon as the secure connection was established, he answered, "Major Fowler, NMCC DIA Desk."

A familiar voice boomed out at him from the handset. "Hey, Lester, this is Russ Allen, Echelon Center! Got another interesting Rosemary intercept for you. Good news, bad news kinda deal—again. We picked up an UHF satcom transmission, clear voice. Your man in the Sinjar Mountains survived the nuclear event, but EUCOM lost contact with him before they could set up an extraction. I sent over a transcript."

Fowler shoved aside the code-word summary report. "Roger, Russ. I was reading the EUCOM summary when your copy came through. But thanks for the heads-up."

"I'm not hearing a lot of enthusiasm from your end. Is it the crappy encryption algorithm on the phone, or did you get passed over for promotion?"

Fowler crumpled the report and dropped it into the red-striped classified waste bag. "The phone's okay, and if I don't get this right, I can forget making light colonel. This is a for-God-real problem. Since the nuclear event report, all overflights into Iraq are canceled. Nobody wants the world to think we had anything to do with the radiation drifting out of the area. So my man's on his own."

"Just going to let him sit in the middle of that mess, huh?"

"Yep." Fowler stared at the handset. Nothing else of substance to say. He stared at the message on the screen, the list of associated names on the sidebar. But maybe there was something he could do. "Listen, Russ. Gotta go. Gotta make a call."

He put down the phone, retrieved the crumpled message and glanced up at the clock with Riyadh time, a lingering vestige of the Gulf War still hanging in the command center. *Someone else in the DIA should know what's going on. Need to know, sort of.* Wouldn't hurt to roust out Houston.

And then a call to Germany, see if he could located Baker, Susan's father, hopefully his future father-in-law.

CHAPTER 25

Mesmerized by the smell floating out from the hut, Devon resisted the urge to throw the inoperative transceiver down the slope. He stuck his head inside the doorway and found Granwin squatting by a tiny fire, holding the almond can over the flames.

"Instant coffee, from one of the little packs," she explained. Her tone was apologetic, like she should be fixing him a gourmet breakfast. She held out the remainder of a hard cracker smeared with red jam. "I heard you talking and looked out. Is that thing a radio? Is someone coming to get us?"

He chewed the dry cracker and washed it down with the lukewarm coffee from the almond can. Strong and sweet, it smelled like coffee. Taste was something else.

"I talked to Bert Baker. He knows where we are, but the batteries ran down before we could set up anything. Our best bet is to sit tight. Bert won't let us stay out here under duress. He knows you and Arif are with me, and about the mountain."

But Baker was going to eat schnitzel tonight, with a couple of foamy drafts. They were down to one unopened MRE and the accessory pack remnants, orange-flavored beverage mix and dry crackers left from the night before. Granwin took back the can, and they sat, silent, watching the flames and exchanging sips of ersatz coffee.

Devon pulled the medallion from his pocket and inspected it closely in the flickering light. He squinted to read the words circling the edge again. The basalt bas-relief in the center depicted a kneeling man with chains dangling from his wrist. He handed it out toward Granwin. "Baker wanted me to give this back to you. Where did you get it?" he asked.

"Grandpère left it to me, for Albert. Albert wouldn't wear it. He said it was too delicate for a fighter pilot. I think he was just too proud. He always wanted to be recognized for what he did, not what he might represent." Granwin's voice shook as she replied.

"I know it's very precious to you. Where did your grandfather get it?"

Granwin shrugged her shoulders. "Grandpère collected many antiques over the years, especially Wedgwood. As he died, he placed it in my hand, like this—" She folded his fingers down over the broach. "—and I hid it from the thieves."

Devon opened his hand and inspected the piece, front and back. "Looks real, classic Wedgwood."

"Oh, I'm sure it is. Grandpère had an affection for Wedgwood pottery. Albert researched the medallion, and it turned out to be rather famous. Josiah Wedgwood himself commissioned it for the Society for the Suppression of the Slave Trade. Most of the pieces went to America to your Ben Franklin, so Albert told me."

He shook his head in admiration. "Wonder how your grandfather got his hands on this one?" He dropped the medallion into Granwin's hand. "You save it. For your kids to remember Albert by."

She slowly shook her head, and he wished he had said it differently, then she nodded, whispered, "Yes. For Albert," and sipped the last of the coffee as the door brightened with the dawn. Outside, a bird shrilled in the clear air.

Granwin cocked her head. "Listen."

Devon felt a vibration in the air, more than a birdcall.

"A helicopter? Perhaps they have come for us already." She started to get up.

He put his hand on her shoulder. Granwin's face was pallid. Never one—at least in the few days he had known her—to wear makeup, in the gray morning light she looked even paler than normal. But, despite the tired lines, she still had a determined look deep in her eyes.

"Careful. Could be help, or it could be trouble," he warned.

Devon had been around too many explosions lately to trust his hearing of the faint beat in the distance. "Wake up Arif and get ready to go. Whoever, whatever it is, we might need to run."

The sky had opened to a clear blue when he stuck his head out of the hut. Already the night's rain was steaming from the ground. Twirling wisps of vapor rose and caught the thermals swirling up the rocky slope. A helicopter approached out of the sun, then turned to settle where the slope flattened out, about a hundred meters away. Brown, bulbous and squat, one of the old Soviet helicopters, Devon could see it vibrate, rocking back and forth on its three wheels.

Four men jumped out, three of them carrying guns. The rising sun glinted from a container carried by the third. The three with guns crouched and ran under the whirling blades, dropping to their bellies when they were clear of the helicopter.

Far beyond the soldiers, a big six-by-six truck and a smaller truck sporting a pedestal-mounted machine gun wove through the limestone outcroppings and churned their way up from the valley floor. Wheels spinning on the slick marl, both vehicles slid to a stop between Devon and the helicopter. At least a dozen soldiers spilled from the two vehicles and ran to join the men from the helicopter. When Devon stepped out from the rock hut, carefully shielding himself from their view, he spied the soldiers' objective. The white Nissan lay on its side another hundred yards down the slope.

A solitary soldier remained behind the machine gun in the bed of the small truck, swiveling the barrel back and forth in the direction of the disabled Nissan.

"Renée! Get Arif," Devon whispered. He kept his eyes on the soldier behind the machine gun. "Come on. Gotta go."

"We're ready," Granwin answered from close by his shoulder.

Bedraggled and smeared with the muddy mixture of brown desert grime and fine gray dust, Granwin stood in the doorway, tip of her tongue in the corner of her mouth as she slung her tote bag over one shoulder. Equally as dirty, Arif stood beside her with his rolled prayer rug under an arm.

Devon grinned at them, trying to remember how his confident we-can-do-this grin worked. And how in hell they going to do it?

He stepped back in the long morning shadows, hidden from the soldiers, and picked out a route from their hiding place to the trucks. A rain-washed ravine zigged and zagged down the slope to within ten or twenty feet of the trucks. Beyond that last gap was open slope, bare rock and a patch of scrub. He squatted down, holding back the groan when his hip joint popped. "Arif." He looked into the boy's eyes, wide and brown and innocent. "Today is your first day as a brave. Are you ready?"

Arif solemnly nodded. "Are you going to take a scalp?"

"Nash!"

Devon held up his hand, shaking his head at Granwin's protest. "No scalp. See the smaller truck down there? Both of you?"

They nodded.

"We're going to ease down that ravine. Hurry, but be quiet about it. Then, when I tell you, Arif, I want you to walk out so that soldier standing by the gun can see you." Devon pulled Arif to the door and pointed to be sure the boy understood. "Get his attention. Ask him if you can have something to eat, anything.

"Don't run or act crazy because I don't want him to yell or start shooting. Just make him think a hungry kid is curious. Get his attention away from the ravine, and while you're distracting him, I'll come up from the back of the truck. Understand?"

"What then?" Granwin asked.

Devon ignored her question, knowing she knew the answer. "Then get in the truck. I'll cut a brake line, do something to the other vehicle, and we'll get out of here.

"The helicopter? And the soldiers?" she asked.

Devon looked at Granwin and shook his head. Why did she have to bring up the hard questions? "You just get in the vehicle. I'll take care of them." *Somehow.*

Devon slid into the ravine, then turned to help Arif and Granwin. Crouched so his head stayed below the lip of the ravine, Devon led the way in an awkward duck waddle, hip screaming, hands on the side of the narrow ravine, feet sliding over the rain-washed granite. When they had gone what he judged was the closest point to the trucks, Devon stopped and peered up over the edge of the ravine.

The soldiers had formed a crescent around the Nissan and were moving toward it, weapons at the ready. Time was getting short. He turned and whispered, "Arif, you stay right here. When Renée and I get to that big rock—" He pointed down the ravine to a boulder. "—I'll give you a wave, and you climb out and put on your act."

"Okay, Chief."

Devon gave him a pat on the back. "Go get 'em, brave."

When Devon and Granwin reached the boulder, Devon turned to Granwin. "Watch what happens. When the soldier goes down, you come out fast, grab Arif and get him in the truck."

"What if something happens to you?" she asked.

"Then try to get him out of here the best you can." Devon waved back at Arif, squatting back up the ravine.

When Arif scrambled out and started toward the soldier, Devon wormed his way over the lip of the ravine and belly-crawled toward the vehicle, gritting his teeth when he crawled over a dried buckhorn, prickly with thorns. He froze when a horned lizard as big as his leg flicked a droplet of dew from the tip of a thorn, then scurried off with a rattle of stones and dried branches.

Devon waited and baked, exposed to the rising sun and the soldier on the rocky ground.

"*Min fadlac,*" Arif called out and waved at the soldier, a big grin plastered on his face.

Great timing, but don't lay it on too thick. Most adults didn't take kids seriously, anyway, he remembered, and this guy wasn't either. The soldier reached down and hitched up his web belt, sagging under the weight of canteen and a half-dozen grenades dangling from his shoulder harness, then waved Arif away, wagging the long barrel of the machine gun in his direction, yelling back in Arabic.

Devon eased to his feet and crept the final ten yards to the vehicle, an old Land Rover. Devon stopped behind the Rover's side rails. His stomach boiled, the MRE chili beans working overtime. Devon pushed his discomfort to the back of his mind and shifted his feet, feeling with his toes for a good grip on the slick, chalky soil, mouth open and nostrils flared as he tried to quiet his breathing. He reached into his hip pocket for the knife and eased it out.

Does it click real loud when it opens? Last night was a blur. He had no memory at all of the knife opening, only the sharp tingle when he pricked his thumb, and of Arif's eyes, big in the light of the fire.

This was insane. He really wasn't a brave. He was a farmer, and at best, an ordinary soldier. He had only killed once with a knife—the woman in the desert. Devon shook his head and pushed the old memories away. He had brought Granwin and Arif too far to go back. And he had promised Sara. He found the knurled button with his thumb and flipped open the blade.

The blade locked open with a loud, metallic click. The soldier casually turned his head just as Devon sprang for him. The soldier twisted, reaching back for the machine gun. Devon locked his fingers in the soldier's web belt and jerked him over the side of the Rover, grenades flying in every direction. The soldier's feet caught on the side rails, and he went over face-first, arms flailing, calling out in Arabic. His yell abruptly stopped when he slapped the ground. Devon pounced on the man's back, pulled his head back, and slid the serrated blade under his throat.

"Nash, please." Granwin emerged on all fours from the ravine. The furrows returned to her forehead as she stared at the man's face. "Must he die?"

The body underneath Devon lay still. It was too late to take *coup*. The soldier's soul had already left to join the eagles or the lizards. Devon rolled the body over. The soldier's head flopped un-naturally on his neck, and a bloody face stared back, not seeing. Devon rested his fingers lightly against the soldier's chest. The last feeble beats pulsed through the body; his arms trembled, then fell limp.

Devon finally answered Granwin's question. "Yes. For Arif." Devon sliced one of the straps on the dead man's harness and caught a can-shaped grenade that fell loose, then climbed to his feet. "And for you." He snapped the knife shut and turned so he could see over the side of the Rover.

Arif stood alone on the slope looking back at them. Behind Arif, one of the soldiers pointed back toward them, waving at the helicopter. His shouts carried over the distant swishing of the blades as several of the men sprinted in their direction. Others jogged up the mountainside toward the huts, moving to flank them.

Devon sprinted toward the big truck, yelling at Arif as he ran by. "You did good. Now go jump in the Rover, scout." Arif just stood there as Devon ran past.

Devon fumbled the old underwear bag of pipe tobacco out of his hip pocket and worked the frayed rubber band off as he ran. He double-wrapped the rubber band around the grenade's butterfly handle and pulled the pin. Across the slope someone began shooting, short bursts, flat pops, the old AK noise. Devon twisted the gas tank cover from the truck and dropped the grenade down the filler throat, then snatched open the truck door. When he climbed up the high step, undisciplined soldiers' litter greeted him. The cab reeked with the rancid smell of old food, sweat and oil. He slid behind the wheel and scanned the dash.

Where's the ignition?

No ignition key—switches and gauges labeled in scribbly Cyrillic. The only thing he could make out from the dash was a nameplate with '*Ural*' in Roman letters. Bullets rattled against the door, slapping it against his leg. How long was the rubber band going to last in the gas tank before it dissolved and released the butterfly handle? Seconds, minutes? Was the grenade a white phosphorous or fragmentation? Or was it only a smoke grenade? Or did it matter? Any one of the three would play hell in the gas tank.

He wiggled the shift lever to make sure the *Ural* was in gear, then mashed his foot down on the old-style floor starter. The truck lurched forward. He held down the starter, and the truck moved a little faster, flywheel teeth grinding against the starter bendix. He tried to turn the steering wheel, but the tires were too deep in the sand. A little more grinding and the truck jerked free from the sand, rolled a few slow yards downhill, then a few more. A crewman leaned out of the helicopter door and stared at the swaying truck, then swung his machine gun around.

Devon snatched his head back as a stream of bullets ripped the mirror from the side door, cracked over the door and through the cab. Glass shattered and sprayed over his face and arms, leaving only the windshield's metal frame behind. An electrical smell added itself to the others odors in the cab. Bullets tore through the sheet metal and clattered against the engine block. A fender flew by, ripped from the truck frame. The same smell that had raised the hair on his neck in the desert, the addictive essence of gasoline, washed over him.

Suddenly clear of the loose sand and rolling across slick shale, Devon felt the steering wheel turn. With both his hands pulling across the top of the steering wheel, the truck gradually angled back toward the helicopter, skidding when it crossed a patch of slick granite. He slapped the transmission out of gear and strained against the wheel with his upper body. Now the helicopter squatted directly ahead, aligned with the bullet-scarred nose of the truck.

The old Russian truck gathered momentum in a life of its own. Devon kicked the door open and vaulted out into the stream of tracers pouring from the helicopter. His leg crumpled when he hit the ground, and his head slapped hard granite. He sprawled there for a moment, stunned, cheek against the cool rock. Devon pushed himself up with his hands and shook his head, sucking in big gulps of air trying to get his breath back. Bullets ricocheted off a patch of shale, splattering him with soft chunks of limestone as they whined over his head.

"Get up, Chief." Small hands tugged at his arm. "Hurry. They're coming."

Devon pulled his feet under him and let Arif push him toward the Rover. A bullet grabbed at his shirt. Another cracked by his ear.

"Come quickly," yelled Granwin. She was behind the Rover's wheel, racing the engine.

Devon tumbled over the side rails and into the short bed. Arif piled in on top and they both curled around the machine gun pedestal mount as Granwin slewed the Rover around and gunned it down the mountainside, swerving back and forth as they raced away from the bullets.

Devon raised up to look back. "Please, Lord!" he pleaded.

The *Ural* was careening toward the helicopter. He reached over his head, grabbed the pistol grip and struggled to his feet, swaying behind the machine gun. He reached out for the end of the ammo belt, fumbling with the gun's cover latch. The Rover bounced and fish-tailed, throwing Devon back into Arif and spilling the ammo in a twisted tangle in the bed, loose grenades bouncing around them like pinballs.

He climbed back up to see the helicopter's blades blur as the rpms rose. Ever so slowly, the ungainly bird lifted clear of the ground, clawing to clear the *Ural* lumbering on a collision course down the slope. The firing stopped as the soldiers on the ground watched the helicopter struggle to rise. One raised his rifle and shook it over his head as the helicopter tilted, nose forward, slipping down the slope away from the truck. The *Ural*'s battered cab slipped under the tail rotor and, for a moment, the helicopter hovered safe over the *Ural* as it passed underneath.

The truck humped its back, then exploded, surrounded by a greasy orb of flame. A chunk of bodywork shot up into the tail rotor. The helicopter suddenly spun back into the center of the fireball. A second blast thundered across the mountainside and the helicopter disintegrated into a tangled mass of wreckage, tumbling down the slope leaving a trail of flames and debris scattered across the mountainside.

Devon looked at Arif, hanging on to the pedestal with both arms. "We're home free, scout," he yelled, grinning despite the cuts stinging his face.

The dust kicked up by the Rover soon obscured the wreckage and fire. Behind them, the shallow ruts left by the vehicles going up the mountain crisscrossed their tracks coming down. Devon twisted around and let the wind blow the dust, dirt and blood from his eyes.

Granwin had wrapped her shawl over her blond hair and around her neck, looking all the world like an Arab as she headed away from the sun, toward Syria, following a narrow track. She slowed as the slope leveled out and turned onto one of the roads paralleling the barren fields, holding just enough speed to keep the billowing dust from catching them.

Devon pulled a pair of loosely filled sandbags back to pad the bare metal frame separating them from the driver's compartment, then slid back down and pulled Arif close.

Arif looked at him with concern. "You have blood on your face. Did you get shot?"

Devon gingerly touched his face, feeling the dried crusts of blood. "No, scout, just some scratches." He blinked, hoping the irritations in his eyes were just dust. Everything felt in place. "How about you? Everything okay?" Devon asked.

Arif grinned. "Bullets flew all around, but Allah spared us, blessed be to Allah."

They both grimaced as Granwin swooped down into a dry riverbed and the Rover flew up and out. They floated above the truck bed for an instant, then slammed back down on to the sheet metal.

"*Inshallah*."

Devon nodded, more inclined to credit blind luck. He had heard *Inshallah*, "God's will," used so often as an excuse for incompetence that he had thought he never wanted to hear it again. Coming from Arif at this moment, however, it actually made sense. But God had not been kind to everyone. Devon wished he had Arif's belief—that all he had to do was to pray and the boy in the desert would be alive. As Arif bounced against his chest Devon thought that perhaps, just perhaps, this whole event *was* God's will.

"Sorry you had to see the soldier die. I—"

"I may have killed also." Arif's interruption silenced Devon. "Sheik Murshid." Arif stopped, looking into Devon's eyes.

Devon waited, realizing he was family now. He and Granwin were all Arif had.

"He took me back to the villa. He said I was to live with him, forever. I ran from him and tried to drive away. He stumbled in front of me, and I hit him with the truck. I couldn't stop. I think he is now dead." A single tear appeared in the corner of one eye, quickly wiped away.

Devon put his arms around Arif and pulled him to his chest. "He was wrong. They were all wrong, Arif. You don't worry." He raised Arif's chin. "Look at me. Have you prayed yet about this?"

Arif shook his head.

"You pray. Allah knows you were right, and will forgive you. Doesn't the Koran talk about Allah's forgiveness, and how he alone will judge good and evil?"

"Yes." Arif wiped away his tears.

"You tell me after you pray. I bet you'll feel in your heart that Allah has judged you, and you did the right thing."

Arif laid his head on Devon's chest and they both fell silent, bouncing with the jolting ride across the desert. Arif had placed his soul in the care of Allah. Devon placed his in the hands of Granwin and fell asleep.

CHAPTER 26

"You two braves wake up."

Devon squinted at the flashing light. Overhead a burning noon-day sun flickered between swaying palm fronds. Sweat soaked through his shirt where Arif's head had rested on his chest. May and summer in Mesopotamia were fast approaching.

Groggy, he pushed up on his elbows, wondering where they were. Granwin had pulled into a small depression, a mini-oasis with one lonely, stunted palm. A hint of dampness darkened a pocket of sand at the lowest spot under the shade of a rocky overhang. "Where are we?" he asked.

Granwin shrugged her shoulders as she pulled her dirty tote bag from the Rover. "Still in Iraq. But close to the border."

Devon gingerly let himself slide over the side of the Rover, testing his leg. It felt bruised and stiff, but nothing was broken. He scrubbed at his beard and stretched. His lips cracked, parched with the heat and dryness, but personal aches and pains weren't the big worry for the moment.

Men had been left alive on the mountain, men who would want to find them. Devon looked back toward the mountain range. The Rover's tires had left faint parallel indentations in the flint scree covering the ground. For an astute tracker, the impressions wound directly to the lone palm, good as a boulevard marker. As he stared into the desert heat, the tracks vanished, illusive in the shimmering glare. They would just have to trust the Iraqis didn't have a Bedouin tracker who knew this patch of desert.

He checked the Rover. Nothing shiny in the sun to give them away to an overhead observer. Over time, the battered vehicle had obviously been painted with several coats, the latest a dirty tan. Along with the collected dust and dirt, the uneven paint made for good desert camouflage, except where a row of fresh bullet scars exposed layers of brown and black. A rusting .30-caliber US M1919 machine gun drooped from the pedestal mounted in the middle of the back bed. Right hand drive, the Rover had perhaps once been a Brit Special Air

Service desert raider. It was missing the two side-mount spare tires and the windshield, but the engine had sounded good on their escape.

"Yow!" Devon pulled his bare hand away from the searing hot metal of the hood. "Motor stables will have to wait until it shades off a little more."

"Motor Stables?" asked Arif. "Such as where horses are kept?"

"Yep. It's an old army term, from when the cavalry took care of their horses." Devon patted the Rover.

Arif squatted in front of the Rover, wiped a layer of dust from the bumper and traced a line of Arabic letters. "This says the truck belongs to the Kuwait Army." He held up two grenades, both the old Mk. 2 serrated fragmentation types, one in each hand. "What are these?"

"Spoils of war," Devon answered, taking the grenades and carefully folding down the safety pins. He remembered a photo of his dad, festooned with the old-style grenades, and his letters about how unreliable the old Korean War ammo stocks were, half duds, and how glad he was to get the new baseball-shaped grenades. Devon wondered if these two were duds as he hung them from a length of wire strung across the dashboard.

"Don't mess with these," he admonished Arif.

Devon shook the two gas cans strapped to the sides. Neither had been punctured in the shooting and both felt full. "They kept the Rover in good condition." A pair of dripping water bags hung from the rear bumper. He smelled the water, took a cautious sip and spit it out, then splashed a handful over his head and face. The cool water soothed the cuts across his face, but brought the attention of a swarm of flies. He swatted at the irritating insects and started up the side of the depression to take a look to the west.

"Stay low!" Granwin motioned with her hands.

Devon dropped to his knees and crawled up the rocky slope. Except where the wind had gathered the sand in scattered pockets, the landscape was all rock, boulders or fine, sharp flint, pink and shimmering in the heat. He cautiously poked his head between two crumbling rocks, a natural portal. An endless run of desert spread toward the south. A row of poles marched off to the right. "What are those? Telephone or power?" he asked.

Granwin joined him, on her hands and knees. "I believe they mark the Syrian border. The posts extend a few hundred yards either side of the road." She squinted in the sun, staring out at the posts, brushing away the congregating flies. She wiped the sweat from the tip of her nose with the corner of her shawl, then pointed to their left where the road shimmered in the noon sun's glare about half a mile away. "I don't see any wires going to the crossing."

Devon shifted so he could see where the row of posts intersected a paved road, undulating across the desert, floating, then sinking down into the expanse of dry gravel. As he stared, the sun seemed to intensify, leaving everything either black or white in its glare. In the far distance, a truck floated across the desert, disappeared, then reappeared, a mirage. Closer, shimmering but real, the metal roof of a small building on the near side of the poles mirrored the sun. An ancient mud building sat on the other side, the remnant of an old blockhouse. As he watched, a man walked out of the blockhouse into the desert, dropped his pants and squatted.

"Border control?" Devon asked.

"Yes, I would expect so. But very inattentive, on both Iraqi and Syrian sides. As soon as I saw the buildings, I turned to the side, then pulled in here when I found the depression. No one came out or seemed to notice." She motioned toward the man squatting in the sun. "He's the only one to come out to the desert side. On the roadside, big trucks stop for a moment, then go on through. Some don't even stop. We are too far away to hear anything more than the loudest of the trucks."

"Oh, good." Arif had plopped in the shade of the overhang. He held up a bag of candy—a leftover from their MRE feast. "May I eat this?"

"Sure." Devon felt his stomach growl.

Rations had been so short since they had left the villa that he would welcome even some of Ian's stew. A big glass of Grandma's ice tea would be even better than the Irishman's rye. Close, but the tea won out, especially with tinkling, cold ice cubes. Saliva ran at the thought of food and cold tea. "Anything else to eat?"

Granwin dug through her tote and came up with the one unopened MRE and a half-liter of bottled water. "I saved this. I suspected we might need it. Here." She held out a small bottle. "Iodine tablets. For the water bags."

"Where'd you get these?"

"Survival in the Middle East means water is more important than guns. Women remember that." She offered him the MRE packet.

He shook his head. "You share the meal with Arif. I've been living too high on the hog. Bert said I was getting fat." He dropped a tablet into a water bag and shook it, then repeated the process with the other. "We'll need this before we get out of here."

"And you will need your strength." Granwin looked at him with those concern lines across her forehead again.

"I'll find us a high-class restaurant." He unfolded the worn map.

A couple of weeks—a lifetime—had passed since Houston had thumped the little dot on the map and explained to him that Irbil would be his new home. But Houston hadn't said anything about hightailing across the whole of Mesopotamia. They were a long way from Irbil and the mess hall where he had first met Granwin. He traced their route over and across *Jebal Sinjar* to his estimate of where they were now, at least fifty miles from Sinjar. Granwin had probably driven over a hundred miles, weaving around the fields and across the slopes.

"I didn't know you could drive. All those miles I covered chauffeuring you around the mountains. You didn't need me for any of that, did you?"

"Some of the customs are useful." She smiled, sunburned nose and all. "And I didn't know you gave advice on praying, especially to Allah."

Devon couldn't help but return the smile, but changed the subject back to where they would go next. "You know anything about Syria?"

Granwin frowned at him. "Didn't you hear a word I said to you this past week?" She took a sip of water from the bag. "I lived in Tadmur for many years with Grandpère."

Devon brought the map over and spread it on the ground beside Granwin. "Where's this city of Tadmur?"

"Northeast of Damascus." She pointed at the cluster of spots south of the high ground labeled *Jabal Abu Rujmayn*. "Here, where it says Palmyra on your map. Palmyra is actually the name of the ancient ruins where Grandpère searched for the Image of Christ."

Devon studied the map. "Mostly desert from here down to Tadmur. If we drive all night, and don't run into trouble, we can be there before dawn. Know anybody there who would help us?"

Granwin smiled and brushed her hair back from her face. "*Mais oui, monsieur*. Where I may also bathe and wash my hair." She turned to Arif. "And you can wash your face, too, you dirty little boy, and eat more than sweets."

Arif smiled at her, busy unwrapping a piece of candy.

Granwin sat up. With the decision to head toward Tadmur, her frown lines had disappeared. "Aunt Jeannine still lives in Tadmur. We will stay with her and find our way from there." Granwin gathered her skirt, mud-caked and dust-covered, around her knees and rocked back and forth. "Grandpère used to tell me stories of the *Résistance* and how he and Jeannine had sabotaged the *Boche* rail lines coming up from Galilee. She will know exactly what we should do!" She grinned so widely her lips cracked, and she flicked her tongue at a hint of blood in the corner of her mouth.

Devon folded the map, stuffed it in his pocket. "You and Arif eat and drink the rest of the bottled water." He sat in the wavering shade. "We'll go visit your aunt when as it gets dark." He leaned back against the soft sand, closed his eyes and laid a rag over his face, a minor barrier between his skin and the pesky flies. Soon he dozed, at peace, as strawberries and Coke floats danced through his mind. Then old Mr. Crow cawed from the rooftop as the Tuscarora began their dance.

CHAPTER 27

A distant drumbeat throbbed beneath his head and coursed through his body, irregular, closer. *Tuscarora?* Devon snatched the rag off his face and rolled to his knees. Across the depression, Arif was pounding the sand with a jack handle, thuds changing to a sharp clang when the handle glanced off a buried rock. A stubby viper undulated across the sand toward Arif's feet, stopped, head and neck poised back in a sharp S.

Devon, Arif, and the snake all seemed frozen for a moment, then the snake struck in a blur. Arif smashed down with the handle and jumped back, all in the same moment. Devon sprang to Arif's side and swung him by the waist up into the Rover's bed. The snake writhed in the sand at his feet, head crushed.

"What's going on here, scout?"

Arif pointed down to the mangled remains. "It was only a snake. I am not afraid of snakes."

"Okay." Devon stood for a moment letting his heart slow to a normal cadence. "You took care of it." A second snake slithered away into a crevice in the rock. The tail of a third flickered into view, then vanished into the rock face.

He took the handle from Arif. "No more loud noise. We don't want to alert the guards." Devon watched the buildings straddling the border. No one seemed interested. Devon looked more closely around the depression, appalled they had bedded down in a viper nest. Grandma's view of the spiritual world included vast good and vast evil. She always associated snakes with evil, and nearly beat him purple when he'd hidden away a garden snake as a pet.

Granwin sat soundlessly in the passenger's seat, her shawl draped over her head, shoulders moving back and forth. She had slept through it all.

A lilting voice of a female vocalist floated out over the hard-packed sand from the border station and Granwin stirred, pulled the shawl back. She stood, stretched her arms out to her sides, turned to Devon and smiled. "Did you rest?" she asked.

"Yep. All rested." He took a long drink from one of the water bags, then splashed a precious thimble-full over his face and shook like an old dog, clearing his head of snakes and crows and nuclear explosions. The depression was in full shade now, the dropping sun blocked by the rock perimeter.

First, he checked over the Rover, then tackled the old machine gun. Finally cool enough to touch, the metal parts retained enough heat to remind him how short life could be in the desert without water and cover. He found his face rag, shook it free of sand, wiped the bolt clean and reassembled the machine gun receiver under the pink glow of the late afternoon sky. Sweat dripping from his nose, he worked the charging handle back and forth several times, then pulled the ammo belt through and chambered a round. The gun should fire, at least once.

He vaguely remembered from his weapons orientation classes that adjustment of the headspace on the M1919 was critical; the cartridge could burst if it were set too loose. But that was all he remembered except that the instructor was a grizzled vet from the Koran War, a big scar across his nose. Devon had wondered if the scar was from bad head spacing.

"Devon. Look, the lights. I think they are searching for us."

Devon stood in the back of the Rover so he could see out across the desert. The setting sun silhouetted the border station's metal roof within a huge orange ball, pierced by the darting lights of vehicles sprinting up and down the road.

The lights occasionally turned to run down the pole line, then circle back to the road, weaving all around them, staying far enough away that the buzz of the flies was louder than the motors. Beyond the poles nothing moved across the desert, an enigmatic mingling of shadows and deeper blackness. Overhead a haze of pink dust kicked up by the circling vehicles floated across the evening sky.

In the other direction, vehicle lights flickered around the distant slopes of *Jabal Sinjar.* A line of green tracers arced from the distant slopes to fall into the desert in the direction of Sinjar, so far away as to be unheard. He hummed while he watched the wheeling vehicles, feeling for the rhythm, a pattern of movement. Was this all for them? As darkness fell, the intervals between vehicles running along the pole line increased.

"Everybody got their stuff and ready to go?" Devon asked.

Arif climbed into the passenger seat. "Ready, Chief."

Granwin slid back behind the wheel and started the engine. "Whenever you say." She pointed at the poles, already hard to see in the fading light. "Straight across?"

"Yeah. Sounds good to me." Devon leaned forward against the pedestal mount, staring back toward the border control buildings, watching for anything out of sync. A vehicle turned off the road, following the daylong pattern, then gradually lost shape in the falling darkness as it approached. By the time it passed their hidey-hole, twin headlight beams were the only indication of the vehicle's progress. "Just as soon as this one clears and turns back behind us, roll on out."

Granwin's reply was a silent nod.

Devon waited, humming an old chant under his breath, more a beat than a tune, his own war drums. The stars, one by one, emerged through the dust, brighter now as the vehicle lights vanished behind them.

"Okay, folks. It's time for us to go."

Granwin eased the Rover out of the depression and headed toward the pole line. As they approached, Devon could see the poles were at best symbolic markers, spaced a hundred or so yards apart. Devon stood behind the machine gun, wondering if either the Iraqi or the Syrians had taken the Gulf War seriously enough to mine the border. He decided that ignorance was bliss in this situation, and was glad they were riding across the gravel with their lights out. Too much knowledge could scare a person to death. Even so, his legs trembled as they passed between the poles and headed away from the rising moon. He decided mines would probably kill too many smugglers, bad business for either side, with traditions that far pre-dated any of the current politics.

"*Ahlan Wa Sahlan*," Granwin said as she gradually gained speed, the moving ground a pink-silver blur around them.

Devon leaned down toward Granwin. "What did you say?"

She flashed a smile up at him. "Welcome to Syria."

Directly ahead, the moon cast a dark shadow, hiding the immediate track in front of them. "Slow up a bit. The map showed water running down to a lake somewhere around here. Don't want you to drop us off a cliff."

Arif looked back over Devon's shoulder. "Chief, I have never seen the moon with color like this. Is there something wrong?"

Devon turned and stared at the moon, glowing with an odd pink sheen. "The dust in the sky. Maybe from the explosion in the mountain."

Granwin slowed, the Rover's engine no louder than the crunching gravel beneath their tires, interspersed with a soft hiss as they ran across infrequent patches of sand.

Beside her, Arif leaned forward, staring out into the moonlit desert. "Something in front of us," Arif announced, and Granwin slowed to a crawl.

Devon hopped down and walked ahead of the Rover. He held up his hand at the edge of a deep *wadi*. Maybe his estimate of making two hundred kilometers before dawn was a little optimistic. He turned to his left, waving Granwin to follow. After about fifty paces he came to a cut that led down into the *wadi*.

Devon waited for Granwin to pull up beside him. "Wait here, and I'll see if this gets us across." Her hand trembled on the steering wheel when he touched her. "We'll be safe soon. *Inshallah*."

She switched off the engine. "Nash Devon, you are the most exasperating man. Go find our way, but don't come back too quickly. I must use some of the toilet paper."

A man-made ramp provided access down into the *wadi*. Apparently, someone used the track on a regular basis. Shallow tire impressions led the way to a layer of soft sand in the bottom, then diagonally across and up a steep climb out the far side. When he returned to the Rover, Granwin was back behind the wheel.

"The cut goes all the way across, but it's very steep, going in and out. You want to drive or should I?" He had underestimated her in so many things; maybe she was even a better driver.

She didn't hesitate. "You take it across." She took his shoulder and slid from the seat. "Come, Arif. We will watch Mr. Devon show us how to drive."

Devon sat behind the wheel for a moment, shifting in and out of gear with his left hand. He put the transfer case in low range, backed the Rover to align it with the cut, then eased it down the ramp, coasted across the flat bottom, then up-shifted to second and climbed out the other side.

Too easy. He turned off the engine and listened. *Just a whisper of wind.* He twisted to look behind them. A black speck flashed between him and the rising moon.

"Get in the *wadi*!" he called out to Granwin and Arif.

Their heads slid back down out of sight as he jumped over the seat and swung the machine gun around to track back over the faint pole line. He searched the sky, knowing his hearing was not as good as his eyes, listening for the sound of a helicopter as he searched with his eyes.

It silently dove toward him, filling the sky. The rusty gun pivot screeched when Devon jerked the barrel skyward and pulled the trigger. Air whispered through a bird's white-tipped wings, massive as it swooped low, dipped into the *wadi*, then soared up and away, turkey-like head silhouetted for a moment against the pink moon.

"Did you see the bird, Chief? Was it an eagle?" Arif asked. He sprinted up out of the *wadi* and jumped into the Rover. "I thought it was going to carry me away. Huge, huge wings, wider than the truck!"

Devon sat back against the seat. "Sure was something big, scout. Too dark tell what. Back home, I would have said it was a soaring turkey. Out here, maybe a great bustard." If he hadn't forgotten and left the gun on safe, a dead great bustard.

"Scared me to death," added Granwin as she took her place behind the wheel and started them back on the track, heading west, away from the border.

"Me, too." Devon reached up and felt along the cold steel, searching for the safety he had not disengaged. On the right side of the machine gun, his fingers slid over the bolt handle. "Half-cocked," he muttered in disgust.

The old Special Forces sergeant had unsuccessfully tried to impress Devon with that bit of military trivia one sweltering day on the Fort Bragg range, air heavy with pine rosin. The World War II vintage Browning didn't have a safety. One pull of the handle put it in half-cock, the second made it full-cocked and ready to fire, thus at least one source of the term, "going off half-cocked." Now he knew what the sergeant had meant. Thank God the big bird had reminded him of the lesson, not an Iraq or Syrian helicopter gun ship. Something else to think about as Granwin steered them toward a distant star.

"Nash, look ahead. Another *wadi*. What do we do? This will take us forever."

"Go ahead. Slow. We'll just take 'em as they come." Stoic time again.

The moon had risen high enough over his shoulder that Devon could pick out a hint of a worn depression weaving between the low scrub, leading toward the *wadi* twisting across in front of them. From his vantage point standing behind the machine gun, Devon could distinguish irregular tracks, man or animal, not tires, running across the *wadi* bottom. As Granwin eased the Rover down the slope, a light flared far up the throat of the *wadi*.

The light died, leaving a glow, bobbing as it approached. Voices echoed down the narrow walls.

"Stop and turn off the engine!" Devon whispered.

When they leveled out on the flat bottom of the *wadi,* Granwin reversed the Rover, backed them into a corner and killed the engine. The old truck groaned and ticked as the engine cooled. They sat and waited, hidden in deep shadow.

A slow procession emerged from the darkness and marched steadily toward them.

"*Jamal,*" whispered Arif. "Camels."

The line of animals shuffled past, feet plodding in the loose sand. The lead camel grunted and wheeled to go up the way the Rover had come down. At the far end of the line, the bobbing light glowed brighter. The acrid smell of burning hashish floated through the night air.

One of the camels snorted and jerked away from the line, only feet away in the middle of the *wadi*. A voice cried out, and the glowing butt bounced closer. Devon clutched the pistol grip and tried to shrink behind the gun mount when a man, robes a silvery wraith in the moonlight, screamed at the camel and pulled it back into line. Abreast of them, a camel broke loose and kicked out at the Rover, thumping the fender with a broad hoof.

Suddenly, a beam of light flashed out, pinning them to the side of the *wadi*. Devon pointed the machine gun toward the sky and triggered off a deafening burst. The light tumbled away, flung aside as the machine gun spat a line of tracers toward the stars.

Granwin started the Rover and hit the lights. The headlights illuminated a scene of pandemonium around them, rearing pack camels and robed men, arms raised to shield their faces from the light. Granwin gunned the Rover, heading for the far side of the *wadi* and the startled string of heavily laden camels.

The camels wheeled and scattered, wild-eyed as they bolted from the lights and roar of the engine. Packs burst open flinging boxes and bales across the ravine. At the top of the far bank, a man fired, muzzle flash probing in their direction, the crack of the bullet too close. The Rover fishtailed up the side, spewing sand back over the camels and bursting by the startled man. All four wheels left the ground at the top, and the engine raced until they slapped back to the ground, slamming Devon to the bed of the Rover. His shoulder popped, stretched past ordinary limits with his fingers clamped around the machine gun pistol grip. Devon dragged himself up, spun around the pedestal mount and fired another short burst back high over the *wadi* as the Rover wove between the low bushes that popped up out of the night.

Devon stared back as they raced across the desert. Nothing seemed to be following them. He leaned down close to Granwin's ear. "Switch off the lights. We don't want to attract any more attention. Likely smugglers. I don't think they want to fool with us either."

Granwin turned off the headlights and eased up on the gas.

Nothing but darkness, black and blacker after the headlights and muzzle flashes. Devon blinked, eyes still sparkling from the gunfire and bright lights, hearing numbed from the rattle of the machine gun. He started at the passenger seat. "Arif!"

Granwin slammed on the brakes and they slid to a stop. "Where's Arif?" she asked.

"I don't know. He must've fallen out. Go back, quickly, before the smugglers find him. Lights on."

Granwin spun the Rover around and launched them back toward the *wadi* like a rocket. She flipped the headlights back on, close-set beams arcing through the sky with every bounce of the Rover. A muzzle flash spurted their way, followed by the rip of an automatic weapon. "Slow down. The smugglers think we're coming back for them. Was Arif in the Rover when we cleared the *wadi*?"

"I don't know. Lord, Lord, Nash, have I lost another boy? Do they have him?"

Her wail cut to his soul.

"The boy's okay." He had promised Sara and Arif, himself. "He's out here in the desert somewhere. You know Arif. He's either waiting for us or leading the caravan by now." He scanned the moonlit desert on each side as they accelerated back toward the *wadi*. They both ignored the gunfire. "Turn off the lights. We can see across the desert better by moonlight."

Granwin killed the lights, and the gunfire slowed, then ceased. Granwin drove slowly, the only noises an even rumble of the engine, the occasional slap of a thorn bush and the whisper of the big tires rolling across the flint.

Until a sharp whistle cut through the night.

"Stop," Devon whispered.

The Rover rocked to a standstill, engine off, before Devon could finish the word. Devon had heard that whistle before. He swiveled the machine gun to the left, listening.

Thud, shuffle, thud, shuffle.

Devon strained his eyes, trying to distinguish the lumps of bushes from his imagination in the moon glow. A camel materialized from the thorn bushes, its peculiar rolling gait almost silent in the still night air. It slowed to a walk as it approached. Devon could hear a soft voice urging the camel until it stopped beside the Rover. The camel pulled its head away from the Rover and blew, a long flutter of its nostrils.

"Tired of being a brave already? You want to be a cowboy?" Devon asked.

Arif grinned down from his perch. "Can I keep him? He obeys very well, kneeled for me to climb up and everything."

"Arif, get down from that camel and get in this truck this minute. Are you hurt? What happened—?"

"Enough talk," Devon interrupted Granwin's scolding. "Come on, Arif. You've gotta leave your buddy and go with us."

Devon helped Arif slide out of the camel saddle and into the Rover. When Devon slapped the camel on the flank, it snorted at him, turned and trotted off toward the *wadi*, slowing after a few steps to a measured walk.

"*Mass salaam*, goodbye," Arif called out after the camel. He climbed back into the passenger seat. "I was afraid you had left me. When the truck went up the hill, it threw me to the ground. The men yelled and ran around shooting, all acting crazy."

He nodded his head. "I was scared, but they yelled to each other that we were the police. I think they were more afraid than we were. They all ran and left the camel behind, so I tried to catch you. But when you turned out the lights I didn't know which way to go. How did you know I was here?"

"I prayed," answered Granwin.

And I, thought Devon.

CHAPTER 28

Leaving the smugglers far behind, they bypassed a small town and splashed across a shallow stream until they came upon an intersection of paved roads. Granwin backed away from the intersection while Arif trotted closer to read the signs in the full moonlight.

In a moment, he was back. He pointed to their right, toward the Big Dipper and the North Star, low over the horizon. "That way points to *Al Hasakah*. The sign the other way says Damascus," he reported. Arif jumped up into the seat. "Which way are we going?"

"Toward Damascus." Granwin put the Rover into gear and pulled out onto the road. "Tadmur is on the road to Damascus."

She soon had them up to highway speed, heading south into the night, then turning back more westerly, led across the empty desert by the setting moon. In less than an hour, lights brightened the horizon ahead of them.

"Should we bypass the town?" she asked.

Devon visualized the map. "Should be *Dayr az Zawr*. We'll have to find a way over the Euphrates River and get past an airfield on the other side. Go to the left to where the river broadens out, and maybe we can find a ford."

Granwin slowed and eased them off the road. Lights passed to their right, then vanished in a thin mist. Soon they came upon a glistening ribbon of water. Vapor clouds floated over the river, sliced through by slivers of moonlight.

"Now what, Nash?"

"I know," piped up Arif. "You must back up and go like the devil." His teeth shone in the moonlight.

"Shame on you, Nash, teaching the boy such profanity."

Devon could sense her frown in the moonlight.

She turned to look back at Devon. "Is he correct, then? Just 'go like the devil?'"

Devon had to laugh. "Put it in low range and wait. Let me see how deep it is. Most likely any bridges in the town will have some kind of armed guard. Crossing here might be our best bet. Spring floods have pretty much gone down." He walked along the marshy bank until he stumbled across a set of ruts. He stared through the moonlight trying to see into the shadows waiting on the far side, shivering in the damp air.

Tendrils of mist rose from the water, and a family of frogs began croaking, one, then another, until the riverbed echoed with their grunts and calls. Even with his artillery-dulled ears he could hear the whine of the mosquitoes rising from the muck. He waved Granwin over, and the Rover growled up in response, silencing the frogs.

"Tracks lead into the water, so it must be a ford. I'll wade across and you follow. But stay back and give me plenty of room in case the bottom drops off."

The river was kind. Cold water washed around Devon's ankles, but the bottom stayed firm. A breeze pushed down from the mountains, enough to disturb the mosquitoes. At the far edge, he let the Rover ease past him, then climbed into the back. When they topped the bank, a row of shanties popped up in the night. A dog began barking, yips more insistent as they got closer. The feeble glow of a lantern wavered through the darkness about the time they rolled up onto a paved tarmac.

Granwin slowed and pulled the transfer case back into high range, then gunned the motor and accelerated past the shanties and the bright lights of a distant airfield. She slowed when they came to a signpost.

It whipped past in their lights, a highway marker in Arabic. "Arif, could you read the sign?" Devon asked.

Silence. Arif's head nodded against the back of the seat.

"It said Highway Number Seven," Granwin answered for the sleeping boy.

Devon leaned closer to hear as she accelerated back to speed.

"It's the main highway to Damascus and Tadmur."

Devon looked up at the moon, now in front of them and heading quickly toward the horizon.

"Hold on," shouted Granwin as the Rover bounced down the road shoulder.

An oncoming truck, a big dual trailer monster with canvas covers flapping over the cargo beds, whipped past with a rush of turbulence.

"Jesus, did you see that coming?" asked Devon.

Granwin's voice had a catch in it. "No, not until it was on us." She paused, as if gathering her breath. "The driver didn't have any lights on—a common practice across the Middle East. Drivers think driving cark saves the batteries, or lights, or something. I should do the same or we'll draw attention." She pulled back up onto the pavement, switched off the lights and slowed in the sudden darkness, then gradually speeded up as she became more accustomed to the moonlight.

Devon patted her shoulder. "Let me know if you want me to drive."

There was a long pause before she answered. "I want you to stand by the damn machine gun and kill anyone who tries to stop us." Her voice was firm again.

Devon settled back and watched the road, squinting against the wind in his eyes. The sky behind them was tinged with a hint of pink when the houses and stores and roadside trash of a small town appeared ahead of them.

"*Gendarmes,*" Granwin announced.

She cut the engine and coasted past the single light in the town, a blue light at the top of a pole marking the police station. Devon tracked the station door with the barrel of the machine gun, but no one appeared. They silently coasted all the way to the edge of the town, rolling slower and slower. When they had almost come to a stop, Granwin engaged the clutch and let the engine catch.

"Go slow." Devon hopped off the Rover and snatched up a melon lying in a basket by the front of a shop, then sprinted to catch up. He was back in the back of the vehicle before he realized the stiffness had left his leg and thigh. "Go!"

Behind them, a light flickered and a voice shouted from the shop.

"Fool. You know how they treat thieves here." Granwin's anger carried over the wind.

Devon grinned as he jammed the melon into a corner so it wouldn't be under his feet. Stealing watermelons had always been one of his specialties. Grandpa had grown melons in a patch by the old chinaberry tree, just enough sand mixed in with the river-bottom loam to keep the nematodes from eating up the watermelon vines. On a hot summer day, a busted melon, especially a forbidden one, was better than lemon pie with real meringue.

The light faded from view as the road curved around the last building of the town. The Rover accelerated over a swell, dipped down, then back up, the rolling ground a sudden change from the flat desert and *wadis*. To their right, low mountains took form in the pre-dawn light.

"First chance, turn off the highway and take us up into the hills. We're not going to make Tadmur before light. We have to hole up somewhere for the day."

Granwin nodded. “I know these mountains. I will find us a good place.”

Around them, the rolling ground began to take form. Phantoms turned into bushes and stunted trees where the desert fought its way up the slopes toward the greenery. At each crest, Devon gripped the machine gun tighter, expecting to see a truck full of soldiers barreling down the highway toward them.

Ahead, a distant vehicle flashed over a rise then vanished into a dip. Devon stood up in the wind and braced himself behind the gun as Granwin turned off the pavement and bounced along a track leading up into the hills. Rusty dust floated up behind them, its natural tint deepened by the early slant of the sun easing up over the horizon behind them. Granwin stopped in a depression, let the vehicle pass by unseen, then put the Rover back in gear and started toward the low range of mountains.

“Are we there?” Arif scrubbed at his eyes. “I’m hungry.” He stood on the floorboard and looked over the narrow hood. “And I need to go to the toilet.”

“Almost to a safe place, Arif.” Granwin wound through a maze of crisscrossing trails, steadily heading toward the west, cutting over the ridgelines as the sun rose higher and the slopes became steeper. A profusion of bushes and low trees clinging to the sides of the bare slopes slowed their progress to a twisting crawl. They emerged from a thicket to face the carmine face of a sheer cliff, a dead end. Granwin pounded the steering wheel with her hand. Arif hopped down and slipped behind a tangle of bushes.

“What’s the matter?” asked Devon.

“For the moment, I’m lost.” Granwin stood up on her seat and looked across the ridgeline sloping away from them down to the valley.

Devon stepped across the seat to stand on the hood. Several miles away, a line of faint shadows marked an irregular row of columns flanking an ancient road. Low ruins flanked the line of columns. Too symmetrical to be natural, the columns glowed vermilion in the early sun. *Why is everything the color of blood in this forsaken land?*

Below them Highway Seven snaked beyond a small airport and vanished into a neatly laid-out town. Parallel to the road, a dark line emerged from the western desert and disappeared into the rolling hills on the other side of town. Dust rose up into the sky from a cluster of lights, an open mine operation of some sort. Groves of tall date palms wandered through the town, probably tracing an underground aquifer. An airplane took off from the airport and turned their way, skimming over slopes covered with thickets of tangled tamarisk trees and thorn bushes.

Devon hopped to the ground. “We’ve got to get under cover. I’ll scout around for some place to hide for the day.”

Granwin turned, teeth glittering in the sunlight as she flashed her old smile. “Get back in. I know where we are now.” Granwin pointed toward the red columns. “See those ruins? They mark the old boulevard of the ancient city. We must continue around the side of the mountain until the row of columns point directly at us.”

As soon as Arif was back in his seat and Devon behind the machine gun, Granwin put the Rover in gear and eased around the edge of the cliff, scraping along the wall until they emerged on the far side where she picked up a new trail, a single rut. “Watch for goats. They, and their herders, should be the only ones on the mountain.” She cut back and forth across the tangled trails so that they gradually moved across the slope. Devon kept the machine gun trained in the general direction of the circling airplane.

“Soldiers!” Arif pointed over the ridge to twin columns of dust. Two trucks popped over the crest.

Granwin gunned the motor. She spun the wheel and turned into natural cavern in the side of the mountain. “I found it.” Her voice was triumphant as she turned off the motor.

Devon blinked at the sudden darkness. “And just in time, I’d say.”

“Where are we?” asked Arif.

“Safe, child. This is a very safe place,” Granwin replied.

Devon stepped back and cautiously looked out of the cave, scanning the mountainside and sky above. The plane was a distant dot to the southwest. The trucks continued along a faint trail, working their way down toward the airfield until they were specks in the distance. While he watched, they and their dust faded from view. The tick of the Rover’s engine echoed back from the narrow cave walls.

Devon turned back to the cave. “Where’s Renée?”

Arif pointed toward a dark shadow, a recess in the cave wall.

Devon leaned against the Rover. It had been a long night. “Renée, what you doing?”

Her voice reverberated as she walked deeper into the cave. “Grandpère brought me to the caves many Sunday afternoons. His main work was in the ruins below, but his personal curiosity remained here in the hills. He suspected the icon he sought was hidden in one of the caverns, perhaps buried with an old Christian.”

Arif clutched his prayer rug under his arm. “May I go outside?”

"Sure. Go ahead. If the airplane or trucks come back, give a whistle and hide in the shadows. Be still and quiet, Scout, and they won't spot you." Devon held up the melon. "Breakfast will be waiting for you when you come back."

He flicked open the knife and sliced the stolen melon. Green skinned and soft pulp, not the sweet-smelling watermelons from grandpa's special patch, but edible as he sampled the pithy meat.

"Granwin, come get some melon."

She was kneeling in a small recess in the side of the cave wall. Devon stopped when he saw she had her cross in her hands, head bowed.

After a moment she looked up and smiled at him. "Grandpère's grave."

Devon bent close to read the words, *Jean Roussel, 1902-1970*, chiseled in the rock wall, almost hidden in the lichens covering the old rock. "Doesn't say much."

"The Arabs established a free government of their own in Damascus after the Great War. Perhaps you've read of the Arab nation in the writings of the British officer, Colonel Lawrence. Afterwards, the French and British governments, sanctioned by the League of Nations mandate, sabotaged the Arab alliance.

"To this day, many Syrians have harsh memories of the French occupation. So Jeannine suggested a simple marker which would not draw attention to Grandpère and his work, and a resting place that would not attract desecrators." She shook her head. "I didn't expect to see his grave again in my lifetime."

"You never travel to Syria?"

"Not with the troubles. I visited Aunt Jeannine once, several years after I married Alfred, but I am no longer welcome in Syria." She laughed. "About as welcome as you are, I would expect."

Devon squatted down beside her and handed her a slice of melon. "Could you get us into the British consul in Tadmur? Would we be safe there? Or should we try to make it to Damascus and the American embassy?"

She bit off a chunk of fruit and chewed for a moment before she answered. "You sound like Arif with his questions." She wiped her hands on her skirt, then rearranged the rocks covering the mound at the base of the wall. "First, I think we should find Aunt Jeannine's home once it becomes dark." She dabbed at her mouth with her skirt tail and made a face at the dust. "There we can eat, bathe and find out if it is truly safe for us to go to the consul's office, or if we should try to get to Damascus and your embassy."

Devon left Granwin with her meditations and walked out to the mouth of the cave. He looked across the valley, eyes shaded against the morning sun, and searched for a path down the mountain. The tamarisk trees glistened, dew sparkling from their fine green leaves. Tiny blossoms gave the trees a hint of color. Half-hidden under the trees, trails twisted across the hills and down toward the valley and town. To his surprise, the ground he thought barren shimmered with green.

The line, now discernable as a huge petroleum pipeline, skirted the town leading off to the east. A helicopter climbed up from the airfield and circled over the distant ruins. Sightseers. Or searchers.

"Arif!" Devon stepped out of the shadow, looking around to make sure the boy was not out in plain sight.

"I am here, Chief." Arif sat cross-legged on his prayer rug just outside the cave's mouth. He studiously ploughed the ground with a stick, trapping a large beetle in a miniature tank trap. He broached the trench wall and urged the beetle out of the opening.

Devon squatted beside him. "You finish morning prayers?"

Arif nodded.

"Just thinking?"

Arif took a deep breath. "Yes." The beetle crawled over the stick. Arif looked up at Devon, eyes wide in his dust-covered face. "Are all Iraqis evil? Is Islam evil?" Arif asked.

"No, of course not. Bad people grab power any way they can. Some use money, some the sound of their voice, some use religion—Jews, Christians, Muslims, even atheists. You stay true to the teachings of the Koran as long as you are satisfied they lead you the right way. You know many good Iraqis and Muslims, don't you?"

Arif looked up at Devon and nodded. "But soon you will go back to America and Mrs. Granwin will return to—" He shrugged his shoulders. "—England, or France, someplace else." He stared back out at the circling helicopter. "Where will I go?" His voice was soft with resignation.

The answer was easy and quick. "You'll go with me."

Devon suspected that if he walked away from the mountain and left Arif alone on the slope, the kid would survive, beat them all like he killed the snake. But he wasn't leaving Arif anywhere. To hell with promises. He would do this just because it was right.

"Truly?" Arif's grin was worth any risk.

"You betcha." He handed Arif the knife. "Now come inside and eat some melon. It's all we've got. Tonight, we'll go into town, find

Renée's aunt and eat good." He pointed toward a scattering of goats far down the slope. "If we don't find her, we'll have goat stew up here."

Inside, Arif carved his way through the melon while Granwin sat on the ground with bits of rock scattered on the ground around her. She pushed them back and forth, stared at them, rearranging until the puzzle from the monastery was back together. She pulled the remnant of Devon's notebook from the tote bag and began copying letters from the fragmented tablet. "Remember, you told me it was simple," she said.

"What was simple?" He sat beside her after scanning the rocks for snakes.

"The riddle." She pointed at the rocks. "The words on the box and scratched on the rock were the key. I solved the code last night. I was checking to make sure I had not misread the words in the bad light." She held out the notes. "See."

"No, I don't, smart aleck. What are those letters, Greek?"

"Yes. Classic form, typical of artisans, in the style you see throughout Syria and Mesopotamia attributed to the beginning of Christianity. Wait a moment." She crossed out a selection of letters and substituted a new row below them, and nodded her head in satisfaction. "Now to translate to English for the ignorant masses." She added a third row of letters below the others and handed him the notebook.

Devon slowly deciphered her smudged pencil marks, reading the words out loud. "The Image of Christ lies behind the green water, the way to the light, the way to everlasting Christ, Son of God and father, savior of—" He paused.

"Caesar Philippi. At times you try very hard to convince me of your ignorance. The town's modern name is Baniyas, south of Mount Hermon. Look it up on your map. Finish reading, then tell me what you think it all means."

Devon continued. "—some obscure town for which I will take your word." He read on. "In the shadow of the mount of Moses, love of God, man, woman and child are proclaimed to all." Devon shook his head. "I don't understand any of this. Is there some special meaning? Where is the green water?"

"I have no idea what any of it means," Granwin replied. One-by-one, Granwin picked up the pieces of marble and began placing them randomly in with the litter of stones mounded under the inscription.

"Don't you want to save the tablet?"

"I will save it the way it should be saved. Grandpère searched all his life for the image." Now it was her turn to shrug her shoulders.

"The tablet may be the icon for which he searched. I don't know, but these are the first words I have seen, in all my years of searching, that mention the Image of Christ. So it must mean something. Even more to Grandpère than to me. He dug his entire life in these deserts, searching for the roots of Christianity."

She buried the marble fragments under other bits of rock and sifted a handful of dirt over the mound. "I will not deny him, even in death, this treasure. I give them to his memory and leave them here in his safekeeping." She took the notebook back and put it in her tote bag. "Besides, I now know the words. Perhaps, someday I may understand their meaning."

CHAPTER 29

Arif stood and shook the dust from his rug, evening prayers completed. Below them, the town was quiet, the last shrill *muezzin* finally silent. Devon topped off the Rover with gas while they waited, emptying one of the cans. Before long, Arif was asleep in the Rover's passenger's seat. Granwin sat silently behind the wheel, eyes staring into the dark.

Devon leaned close to Granwin. "Close your eyes for a few minutes. We'll go after midnight when everything is quiet." As he watched, the last shop lights dimmed, leaving only a solitary streetlight to mark the center of town. One by one, lights in the outlying residential quarter went dark. The distant airfield lights flicked off, all at once, until only a line of green markers lined the runway.

Devon leaned back against the side of the Rover, but sleep escaped him. Too many unsolved puzzles running through his head. Outside, the moon rose, the crescent filling, an even deeper pink than the night before. Shadows broke the slope below into a series of jagged fissures, softened by a scattering of trees. What had happened to all the gently rolling hills and trails he had mapped out in his head?

When the moon started toward the horizon, he looked over at Granwin, now awake and watching him from the driver's seat. "Ready?" he asked.

She nodded.

He pointed at the faint trail they had agreed upon when it was still light. "Go easy. I'll try to guide you as well as I can."

Granwin rolled the Rover out of the cave mouth and followed Devon's twisting directions down the slope.

He leaned forward, hanging on to the machine gun, searching out the ruts he thought he had memorized. Darkness enveloped them when a heavy cloud rolled across the moon, leaving them perched at the edge of an abyss.

"Hold up. I can't see a thing."

Granwin slowed the Rover to a stop, and they waited until the pink wash of moonlight flowed back up the slope.

The air warmed as they dropped down the mountain, weaving back and forth from ridge to ridge, searching out the worn trails. Below them, a helicopter took off from the airfield, landing light sweeping across a low row of houses not far down the slope.

"Stop!"

Granwin turned off the engine and they waited.

Patience, Grandma had said when he had disturbed the water with a skipping rock. Patience marked a true Indian she had said. Devon tried to regain some of the patience she had beaten into his rebellious butt. Soft night sounds, bird twitters and the hum of insects floated around them. Devon watched the helicopter circle. He drew a deep breath. A dusty smell rose from the desert, carrying a heavy aroma of a flowering fruit. Apple, fig, something exotic. He wondered if pomegranate blossoms were fragrant. Damn, what an agricultural expert he was.

The helicopter climbed, crossed over the moon, then rose higher and turned south, toward Damascus.

Devon realized he was holding his breath. He slowly exhaled. "Okay, let's try it again," he said.

Granwin eased the Rover along the ill-defined trail. Limbs slapped the sides of the Rover and brushed over Devon, lost for a moment in the tangle of low trees.

"What're those?" Devon felt impelled to whisper as they glided by a ghostly structure set into the hillside.

"Tombs. The hills are full of grave sites, many very ornate, all robbed bare for many years, since I was a child."

The air filled with an aroma that reminded Devon of the American southwest as the tires crunched a low bush. Was it mesquite? A deeper black appeared ahead, jerking his mind back to the trail. "Turn right!"

Granwin twisted the wheel, and the Rover slid sideways. Thin limbs whipped across Devon until the Rover crunched to a stop, tangled in the low limbs of a tree. Granwin reversed, hung for a moment. She gunned the engine and the tires dug into the rocky ground. A heavy branch snapped and the Rover pitched free with a jerk. Granwin eased the Rover back on the trail. Cautiously, they moved forward. Devon glanced down.

Arif slept in his seat, oblivious to their haphazard trek.

Without warning, they came upon a wide track. Granwin speeded up and turned toward the town lights. Devon stood erect behind the machine gun, more for show than looking for a fight. Shooting was the last thing he wanted to do. Granwin slowed, then eased them up and over an earthen mound. Widely spaced floodlights gave out just enough light to see they had crossed over the pipeline Devon had spotted from the cave mouth.

When they entered Talmud, the streets were neater than most, certainly cleaner than Baghdad or even Riyadh. No piles of trash, no scraggly dogs, no rubble, and not as much new construction as Devon was accustomed to seeing. If Riyadh and Baghdad were representative, construction cranes and scaffold-surrounded buildings were as much the norm in Middle Eastern cities and towns as in the West.

Here, or at least in this part of Talmud, the owners were content to leave the town as it had been for years. On each side of the street clusters of homes and shops began to show more detail as the moon dropped toward the distant hills, replaced by the building grayness of dawn. At the next corner, a startled face in a window stared at them for a moment, then withdrew, apparently unwilling to have an early morning discussion with an armed patrol.

Granwin slowed the Rover to a crawl, reading the signs at each intersection. She turned up a narrow street bounded on each side by stucco walls. The rumble of their engine reflected off the walls, glistening white when they passed the occasional streetlight.

Devon lurched against the machine gun at an unexpected stop in the middle of a narrow alley. Granwin slid from her seat, engine running, dropped to her knees by the curb and picked at a chunk of rock set in the wall. She frowned, replaced the rock and shuffled to the side to dig her fingers under a second.

Devon turned his head back and forth, looking from one dark end of the alley to the other. "What are you doing?" he whispered.

A shadow flitted across the far end of the alley.

She replaced the rock then climbed to her feet to unlock a small door set in the wall beside a larger gate. A moment later, the gate scraped opened just enough for Granwin to slip back out. Without a word, Devon dragged the gate wide and Granwin drove the Rover through. He scanned the alley. No one in sight as he closed the gate behind her.

Granwin parked in the far corner of a small courtyard under the dark shadow of a vine-covered trellis. She killed the engine as Devon slid the gate shut, then walked to the center of the courtyard. He stood silently for a moment, listening to the sounds of the town. No sirens, no loud voices, no pounding on the gate. A solitary dove cooed from the far corner of the courtyard, turning and strutting, stopping to stir dust up into the first rays of the morning sun.

Granwin, her smile widening, surprised Devon by pulling him close and putting her hands on his shoulders. She stood for a moment, her eyes searching his face, then slid her arms around his neck and pressed her body against his. “We’re safe, Nash. I have brought us to a safe place.”

Devon put his arms around her waist, holding her lightly, not sure what she intended. Was this affection or just relief? Whatever, he was afraid to speak, to spoil the moment for her, for him. Far away, a cock crowed. Devon closed his eyes and let the smell of her hair, the dusty pungency of desert sage commingled with unwashed body smells, his and hers, sink into his brain.

Desert sage. That’s what the broken bushes were. Not mesquite. “Sage,” he whispered.

“Sage?” She looked up with a question in her eyes.

“The smell in your hair. It reminds me of Nevada. Sagebrush.”

She smiled. “Playing Indian?” She stepped back and looked up at the silent house.

“I take it this is your aunt’s house.”

“Yes. I lived in this house for—” Her voice had a tiny catch. “—many years. Too many to forget Grandpère’s habits. The key was his, left there all these years.” She took a deep breath. “Stay with Arif while I see if Aunt Jeannine is alone.” She pulled away and vanished into a small doorway leading into the house.

Overhead, the sky evolved to a cloudless pale blue as he waited in the middle of the small enclosed courtyard. Glistening green fig trees grew in each corner of the yard—the fruit, tiny green spheres, weeks away from ripening.

Arif had slept through the trip, slumped back against the seat cushion. Down by his feet in the footwell a rusty frag grenade lay abandoned beside several small figs, probably scraped from the orchards in the drive down the mountain.

Devon fished out the grenade and slid it out of sight behind the driver’s seat.

Empty windows in the neighboring houses looked down into the courtyard, but none of the neighbors seemed interested. Upstairs, a murmur of voices floated through a window, muted by a partially closed shutter. Devon heard the throb of a helicopter in the distance and stepped back under a tangled grapevine, lush with big, green leaves and tiny, immature grapes.

Arif still hadn’t stirred. Curled in the seat, his shoulders moved with each breath.

Devon gently shook Arif’s shoulder.

Arif stretched, scrubbed his eyes and looked around. "Do they have anything to eat here?"

Over their heads, a shutter banged open just as a calico cat leaped from the courtyard wall, thumping down on the hood like a bass drum. The cat arched, stretched and began licking a long rear leg, ignoring Devon and Arif. Granwin's face appeared overhead, beside an older woman with long, gray-streaked black hair glistening in the sun. Granwin leaned out the window and waved them up, then stood back for the other woman to pull a curtain over the window.

"Come on, scout. I bet they've got something for you to eat up there." Devon lifted Arif out and led him, still half asleep, up the narrow stairway. The two women were pulling plates from a wheezing refrigerator, loading a small table set in the middle of the floor. Three other doors led off a back wall, one to a bath, the other two rooms too dark to tell what they held. Devon supposed they were bedrooms. He wondered if anyone else stood waiting in the darkness.

"Nash, this is Aunt Jeannine." Granwin beamed, turning to the older woman. A dark robe covered Jeannine from shoulders to the tiled floor. Tangled hair fell to her shoulders and half-covered her face until she swept it back with her hand. Her face was sharp, desert-Bedouin hard, with the nose of a hawk that she held high as she stared back at him through coal-black eyes.

Devon decided this was the time to put on his polite cap and tried his most civil French. "*Le bon matin, madame. J'espère que vous soyez bien. Vous remercier beaucoup pour votre hospitalité.*"

Jeannine looked at him like he had spit on the floor, a frown on her face. Devon knew he hadn't said anything vulgar, just a good morning-hope-you-are-well-thanks-for-your-hospitality phrase right out of the textbook. What the hell was he supposed to say?

The old woman shook her head, gray hair swishing across her face, and replied in English, "Did you learn your French in a bordello?"

Granwin giggled like a schoolgirl, then laughed, her old laugh from the first day he'd met her. She flopped back in a chair by the table, tears running down her face.

"You must speak English, so I can understand you." Jeannine shook her head. "What a terrible accent." She looked at Granwin. "Did you teach this American to speak French? He speaks worse than the colored man you brought to see me."

Jeannine scowled down at a bewildered Arif, spoke to him in Arabic and pointed to a small sink between the refrigerator and a stove. Arif dragged a chair over and proceeded to wash. Equally bewildered, Devon joined him. Arif gave him a slight shrug of his shoulders.

"Here, boy. Sit and eat, then rest." She motioned toward the window with a swirl of gray hair. "I see the truck with the gun in my courtyard." She stared at Devon. "It must be stolen. What has happened?" Aunt Jeannine spread a bountiful table as she quizzed them, bringing bottles of water from the refrigerator. "Are the police after you? What are your plans?"

Granwin ignored all Jeannine's questions, tore a hunk of unleavened bread from the plate-sized sheet and piled it with hummus for Devon. "Try this. It's real food, not from a plastic bag."

Across the table, Arif made short work of a plate of leftover dough balls. Mouth half-full, Arif offered one to Devon. He cautiously bit into it to discover a thin crust hiding a spicy meat stuffing. But best of all was the chilled mineral water.

Granwin chewed for a moment, then finally answered Jeannine in French. Devon had always had an idea that he spoke French pretty well, but he only caught the odd phrase, not enough to clearly understand except for the Anglicized words like "atomic" and references to Hussein and a nod toward Arif accompanied by a sad face.

He finally cleared his mouth enough to interject his own question. "Does *la dame de la langue aiguë* believe we can make it to the American Embassy in Damascus?"

Jeannine closed her eyes and shook her head. "You are an American, truly, so rude." She stared at Devon, eyes narrowed, then turned to Granwin. "Do you forget you are French, or perhaps today you are British? You change like the little lizard on a leaf and I can't keep track. Now you want to go to the American embassy, where—in Damascus, *chéri?*

"*Oui*, the American Embassy on *Rue al Mansour*. If we go there, we can take care of Arif. At the British or French embassies, I don't know what will happen to the boy."

Jeannine's scowl seemed to spread. "Is he a child of Islam?"

Granwin nodded. "Yes, but we have promised to care for him."

"You say his father is dead? And his mother?" Jeannine took Arif's face in her hand.

Arif's eyes flashed from Jeannine to Granwin, finally swiveling over to Devon as they spoke.

Granwin shook her head. "She was killed. We barely escaped with our lives."

"By the Iraqi police," added Devon. A less-than-half-truth, but easier to explain than a renegade Pakistani colonel.

Jeannine shook her head. "The boy should stay with me. It is not right he should go with you, or especially with the American. Who will see to his prayers?"

"No. He's my responsibility now. I'll make sure he is taken care of. In all ways." Devon reached across the table and put his hand on Arif's small shoulder. "That okay with you, Arif?"

Arif's eyes flickered from Jeannine to Granwin. He looked up at Devon, face solemn, and nodded.

Devon looked across the table at Jeannine. "But we do need your help. Can we use the Rover to get to the embassy?" He asked Granwin, silent through his exchange with Jeannine. "Does that make sense?"

Granwin pondered for a moment. "Makes as much sense as anything else we have done." She stood and poured Devon a cup of thick coffee.

The morning breeze fluttered the faded window curtain while a single vehicle puttered down the alley.

The town was quiet, much quieter than Devon had expected. He suddenly wondered if the townspeople had been warned to take cover from fallout. "Has there been any special news from Iraq?" he asked.

"*Oui.*" Jeannine gestured toward a small television. "*Al Jazeera*, the television news program, speaks of more bombing by the Americans and many people killed." She looked at them sharply. "Part of your affair?"

Devon shrugged. "No, I don't expect so. What did they say was the targets?"

"The news reported a large explosion, without any details, no mention of *atomiques*."

"We should rest, then leave when it's dark." Devon shook his head. "We don't intend to implicate you in anything." Devon sat back and looked at Jeannine, wondering if she was going to cause trouble with Arif. "You'll help us?"

Jeannine shrugged. "You give me no choice."

Her words said she would help, but the look in her eyes left Devon wondering.

CHAPTER 30

Jeannine's sour mood had spoiled Devon's appetite, but the boy's seemed to be undeterred by the conversation. Devon sipped the bitter coffee while Arif attacked everything Jeannine laid on the table.

"Come," Jeannine said to Granwin, and the women left the room, leaving Devon with Arif, his coffee and serious doubts that they had sheltered in the right place. Jeannine's reaction to Arif bothered him. Was she going to cause a problem? She was family, at least Granwin's. Listening to the happy chatter from the back room, he tried to sweep his concerns from his mind, but something kept nagging him.

When the women returned, Jeannine wore a sweeping gray dress and an embroidered shawl over her shoulders, much the Middle Eastern woman with her hair pulled back in a bun and held by a long, turquoise comb. "I am going to the market. What specifically do you need?" Jeannine asked.

Devon deliberated for a moment. "White paint, enamel, and a brush, if it's not too expensive."

Jeannine shrugged. "To be rid of you, no price is too high." She turned to Granwin. "*Chéri*, look in my *commode*. I think you will find a skirt and blouse to fit. Your lingerie, you will have to wash, and for the boy also. I have nothing here that would fit. The men at the market would ask too many questions about clothes for those two. Paint—" She waved her had around the room. "—Goodness knows I needed to paint for years." She looked at Devon. "And for our linguist's benefit, a *commode* is not a toilet. It is furniture with drawers, for clothes, *comprendre?*

"*Oui, madame. Merci*," Devon replied.

He followed her down to the courtyard, peeking up and down the street as Jeannine left, then securing the door behind her. The everyday sounds of people hurrying to work on foot and on bicycle, exchanging quiet words, reverberated from the stucco walls as he began. He focused on the rusty bolts, pushing away the images of Granwin strapped soundless in the reactor room chair, Sara in his arms with blood pulsing from her wounds, with work and sweat. He dismantled the machine gun, carefully cleaned it, then turned to the mount.

"Damn!" he exclaimed. The last rusted bolt snapped off, releasing the pedestal mount from the Rover and scraping his knuckles to the bone. He stopped to stretch and wipe his eyes, scanning the sky above. A soaring pair of buzzards wheeled overhead. White cumulous clouds were building in the background, an unlikely promise of rain. He leaned back against the Rover, still cool under the shade of the trellis. Heat radiated back from the concrete pavers. Closer to the Mediterranean Sea, the temperature was much warmer here than in the Iraqi highlands they had just left.

A screech disrupted the quiet of the morning, the squall of the small entrance door opening. He laid his hand on the dismounted machine gun. The ammunition belt hung several feet away, draped from the grapevine.

"Assistance, *s'il vous plaît.*" Jeannine angled through the opening, shopping net dangling from one hand, a bucket of paint from the other. "Close the gate behind me."

Devon took the paint and brush and worked the rest of the morning alone with his memories, pausing only when a vehicle rumbled by or footsteps clattered down the alley. Devon let Granwin have her time with Jeannine while he took care of the Rover. He forced his mind to dwell on the good—Arif's off-key attempts to whistle the complex lilting tunes that floated from the radio, Granwin's arched eyebrow and smile—all the time with one eye on the alley door, waiting for it to burst open.

The late night drive across the desert and down the mountain finally caught up. Devon relaxed for a moment in the paint-splattered seat. Grape leaves slowly twisted in the afternoon breeze, dipping over the walls, glittering in the sunlight and teasing his eyes until he dozed off.

"You missed lunch." Arif's voice woke him.

Devon snapped his head up and rubbed the crust from his eyes.

Arif held out a condensation-covered bottle of cold water and a platter of bread, cheese and olives.

Devon splashed some of the water over his face. "Thanks, scout. Everything okay upstairs?"

"They talk too much. Can I paint?"

"Knock yourself out, kid." Devon pointed toward the brush and paint, and Arif fell to, adding his touch to the impromptu paint job.

Devon picked up the machine gun and ammunition belt. He carried them back under the shadow of the trellis where a sagging door revealed a large room under the house, an old stable from the smell and bits of old straw underfoot. He carefully arranged the gun and ammo on a shelf along the back wall beside a wash sink, laid out so he could deploy the weapon if someone burst in. He shook his head. Holding off the hordes with ammo belt over one shoulder and machinegun in hand like Audie Murphy? No, he wasn't a hero, not the kind Murphy was.

An old portable radio caught his eye, perched on the edge of a narrow shelf over the sink. When he clicked on the radio, a serious Arabic voice boomed from the speaker until he quickly snapped it back off. Devon glanced out the door to see if the noise had attracted anyone.

No one else appeared. Devon joined Arif and the calico in the courtyard.

Arif stepped back from the Rover, brush in hand, a pensive look on his face as he touched up a fender, then added a spot of white to the tips of the calico's ears as it wound around between his legs.

Devon held his tongue. The cat didn't seem to care in the least, and the boy's grin was worth the minor evil. Let him have a tiny bit of fun. Devon just wanted to get Granwin and the boy out of reach of the Iraqis or whoever else wanted them. He unstrapped the two gas cans.

"Give these a whack." He pointed out the tan spots on the Rover where he had removed the cans, then fished out his Zippo, dipped it in the full can and let it soak up a load of gas. He sat the lighter on the floorboard of the Rover to dry before he strapped the can back on to the Rover.

"What do you think?" he asked Arif.

Arif, splattered with about as much paint as the Rover, nodded in approval. "I believe it is painted very good." He looked up toward the window where the kitchen smells were floating down, making Devon's mouth water. "Do you think we will eat soon?"

"Probably. Why don't you go on up and wash?"

"But I bathed this morning. And again for noon prayer."

"You want to eat?"

Arif's head nodded, even more vigorously.

"Then upstairs. You tell Renée you want to clean up. She'll probably give you something to eat on the way."

Devon put away the remaining paint and wiped his hands as Arif bounded up the stairs. He wondered how the boy's grief would work itself out. Since he had told Arif that Sara was dead, the boy occasionally drifted off to a far place, but most of the time he kept his grin intact. As long as they were on the run, driving at night and staying busy, he would be all right. Devon remembered his loses. When times got easy, difficult thoughts would return.

Devon turned back and looked over the Rover. Vine, trellis and Rover all shared the white paint, but at least it didn't stand out as a military vehicle with the machine gun stashed in the stable and the mottled tans covered by more-mottled whites.

Surface camouflage was the easy part. Dealing with the people was the catch. Syria had been an unlikely and minor ally during the Gulf War, pressured into joining the coalition by Saudi's largesse and subtle diplomatic maneuvering by the Egyptians, a suggestion of the old Arab League solidarity. Whatever the reasoning, Syria's participation had nothing to do with friendship toward the United States, England, or France. Too much modern animosity still bubbled from America's actions in Lebanon and support of Israel to ever think an American would be welcomed in Syria, at least by the government.

Devon suspected the Arab political memory reached all the way back to the betrayal of the infant Confederation of Arab States promised by Lawrence and others after the Great War. Individuals likely had the same diversity of views as everywhere else in the world. But outside of family or clan, trust was hard to come by, much like the Lumbees and the tarheels of Carolina.

A taxi driver in Damascus with a cousin in New York who wrote home about all the TVs and good living—never mind the slum he lived in—and the Damascus cousin was suddenly willing to be a very good friend with Americans. But the melon grower who'd had a brother killed in the Golan Heights still searched for revenge. Devon stopped to listen to a vehicle putter down the alley. Who knew which one just drove by?

Or lived next door? He scanned the adjacent houses, the white stucco taking on a pink glow as the evening sky began shading toward a deep rose. TV antennas poked up from roofs all along the street. Across the alley, a black cat leaped up to a window sill, then disappeared in the dark shadows cast by the overhanging eave, causing a row of turtledoves to twitter nervously on the drooping power line.

Music drifted down the alley from a radio. Arabic lyrics, soft and indistinct over the background of a stringed instrument played much like a mandolin—a reminder of Grandma and her Saturday night Oprey show. Bill Carlisle yodeling and singing bawdy songs from her old Motorola, Grandma slapping her knee, Grandpa grinning at her as he rocked.

Lord, I never thought about it, but they probably even made love, were in love. How had he missed such an important part of his life? All too busy being his own person.

"Nash." Granwin's soft voice floated down from the window. She leaned forward just enough for Devon to catch a glimpse of her crooked grin. "Time to wash before supper."

The bath was small and neat, hooked rag rug damp where the others had finished earlier. This was all too domestic. *Too many cute cats, too easy.* He had searched the rooftops for the crow, but at least that omen had left him alone. When he looked into the mirror, he realized Arif wasn't the only sloppy painter. White flecks specked his dark beard. Two nights without shaving and the stubble was already covering his face. He scraped the paint from his whiskers with his fingernails and quickly scrubbed his body in the lukewarm water filling the narrow, tiled tub.

A pair of black trousers and a long-sleeved white shirt hung from the back of the door. The pants were snug in the waist and a bit too long in the hem, but close enough to wear. And would save time. He would already be dressed for his funeral.

The others sat at the small table, waiting for him.

"Have you had *samak* curry before?" Granwin asked. "My favorite. Jeannine fixed it special for me—for us."

"What's *samak?*" Devon asked.

"Fish, fool!" Jeannine shook her head at his ignorance.

She served up sautéed fish fillets in a curried mixture of vegetables. Steam rose from the platter as she ladled out the fillets onto beds of rice covering delicate Wedgwood plates, chipped by years of wear and everyday use.

Arif ate almost as fast as Jeannine could fill his plate.

"Eat some of your rice and vegetables, *garçon qui mourir de faim.*" She paused to ladle a fillet from a cast iron skillet to Devon's plate, searching around the thick stock for a large selection.

Arif stared at the old woman, hand paused halfway between his plate and his mouth.

Devon laughed and picked up a slim green pickle. "She just said you were a starving boy. Go ahead, eat. The food smells delicious." He waved the pickle at the old woman. "Is this spicy-strong?" The bouquet of curry and garlic filled his head.

"*Non bête.*" Jeannine covered his fish and rice with the thick sauce floating with finely chopped carrot, celery and onion. "They are sweet gherkins." She crooked her little finger at him. "We call them 'lady fingers.'"

"While I painted the Rover, did you two figure out how to get us safely to the American Embassy?" Devon asked.

"Jeannine suggested a way." Granwin smiled at her aunt. "The foreigners here are either tourists or archaeologists. No Americans are allowed in at the moment, but Aunt Jeannine told me there are a handful of Western researchers. Most local police will not care about the difference between a German and an Englishman." Her nod turned to a shake with the addition of a frown, that old brow-creaser she scrunched up when a problem perplexed her. "But an American would be pressing the matter at bit."

Jeannine shook her finger at Devon. "Above all, do not let him pretend to be French. His terrible accent will betray you immediately. Now eat, or your food will get cold."

Granwin nodded in agreement. "I have my British passport. We could travel as archeologists from Palmyra, returning to the British Embassy on some excuse. That should get us into Damascus. Unless we are stopped by the military or the federal police, we shouldn't have a problem." But her frown hung on.

Devon paused with a forkful of fish halfway to his mouth. "How about I say I lost my passport? Real enough."

"Risky enough, I would say," was Granwin's retort.

"Do I need a passport?" asked Arif.

Devon looked from Granwin to Jeannine. "Do kids have passports in Syria?"

"No," she said. "But they are usually Syrian children traveling with their parents who have proper identification."

Neither Devon nor Granwin had a quick answer to her sharp comment.

"Since Arif speaks such good English and Arabic, you could say you hired him to interpret." Jeannine looked at Arif, head cocked on one side. "But his Arabic is not of Palmyra. You must say he is from—" She hesitated a moment. "—Gaza. He will be a Palestinian, a refugee. None of them sound the same, none claim a real home, only a home in their mind."

Devon frowned. "Too complex. But I can't think of a better cover." He pointed a pickle at Arif. "You're a smart kid. Think of a story. I'll back you." They grinned at each other, and Arif nodded his agreement. Devon dug below the fish for a large forkful of rice and vegetables. The curry mix quickly filled him, soothing, something that would put him to sleep, dreamless, no crows, no snakes, maybe just a friendly dove to guide the way.

Jeannine's eyes flicked back and forth from Granwin to Devon as they ate and talked over the route and their cover story. Why did Devon sense a feeling of… He wasn't sure what, other than something hidden under the old woman's dark lashes. She turned away from his stare to clear away the dishes and wipe up, shaking her head as they talked as if she didn't give them much of a chance with their scheme.

Arif's head bobbed over his plate, sinking dangerously close to the crumbs of curried fish and scattered grains of rice left on his plate.

Jeannine urged Arif from his chair. "Renée, *chéri,* turn out the lights when you finish. I have secured the downstairs door."

Arif blinked, head nodding, as Jeannine led him from the room.

Devon rested his chin in his hands, elbows propped on the empty table. "I guess we're all as tired as Arif. At least you have reached the safety of family. Is Jeannine your father's sister? I don't see much resemblance."

Granwin laid her hand on his arm and softly laughed. "Jeannine joined us after mother brought me here to live with Grandpère. Born and raised in Syria, as a child she came to work for Grandpère, first as a maid for mother and a nanny for me. Then she became Grandpère's mistress. They never married. He would not adopt Islam, and she refused to become a Catholic."

They sat in silence for a few minutes.

"Is there a telephone?" he asked.

Granwin shook her head. "No. I expect it is too expensive for Jeannine with the little money left by Grandpère." She bent down and dragged her dusty tote bag from beneath the chair. From inside the bag, she pulled out the transceiver. "Perhaps you can contact someone on this?"

"Wonderful!" Devon was amazed she still had the set. He hugged Granwin with one arm as he took the transceiver and held it up like a trophy won in a great race. "I thought I'd left it on the mountain." Devon turned the box and tangled wires over in his hands. The transceiver seemed to be intact, all the cords and knobs in place. "You're a love!"

When he looked at Granwin, her expression was—then his words echoed back in his mind. He carefully placed the transceiver on the table and took her face in his hands. "Let me see if this thing works. Then we'll talk some more." He sat at the table, opened up the transceiver and removed the battery, a common nine-volt cell.

"Will you be able to talk with Mr. Baker again?" Granwin asked.

"We'll see."

CHAPTER 31

The door to the moon-lit yard opened easily to his touch, unlocked despite Jeannine's comment. Devon stepped out to a half full moon ballooned up over the roof of the house across the alley, rising against a backdrop of indigo sky and faint stars. The desert breeze blew over the courtyard, dry and chill. Warmth still radiated from the pavers and stucco walls. He found the Zippo in the dark where he had left it on a gas can. He felt his way into the stable out of sight from the neighbors' rooftops. He blew off the excess gas and sparked the wheel against the flint until the wick caught. The gasoline blazed high above the lighter, smoke trailing upward from the yellow flame toward the low ceiling.

Devon stepped across the flickering shadows to the shelf. He snapped the lighter shut and felt in the darkness for the old radio. He pulled the back cover off and smiled in the dark as he snapped out the small battery, a nine-volt. When he turned, the door was a black frame around a smattering of stars glittering through the grape trellis. Outside, the starlight and moon glow reflected from the dull white of the Rover, sufficient light to clip the battery to the wire leads and slip it into the bottom of the transceiver.

He closed his eyes and visualized where the sun had set—over the trellis, against the back wall, fixing west in his mind. He opened his eyes and searched the sky for the North Star, imagining where the satellite circled overhead. Devon positioned the transceiver on the Rover's hood and angled the flat antenna plate toward the southwest, just over the neighboring roofs. He held his breath and clicked the power switch. The transceiver LEDs glowed, powered by the radio battery.

Devon figured he had only minutes before the battery gave up. He hit the transmit button. "Deacon, this is Chief." The low hiss droned back in his ear. Devon balled up his fist on the fresh paint, willing his fingers not to immediately punch the button again and waste battery power transmitting. If Baker, or anyone at EUCOM, were monitoring, he'd eventually get an answer. If he was actually transmitting. He clucked into the microphone. No return.

He checked the frequency settings. *Damn!* The receive frequency was off by a hundred kilohertz. He flicked the knob until the correct setting glowed back through the LED window. He pressed the transmit knob and repeated the call, shifted the antenna position slightly and called again.

The moon fought for recognition, a pale rose-colored disc as it climbed over the low roofs, accompanied by a bright star, more likely a planet with its steady glow not intimidated by its bigger neighbor. Size and importance were all relative, like him and Granwin and Arif, just tiny stars trying to shine through the darkness.

The hissing stopped and a nasal voice called from the earpiece. "Chief, where are you located? Your exact location?"

Devon grinned, put the microphone masquerading as a probe close to his mouth, then stopped and stared at the set.

Baker had said they could read his location. The correct question should have been, "What are you doing there?" not "Where are you?" *Damn it to hell!*

A flutter of wings caught his eye as the row of doves jockeyed for position on the power line. He searched the rooftops, looking for the crow, following him around with its mocking call. *Piss on the crow!*

"Deacon, what color was Tug's hair?"

No response. Devon stood in the dark, listening, waiting, his high hopes plummeting.

The high-pitched voice whispered back, "Say your location again, please."

Not Baker's voice, not even whispered through the tiny earpiece. *EUCOM?* Anyone there should be receiving his location. This was someone else, someone he didn't really want to talk to. He pressed the power switch, and the red LEDs vanished. In the distance, a *muezzin* called out to the faithful. One last chance for redemption before bed.

He slid the bolt home and tried the door, making sure the bolt was securely seated this time before he felt his way up the dark stairs. When he reached the top, he stood for a moment, listening to the rhythmic, off-balance hum of the ceiling fan. He turned the old porcelain switch on the wall and the fan slowed to a stop, leaving only sounds of sleep—soft breathing, a half-snore. Jeannine had taken Arif to the front bedroom, so he supposed the women were there. He made his way to the back bedroom, stripped and felt for the bed in the small room.

Spring was late arriving in Maryland. Allen had left home early for his night shift, afraid the narrow lanes leading to Mapes Road and Fort Meade would be impassible if he waited until his regular time. Night shift sucked, but was the price paid for pissing off the boss.

The early spring ice storm had crusted to glaze ice, but the roads had been clear. Then, sure enough, he had busted his ass trudging in from the parking lot. He hung up his coat, rubbed the strained muscles in his back and stopped to get a cup of steaming coffee, ears still stinging from the bitter cold walk across the parking lot. The hot coffee clouded his glasses when he held it to his face, eyes closed until the soothing warmth dissipated and his glasses cleared.

Terry Robins, his day-shift counterpart, waved at him from the central workstation surrounded by analysts, each staring at individual computer screens and listening intently to a set of headphones.

"Heard the weather report and worried about you, Russ." Robins tapped his computer screen. "Got one here I knew you'd want to personally work—one of those Rosemary messages." Robins rolled his chair to one side so Allen could see the message and sidebars.

Allen quietly read the brief transcript: Chief's call to Deacon, an ambiguous reply, the sudden termination of the call. "Get the transmit locations?"

Robins nodded. "Got a good location on the initiator. Call sign Chief's set has the embedded GPS location. Placed transmitter in—" Robins leaned closer to the screen. "—Tadmur, Syria, northeast of Damascus. No correlation with our database, so the transmitter's not on a known military or government installation. One minor commercial air field is close to the coordinates, but nothing listed as strategic."

Allen shook his head. "How about the response?"

"I figured you'd want to know, so I ran an analysis and correlation. Transmission came from the general vicinity of—" Robbins ran his finger down the screen. "—here. Old listing calls it Saad Sixteen, an Iraqi research facility, now doubling as a secret police command center outside of Mosul. *Amn al Khas* secret police technical signature. No, that's not right, not their secret police. The *Amn al Khas* are the guys Hussein uses to guard the WMD research facilities. Probably associated with the mountain your Rosemary guy blew up, or had blown up under him."

Allen compared the latitude and longitude with the computer-generated map of known Iraqi military facilities flashing in red on an adjacent console. "I agree. Has all this gone over to the Pentagon?"

Robins nodded. "Yeah. But I haven't called yet to verify receipt. Held off to see if you were going to make it to the office through all that crap. I thought you might want to make the call."

"Thanks, buddy, I sure do. Let me make the verification, then we'll do our shift transfer and you can get out a little early. No use both of us standing around. The roads aren't bad yet, but the parking lot is like a goddamned sheet of glass." Allen picked up the secure phone, flexing his stiff fingers. It was so cold in the air-conditioned computer haven that the telephone handset was like ice to his touch. Or was he chilled by the information? He cradled the handset against his shoulder and wrapped his fingers back around the coffee cup.

The phone answered as soon as the crypto synced. "Major Fowler, DIA desk."

"Les, this is Russ Allen, Echelon Ops. There's a problem. Seen the Rosemary report, couple of hours old, date time group 032243 Zulu?" It didn't take Allen long to confirm that the brief transcript and locations plots were all the information either of them had.

In the Pentagon, Major Lester Fowler tapped the secure telephone handset down on the base just long enough to break the connection to the NSA Echelon Ops Center and punch up the EUCOM Headquarters tactical operations center in Germany. Nothing was going right. The bosses were telling him hands-off, to let Devon get out on his own. Now the Iraqis had tracked him to Syria and were trying to reel him in.

That just isn't right.

A female voice answered. "EUCOM Command Center, Petty Officer Ramirez. This line is not secure, sir."

"Master Sergeant Baker, please. This is Major Fowler, ANMCC." Fowler drew small circles on his pad as he waited, then connected them with narrow straight lines.

"Sergeant Baker's on break. Can I take a message?"

"Have someone get him for me, please. I'll wait. This is important." He broke the pencil point off on the pad.

"That'll take a few minutes, sir. He might be down the hall in the snack bar."

"I'm the DIA desk officer. This pertains to an ongoing code-word operation." Fowler's full-ranged baritone made his mother cry whenever he broke into *Ol' Man River*, and he knew how to effectively use the power of his voice, especially over the phone. He turned on his best preacher's inflection, the one telling the brothers they were going straight to hell. "Get him on a secure line, right now, please, or put your watch chief on."

"Stand by, sir," was her quick response

Les reached in his desk drawer for a fresh pencil as he waited. He let his worries about Devon slide to the back of his mind, replaced by a classic Satchmo Dixieland melody, humming the harmony and tapping out the bass beat, disjointed memories drifting to June's framed photo on his desk until the phone thumped at the distant end.

A throat cleared in the background, then a hoarse voice came on the line. "Major Fowler?"

"Fowler here." Satchmo had left the Pentagon.

"Hey, Les, this is Joe Gunther. How's spring in the big city? Cherry blossoms out yet? I sent Ramirez to look for Bert. You want to hold on? She thinks he might be just down the hall at the vending machines."

"Sure do, Joe, thanks. I appreciate your help." Fowler tapped his new pencil, carefully letting the point hit the exact center of each circle. "No cherry blossoms yet, just a late freeze back here. You sound like you need to go over to the Rod and Gun Club and knock back a couple of shots of *Jagermeister*."

"Best idea I've heard all day, Les. Damn cold's killing me. It's rained all spring here in beautiful Bavaria— Hold on."

The phone thumped again and a new voice came on the line, as clear and deep as Fowler's own. "Sergeant Baker, sir."

"Pops, how's your leg getting on?" Fowler smiled, relieved he had caught up with Baker.

"Hey, little Lester! Doing fine, bro. How about your own self? And your momma and my little June? Hope it was something important to hustle me back here in the middle of my break. You got little Ramirez's bellbottoms all in a knot chasing me down."

Fowler scanned his phone indicators. "Can you go secure on this line?"

All humor left Baker's voice. "Going secure at this time."

The lights confirmed the crypto handshake, and Fowler cut to the problem. "Is anything going on to extract Devon from your end?"

"No. I was told hands off. You big boys would take it."

Fowler could hear the surprise in Baker's voice. "Nothing going on here," Fowler replied. "Lord, have we left Nash on his own?"

"The intel folks closed down my ops here and implied Nash was clear. Lord Almighty, they even sent down orders for me to go to Frankfurt tomorrow and fly back to the world." Baker's voice got quiet, as if he didn't want the others in the ops center to hear. "What's up? You got news on the situation?"

"Bad news. That's why I called you. Is there anything you can do to get him out?"

"I don't have any way to contact him from here. They even took away my radio. Eyes-only message said the operation was being managed directly by Washington. I've just been killing time here in the ops center playing soldier again. You there, man? Tell me what's up."

"Pops, I feel bad. After I passed your request through to divert Devon to Iraq, I've been kind of monitoring what went down. It ain't so good."

"Where is he?" Baker asked.

"He transmitted last night from Tadmur, northeast of Damascus. Blind call. To you. The only answer came from inside Iraq, the *Amn al Khas* outside of Mosul. Devon blew off the rag-heads, but so far as I can tell, no positive action is planned..."

"Son of a bitch! And nobody in Washington is going to do a thing?"

"Boss says hands off. It's a strategic show now, all White House and State. Passed me a CIA White Paper that advised letting the Iraqis stew in the European reaction to the nuclear incident, and predicted the rest of the Arab world would turn against them." Fowler felt like a bucket of cold water had dumped over his head. "Nobody's going in for him, are they?"

"We ain't done yet. Listen, you hug June for me, son. I don't think I'm going to make my flight, at least not one coming your way. This is one of those times I'm glad I'm retired, contract DIA civilian-pretend-to-be-soldier, not real Army anymore. I got one more card to play."

"You take care of yourself, Pops. Call me when you get where you can." Fowler hung up the phone, wondering if he had sent Devon a trip too far.

Houston closed his eyes as he listened to Baker, wishing he had taken early retirement before he accepted this rat-shit assignment. He had dreamed attaché duty would be neat after a career in the air. So far it sucked, at least in the Middle East.

As soon as Baker rang off, Houston dialed the Embassy Marine Quarters. *How am I supposed to make this seem like a normal part of embassy operations,* he wondered.

After a single ring, a sleepy voice answered the phone. "Sergeant Gonzales, sir."

"How's that new stripe fit, Gonzales? Told you joint operations could pay." Houston slid his hand over his smooth pate as he explained what he wanted to the Marine. "Wear a sidearm and be prepared. But I don't think anything odd will go down. I just don't know, though, okay?"

Houston nodded at Gonzales' response then punched the intercom button. "Birdi, come in here, please. And bring Major Devon's file with you."

Houston leaned back from the intercom and scrubbed his bald head with both hands. *Amateurs.* The whole operation backfired and had gone totally to hell. Why had he ever agreed to pin this job on his old friend? In his heart, Houston knew the answer. *Because Devon could piss on the fires of hell and come out the other side.* A little stinky, perhaps, but come out. Now, through the careful neglect of the agency, the fire was creeping up Devon's pant leg. Houston could smell the stink.

Birdi Flowers stood in the door and smiled at him, a bit of a wistful look on her face. In contrast to the rest of them, himself included, Flowers was no amateur. He held out his hand and took the folder from her, the one with the smiley face drawn on the cover. "Shut the door, Birdi, and have a seat." He waved her to a chair, the same one Devon had squirmed in.

She shut the door and sat down, pulling her knee-length skirt even lower. Sergeant Gonzales appeared outside the door, his stocky frame filling the glass half of the door as he turned his back to the room.

Houston let his eyes run over Birdi's body. If she carried, it sure didn't show. Now he was being paranoid. Who would want to be armed on the embassy grounds? *Someone who could be beheaded if I turn her over to the Saudis, for one.*

Houston really didn't want to play this card. He'd been holding it for over a year, waiting until he could reap some grand *coup*—get promoted, get fired, do anything to get away from the smiling Saudis. But the time had come to lay it out.

"I know who you are," he said.

"I expected your call sooner." Her answer was as matter-of-fact as his statement. Flowers took a deep breath. "I was told there were phone taps, and wondered when you were going to stop my operation." Her Jersey accent had suddenly evaporated, her articulation accentless, totally neutral and, even more amazing, calm.

She daubed at the beads of sweat on her upper lip, the one indication that she realized the seriousness of the conversation, the meaning of the broad back in camouflaged utilities leaning against the door glass, butt of the holstered Beretta visible through the glass.

Houston shook his head. "I don't know a lot of details. Like I don't know if you are a minor operative or a Mossad mucky-muck." He paused, waiting for her answer. None came. "I don't need you to go to jail, so talk to me."

Flowers glanced at the door, then took another deep breath, obviously resigned to silence and whatever fate he brought down on her.

"Don't play with me, Miss Flowers, or whoever you are, and maybe we'll both come out of this with our skins." He waved the folder. "Devon needs some help. But first, I want you to help me find out exactly where he is. I want to work with you," he said.

Flowers' eyes brightened.

He picked up the phone "Call your contact in Damascus."

She kept a blank look and didn't take the offered phone.

"Don't dance with me. Devon's somewhere in Syria. I want to know where, and what he's doing. And, most importantly, can we get him out? Don't make me make a call neither of us wants to happen."

Flowers looked at Houston for a moment, then held her hand out for the phone. "Tel Aviv will have a shit-fit. Do you think Washington will mind?'

"They'll mind, but I won't. Make the call. Who'll know?"

"Hurry, please, I'm getting cold."

Devon patted the bed, confirming it was already occupied and he wasn't having some imaginary wet dream. He quickly slid under the light sheet. Granwin put her arms around his neck and pulled him close, kissing him lightly, then more insistent as their bodies warmed.

"You need a shave."

Devon kissed her back. "I didn't see a razor and mine's in Iraq. Want me to go get it?"

"No. You stay right here where we're safe." Her breath smelled faintly of lemons and mint, garlic and curry. The olive oil had softened her lips, soothing the desert-dry cracks.

He kissed her lips, the tip of her ear, and pulled her closer against his body. "This is nice." He felt himself growing as they pressed together, her moistness opening to his need. "But I wasn't expecting you here."

"Arif said we should be a family. Despite the passport and blond hair, I am French." She giggled. "Especially in bed."

Devon ran his hand down her side, over her ribs, and hips. She shivered as he stroked her body, and trembled under his kiss.

"If we are going to be a family, I have a very important question to ask."

She pulled back enough so he could see the glow starlight reflected in her eyes.

"Will you marry me?" he whispered.

She smiled and pulled at his shoulder, urging him to roll over until his body covered hers, her warmth flooding him from head to toe, her arms encircling his body, pulling him tight.

In a moment, he had her answer.

CHAPTER 32

Devon stared the door at the bottom of the steps and the open bolt. He hadn't heard a sound from outside since the call to morning prayer had roused him from the warm bed and the tangle of Granwin's arms and legs. He eased the door open. Cool morning air brushed his face, thick with morning mist laden with dust. The courtyard was empty. Beyond the walls, the alley was silent.

What day of the week was it? Was it the Muslim weekend? He had totally lost track. He stepped out, closed the door behind him and looked up at the sky. The sun, silvery behind a haze of dust, had just cleared the house across the alley. Overhead, the turtledoves cooed on the power line, white-tipped tails bobbing as the morning breeze stirred.

"Nasty, isn't it, Nash?"

Devon spun, crouched, and slowly stood.

Khan, a cigarette in one hand and his old Webley in the other, sat in the Rover, a burnished metal briefcase in his lap, reminding Devon for a moment of Kilborn.

"Dust blows from the open pit phosphate mines outside town. The way the desert wind picks up the dust reminds me of your El Paso, debris from oil refineries and concrete plants all mixed in with the desert dust. We sure do know how to pollute, don't we?" Khan blew a long stream of smoke up into the grapevine.

"You, Devon, especially made a mess of Facility Number Seven. For a while, I prayed to Allah that the radioactive spew would bring a quick death to us all." He shrugged. "But the mountain held most of the radiation in. Good facility design, what'd you think?" Khan flipped the cigarette to the ground, swung out of the Rover and ground the butt under his foot.

He waggled the briefcase toward Devon. "Speaking of designs, I've got your notes in here. Unfortunately, Dr. Kee did not survive, and they need a little elaboration. I'm sure you'll oblige me."

People had died, good people, and still this asshole has the notes. Devon searched the rooftops for the crow.

"You're quiet this morning. Did you actually think you'd escape? This is my world, Nash. Not cowboy land. The old woman—" He saluted the open window. "—she couldn't wait to call her contacts to give you up." He thumbed back the Webley's hammer as the door opened behind Devon. Granwin, hair in a tangle, and Arif stumbled from the doorway as the door slammed behind them.

A moment later, the curtain flew back from the upstairs window and Jeannine leaned out. "Get out, *houri*!" She waved at the group below. "Take the child and raise him in sin, as your filthy grandfather forced me to live." She pointed at Khan. "Soldier, take them and get them away from my house."

Khan holstered his pistol and straightened his tunic. "My Syrian *Mujahideen Al Ahad* brothers tell me she was taken from her home as a child and sold to the Frenchman—" He pointed at Granwin. "—That one's grandfather, as a slave. Since then, she's helped the cause in many ways...even arranged the old man's execution." He motioned toward the Rover. "Come, all of you. I have to return to Pakistan tonight."

Devon put one arm around Granwin's shoulders. Her face was blank as she stared up at the empty window, tears running down her face. He put his other arm around Arif, staring across the courtyard at Khan.

Arif looked up at Devon. "Mother said he was the evil one," he whispered.

"She was right, scout. Stay alert."

"Cozy family you've made for yourself, Nash. Now let's go." Khan called out in Arabic and the gate squawked on its hinges.

A blur flashed from the stable and into the grapevine, and just as quickly, Khan drew his pistol and fired. The doves flushed in a flurry of wings and a furry body dropped from the grape trellis to the ground.

"Nooo..." cried Arif. Devon grabbed him by the collar and held him back from the twitching calico.

Khan coolly thumbed open the old revolver and replaced the fired cartridge as the gate flew open, pushed by two grunting soldiers, followed by two more with AKs at the ready. Khan yelled at them in Arabic and they stopped.

"No surprises, Nash, or more than a—" He paused to shove the bloody body across the pavers, flipping it over with his toe. "—cat will die." Khan waved the men back to a truck parked in the alley. "Come, Nash. You may drive. You, boy." He motioned to Arif. "Get in the back of the truck."

Khan stared at Granwin for a moment. "I should leave you for the woman. She'd have her own justice for you. But I recall Nash is much more inclined to speak freely if you're present." He motioned toward the Rover. "In the back with the boy." He impatiently waved the heavy pistol. "And no more heroics."

Khan slid back into the passenger seat and put the briefcase between his feet.

Devon followed Khan's directions, retracing their route out of town, but this time turning toward the airport.

Khan turned to Arif. "Boy, why do you not kill the American? He has dishonored your mother." Before Arif could answer Khan twisted until he could see Granwin. "And you. Why do you sleep in sin with a man so dishonorable? You must have a mind of your own. Why do you let this man defile you?"

Granwin was silent.

Devon glanced down at the frag grenade dangling from the wire.

Khan reached down and slid grenade off the wire. He dropped his pistol in his lap, then pulled the safety pin from the grenade and waved it at Devon. "Do you think I do all these things for my glory? My life is of no great importance. I do all this for the *Al Ahad*, the Brotherhood."

He turned back to Granwin and Arif. "I pray to Allah that I shall be worthy, and that He will forgive my sins. I believed I was better than you when we first met, Nash, in Oklahoma. My pride, fueled by your arrogance, led me to the little skinny one, Rachel. She was not a very good lover, was she?"

Devon's grip on the steering wheel tightened and his mind whirled.

"Your American snobbery, your vulgarity, all tempted me to sin." He laughed. "Would you believe your wife even preferred me to you? I know I'm more handsome, but even so, that is the way of western women to be careless with their virtue." He worked the pin back into the grenade and dropped it into his pocket. "Turn here, and stop by the operations building." Khan pointed toward a white building at the edge of the taxiway.

Devon slowed to a stop, numb from Khan's words. A white Dauphin with UN markings sat about fifty yards away at a refuel point. The truck with the soldiers pulled up beside them.

"Out. Go." He waved Arif and Granwin toward the Dauphin. "Get in the helicopter."

Granwin and Arif walked over to the Dauphin, leaving Devon alone with Khan. A man in overalls drove up in a tanker and began refueling the helicopter.

"You'll pay a great price for the destruction of Facility Number Seven, Nash, but despite what you've done, I have won. Your life—" He pointed toward Granwin and Arif standing by the helicopter. "—and theirs, depends on your cooperation." Khan laid the briefcase on the hood. "Your designs will be very valuable to my friends. By tomorrow, you'll be in the Pakistan National Development Centre, assisting in the next upgrade to the *Ghauri*, our latest ballistic missile." He pulled a pack of cigarettes from his pocket. "You still smoke your grandfather's pipe you were so proud to carry?"

The biting smell of aviation fuel washed over Devon as the service man splashed gas on the ground trying to get the nozzle plugged into the Dauphin. "Yeah, same old pipe."

"Smoke, then, while we wait." Khan patted the briefcase. "Watch the papers for me while I'm gone." He grinned at Devon, the old scar twitching, lit up his cigarette and sauntered over to the Syrian truck, talking to the soldiers.

As Khan walked away, Devon felt under the driver's seat until his fingers found the cold iron of the remaining fragmentation grenade. While Khan talked to the soldiers, Devon worked the grenade from between the seat cushion and the metal frame and dropped it into his pocket. No rubber band. How was this going to work? Khan had pulled his billfold out and was counting out a series of banknotes to one of the men.

"Bastard," Devon muttered, blinking back tears from the gas fumes. Khan's back was still turned. Devon wrinkled his nose, the old hairs standing up again. The smell was regular automotive gasoline, not aviation fuel. In the back of the Rover, Granwin's black shawl lay draped across a gas can, one end stuffed into the can. Gasoline had begun to wick down the loose fibers.

Granwin had been busy while Khan harangued.

The Dauphin's twin turbines stirred up dust as the drooping blade tips flexed and began to turn.

"Nash," Khan yelled at Devon. "Take my briefcase on board." He pointed at the briefcase and waved Devon toward the helicopter.

Insolent son-of-a-bitch! So he thinks he has me, Renée, Arif, all of us, the designs, everything under his absolute control. Devon pulled out his Zippo, thumbed the wheel, and tossed the flaming lighter onto the shawl. The fabric smoldered for a moment, then smoky flames raced toward the mouth of the can. Devon grabbed Khan's briefcase and sprinted toward the helicopter.

Granwin stared at him through the open doorway as he threw the briefcase under her seat. Her eyes were full of questions. The pilot and copilot, focused on the gauges, ignored him. The Rover suddenly belched a torch of flame into the sky, splattering the soldiers with burning gasoline.

Devon felt the rotors begin to pick up speed as the crew stared across at the mayhem. Devon yanked the grenade from his pocket and yelled at the crew. "Everyone out!" He waved the grenade at the pilots. "Out. Get out!" he roared.

They looked back at him, frozen in their seats.

Devon shoved the hand grenade under the pilot's nose with a finger through the pin. "Arif, tell them to get out of the helicopter or I'll blow us all up."

Arif screamed in Arabic, joined by Granwin. Both doors opened, and the pilot and copilot rolled from the helicopter as the Rover exploded with enough of a whomp to rock the Dauphin. The explosion slammed Khan face down on the tarmac. He scrambled to his knees, surrounded by flames.

Devon scrambled over the console into the left seat. Across the runway, the soldiers had vanished. Khan climbed to his feet, staring across at the helicopter. Devon dropped the grenade into a shirt pocket and grabbed the controls. He twisted the throttle, the rotary control on the end of the collective under his left hand, bringing up the blade revs. Devon raised the collective and the Dauphin shuddered and started hopping around on its wheels, turning to the right. He gave the throttle control another twist and toed the left rudder pedal. Behind him, Granwin and Arif's incomprehensible voices shrilled against the roar of the turbines.

Khan was on his feet, pistol dangling from one hand as he cocked back the other in a throwing motion. Devon yanked the collective up and pushed the stick between his legs forward, pointing the Dauphin down the short taxiway.

Agonizingly slow, the helicopter began to roll. Devon glanced at the gauges. Compass, altimeter, gyro, some he recognized, most he didn't. Why should he? He had never flown a Dauphin in his life. All he could do was get the damn machine to languidly roll down the runway.

Another explosion rocked the Dauphin. Something whizzed through the flapping door and smashed into the instrument panel, shattering a gauge face above his left knee. The Plexiglas beside his face exploded, slapping his face with chunks of plastic. Khan's aim was getting better.

Devon tightened his grip on the collective and slowly bent his elbow, raising the collective higher. They needed to get off the damn ground. The helicopter lurched up into the air, then fell back, bouncing on the taxiway. The helicopter climbed again as he pushed the cyclic forward, now rolling faster down the taxiway, suddenly off the tarmac and bouncing across bare dirt. Sand and dust swirled all around and into the cockpit. Blinded, Devon pulled the collective up and suddenly the Dauphin responded, lifting clear of the dust, rising, leaving his stomach on the ground. The runway flashed under them, then the roof of a building.

Devon pushed the cyclic forward another fraction and glanced at the instruments. The altimeter was spinning; they were still climbing, fast. He bumped the collective down. The ground below seemed to be keeping its distance, but they were moving fast enough that the town below them was a blur of roofs. The rate of climb indicator stabilized. Altimeter indicated about thirty. *Too damn low.* Then he remembered—meters—they were at about eighty, ninety feet. *Good, just don't clip any power lines or towers, but keep it below the radars.*

He glanced left and right out the windows. The highway dipped out of sight into a saddle, then up and across a long ridgeline rising up to the right. To his left, harsh brown desert shimmered in the morning sun. If the sun hadn't reversed course, they were heading southwest toward Israel. He twisted his neck for a quick check. The two doors to the cockpit were closed, blown shut by the airflow. He looked back into the cargo compartment. Arif was straining at his seat belt, craned forward to look out the open cargo door, wind whipping his shirt collar around his face. Beside him, Granwin's eyes were squeezed shut, her hand to her throat. Devon hoped she had it on her cross and was praying for them. Or that after Khan's yammering, she and Arif at least didn't hate him. Or maybe they should. The way he hated Khan.

Devon wondered how much Khan was working within the system or if everything was one big Islamic conspiracy, this *Mujahideen al Ahad.* Why was his life now all questions with no answers? But they had escaped, for the moment. *Over Syria, but away from Khan. Screw you, crow.*

A gust from the desert pushed the helicopter, tilting it to the right. Devon gently eased it back level and to the left. No use slamming into the low mountains, or slipping over and ending up in Lebanon. He racked his memory for anything about the Dauphin that could help him control it. He had been too focused on his own miseries to pay attention to the helicopter on the short flight going into Irbil on the Commission bird. His few stick hours in flight school with the sturdy old Vietnam-vintage UH-1 Huey didn't count for much now. He finally recalled the Dauphin cruised at about a hundred knots with a range about three hundred nautical miles. The fuel had just been topped off, so they should be able to make it to the coast.

He just had to keep in mind the two guiding principles for piloting helicopters. First, they are inherently unstable aircraft. Unlike fixed wing birds, take your hands off the controls for more than an instant and the damn things tried to crash. He had proved that aeronautical fact to his and his instructor's satisfaction. Enough that they had busted him out and told him not to return to Fort Rucker. Not so much for crashing. The instructor had told him he was tired of Devon's attitude. Too much talk about flying with the eagles and not enough study—a nutso case. *Not nearly as nuts as flying this barge across Syria.*

Another gust of wind reminded him of the second principle: be gentle. *So easy to say.* Hours of riding behind the Blackhawk pilots, watching them dance over the pedals, caressing the cyclic and collective controls, grinning behind their Ray Bans, he sometimes wished he had made it through flight school. Now he was going to do a little on-the-job training.

Devon forced his grip around the cyclic to relax, maintaining just enough pressure to the left to offset the desert winds trying to blow them to Ankara. Devon tried to visualize the ragged travel guide folded in his pocket. The ridgeline should end just before they got to Damascus. He could cut across and head east, toward Lebanon and the coast.

Ahead, a large jet climbed into the sky from the ragged skyline of a distant city. An airport in this part of the world probably signaled air defense, probably more Russian SAMs. Devon edged the cyclic to the right, hugging the rugged side of the ridgeline as closely as he dared, roads and houses flashing under his feet.

Devon jammed the pilot's discarded headset onto his head, working it with his left hand until one of the pads covered an ear and the boom mike was in the vicinity of his mouth. He toggled the push-to-talk switch. "Mayday, mayday, this is UN helicopter enroute to—" Devon hesitated. Where the hell was he going? "—Damascus. Any American stations monitoring?"

He glanced at the control panel by his right leg. He had absolutely no idea how to operate all the radios transponders and other electronics. Not even an idea how to flip the radio to guard frequency.

The ridgeline fell away and Devon banked the Dauphin to the right, bringing the sun to his back and hopefully putting the unseen coast on his nose. A lush valley flashed under the clear Plexiglas beneath his feet, greens vivid under the clear sky. Ahead a distant range of mountains rose much higher than the low ridgeline he had just used as cover, snow-flaked tops half-hidden in an approaching line of clouds. If he remembered the guide correctly, the green was Bekáa Valley. Beyond the valley lay the Lebanese mountains, and beyond them, the Mediterranean Sea.

Just then a dark shadow flashed over the controls and the helicopter rocked violently. Devon tapped the pedals and eased the cyclic back and forth against the pitch and yaw, trying to keep the tail rotor from swinging around and leading the parade.

"Gentle, like rocking a baby," he whispered.

He searched the instrument panel until he found the artificial horizon, a big ball with a line indicating how far off level he had pitched the helicopter. He focused on the instruments, not trusting his eyes to look out until he had the helicopter back on level flight. The big ball finally stabilized, and Devon craned his neck up and back over both shoulders, searching.

A stream of tracers flashed by on the right, followed by the whoosh of a jet and the bone-shaking jarring of his tailbone on the hard seat as the helicopter bounced up then plunged toward the ground. The arrow shape of a MiG banked just ahead, tail low, flaps full, trying to slow enough to get a good shot at them.

Devon clenched his jaw while he sawed at the controls, fighting to keep the Dauphin in the air. He buried the cyclic into his stomach. The helicopter staggered as he climbed, then dropped them down on the far side of a glimmering tangle of power transmission lines. He yanked the helicopter into a hard bank, the Dauphin fighting him, shuddering, tail waggling around until he got the pedal pressure worked out. He snuggled close in beside the power lines and followed them toward the growing skyline of a city.

The MiG roared across his path, pitched up and climbed toward the sun. Devon thought his biceps would explode as he tensed his muscles at the same time he tried to keep the control movements steady and easy.

"Gentle, my ass," he muttered as the helicopter dove toward the ground.

CHAPTER 33

They flashed dangerously low over a minaret and dropped down until he was buzzing over the tops of cars and trucks, heading down a wide highway toward town.

"Turn at the next light to get to the embassy."

Devon jumped in his seat at the voice in his ear. "This Damascus?" he yelled back.

Granwin leaned closer and pointed to the left. "Yes. I recognize the stadium."

They flashed by a big sports stadium. Devon fought to keep them low as a line of tracers rose up from the next intersection and behind them before he could react. Ahead, crisscrossed streams of tracers reached up into the sky, a wall of fire coming up from an open park by the street. He eased the cyclic to the right, angling across the city, cutting diagonally across the rooftops, making it harder for anyone to report their whereabouts and course from the ground.

At least the interceptor had pulled off and wasn't shooting at them over the city. If only they could stay away from anything significant enough to protect with antiaircraft emplacements.

Below, an old walled section of town came up and Devon pulled further to the right, staying over the homes and small street-side shops. He glanced back. Granwin was still by his shoulder, but their cover had run out. The ground passing under his feet held fewer buildings. Green fields scattered between areas of parched rock and an occasional house, scattered farmers and livestock took the place of city streets. Granwin's arm pointed ahead. A tall mountain rose up from the rolling hills, high enough that the top glistened with snow.

"Mount Hermon," she shouted in his ear.

"Too high to go over. Which way do you suggest, left or right?" Devon yelled back.

Granwin paused. "Probably left. Right puts us in Lebanon, not much better than Syria now that the Israelis have pulled out."

"Left puts us in Israel, yeah?"

"Yes." After a pause she added. "After you cross the Golan Heights."

"Is it still dangerous?"

"It's been a military barrier between Israel and Syria for many years with much fighting. Druze villages along the slopes." She bent across him, reached down and pulled one of the harness straps over his chest. She searched for an opposing strap, finally finding each end and snapping them into the four-point harness until he was secure.

"So, we go to Israel, low and fast. You better get back and put a seat belt on, too." He wiggled against the loose straps. "Now," he added, milking all the speed he could from the fleet Dauphin. Ahead and to the right, a dust plume marked the route of a fast moving vehicle, probably tracked, probably armed to the teeth, on an intercept course, closing too damn fast. The Arab bloc had too many old Soviet weapons, including the track-mounted SA-9 with infrared guided missiles. He pushed the Dauphin closer to the deck.

Telephone poles whipped by on his left, just below the whirling blades. Below, a pickup, probably driven by a war veteran leery of Israeli fighters, veered into the ditch as they closed. Out to the right, the dust trail boiled to a stop. The plume of a missile launch emerged from the dust and streaked toward them.

Devon crowded down even closer to the ground, posts whipping past on the left, a face on a bike a blur, a house roof too damn close to the forward edge of the blades clawing at the air. Ahead, a large truck barreled toward him, a fine layer of dust and exhaust haze trailing behind it. To the right, the missile disappeared in a glint in the Plexiglas, leaving him to guess at its trajectory. He jerked the collective up, snapped the cyclic over and shoved the collective back down so the helicopter was on the left of the road and wire line, and the oncoming truck was, with any luck, between them and the oncoming missile. *Inshallah.*

He crowded the ground, hopped up and over a farmhouse, focused on the truck, medieval jousters holding to their lanes, armored steeds frothing as they closed. Devon squeezed the air between the helicopter and the ground.

The truck erupted in an explosion just as they met. The blast slammed the helicopter to the left, toward the fields. Devon fought to keep the helicopter from yawing and digging the whirling blades into the ground. He jerked at the controls, snatching them away from the ground and a near roll. Granwin's scream pierced the howl of air, the bellow of the missile detonation behind them. The Dauphin tipped to the right toward the silver wire line, dove down toward the road, almost going under the wire. Devon fought to retain control, to not overdrive the helicopter. *Relax, relax, gentle...Bullshit. Fly like the eagle!*

Still too close to the ground, Devon forced his mind blank and let his reactions fly the helicopter. He jockeyed the controls until the indicated airspeed wavered around the two hundred kilometers per hour mark, palm trees blurs passing by on both sides. The terrain transitioned from flat fields to rolling orchards with low trees, shadowy ravines and rising hills, with a distant glint of a river. Directly ahead, the chalk-white lumps of a row of houses twisted along the road. Tiny figures scattered toward the houses.

"Okay?" he yelled back over his shoulder.

"Go like the devil!" Arif's shrill voice answered back.

Devon laughed, tears starting to squeeze from his eyes at the reply. He clamped off the laugh. A man stood on a rooftop, dead ahead, a tube on his shoulder. Devon dropped down so they were skimming just over the unpaved road, whirling blades at the man's level. *Let's see how this son-of-a-bitch plays chicken.*

A puff of smoke bloomed from a rocket launcher just as Devon jerked the helicopter up and over the house, so close he could see the man's eyes as he threw down the launcher and dove off the roof. The man had fired at them.

Devon tensed, waiting for their world to fall apart. No explosion, but the Dauphin shuddered and lost power. An unnatural grinding yowled from the turbines overhead. Maybe an old RPG-7, impact fuse shorted out, or maybe a dud, but the turbine had swallowed it.

A faint fog of his short-lived training returned. Devon pushed the collective all the way down and eased the cyclic back. The Dauphin slowed and started falling, diving toward a high embankment topped with glimmering barbed wire, fast—too fast.

"Ah, shit!" Devon blurted out. Beyond the embankment, morning vapor rose from a field, empty except for a solitary cow directly in their path, staring with great concern as the helicopter hurtled toward her. Shorter than a football field, the other side of the field dropped off into the shadows of a deep ravine. The plateau beyond the ravine glittered with small lakes.

Devon danced with the controls and held the Dauphin level, letting the bird fly, keep its forward speed. An instant before impacting the bank, he eased up the collective and yanked the cyclic back into his belly, bringing the nose up into a flare. The air caught them like a cushion, pressing Devon down into his seat and marginally slowing their decent as they flashed over the bank. A tangle of wire flashed by under the Plexiglas nose, missing by inches.

A sudden wish that he'd strapped in tighter flicked across his mind when the helicopter suddenly staggered, hurling Devon against the harness, a snapping sensation flowing up through the controls into his hands, accompanied by a wrenching sound from the tail. Below his feet, the ground raced toward him and slammed into the bottom of the Dauphin. The Plexiglas under his feet shattered. Shards of plastic, metal and dirt exploded around his head. He gasped for breath as the loose belt bit into his chest and his ankles slammed up against the instrument panel.

Dirt and grass and shattering Plexiglas pelted him as the Dauphine bounced and tumbled across the pasture. The aluminum skin screeched as it shredded away from the frame. A brief glimpse of the horizon twisted by as the crash ripped him away from the seat. He gasped when the pressure across his chest vanished. Devon slammed up into the top of the cabin, bounced back, crashed against the control panel, and felt his leg crack across the cyclic, then floated free, spit from the jaws of death.

He lay stretched across a soft cushion. Devon wondered if they had lined his casket with velvet or satin. Were the gunshots the honor guard? Was Grandpa here with his faded bandanna?

Devon shook his head, then stopped when the movement shot jolts of pain through his head. Pain radiated from his chest. *I hurt too much to be dead. Not even time for a heart attack, too busy crashing stolen helicopters.*

"Chief, Chief."

Devon opened his eyes. Arif was bending over him, wiping dirt from his face. Devon turned his head and spat out a mixture of blood and dirt. He wiggled his tongue around his mouth until he could talk. "Hey, scout, we're alive. How about that?" His voice croaked like a poor frog imitation. He blinked up into the sun. "Where's Renée?" He looked at his hands. Shaking, dirty, but still there on the ends of his arms. Lordy, lordy, Granny would say.

"I'm here." Granwin slid down the side of the tilted wreck and stumbled over to them, rubbing her hands over her arms as if she were checking to see if everything were still attached. Her blond hair looked like a teenager in a mall, red-dyed spikes standing on end. All she needed was a little purple tint. Then he realized the red was damp blood.

"Renée, is your head all right?" Devon let the two of them pull him to his feet.

"Still on my shoulders, no thanks to you. Now get up."

Twenty feet away, the smoldering Dauphin lay twisted across a shallow furrow dug by the sliding helicopter. A single helicopter blade protruded from the ground directly in front of the wreckage. Its shadow fell over a cow. She stared at them for a moment, chewing her cud, then dropped her head back down searching out the sparse spring grass. Devon dug the loose dirt from his ears. "Are those voices?" he asked. He stared at his fingers, dark with blood and loam. His left ear felt like it had been torn from his head. His ears rang, echoing back Arif's reply, mixing them in with other voices and reports. "What?"

Arif tried again. "People shouting and many gunshots. I think they are coming to get us."

"Like hell. Come on." Devon turned, caught his foot in the loose dirt and fell back to his knees. He stopped to feel the soft clods of dirt under his hands. Good soil, farmed forever, rich, tainted only by the smell of fuel dripping from the wreck. He shook his head and looked around the debris. "Where's the briefcase?"

Granwin grimaced and clutched at her side. "Leave it, Nash," she pleaded. "Whoever shot us down will be here shortly." Her voice had a tinge of panic. Frown lines surrounded her eyes, enough to show through the dust, dirt, and blood.

Devon was still having a hard time drawing a deep breath against the soreness binding his chest. "The briefcase. Too important to leave. Sara died for it. Others, many may die if I leave it behind."

He staggered back to the wreck, climbed into the opening where the sliding door had been ripped away. He slid across the cabin floor, now tilted at an impossible angle and searched the wreckage. No briefcase. The seats were a tangled mass of tubes and straps and twisted metal. Thank God, Granwin and Arif had survived, tangled in that mess.

"Nash, over there." Granwin's yell penetrated the ringing in his ears.

He hauled his way back to the doorway. She pointed toward the cow. The metal briefcase glittered in the sunlight, half covered by churned up dirt.

He clawed his way out of the wreck, and by the time he was back on his feet, Arif had dragged the briefcase over to Granwin. "Good work, scout." Devon snatched up the briefcase and grabbed Arif's hand in his other. "Come on." He led them toward the ravine. "Know where we are, Renée?"

"Not really. But we're close to Israel." She pointed to their right. A mountain, the same snow-tipped peak that had loomed in the

Dauphin's Plexiglas, now dominated the horizon to the north. A series of small snow-fed lakes glittered between them and the mountaintop. "We don't have far. The border is close to the line between Mount Hermon and the Sea of Galilee."

"Surely they outpost the border up here." Devon thought about the UN mandates the prim Englishman had given him to study far away in Heathrow's Terminal Three. "If we've made it to the Golan Heights, the UN's got a force posted somewhere around, a barrier between Syrians and Israelis."

Devon shook this head. He couldn't stop the buzzing and whirring in his head. Dizzy, he dropped to his knees and held his head still for a moment. There was more to the ringing in his ears.

"Look!" Arif pointed into the sun.

Devon watched helplessly as a white helicopter circled around them, UN markings a blur but unmistakable on its sides.

"Thank God," Granwin said. "I can see the commissioner."

Devon, expecting Khan and his Webley, was confused. "Who?" he asked.

"From the High Commission office in Baghdad. Commissioner Aragon. He must be here to rescue us," she answered, a look of pride on her face. "He is a true Frenchman. He has dared the danger to save us."

Devon looked at her. "Aragon. You know him?"

"Yes, silly. I at least know who he is. He is a very famous person in France. I have seen his picture in *l'Humanité* many times. Only last year the newspapers described Monsieur Aragon as a *financier* of large companies, very generous for stepping aside from his company positions to assist with the UN's humanitarian efforts. Even more significant, he is named for a great French poet."

The helicopter swooped to a landing on the far side of a narrow ravine and several men jumped out. Devon could see that at least two carried rifles.

Granwin waved at them.

Devon muttered, "Ah, shit," when the rifles swung in their direction.

"Get up, man. We can leave safely." Granwin's voice was giddy with relief.

A bullet cracked over their heads.

The cow tossed her head, tail swishing at the fly she thought she heard flicked by.

Devon turned to see a man standing on top of the bank, rifle aimed in their direction.

The cow turned and started a slow amble, then broke into a full trot, teats flinging from side to side as bullets tore into the field.

"Get down," Devon shouted over the crack of bullets, pulling Arif down beside him. "They aren't here to rescue us." A bullet smacked into the ground with a thump and splatter of dirt, confirming his suspicions.

The splatter of bullets apparently convinced Granwin. "Quickly. This way," she called out, and led them to the edge of the ravine. Devon and Arif followed, sliding and stumbling down grassy slopes to the cover of several palm trees lining the banks of a shallow stream out of sight of the men above. She grabbed Devon and pulled him in the opposite direction when he started to follow the flow of the water. "No, no. To the falls."

Devon pulled at her arm. "Downstream will take us south to Galilee and Israel." Angry shouts echoed across the steep sides of the ravine, seemingly all around them. "We'll find the Peacekeepers if we run. Come on. Don't give up on me now."

He looked down at Arif. Covered with dirt, an angry welt across his forehead, the boy's hand trembled in Devon's grip.

"No, Devon," Granwin insisted. Her voice was calm and soft. She tugged at him and pointed in the other direction.

Devon looked upstream. A torrent cascaded over the rocks and down the slope, breaking into separate rivulets only to reunite and crash against a jumble of glistening rocks, again becoming a pastoral stream flowing toward the Galilee. The water sparkled, tinted an emerald green against the moss-covered rocks.

"God has brought us here, Nash." She grabbed his arm and pulled him into the shallow pool at the foot of the waterfall and on toward the rocks. "Remember the words?" She closed her eyes, held her blood-streaked face to the sun and recited. "The Image of Christ lies behind the green water, the way to the light, the way to everlasting Christ, Son of God and father, savior of Caesar Philippi.

"In the shadow of the mount of Moses, love of God, man, woman and child are proclaimed to all." She waved her hand at the green-tinged water, the snow-covered mountains barely visible over the lip of the ravine. "Have you no faith, man?" she asked.

Devon yanked his arm back. "Don't let blind faith kill us, Renée."

Arif pulled his hand from Devon's and walked up to the base of the waterfall. He stood, looking up at the shimmering water, droplets refracting tiny rainbows of light, stepped forward and vanished.

Granwin took his arm in both of her hands. "I trust in God and little children, Nash. You can trust in my faith."

A shrill screech mingled with the soft sounds of the water. Devon bent his head back. Far overhead, a bird wheeled across the sun. Was it the crow come to escort them to hell? The circling bird folded back its wings and dove, cleaving the air like a missile. Suddenly its wings spread, talons extended, and the bird pirouetted in the air to settle on a protruding root. A rainbow stretched across the mist kicked up by the waterfall, arching over the bird. It cocked its head and peered down at them, then spread its wings and swooped low over the water and on down the ravine. *Not a crow, a hawk. Bless you, Grandma.*

Devon pulled Granwin close and nodded in agreement. "All of our gods are here."

A grin replaced her frown, erasing the furrows of worry and doubt.

Enough. He shoved her toward the base of the waterfall. "Come on. Let's find Arif and lose those guys up there."

He followed Granwin under the water and into the dark shadow of the waterfall. He stood for a moment letting the chill water, snow melt from Mount Hermon, wash over his head. These were the headwaters of the River Jordan. And he had never been baptized.

CHAPTER 34

Without a word of explanation, Dan Sever, spook-natty in his blazer and regimental tie, dropped a sheet of paper on Fowler's desk, spun on his heel and walked away, tasseled loafers clicking on the linoleum tiles.

"Shit almighty," Fowler muttered as he scanned the paper. *Before this is over I'll be the pariah of the Pentagon. Better brush up my resume. No more below-the-zone promotions for me.*

Unlike most of the documents strewn across Major Fowler's desk, this one was devoid of any classification marking. He scanned the sheet, more like a computer printout of a news agency wire report than a desanitized-to-protect-the-source summary from Central Intelligence Agency headquarters. Most of the shit Sever dropped off fell into the 'burn before reading' category, but this one caused Fowler to pick up his phone and punch in the number Colonel Houston had emailed to Fowler's home computer.

Fowler was only mildly surprised when Baker answered with a gruff "Hello."

"Hey, Pops, how you doing?" Fowler had no idea where the other end of the line terminated, or of who could be monitoring the conversation.

"Hey, yourself, bubby. What's up?" Baker's voice on the other end had a somber sound to it.

"Just got a piece of paper. Says we need to listen to Syrian air controllers a little closer."

"I can do that, son. But I need a hint."

Baker's voice was lower than usual, the bass almost bottoming out. Fowler wondered if his friend was fatigued, or— No "or." Fowler acutely remembered that Baker had personally dreamed up this scheme and shopped it around the Agency. Fowler had bought in, taken it on for his own, really sold it to his DIA bosses. Now he had to do something to help.

"Pops, remember Brother Guillespie, big ol' fat dude, and him talking about Jesus and Peter and James, all in their white raiments, going to the Transfiguration, all the time Brother Guillespie sweating like a pig in his white suit he was so proud of?"

"Sure, son. 'Cept you forgot John. Not John the Baptist, but the Lord's brother John. He was there, too. Climbing the mountain. Climb to Jesus, Guillespie used to say, and put more in the collection basket."

God help us, Pops sounded truly tired. Fowler wondered if he was ever going to get this across without just blurting it on the non-secure line? "Yeah, Deacon. But 'member how he'd tell the story, stompin' across in front of the congregation, yellin' and pointing up at the sun shining in the high window, the stained glass one with the mountain?"

"Why don't you cut to it, son? Ain't got time for AME reminiscences."

"Brother Guillespie used to yell 'Follow, follow our Lord Jesus' footsteps.' The mountain he was talking about?" The phone hummed back at him. Fowler waited.

"Okay, I'm with you. Now what?"

Fowler took a deep breath. "Some folks here think Devon is in the same place. Unattributed source."

"That all you got?"

"That's all." God knows he had searched and listened. "Not a peep otherwise."

"Okay, bubba. I'll see if it's enough."

Baker hung up the phone and turned to the tough-looking brunette in the dark khakis with the pips on her epaulets. "Captain Flowers—"

She brushed her long hair back from her face. "I'll call you Bert. You call me Birdi, okay? I may be wearing an Israeli uniform, but I was born in Harlem. Not sure how long I'm going to able to keep it, but I have dual citizenship. I still believe in the United States, too. It's just that family counts, sometimes more than anything else."

She shrugged her shoulder, showing off the captain's epaulets. "These have more to do with family than country. And I've never found that my two countries' policies differed in many ways." She pushed her chair back from the desk in the Israeli command center and took a clipboard over to a large wall map where she stretched up on her toes, face close to the northern tip of Israel, stretching the khakis taunt over her buttocks.

Baker sat back and admired the view, scratching his exposed big toe with the tip of his crutch. By God, this no-nonsense woman was going to make him forget his thinning gray hair, give him a little juice. Following the old cliché, her transformation from blond to what appeared to be a natural brunette had even made her seem smarter. *No, not smarter...maybe more in control, but that probably had to do with her being back in her own 'hood.*

He pointed his crutch at the map. "Friend of mine thinks Devon could be around Mount Hermon. Could he have gotten that far since the radio transmission your AWACS bird—what do you call it—the Phalcon, reported? Long damn way from Palmyra. Hermon is way the other side of Damascus from the reported radio contact."

She shrugged her shoulders, this time with a tilt of her chin that indicated she didn't know for certain either. "We also received a report of gunfire in downtown Damascus and a SAM launch south of the city, close to the highway leading to Sassa, here, in Syria." She pointed at a spot high up on the map. "I checked. The Israeli Air Force has no operations over Syrian territory, so the Syrians weren't shooting at Israeli assets."

She pulled the scrap of paper from the clipboard, folded it and put it back into her breast pocket, a tight fit. "Based on a Phalcon radar early warning indication, the command center sortied IAF interceptors searching for a low speed, low altitude aircraft approaching UN disengagement force positions in the Golan. Pilots reported no contact, so the aircraft were recalled before they attempted an overflight and the political hurrah *that* would create."

"Can your Mossad connections get us to the Golan?" Baker asked. "I don't have anything better keeping me in Nazareth. My leg stiffens up sitting around. I need a little exercise."

She laughed. "More exercise, huh? I'd have thought our little escape and evasion act maneuvering around Israeli customs last night would've gotten your blood pretty well stirred up." Then she nodded her head, a more serious look on her face. "I think I can access considerably more operations assets in Israel than when Colonel Houston introduced us in Riyadh. In fact, I know I can."

She picked up the phone and smiled across at him. "When we close this file, I'll buy you a drink to thank you properly for your fine escort service out of the Kingdom. At best I thought I was going out in handcuffs. At worst I worried a bit about being turned over to the Saudis."

"Sounds good." Baker wondered if it was any great sin for a duly baptized African Methodist Episcopalian deacon to mess around with a Jew. Probably not if she were an officer in the Mossad. If she got Devon out, he'd even buy the drink.

The mist-filled air swirling around behind the waterfall chilled Devon to the bone, leaving him shivering in his wet clothes but somehow rejuvenated.

The small room behind the waterfall glowed with a strange luminance as the sun danced over the flowing water. Refracted rainbows flowed across the walls, the colors rippling over Granwin and Arif, flashing and sparkling over Granwin's eyes.

Devon let his pupils adjust to the low light before he scanned the blank wall behind them. "Is there a place to hide back away from the water? The locals are sure to know about this place." They huddled together against the moss-covered rock, ankle deep in flowing water. Faint voices made their way through the rush of water. "Sounds like they're getting closer."

"Chief, I think there is a way…" Arif's voice faded as he wiggled into a hole under a protruding ledge.

"Is it big enough for the rest of us to get through?"

Granwin's answer was to drop flat and follow Arif. Devon knelt in the slick mud. The grenade dropped from his shirt pocket and Devon realized the pain in his chest wasn't a heart attack, but a bad case of grenade imprint. He snapped open the briefcase and dropped the grenade inside.

The shouts grew louder outside the thin screen of water as Devon shoved the briefcase through the hole and slithered after it, shoulders and head scraping the edges. He cleared the hole and stood, wiping away the layer of mud, and held his hand over his head to keep from bumping the rock. When he stretched his arm, his fingertips barely touched the cool rock. Enough light filtered in to illuminate a large cavity, so large the light gave out before the back wall appeared.

Granwin leaned against him and shivered.

"Cold?" he asked.

Her answer was a nod as she buried her face against his chest.

They both jumped as a shout echoed through the room. Someone had followed them under the waterfall.

"Chief," Arif whispered. "They have found the overhang. The one shouting thinks he has seen tracks into the cave."

Devon gently set the briefcase by his feet and put his other arm around the boy.

"End of the trail, scout. Listen to me. You tell those guys out there I dragged you along, pretend you don't know me, then run like hell the first chance you get."

"I run like hell, but not that way," Arif replied. He pulled away from Devon's arm. "I'm staying with you, wherever you go."

In the faint light Devon could tell he had his mother's brown eyes—big, soft, and burning with determination.

"Look." Arif reached up to a narrow ledge, slowly moving his hand, then snatched. He held up a small snake by the head, tail wiggling. "Here is something for them to follow." He tossed the snake into the flowing water for it to disappear into the pool. A short screech, then the voices outside grew louder.

"Careful, Arif." Devon shivered at the boy's nerve. "Come on, let's get away from these guys."

Devon picked up the briefcase and led them back into the blackness, facing into a slight breeze as he shuffled across the inclined rock, hand out in front, reaching for the back wall, hoping the snakes had gone to lunch. He didn't have Arif's knack. Or will.

He stopped and Granwin bumped into his back, slipping for a moment on the wet rock. Droplets of water ran down Devon's back where she squeezed a handful of wet shirt.

"Hey!" Devon called into the void ahead. Behind him, Granwin jumped at his low shout.

Devon strained his ears, playing bat, trying to decide how far back the recess reached. The faint hint of an echo suggested the cave reached far back into the mountain. Behind them, he could distinguish two separate voices outside the hole. He continued walking, feeling with his toes as he shuffled forward in what was now total darkness.

He jammed his knuckles against the wall as the rock corridor curved in front of him. "Damn!" The rock angled away as smooth as glass, likely an old water chute. Underfoot, chill water soaked through the seams of his boots.

"Renée, you got a good hold on Arif?"

"Yes." Her answer was muffled, face against the back of his shirt.

"I think this passageway leads back into the mountain." He let his fingers slide along the wall as the incline steepened, enough that Devon's knees began to ache. The distorted voices behind them caused him to quicken the pace. He looked back, but the light from the entrance had disappeared.

"Are we turning or is my equilibrium all screwed up from the crash?"

"It goes to this side." Arif patted the wall to Devon's left. The slight reverberations of their voices suggested the passage was narrowing as it turned, the radius of the curve so sharp Devon had trouble fighting off the whirling in his head.

"Where will this take us?" Granwin turned him loose. Her breath was short, almost a pant.

"Renée, are you feeling all right?"

"My ribs hurt, but nothing to stop us. I only wonder if we are only going deeper into a trap. Or worse, if we will be lost in here forever."

He could hear her fingernails sliding across the rock. He closed his eyes and held his face up. No sense of a breeze. He wondered if the passage had forked behind them, and if he'd led them into a dead end. This was one time he wished he hadn't listened to Grandma and her tales of the watery underworld, filled with demons and the very forces of evil. And Arif's snakes. "Come on. This passage has an end. Let's find it, hope it comes to an opening. If not, we'll keep looking until we do find a way out."

Devon led them deeper into the cavern until his right shoulder scraped along the wall. A few steps later, he choked back a curse when he cracked his head against a protruding rock.

"Nash?"

"I'm all right. Feels like the passageway is getting smaller. Definitely getting tighter." Cold rock brushed both shoulders, so close he had to twist sideways to sidle past the overhang. The passage twisted and turned, but he sidestepped along as it narrowed, pressing against his body. Twenty or so steps beyond the overhang, the ceiling sloped upwards under his hand, but the floor matched it with an even steeper angle. Suddenly, the rock wall fell away from his right shoulder, opening up the passageway. "Stop here for a moment."

Arif crowded up against his legs in the darkness, shivering.

"Stop and rest. Let me see what's going on."

He shifted the briefcase to his left hand and held it out so it scraped along the wall, a harsh metallic grind that put his teeth on edge. He stretched his right out into the dark, fingertips extended, feeling for the far wall. He shuffled through the dark, sliding his feet across a rounded trough carved in the middle of the passageway, etched through the years by the ice melt from the slopes of Mount Hermon flowing down to the River Jordan and on to the Sea of Galilee. The squish of his boots as he crossed the trough hinted they were still following the watercourse.

Devon wondered what they would find at the end. *An underground lake? An impassable torrent?* He stopped and whistled softly. Two different echoes seemed to come back.

He took another step and the trough smoothed out about the same time the floor resumed its incline. "You guys still back there?" he called out.

"No. I got tired and went out for tea. Yes, we're bloody well here. Now quit mucking around and come get us," Granwin answered.

"I think there's a split here." He put his back to the left wall and shuffled straight across the corridor, splashed through the water trough until his outstretched fingers touched the cold rock of the opposite wall. "Passageway to our left angles back up. The right side is grooved, washed out, still a trace of water flowing down."

He put his back to the wall and started back, pausing as he slid his feet over the slick trough. He stopped, blackness whirling around him. *Which way does the floor slant?* He felt disorientated, dizzy, panic rising, and dropped to a knee. The briefcase clanged against the rock floor, a reminder of why they were running like rats up a pitch-black tunnel to nowhere.

"Nash?" Granwin's voice sounded miles away.

"Right here. Put your hand on the left wall and come up this way." He stood, willing the swirling stars from behind his clenched eyelids, and inched over to the wall until Arif and Granwin huddled up next to him, their wet clothes clammy against his arm. "This could go on forever. Why don't you guys stay here where it's dry and wait here for me to explore this side corridor? If it dead ends, you won't have to come all the way back to try the other way."

"Chief, can I go—?" Arif's voice trailed off.

"What, scout? I'm open to any suggestions. I'm not much of an expert of caving." Their voices reverberated up and down the corridors.

"I don't want you to leave me. I want to go with you."

Devon sensed a bit of a quaver in Arif's tone.

"But if you tell me to, I'll stay with Mrs. Granwin."

"I'll settle this discussion. We'll both go with you. If we have to come back, we'll come back together." Granwin's declaration was final.

"Grab my belt, then, and let's give it another try."

Devon waited until Granwin wiggled her fingers under his belt, then led them deeper and higher into the mountain. The ceiling scraped Devon's head, forcing him to crouch, then drop to a crawl, pushing the briefcase in front of him. The dry rock scraped along his back, forcing him lower and lower, at the same time closing in on both shoulders, squeezing closer with each shuffle forward on hands and knees.

About when he thought he was going to have to go to a full crawl on his belly, the ceiling fell away. He struggled through a narrow opening and climbed to his knees, stifling a groan as his joints popped.

The echo from a short whistle suggested an open room, not big, but at least wider than the narrow passageway they had just traversed. Devon carefully stood, then pulled Granwin and Arif up behind him. "You guys see a glimmer anywhere? We've gone far enough we should be close to the surface." He shifted the briefcase to his right hand and followed the rock wall around to his left.

The briefcase clanged against a solid object. "Watch out. There's something in the way." Devon ran his hand over the large obstruction. Smooth, squared corners, chiseled indentations across the broad top. "This is manmade!" he exclaimed. "Polished rock."

Arif patted his hands around the rock. "I think this is a place of dead people," he solemnly announced.

Devon continued talking as he followed the curved wall. "The rock wall has been chiseled smooth. I can feel the tool marks. And here!" *A way out?* "Feels like plaster, like someone has plastered over rocks on this side. Then more chiseled rock, then the wall smooths out again, powdery like someone has painted over the rock." He continued around the chamber until he passed the narrow entrance they had entered through, then bumped into Granwin. "It's almost circular, and I'd say only fifteen, twenty feet across at the most."

"Arif is correct." Granwin's voice was as solemn as Arif's.

Granwin's fingers brushed Devon's as she ran her hand along the top of the obstruction in the pitch dark. "This is a coffin and we're in a burial vault. Feel the letters carved into the top of the stone." She pulled Devon's hand with hers along the top.

A light flickered, followed by the sharp bite of sulfur in Devon's nose. The unexpected light glared in his eyes after the intense dark of the cavern. Devon blinked and focused as the flickering light of a match lit Arif's face. Arif held the match up and the light wavered over a small room. A rectangular vault dominated the middle of the floor, leaving an arms-length of space between it and the walls. Otherwise, the room was bare except for—

The light flickered out and Devon wasn't sure what else he had seen, maybe something that looked like a rusty hammerhead on the floor and a litter of rock fragments scattered across the chamber.

"Got another match?" asked Devon. The image of the room drifted around, a ghost his mind remembered from the smoky match.

"It feels like three more." Arif hesitated. "But the others are wet."

"Wait at moment before you try it," Granwin asked. "I think I saw a niche."

Devon shivered as he waited, listening to Granwin's fingernails sliding high along the walls.

"Thank you, Lord," Granwin exclaimed, followed by a dull thump. "Jesus and Mary, save me from myself!"

Devon stared into the darkness, holding his questions while he listened to something rolling across the floor and the soft swish of Granwin's damp skirt as she chased after it.

"An ancient tallow candle," she exclaimed. "Arif, stand next to me so we can light it, and strike another match." A dull glow, then another, then a tiny flash blossomed and just as quickly died out.

"No more matches." Arif sounded as if he had struck out in the ninth.

Devon patted his pockets. His lighter was long gone, blown up with the Rover. "Still got the knife?"

"Yes." Devon could hear the soft whisper of wet cloth as Arif fumbled for a moment.

"Here it is." Arif tapped the top of the stone sarcophagus until Devon slid his hand over and took the folding knife.

"Now it's time I taught you how to be a real Scout." He felt around his feet until his fingers closed around the briefcase handle. He placed it up on the coffin. "Scurry around and see if you can find me a really hard rock, something with a sharp edge, not the sandstone kind that falls apart in your hand."

Devon snapped open the briefcase and fished around until he came across a folded sheet of paper. He ripped the sheet into shreds, as fine as he could tear, hoping these were the sheets on which he had sketched out the warhead design.

"This probably won't catch by itself," he muttered. "Renée, baby, you got any dry toilet paper left?" That would fit right in with his thoughts of Kee and Khan, burning their dreams with ass-wipe.

"Here." Her fingers slid along his arm and pressed a sheet of tissue into his open hand.

Devon ripped up the tissue, added it to the bird's nest of shredded paper. Arif's small hand slid along his arm in the dark, then pressed a sliver of rock into his hand. Devon held the back edge of the knife blade next to the paper. "Got the candle ready?"

"Just light the paper," Granwin replied.

Holding the rock in one hand over the paper, he scraped the knife over the edge of the rock. *Nothing!* He tried again. Either the metal was too hard or the stone not hard enough. He shifted hands, striking with the knife against the rock. More nothing. The knife handle was lightweight, aluminum or some crap.

"Arif, I saw something on the floor by the foot of the tomb, almost like a tool. See if you can find it."

"Here. It feels like an old hammer." The sarcophagus thumped as Arif dropped a heavy object on top.

Devon felt across the top of the slab until his fingers closed around a hunk of metal, so rusted he could feel the top layers fall away as he picked it up. He scraped the loose surface against the edge of the slab until it felt whole. Before he could try it, the lump fell apart in his hands. Useless.

"Wait a minute." Devon felt across the slab to the open briefcase and patted the insides until he found the grenade nestled in a corner. He gripped the grenade, cold in his hand, and tossed it around so the butterfly handle was in his palm. He nestled his fist against the nest of paper and struck the rock edge against the rough cast iron casing.

On the third hit a single glimmer of light reflected from the white toilet paper. He tried again.

A tiny glow spread through the nest. Devon bent his face close to the pile of tinder and blew. Beside him Arif joined in, his breath a whisper in Devon's ear until a flame popped up and ran across a shred of paper. Granwin thrust the tip of a candlewick into the flame, then shielded it with her hand as the chamber came to life. Devon grinned as he fed the remaining shreds of paper into the fire.

Solved that problem. No more nuclear designs.

The crutch into his underarm as Baker hobbled back inside the Israeli military building, ostensibly a supply depot, but in reality a Mossad field operations center. But walking was better than sitting by a phone, shifting from cheek to cheek with his leg up in a cast, or standing at the window watching the quick walk of nervous people on the streets. Baker didn't like the local streets. He felt too vulnerable in his cast whenever he walked the neighborhood. He lumbered past Flowers, plopped down in a chair, and threw his crutch into the corner.

Flowers looked at her reflection in a pane of glass, carefully braiding her hair. "Glad you're back. I was getting ready to come looking for you."

"I'd rather be on armed patrol in Mogadishu than walk the streets of Nazareth. Too much like the bad parts of Bosnia. Too much hate in the young." Baker pointed at the kids hanging over a fence. "I'm just never sure if one of the dirty-faced kids is hiding a bomb, fast on his way to heaven, by being the next *jihad* martyr." Then he realized the implications of Flowers' remark. "Something happening?" he asked.

"We can't go in as Israelis. Plus, I don't think you really want to pass as a Jew." Flowers flashed him a big smile as she coiled her long braid, then tucked it under the beret, transforming her from a sensuous woman to a card-carrying Canadian peacekeeper, medusa insignia on her collar.

Baker couldn't criticize; he was back in his role as a UN mine clearing advisor, dressed out in his Georgia Bulldog sweatshirt and Atlanta Braves cap pulled down tight over his head.

"I've arranged for an Israeli Search and Rescue helicopter from Palmacim Air Base, using the cover we suspect a UN helicopter has crashed. Even the Israeli Air Force can't overfly the separation zone, but they can fly us into the Austrian peacekeeper headquarters in the northern sector of the UN disengagement force area. We'll have to see if the UN Peacekeepers can take us the rest of the way. Ready?"

She was halfway to the door before he could find his damn crutch. He hopped down the gravel path and followed her out to the landing pad just as a helicopter touched down. On his last flight in a Blackhawk, the bird was black and the crew called themselves Nightstalkers. This one was light blue, marked with the blue Star of David and flown by IAF flight officers.

As Flowers put an arm around him to help him into the helicopter, he had a sudden thought that breaking a leg wasn't all so bad.

"You've flown a lot before?" she asked, pulling his seat belt snug and securing his crutch under the seat.

"Yeah, a few times," he answered. *Several hundred takeoffs, not quite as many landings unless you counted rappelling.*

The twin turbine revs built and the helicopter began its rhythmic hopping, the old feeling that the bird was trying to escape the ground. Baker leaned out the open door and let the warm air beat down over him from the helicopter blades. Air assaults were always a good way to pump up the adrenaline. He leaned back in as the crew chief swung onboard, slammed the door, and they were airborne, headed toward the Golan.

Flowers leaned over, mouth close to his ear, and pointed down to a scattering of rusted tank hulks and separated turrets with bent gun tubes littering the rugged terrain rolling under them. "I came up here once before. To see those."

"Why?" He stared down at the ground, very aware of her warm shoulder pressed against his.

"My brother died in one of those tanks in October, 1973, when the Syrians launched a surprise attack, in concert with the Egyptians in the Sinai. That's part of the rationale why Israel is hesitant to give it back to the Syrians. And it was pretty good motivation for a kid to do something useful with her life besides chew gum and play eight-tracks."

Below, patches of green alternated with unmistakable traces of old lava flows and massive boulders. Baker pointed at the odd conical mounds poking up from the ground. "Big anthills if we were in Africa. Are they some kind of fortifications?"

She shook her head. "Natural. Volcanic vents."

"And those?" They flew cross over a bare-scraped hilltop criss-crossed with trenches and sandbagged positions.

"UN outposts. Scattered all over the zone."

By the time Baker got his cast adjusted so the vibration was contributing a pleasant friction to the itchy spot by his knee, the helicopter flared, nose high, slowed and dropped toward the ground and a big X marking a pad inside a barbed wire enclosed compound. White frame buildings painted with blue accents surrounded the landing pad. Snow-covered mountains lined the background, like a panorama for a tourist guide.

Opposite, mechanics worked on a line of white vans with UN painted across their sides in big, block letters.

The helicopter hovered for a moment, then leveled off and crabbed over to set down by a refuel point, turning to bring into view a sandbagged bunker, a hint that the idyllic world around them could rapidly turn to shit. The helicopter settled and the crew chief opened the sliding doors, motioning them away from the aircraft so he could start refueling.

The sun felt good. The blades had slowed and the twin turbines wound down to a slow grind before anyone came out to the helicopter pad to meet them. An officer, Austrian by the gray beret and shoulder patch, and captain by the pips on his epaulets, strutted up and smartly saluted Flowers.

She grabbed a med bag and jumped down from the Blackhawk, leaving Baker to drag his crutch out and hop over the rocky ground, tool bag flopping over his shoulder. Except for the rumble of a truck engine, the compound was quiet, a quaint, whitewashed village set in the shadow of Mount Hermon—a sanitized version of Irbil.

"Captain, welcome to Austrian Battalion. I am Captain Franz." The officer nodded to Baker and hurried on with his report. "Our roving patrols reported a low flying helicopter just inside the Bravo line, the eastern boundary of the sector, followed by an observation post sighting of armed paramilitary activity and what they believe is a crashed aircraft, although it is too far away from their position to be sure.

"Our patrol vehicles are several kilometers south of here at the moment." He shrugged his shoulders in a slight apology. "The patrol will need, perhaps, a further hour until they reach the crash site, so your medical support may be very timely."

Franz made up for short legs with a rapid stride. Baker's armpit chaffed as the crutch dug into his skin, but he kept pace close enough to hear Franz's breathless report.

"The ready reaction force has been tasked by HQ to take you to the site. Stand by for a moment and we'll see what the latest report provides on the downed aircraft." He ducked into a sandbagged bunker sprouting a forest of antennas, and as quickly popped back out and waved for them to follow him to a white M113 armored personnel carrier.

The back ramp was down and several solders pored over a map, evidently tracing a route. Baker exchanged a nod with the men sitting cross-legged on top of the APC. They obviously appraised Flowers' attributes as they waited.

"Captain Flowers, this is Warrant Kendric." The Austrian introduced Flowers to a Canadian NCO with an MP brassard on his sleeve who turned from the map board.

"Sir." Kendric braced and saluted the two captains. Kendric was tall with a sunburned face, big blond mustache, muscles bulging under his rolled battledress sleeves. Captain Franz glanced at a scrap of paper in his hand and marked a spot on Kendric's map. "The aircraft dropped off the Phalcon radar about here, less than three kilometers from the camp, only minutes away."

"Got a radio call from the outpost—" Kendric pointed at a hilltop on the map close to Franz's mark. "—about here. They heard some firing in that direction. Glad you medical folks could make it up here. Our medic's sicker than a buzzard and, other than the one report, we haven't had any contact with the crash site. Don't know what kind of shape the crew might be in."

Or if Devon is one of them, Baker thought, looking around at the wire fence and sandbagged bunkers.

Kendric looked up from the map at Flowers. "You must be new in country?"

Flowers nodded, a slightly terrified look on her face that forced Baker to bite the inside of his cheek to keep from laughing. *Damn fine spy. She should be on Broadway.*

Kendric gave her a fatherly smile. "Don't worry about your safety. We'll take good care of you, ma'am." He patted her on the shoulder.

Watch your hand, thought Baker, as Flowers flashed him a warning look. Baker clenched his jaw and kept a straight face.

Kendric's eyes washed over Baker. "And you?" he asked. The Canadian, obviously a career soldier, took in Baker's sweatshirt and jeans. "American, but no camera. Here for the ambiance?"

"I dig out duds." Baker waved his bag of tools. "I'm on the UN rolls as a mine clearer."

Kendric gave his crutch a look. "Looks like you're not too bloody good."

"Be glad to stay back here if you don't need me." Baker made a show of looking over the compound. "Got a canteen around?"

Kendric grunted, waved them all inside the APC, and yelled at the driver to start up his engine. The big diesel belched a black gob of smoke before Baker could drag his cast through the hatch.

Kendric briefed his team in a couple of barked sentences, then stepped up on the commander's seat. The men pulled on blue-covered helmets, and, before Baker could find a handhold, the APC slewed around on its tracks and headed out the compound gate, dropping him to his butt against Flowers on the troop seats.

Baker closed his eyes and took a couple of deep breaths. Since Mogadishu, riding inside an APC wasn't his thing. Sweat started pouring down the sides of his face. Leaving his crutch behind with Flowers, he levered himself to an ammo box strapped in the middle of the APC, then pulled himself up and out of the open center hatch until he was perched on the top deck. This was a standard issue, M113 APC, except no add-on cupola, not even the US-standard .50-caliber machine gun on the commander's hatch.

In front of Baker, Kendric stood half out of the commander's hatch, scanning the road ahead, constantly talking into a boom mike, directing the driver around a winding road to the coordinates on the map marking the suspected crash site.

Flowers' early morning phone call hadn't confirmed Devon was on board, but the circumstances felt right. Baker wondered who was flying, if Khan was on board. *No use speculating.*

Besides, Baker thought he would go stir crazy if he had to spend another day in the Israeli Defense Force command center, ignoring the other Israeli officers' disdain at supporting an intelligence operation involving an American. Out here he was with soldiers, maybe Canadians who believed he was a straphanger, but hellfire, that's what he was, so enjoy. And maybe find Devon in all this bull-pucky.

Two of the Peacekeepers, one on each side of the APC, kept a careful overlook toward the hills, armed with C-9 light machine guns, the Canadian equivalent of the US Squad Automatic Weapon. The others held Canadian C-7s, bulked-up M-16 rifles with stubby telescopic sights mounted on the carry handles, at the ready. More importantly, every man looked like they knew what the devil they were doing, each covering a sector, even to the rear.

The Peacekeeper beside Baker grinned, teeth pearly against coal-black skin, and reached out a hand. "My name is Rasty. You like the ride on top, eh?" he yelled over, a hint of a Jamaican twang in his high-pitched voice.

"Bert," Baker introduced himself. He pointed down into the tossing APC. "Seen too many RPG holes punched in these cans. Rather ride on top and let 'em blow me off." When Baker glanced down, Flowers smiled up at him, head shaking.

Kendric twisted around and pulled down his headset. "You soldiered, old man? Tanker?"

Baker shook his head and pointed at the parachute insignia on Kendric's chest. "Ground-pounder, with a few jumps. I even got some wings that look kind of like those."

"Canadian?" Kendric's eyes narrowed. "Don't ever remember seeing your face around."

Baker laughed. "Wings were Brit. I did an exchange with the Special Air Service boys."

"Ever been in this Indian country before?" Kendric asked. The Special Air Service comment had seemed to put a bit of respect in Kendric's tone.

"Indian country? Like hostile?" Baker asked.

"Yeah. We're just south of Lebanon, sandwiched between Israel and Syria. Hezbollah freedom fighters like to drop rockets on us for sport. The Druze in the villages act like a bunch of wild Indians with plenty of guns, and I swear to God most of them are smugglers. I was raised on a ranch between Calgary and Red Deer, and I've seen tough country, tough people. Believe me, this is real Indian country."

Before Baker could respond, Rasty shouted and motioned with his rifle.

Baker grabbed at his cap and leaned out into the wind, searching the ground in the direction Rasty pointed, eyes watering as the dust boiled from the tracks and up in his face.

A helicopter lay on its side, split open, in the middle of a field. As the APC rocked to a stop, a man ran from the wreckage, an unrecognizable part in his arms, and splashed across a nearby stream.

"Sweet Jesus, please help us in our time of need," Baker muttered, one hand on his cap and the other gripping the side of the APC.

Flowers climbed up on the ammo box, clinging to Baker's good leg, and raised her eyebrows with a question. He pointed at the mangled wreckage and she nodded, now understanding, eyes wide. Twisted metal and caked dirt partially obliterated the blue UN markings on the tail boom. The main body reminded Baker of a scrap heap. Long strips of skin had been sheared from the main airframe, and the rotor blades were scattered over the field.

One gunner stayed on top of the APC with Rasty and Kendric while the others dropped off the sides or exited the ramp that thumped down behind them. Baker muscled his way down to the ammo box, then followed Flowers across the ramp and over to the wreck, cursing his weak leg and the crutch, slowed even more by the plowed furrows.

Two of the Peacekeepers clambered up and through the gaping hole in the helicopter and into the wreck. One almost immediately popped back up and yelled back at Kendric.

Baker limped up to Flowers, standing there with her so-far useless med bag.

"What'd he say?" he asked.

She shook her head. "No one in there. A few blood splatters, but no sign of the pilot or crew."

The other soldier tossed a logbook across to Kendric, who slipped on a pair of reading glasses and flipped through the pages. "The aircraft was assigned to the High Commission for Refugees." He frowned at the book. "Based in Iraq. What the devil is it doing in Syria?" He pointed across the ravine. "Damn. There's another commission helicopter. Maybe they've already rescued the crew."

Baker dragged his cast to the edge of a deep ravine. To his right and at a slightly higher elevation, water surged out to fall clear for fifteen or twenty feet, then splashed against an outcrop of green, moss-covered rock. One last miniature Niagara imitation over the outcrop, then the water, broken by the fall into a heavy mist, splattered into the bottom of the shadow-filled ravine.

For a moment, Baker caught a glimpse of something moving below. He bent further over the edge, leaning precariously on his crutch. Water swirled around a shallow pool at the bottom of the falls, then flowed between the grassy banks and on toward a distant river.

Baker wrinkled his nose and looked down at his cast, then up at the sky, now heavy with dark clouds. “Lord, is it going to be one of those days?” He hadn’t spent much time on the farm as a kid, but he recognized cow shit when he saw it. And he had confirmation from his nose.

Worn rocks marked a path down the side of the ravine to a pool downstream from the waterfall. Nice biblical scenery, but no Devon.

No Granwin.

No kid.

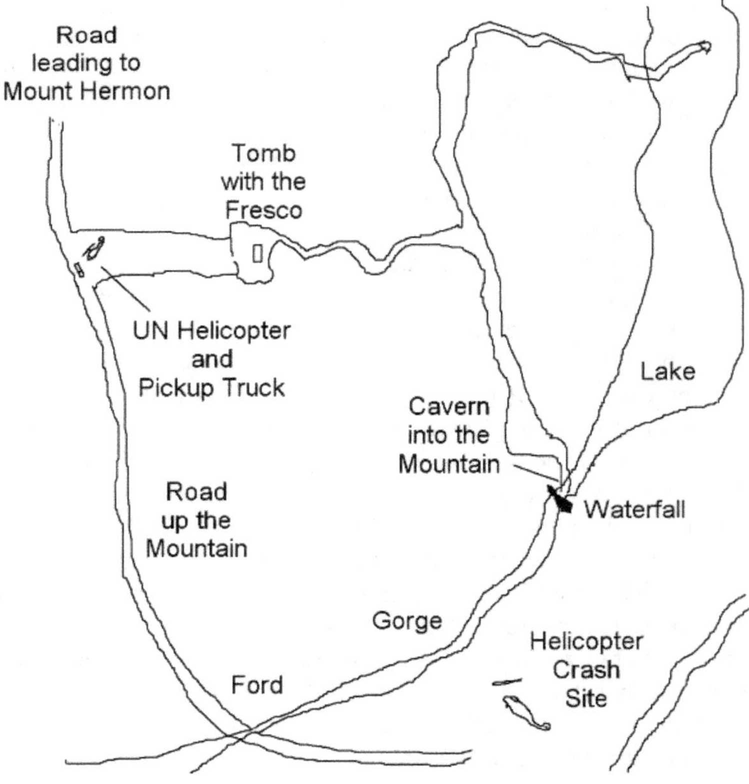

CHAPTER 35

Granwin leaned over the coffin, her face close to the engraving. "Cyrus, citizen of Athena." She translated the lines cut in the stone, word by word to Devon. "This is a Greek-style sarcophagus. Probably a wealthy land owner's remains lie here, entombed perhaps in the time—" She hesitated. "—in the time of the Caesars. Perhaps older. Or younger." She sat down, back against the tomb. "Now what do we do?"

"Good question." Devon gently shoved Arif down beside Granwin, then slid down so the boy was pinned between them.

Arif said something to Granwin in Arabic, and she laughed.

"He doesn't know the word for 'squeeze' in English."

Devon wiggled over on his butt, giving Arif breathing room, then leaned back against the cold stone. The smoky flame from the candle barely illuminated the wall around them.

"I wonder how old all this is?" Granwin asked.

Devon didn't have an answer. He closed his eyes for a moment and let his exhaustion drain out into the cold rock floor.

Arif's soft voice cut through the haze. "Chief, did Mother really sin?"

Devon opened his eyes. Granwin had taken the candle and bent over, face close to what appeared to be a fresco on the far wall, lightly tracing the images with her fingertips.

"We all sin, Arif. Some because they are ignorant, and some because they are plain evil. Most of us, when we realize we've sinned, try to do better and pray for forgiveness. The evil ones just keep sinning. I doubt very much your mother ever really sinned."

"But she slept in your bed. Wasn't that a sin?"

The creaking bed in his mother's room had always signaled Devon when Jason stayed over. He'd known what was going on, so why shouldn't Arif?

"If there was a sinner, scout, it was me. Your mom came to me, yes. But she wanted to make sure you were safe. You don't worry about Sara. She's in heaven now with your dad." He patted the boy's leg. "And she'll be real mad if I don't take care of you, so let's figure out how to get out of here."

"Did I sin when I hit the sheik?" Arif persisted.

Devon shook his head. "That sure wasn't a sin, scout. That was survival. If you hadn't gotten away from him with the Nissan, you wouldn't have saved us from the explosion."

"But I didn't save my mother." The candlelight flickered across his face.

"No." Devon considered Arif's comment. "But I couldn't either. I think we both did our best. Now we've got to keep on going." He felt in his pocket for the knife. "Sara would want us to talk about escape."

"Devon." Granwin's voice had a strange catch to it. "Come and look."

"Later, Renée. First Arif and I are going to dig us out of this tomb." He crawled over to the wall and thumped his way along with a fist-sized rock until he reached a point that sounded soft, then chipped away with the knife, working the plaster away from the rocks, slowly digging out the loose mortar. Arif knelt beside him, digging with a long wooden stave he had discovered on the floor of the crypt.

Devon had dug enough to build up a sweat in the cool air, enough to remind him they hadn't eaten all day, when a tiny pinpoint of light glimmered through the wall. Devon dropped the knife and clawed his fingers into the gap, pulling away bits of mortar and small rocks. First a gleam, then a flood of light bathed the chamber. Devon kept digging until a head-sized hole opened up.

"Thank you, God," cried Renée, as the room glowed with light.

*** crypt map

Warm, moist air, scented with spring blossoms, rushed in. Devon squinted into the bright sunlight. Gradually, his eyes adjusted until he recognized the lilac bushes outside the tomb. When he bent over and peered out the small hole toward the horizon, he could see hills rising from the far side of the valley to disappear into heavy clouds. As he took a deep breath of the fresh air, the clouds drifted apart enough to hint at snow-covered mountain peaks not too far distant.

A shadow flickered across the shaft of light. A man called out and another answered.

"Shhhh..." Devon cautioned. He pulled Arif over to the opening. "Voices outside. What are they saying?" he whispered.

Arif put his ear to the hole and listened for a moment. "They are shouting about hearing voices and digging," Arif whispered back.

"One calls another colonel. They are searching for a way into the mountain."

Devon carefully fit several of the larger chunks of rock back into the hole, enough to obscure the opening, but with a gap that allowed a finger of light to shine into the chamber.

"We'll wait them out," Devon said, and slid back over to the sarcophagus and sat facing the opening. "When it's dark, we'll dig clear and slip down the mountain." He sat back and closed his eyes, arm around Arif's shoulder.

"Nash," Granwin whispered, subdued with the report of searchers outside. "Please, look. This is important." She set the candle on the floor just as the flame flickered out, leaving a wisp of smoke curling around the fresh air whispering through the gap in the wall.

Enough light from the small hole played over the far wall and the fresco to see brown streaks marring indistinct images. Closer, Devon could make out his own finger trails, left, he supposed, when he had circled the chamber in the dark. Devon stared at the fresco, finally resolving the images of distant mountains, the skyline just as he had seen through the opening a moment before. Below the mountain images, a wash of green represented the fertile valley floor while patterns of darker green brush marks signified tall Lebanon cedars. The tops of the distant mountains were dusted white. The background was outlined with black as if to suggest deep shadows in the clear valley air.

"Here. Can you see them?" Granwin pointed at a cluster of images in the center.

Devon squatted and slowly studied the fresco, focusing on the figures. Five people dominated the foreground, the others behind those in less detail. The artist had been a master of shadow and form, sufficient to imply the background crowd included both men and women, using a hint of a broad shoulder and the drape of clothing over hip or breast. Where Devon's hand had wiped across the image, he could see the background layered under the foreground, as if the landscape had been painted earlier, with the figures added as an after-thought.

"Who were they, and why a fresco painted in a tomb? Is the man in the picture the same one buried here?" Devon wondered.

"How beautiful," Granwin whispered. "The artist painted the skin of this man with a dark flesh tone, common with people who spent much of their time outside. But a lighter pigment was used for the woman, suggesting someone who spent more of her time inside, or covered with the robes. Beside the couple he placed an even darker man, leaning on a staff. Look.

"The soft shadows hint that each is cloaked in loose robes, tinted with the same reddish-brown hue used for the distant mountains, perhaps to show they were dirty with travel, or perhaps the robes' natural color. Strange. The men's robes have an added touch of yellow surrounding them so they seem to glow." She knelt down closer to the floor.

"Did you do this?" asked Granwin. She pointed at the pigment in the lower right corner where the green of the valley blended into the brown of the slopes held a distinct pattern, unmistakably a pair of hand prints, one slightly larger than the other, with the tips of their fingers interlocking.

"I don't think so. The streaks across the top are probably where I felt my way around the room, but I didn't put the hand prints on the bottom. Ask Arif."

"Not me."

The shifting light made its way across the handprints to the print of a baby's foot.

Devon laughed. "I know I didn't do that." He pointed at a line of what appeared to be Arabic letters on the opposite corner. "What do the words say?"

Granwin traced the letters, right to left. "I think it is Aramaic." The sunbeam backlighted her head as she bent close to the smudged fresco. Dust motes stirred up by their activity glimmered in the narrow sunbeam. "*Misssh...misshkhaa*?" She sounded out the letters, then bent even closer, nose almost touching the fresco. "*Mshee-Khaa*. Aramaic?" Her voice caught. "Messiah?"

Granwin quickly traced the remaining letters with her fingers, lips moving. She stopped, turned toward Devon. "It says 'Family of the Messiah,' followed by 'Ajax, the healed.' The words are written in Middle Aramaic, the language of the people who lived in this valley, the very language Jesus spoke." She grabbed Devon's arm.

"Nash, God has sent us to this place, to where Jesus taught, on these very slopes." Her voice trembled. Even her hand was shaking on his arm. "The artist who made the tomb, who painted the wall saw him, saw Jesus healing a child. This is a picture of our Lord Jesus Christ."

Arif squatted beside them. "The prophet from the Koran?" he asked.

"The very same one, Arif. His portrait, left here all these years for us to uncover, to bring to the rest of the world. And look." Granwin's finger trembled as she pointed to the figures. "A woman and a child, by his side."

"Did Jesus have a family?" asked Arif.

Devon knelt close by the fresco, his forehead touching Granwin's. His eyes adjusted to the beam of light and he focused on the individual elements of the fresco. "The Bible tells of Jesus' mother and father, brothers, but not a family of his own." Always the skeptic, Devon shook his head. "Surely the figures in the fresco are just the man buried in the tomb, his family, perhaps a wealthy Syrian."

"Oh, no, Nash. Look closely." Granwin voice was soft, almost a whisper in the small chamber.

Devon had whiled away many hours in the backwoods clapboard church, staring at the fanciful figures in the illustrated Sunday school book. In the books, Jesus was always a tall Caucasian with classical, aquiline features and flowing light brown hair.

The symmetry of the fresco focused the viewer's eyes on a man standing on a limestone terrace. Bearded, his hair was cropped close, dark, glistening with highlights. He was slightly shorter than the man beside him and slightly taller than the woman by his side. One hand stretches toward a child kneeling at his feet. The other was around the shoulders of the woman close beside him. Both smiled at the kneeling child. The child's mouth turned up in laughter as the man's fingers, each painted in exquisite detail, touched the child's head. On the woman's hip, a smaller child clutched a white kitten sprawled on its back between the child's chest and the woman.

The cat's eyes glittered, seemed almost alive as the dust flickered in the sunbeam. Even in the feeble light shining through the crack in the wall, the eyes, facial features, the expressions of the central figures were finely wrought, laid in by a delicate brush.

"I don't know if he's Jesus or not, but the woman and the child on her hip belong with the man in the fresco. Even I can see the love in their faces." As Devon said the words, he knew.

Jesus had taught, healed, and loved at this very place, with his family.

CHAPTER 36

Arif coughed and scrubbed at his eyes. "Chief, something smells wrong."

Devon cautiously sniffed at the air.

"Yellow dust is floating in the air," exclaimed Arif, wagging his hand in front of his face. Saffron-tinted particles swirled across the sunbeam in the wake of Arif's motions.

"Damn. They must've popped a smoke grenade down at the waterfall to see if there are any air vents, any other way out of the mountain." The tendrils of smoke whisked toward the crack in the wall. A chill ran down his back.

"Should we plug the outlet?" asked Granwin. The smoke became denser, filling the chamber.

"Yeah. I'll take care of it." Devon picked up a handful of crumbled rock to stuff back in the crack. "We can still wait them out."

He hoped the smoke was just that, and not some of Saddam's mustard gas. He cautiously sniffed at the air as he gathered another handful of rock. Devon had seen too many intelligence briefings with piles of dead bodies resulting from Saddam's use of poison gas.

A rumble from the dark passageway gave warning, followed by a blast of air that surged from the dark passageway and knocked Devon against the chamber floor, followed by a roar that battered his ears. He rolled to the middle of the rock floor, dazed and blinded by the sudden flood of sunlight from the outside as the tainted air swirled clear of the chamber.

The face of a man appeared in the opening, hand fanning at the smoke. He leaned into the hole, then jerked back, yelling to someone. Devon could halfway hear the words, but he couldn't understand. Half-deaf from the explosion, he couldn't understand what the man was saying. The muzzle of a weapon replaced the face. That he understood. Devon rolled to the wall as a burst of gunfire and the whine and rattle of ricocheting bullets filled the chamber.

He shoved Arif behind the sarcophagus and covered him with his own body until the firing stopped, then scrambled to the wall where Granwin lay curled in a ball under the fresco. Devon shoved her across the rock floor toward the sarcophagus then sprang toward the light. The muzzle poked back through the hole. Devon grabbed the hot metal and jerked, the searing pain in his palm firing a buried spark in his soul. Deep inside, the yowl started.

Forgive me, Jesus, the black bear calls from deep in the swamp.

Surprised, the man on the other side fell back, and Devon came away with an AK-47. He flipped it around and triggered off a quick burst.

Through the hole, he could see a dusty pickup truck slide to a halt in front of a helicopter, rotor blades slowly spinning to a halt. When he bent down, Devon saw a man running from the helicopter, a gray canister in his hand. Devon thought he recognized his gait, last seen running across the Iraqi desert, when the man got closer. Then the face of a man he had erased from his memory years ago came into focus.

Tristan Aragon, the smart-assed French commando, now a revered industry giant according to the gospel of Granwin, crouched outside the hole holding a grenade. Devon shoved the AK's muzzle back into the hole, blocking his view.

Can it really be the same Aragon? Devon paused. Perhaps Aragon was here to rescue.

"Tristan," he called out. "Is that you?" Devon squatted, better to see through the small opening.

"Yes, my old comrade," an unseen voice answered. "Since we last met, I have made many important investments in the Middle East. Some of which you have placed in jeopardy with your meddling. Fortunately, we have a mutual associate who has taken it upon himself to ensure you are no longer a threat. Emerge with no more trouble and the boy and the woman will come to no harm."

"Great. Would you help me get them out?" Devon asked. He pulled back the AK. Could he trust Aragon? Maybe he really was here to save them, bring some sense to this, and get Granwin and Arif out of this damned tomb.

In response, Aragon bent close to the hole and stared at Devon for a moment with a humorless smile. He pulled the pin on the grenade, carefully sat it in the opening and stepped back out of sight.

Devon suddenly recognized the battered gray cylinder with a yellow stripe. Another dammed antique, a white phosphorous grenade.

Devon fired the AK. The bullet slammed into the grenade, driving it out of the hole and spinning it across the ground toward the helicopter. Devon dove behind the sarcophagus where Granwin and Arif huddled, Granwin's arms curled around Arif's head.

Seconds later, a flash of light filled the tomb. Devon raised his head to see the helicopter spattered with bits of burning phosphorous and Aragon running across Devon's view, clothing on fire.

Someone outside shrieked, poked a pistol through the hole, and fired slow, methodical shots. The deafening muzzle blasts, the whiz and crack of bullets thudding into the soft walls and ricocheting off the hard granite of the sarcophagus, all but drowned out Granwin's screams.

The firing paused. Khan's face filled the hole.

Devon scrambled across the rough floor to the discarded rifle, jerked it up and pulled the trigger. The AK fired, one shot that slammed into the wall beside the opening and splattered dirt into the hole.

Khan's face disappeared.

Devon jerked the trigger again, but nothing happened, not even a click. He glanced down. The bolt had locked back—no bullets. He threw the AK down and scrambled back to Granwin and Arif huddled behind the sarcophagus.

"Get into the passageway. It's Khan. He'll come back when he figures out I'm out of ammo. Maybe we can lose him in the cave." Arif wiggled into the black hole, but Granwin pushed back against Devon, shaking her head.

"Nash, we can't leave. We can't lose this." She pulled away from his grip.

"The fresco's been here a long time, Renée. If we don't get away, no one will ever know it was here...not anyone who cares." He shoved her toward the black hole. "I can't lose you. Or Arif."

When he spoke the boy's name, she looked at him for a moment then, without a word turned toward the passage and crawled inside. He followed her, scraping the skin from his elbows in his rush to squirm through the narrow opening and slither down the corridor. Granwin and Arif moved ahead of him, ghostly in the shadows cast from the chamber and its portal to the outside world.

"Arif, you there?" he called out.

Ahead the sound of rushing water seemed louder than when they'd first come up the passageway.

"I'm here, Chief. Which way do I go?" Arif answered.

"Put your left hand on the wall and go until the corridor opens up. Stop where the passageway splits." Devon shuffled after Arif and Granwin down the curving rock passageway. Soon the blackness swallowed Arif and Granwin, sounds of their movement lost in the rush of cold water deep in the cave.

Arif suddenly cried out, his yelp unmistakable even with the reverberations.

Before he could stop, Devon tumbled over Arif and Granwin, cracking the top of his head his head against the rough rock. They had stumbled into the old trough, worn slick with years of slowly moving water. Now the water ran faster and deeper than it had earlier. Behind them, voices echoed from the burial chamber. Devon clutched empty air, swept his arms around until he located Arif and Granwin. Together, all three struggled to their feet.

"Jesus, save me," whispered Granwin, shivering in the cold. "What's happening, Nash?"

"More water's coming down from somewhere, maybe one of the lakes on the top of the plateau. Someone set off an explosion, probably below at the waterfall, or maybe dropped a grenade into one of the lakes above. I don't know which. The pressure must've blown out the hole in the chamber and opened up the lake drain. Trying to flush us out." Devon leaned back against the cool rock. "Khan...the bastard is still hunting us."

"Chief." Arif pressed something cold against Devon's arm. "I saw his face and remembered what Mother said. His is the face of evil. I brought this with me, to kill again if I must."

Devon felt the serrations of the old frag grenade in Arif's small hand.

"You didn't tell me Khan was the one who killed my Mother, but I feel it is so. Only men of great evil kill women and children. It is written in the Koran. I heard the meanness in his voice. He is as Mother said. He is evil."

Devon felt the water droplets from Arif shaking his head.

"I do not want to die in here in the darkness. But if Allah decides it is to be, I will make sure the man who killed my mother dies also." The boy's voice held no fear, only defiance. "Then I can stand beside my father and mother while Allah passes judgment on us all."

Devon eased the grenade from Arif's fingers. "You're right, scout. Khan pulled the trigger and killed your mother. You lead Renée to safety. I'll make sure Khan dies. But the only talking you're going to do with Allah anytime soon is kneeling on your prayer rug."

As Devon spoke, the water pressure against his legs increased, washing up over the top of his boots, pulling at his pant legs. "We need to hurry before the water bursts free. You two head on down the passageway. I'm going to stop Khan. Right here."

"Nash." Granwin's determination was replaced by a rising tone of panic and grasping fingers.

"Just keep going down the passage, the way we came. Right hand on the wall and you'll come to the waterfall room, then get on out. If there's someone there to meet you, so be it. If not, keep going down the streambed until you can climb to high ground. I'll look for you when I come out."

Devon pried her fingers from his arm. "Don't worry. I'm coming out behind you. We've come too far and still have too much to tell each other. Go." He shoved her and Arif into the narrow passageway, then turned back toward the approaching voices.

Devon listened for a moment. Voices reverberated down the narrow passageway from the burial chamber. Granwin's voice as she urged Arif downward was lost in the hiss of the water rushing around his feet. Devon stood facing the darkness and voices. He thought of Sara in his arms, blood seeping though her blouse. He intended to keep his promise to her.

What had his dad's citation read? *Gave his life to save those of his fellow soldiers.* Heroic words, and all Devon had to remember his father. Arif already had a dead father, Granwin a dead husband. Who the hell would remember him, stuffed in this pitch-black hole? Was the bear remembered, or just a warm hide for the next winter? He bent the grenade safety pin straight. Hell, no time to be the hunted, the unremembered. Today he had promises to keep.

Every good cowboy movie had an Indian ambush in a box canyon. If need be, this black passageway would have to be his canyon, his Little Big Horn.

"Pancho," he yelled into the darkness. His voice rang hollowly over the rushing water, now up to his knees, forcing him back against the rock. He struggled against the flow. The water pushed him back down the twisting corridor. "Pancho, you really want to know how to destroy the Hindus?"

"Return the drawings and I'll show you how it'll be done," the answer came back, Khan's nearness startling Devon. "And you, damn you, Nash Devon. Come back up here or Allah will send the *jinn* to escort you to Satan and his fires of hell," Khan called out.

Khan sounded close, just beyond the turn. A flashlight beam probed the walls, grew, then stopped on Devon's face, blinding after the stark blackness. He stared back into the light. Granwin and Arif should be almost out by now. He just had to stall Khan a little longer.

"Why, Pancho? Why all the killing?" he called out.

"The *jihad* began long before you and I came to this earth, Nash. As far back as the Crusades, Muslims and Christians have fought one another. Today, you drain our oil and impose the Jews on the Palestinians. Since I was a child, I've watched the Hindus threaten the sanctity of our mosques.

"Now, I am but one of *al Ahad* who resists the infidels. Before, our actions were feeble—one, two, three men, a single bomb. Soon the actions will no longer be disregarded, brushed off like the destruction of your warships, your embassies. Nations will notice—more than notice. Governments must learn to treat the Brotherhood with respect and caution. Or the world will reel from the consequences and reap the pain of retribution.

The sneer was clear in Khan's voice. "Your feeble explosion in the Iraqi nuclear facility was only a setback. The Brotherhood has the will and has gathered the capacity. Soon we will have all the technology needed to destroy our enemies, to obliterate them from this earth."

The water inexorably pushed Devon down the passageway as Khan spoke, the voice and light keeping pace. The curve of the wall shadowed the glare from his eyes for a moment and Devon recognized Khan's heavy Webley dancing in the light beam. The hammer clicked, loudly enough to carry over the sound of the water pulling at Devon's legs.

"I warn you, Nash. You're not the only man who understands missiles. I hoped you'd assist and perhaps even live past this day. But no, no, you continue to be as stupid as ever."

"Pancho, I know Pakistan isn't an evil country. I have Muslim friends. I even thought you were one. Was I that wrong?" Devon knew the answer. Khan had given it to him when he spoke of Devon's wife, but he needed to stall, not for Rachel, but for Granwin and Arif.

Khan's wavering beam of light painted compressed blue and brown layers of rock, worn by years of water flow, a fitting tomb as the water forced Devon down the passageway.

Devon bumped against the rock, the final curve before the sharp incline down to the waterfall. Greeks were buried in this mountain. More than fitting, it was an elegant place to bury a Scots-Irish Lumbee. Grandma would be proud he was this close to the mother of all things. And Momma would be proud he had seen Jesus.

"My government is slow to act. Even today they talk of peace with India. We are led, like America, by men who only think of their own power, not of the people. They even forget the martyrs of Islam."

Khan was worse than a slick-suited evangelist, always preaching. *And he believes in martyrs. Okay, far enough. This is the place I make my stand. What had Aragon said just before he'd fired the Milan? "El momento de verdad," or something like that.*

Devon pulled the pin on the grenade. He held it up so the damp metal glistened in the wavering light. The old iron was cold in his grip. "You're right, Pancho. We were at war all that time I was buying you booze and inviting you over to my house for supper. I was just too naive to know it. I understand now."

He was tired. One boy had died at his hands. Another had died while he stood and watched, letting another man try to save him.The light focused on the grenade.

"Fool!" Khan's cry reverberated through the passageway, suddenly pitch black again.

Fingers dug into Devon's arm, twisting him back against the rock. Khan crushed him back against the wall, forearm against Devon's throat. Devon could smell Khan's breath, sour with fear, his face close to Devon's in the blackness.

"Here's your *jinn*, come for you." Devon let the butterfly handle spring free and the handle twanged against the rock.

"What have you done?" Khan screamed, pushing away.

Another light flashed along the corridor, silhouetting Khan backpedaling through the narrow passageway, water up to his crotch now.

"Too many lies, Pancho." Devon felt the heat on his cold palm as the fuse ignited, burning its way down toward the old-fashioned TNT packed into the grenade. He let the incessant water push him around the curve, then pitched the grenade back toward the sound of Khan's voice. The grenade clanged off the rock wall and the light beam waved wildly across the roof. A spark flashed and bloomed into a pitiful orange glow, all too anticlimactic for such promise. Bits of shrapnel ricocheted off the walls; a deep thunder from the detonation reverberated down the passageway, but strangely, without the killing blast Devon had braced for.

A gush of air pushed against him, building from a whisper to a murmur to a roar. The pressure built, and suddenly, a wall of water hammered against him, slammed him back and forth against the sides of the passageway. Devon had released the mountain's demons.

As quickly as it rose, the water level dropped. Devon spluttered and clawed at the rough rock until he wedged his fingertips in a crack and pulled himself upright and out of the water, amazed he was alive.

Well, shit! Khan had probably lost all patience this time. Devon waited for the next flash of light to spotlight him against the wall, the next rattle of AK fire, the clack and spew of a grenade fuse flying back his way.

Instead, he felt a new rush of air across his wet skin, building to hurricane strength, pulling at his flesh. This time it was for real. He felt the roar coming. Devon turned and tried to run down the black passageway, one hand sliding along the wet wall.

"Arif! Renée!" he yelled into the blackness. No answer. Were they out, or face down in a black corner with the water snakes?

The water climbed up to his buttocks, slowing him to a sluggish waddle, then a solid wall of unseen water slammed against him as he tried to take a deep breath. He bounced against one rock wall, then the other, trying to hold his breath as he the water flung him through the black passageway. The lake was flushing right down this passageway like a giant commode.

He shot from the blackness into a dim chamber, swirling around in the water like an insignificant bubble. Vision blurred, the brightness of the small exit hole flashed by his eyes as the turbulence rolled him across the top of the chamber and ground him against the rock, forcing the last remaining air from his lungs.

Suddenly, he remembered the thunder and lightning of a spring storm crashing around the weather-beaten barn, the old mare and Granddad trying to help her with a breech birth. The foal felt all folded up in the mare, her eyes big with pain has she tried to birth her baby, Grandpa's arms all bloody trying to help. Devon had kneeled down, put his hands on the mare's swollen belly and worked the baby around, gently pushing against the blood-slick hide, working the head around to the birth canal.

The current swirled Devon around and around the cavern, the opening flashing by his eyes as he twirled in the water. He slammed against the wall, then the water pushed him like a hand and he shot toward the light, losing consciousness as his lungs filled with water.

"Please, Jesus, let the foal live," he had prayed that night to the white man's God. By the next evening, the rains had stopped and the new colt, already steady on his slim legs, stood by the mare's side.

Devon slammed against the rock, pressure pulling him like a plug into a crevice. He uncurled and shot through the narrow opening. Light, strangely diffused, danced around in his eyes, starry points floating and swirling through his head. He tried to breathe. Water gagged him, flooding his nose, his throat, choking. The sparkles brightened, wavering over his eyes. Devon stared up at the sun sparkling through the surface.

He fought the malaise and struggled to wave his arms, twist in the water, and get his feet under him. The sparkles dimmed and the water took on a pink tint, like the sunset across the Syrian desert, the last rays of the day refracted through the dust.

His eyes closed and his body drifted with the current, newborn.

CHAPTER 37

The ground around Baker trembled. He pushed back from the precipice with his crutch, stumbling away from the edge of the ravine. Dark clouds tumbled across the sky driven by a fitful wind from the mountains. Splatters of rain pattered on his head. A single shot cracked overhead. Muffled gunfire echoed across the valley. Gray smoke rose from an explosion further up the slope. Once again he was in the valley of death.

Baker wheeled around, searching for a weapon more lethal than his crutch. The dismounted Canadian Peacekeepers dropped down into defensive positions as they searched for targets, rifles at the ready. Brown dirt kicked up as the gunfire increased, now a hail of bullets answered by the Canadians, measured shots from their rifles, long tearing bursts from the two machine guns.

Baker wiped a fine mist that had begun to fall away from his eyes and turned toward Flowers. Her beret had fallen off and her braid had begun to loosen, letting her hair stream back in the wind. Crouched beside the APC, she scanned the mountainside behind him.

"What the devil's going on?" Baker yelled over at her.

Before Flowers could answer, the side of the mountain seemed to heave, rocking Baker back on his heels. He turned back to the ravine, staring across at Mount Hermon in the distance. Hermon was the mountain where Jesus spoke to Moses, not Kilauea doing a tourist eruption show. He didn't remember Brother Guillespie saying anything about volcanic activity when he preached his sermon about Jesus going up on the mountain with John and Peter and James, and coming back all shiny, glowing with biblical wonderment in the Transfiguration of the New Testament.

Baker gawked at the snow-covered peaks, fully expecting to see a full eruption gush forth, spewing smoke and ash and flowing lava, a primeval return to times far earlier than the Garden of Eden.

Down in the ravine, two people ran from beneath the waterfall and floundered through the pool. Something was wrong in the bowels of the mountain. The date palms scattered along the ravine side rocked. Treetops whipped back and forth, tearing at their roots.

Several slowly toppled into the stream to be snatched away by the current.

Baker leaned over the edge and yelled, “Run, run. Get out of there,”, waving with his free arm. He stopped yelling at the two people below, realizing they couldn’t hear him over the roar of the water.

Both staggered downstream until one urged the other up the side of the ravine. The flow began to abate and they climbed onto the bank. At the head of the ravine, the waterfall slowed to a trickle for a moment, then the ground rumbled again, more fiercely this time than before.

Spray exploded, up, all the way over Baker’s head, like an incoming Katyusha rocket had landed in the streambed. A geyser burst from the rocks underneath where the waterfall once fell, driving a wall of water so strong the front edge curled like a wave racing toward the coconut palms lining Haunauma Bay. Except the trees were date palms, and this was the Golan Heights.

Water roared down the streambed, ripping out the remaining palms along the bank and scouring the sparse grass until nothing was left but raw mud. Baker pounded his crutch into the ground, helpless against the fury of the water. The surge swept the two off the bank and carried them downstream and out of sight behind a massive boulder.

Baker ignored the scattered gunfire behind him and hobbled along the lip of the ravine. He plunged over the side, sliding and stumbling down a muddy path to the water’s edge. A man drifted by, motionless in the water. Baker threw aside his crutch and floundered through the shallow water after the man who slowly twisted in the current.

Baker dove after the submerged man, dragging his body through the water with his arms until his fingers closed around the man’s ankle, then an arm. He struggled with the inert body, pulling it up onto to the muddy bank, where he rolled the man over on his back.

Ugly, bearded face and scraggly, black hair streaming water down over his face, the man gagged and spewed up water.

“Glory be and hallelujah!”

Where from, or why, Baker had no idea, but he had fished Devon from the swirling water. Devon coughed, then sucked in a deep breath. Baker felt a sense of elation race through him. He’d pulled a lot of strings to get Devon into this. Thank God he was able to get him out. Baker pounded him on the back until Devon waved an arm for him to stop.

"Bert, thank God," Devon gasped.

"What happened, Chief, inside the mountain? I thought we were going to be blown to kingdom come."

"I flipped an old frag grenade at Khan, deep in one of the passageways. The frag probably just pissed him off, but the explosion must've opened up one of the lakes on the plateau above. Sure made a hell of a mess. Cleaned my clock." He pushed up on his elbows, closed his eyes and shook his head, then looked out over the streambed. "Where's Renée and Arif?"

"Got no idea, Chief. Two other people were down here, but a wall of water washed them around the bend, out of sight. Was that Renée and the kid? Were they with you?"

Devon stood and shook his head, flinging water like a spaniel. He twisted out of Baker's grip and stumbled along a narrow path paralleling the water. "Renée!" he shouted. "Arif!"

"Hold up, man," Baker called out, and tried to follow. He sprawled face down in the mud, and looked back at his leg. Pale gray flesh showed through where the plaster had crumbled and fallen away from his cast. Long strands of gauze streamed out into the water, slowly unraveling as the cast continued to dissolve. Baker levered himself up on one leg using his arms, but when he tried to force another step, his leg gave way.

"Ah, bejesus," was all he got out before he tumbled headfirst into the stream.

Flowers jerked back against the metal doorframe when a bullet thunked into the APC's aluminum armor, just missing the exterior fuel tank by her head. The two men on top of the APC turned their weapons toward the line of barbed wire tangled in the helicopter wreckage and the far embankment. The *poot* sound of a RPG launch quickly followed, simultaneous with the return fire from the Peacekeepers. She dove to the ground and buried her face in the plowed loam as hot metal casings from the machine gun overhead jangled over her arms.

An instant later, the RPG hit, flinging Flowers over onto her back. She wondered for a moment if this was how her brother had died, then blinked dirt from her eyes to see smoke rising from the ground where the RPG had plowed up a shallow crater in front of the APC. Overhead, the Canadian gunners laid down a withering line of fire. The APC engine roared and spit dirt from the tracks as it pivoted toward the muzzle flashes. Flowers rolled clear of the churning tracks when the driver gunned the diesel and the APC lurched forward toward the shooters.

"Captain!" One of the men on the APC shouted at her, holding a rifle in the air. He pitched it in her direction and turned to continue firing at the embankment.

Flowers crawled over to the C-7, shook off the dirt and checked the chamber. She racked back the charging handle, flipping out an unfired round, and let the main spring slam the bolt home, stripping a fresh cartridge from the magazine. *The Syrian bastards.* If they hadn't killed her brother somewhere in this very pile of shit-eating rocks, she'd still be in Jersey, probably hauling a bunch of kids around in a van. Now it was get-even time. She crawled toward the edge of the ravine where she last saw Baker and his damned crutch, dragging the med kit across the furrows by a shoulder strap, rifle in hand.

At the bottom of the ravine water flowed around a treadless tank, red with rust and abandoned in the middle of a ford. Faint ruts marked where vehicles bypassed the wreck to ford the stream. A faint road ran up the side of the mountain past a burning helicopter and on toward Mount Hermon.

Baker, identifiable by his trailing bits of cast and gauze, teetered on top of the tank hulk, leaning on his crutch. Up the muddy road a man pointed a pistol at Baker and a group of people at the edge of the water.

As Flowers watched, Baker launched his crutch like a spear at the man with the pistol. Then everything blurred as Baker tumbled from the tank into the stream. The man's pistol roared, bucking up over his shoulder as he fired at Baker. Spray from the bullets' impacts fell all around Baker as ricochets clanged into the tank.

Flowers took aim with the rifle, trying to still her trembling hands as bullets from the firefight raging behind her cracked overhead. Shaking too much to use the scope, she snapped off a shot. Below, the man firing the pistol looked up, a startled look on his face when the dirt kicked at his feet. Flowers took a deep breath and slowed her breathing enough to center the scope on his face, long enough to recognize Khan, the Pakistani she had managed to avoid in Saudi. As she fired his face disappeared from the scope. She pulled the rifle down, Khan was gone.

Flowers ran for the path and Baker. He wasn't her brother, but she wasn't going to lose a friend, maybe more, maybe less, in this God forsaken valley of death.

Devon gathered Arif and Granwin in his arms, shielding them until he was sure the fusillade of bullets had stopped.

"I wish I had kept the grenade," whispered Arif.

Devon looked up when a shadow washed over Granwin's face. Devon squinted into the sun, then raised his hand to shade his eyes. Khan squatted behind a pile of rubble, his Webley leveled at them. A splash behind them caused Devon to turn in time to see Baker floating away, face down, in the water.

"Come back," Khan shouted when Devon dove into the water after Baker.

Devon stood, knee deep in the water. Baker was gone.

When he looked up the mountain Khan jerked Arif away from Granwin and held him as a shield. Khan stumbled over Baker's crutch then began backing up the mountainside.

Devon walked out of the water and faced Khan, fists clenched, weaponless. "You can't hide behind women and children any longer, Pancho. It's time to end this. Didn't you see the fresco up there in the burial chamber? My Bible says Jesus was a man of love, of family, teaching peace to all people. Do Allah's words in the Koran tell you to throw all of that away?"

It began to rain, a slight mist mingled with the smoke from the fire on the slope above them. Devon blinked, water running into his eyes

Khan slipped, but kept his grip on Arif. "I've listened too long to you and even tried to explain the plight of the Muslim, but you continue with your Christian blasphemy. I will eradicate the idolatry painted in the mountain." With one hand, Khan waved the pistol at Devon and dragged Arif up the hill with the other. "Do not follow us."

"Nash, what are we to do?" Renée's voice was shrill as she struggled to her feet, clutching Devon for support as they stood in the red mud and watched Khan disappear up the slope with Arif in tow. "Don't let him take Arif. Is Khan going to destroy the fresco? Oh, God, what'll we do?"

"Stay here." Devon shoved Granwin toward the wet grass by the road and started up the slope on his hands and knees, crawling bush to bush, up to where the grade leveled off to a natural stage ringed by low scrub.

Flat on his stomach, he slithered his way toward a gap in a thick hedge. Through the thin leaves, he could see flames flickering into the sky to join drifting patches of dirty smoke as bits of phosphorous sputtered in the rain. A charred body lay next to the helicopter. To his right, Devon saw a gaping hole torn in the mountainside, large enough for a man to walk into the tomb. But where was Arif?

"Be quiet, boy, and you'll live to return to Iraq and a new, true life. Continue to help the American and you will die as Allah wills and I obey."

Khan's voice came from Devon's left, behind the row of bushes. Devon crawled forward, easing through the damp shrubbery. Ten feet away, Khan wrapped Arif's hands with a strip of tape and tossed him into the cab of a pickup truck parked precariously close to the smoldering helicopter and its fuel tanks. Khan slammed the door and dragged a large leather suitcase from the bed of the truck, past Devon and toward the entrance into the mountain.

A hand grabbed at Devon's leg. He looked back as a mud-covered Granwin crawled up even with him, pulling herself forward through the bushes until she could see Arif in the vehicle.

"Is Arif safe?" she asked.

As they watched, Arif slid over the seat back and before Devon could answer the truck began moving down the road toward the ford, Arif's taped hands on the steering wheel, the wheels crunching the dry rocks in the roadway.

"He'll crash at the bottom," Granwin whispered.

Devon's vision of Arif crashing into the tank hulk dissipated when the brake lights flashed. Arif, as always, was taking care of himself.

Khan stood directly in front of them, also watching the truck roll over the slope and down the trail.

"Look, Renée," Devon whispered as he motioned toward the rugged skyline beyond the vehicle, the same snow-streaked mountains dotted with tall Lebanon cedars they had seen from inside the burial chamber. "We're at the slope where Jesus spoke to the people. Family, Renée. Family is most important of all. You go see about Arif."

She hesitated a moment, holding his face in her mud-covered hands, staring into his eyes as if to capture his soul. "We'll be waiting for you." The bush crackled as she worked her way back, then slid back down the slope.

Faint peals of thunder muffled the sounds of Renée's departure. Devon inched his way back through the bushes just as Khan dragged the suitcase toward the ragged opening in the mountain. As he passed Devon the suitcase looked more and more like the one from the lab Kee had been so proud of, similar to the one Devon had ripped the warhead from.

If the fool detonated a nuclear weapon, the explosion would tear the top off this mountain and cover the Golan and the streams that fed the Jordan River with radioactive debris. Galilee would become a sea of death, for Arif and Granwin, and every other innocent trapped by Khan's fanaticism, for people on both banks of the Jordon and the Red Sea.

Devon glanced over his shoulder to make sure Granwin was out of sight, then forced his way through the bushes and stood, water dripping from his clothes. He shivered as a cool breezed blew down from the mountains, pushing dark rain clouds across the sun.

"Pancho," he called out.

Khan spun to face him. He pointed the pistol at Devon as he continued to back toward the opening.

"What are you doing? If that's a nuke, you'll kill everybody in the valley, yourself included, and leave the valley poisoned for years."

Khan paused at the tomb entrance. "Ah, Nash. I didn't recognize you for the moment, face all painted like a Plains Indian."

Devon reached up and felt the mud streaked down his cheek. Khan seemed calm, now, as if he had made up his mind about something very important.

"My own father was killed by the British." Khan waved the Webley at Devon. "Today I'll avenge my father's death, and many others." His voice rose to a shout. "I'll find a place beside Allah for destroying this place of sacrilege." His voice softened again, his face composed in something closer to a smile. "My actions will save the boy from sin and life as an infidel. If you, and the *houri*, die here, your atonement will please me."

Khan continued, rambling through all the diatribes welled up in his soul. "You've sinned more than most infidels, Nash Devon. Allah is impatiently waiting to judge you."

What could Devon say to stop him? "Others have died, but we don't have to. The Koran says be charitable to women and children. Would you kill innocents despite the words of Mohammed?" Two steps, three. "Would you kill women and children as easily as you killed the cat?" Khan was a fanatic, but was he totally beyond reason?

Khan slammed the suitcase to the ground and pointed the pistol at Devon, now close enough to see Khan's old scar twisted with a sneer. "You are the wrong one to speak to me of holy words, Nash, of killing. My cousin, the *mujahideen* you knew as Olanti, disappeared while assigned to bring you to Facility Number Seven. He once saved your very life. Did he also die at your hands?

"You're the sinner. I am but your own *mullah* with Allah's true message. Listen carefully." Khan thumbed back the hammer and sighted down the long barrel.

"Lord Jesus, I have killed and I have sinned. But let Renée and Arif live," Devon prayed as he stared down at the barrel.

Khan pulled the trigger and the old pistol jerked in Khan's hand with a metallic clack. Devon heart pounded in his chest, body tensed for the report, the impact of the big bullet that didn't come.

Khan broke open the pistol and stared at the discharged brass in the cylinder, then threw the pistol aside. "Then if not by my hand, by the Hand of Allah." He dropped to his knees by the suitcase, flipped clear the leather straps and threw open the case.

Devon took a deep breath and another step toward Khan and the suitcase. A row of blank LED readouts, interspersed with several small dials, ran across the top of the gray metal container nested inside the suitcase. He caught a glimpse of a polished steel cylinder. This wasn't the suitcase he had sabotaged in the mountain. Below the row of dials and readouts blinked a large indicator light, crimson red in the dark shadow of the building clouds.

Khan flipped aside a shield and placed his thumb on the protected toggle switch. "It looks almost comical, yes, Nash? Like something in an adventure movie."

Devon picked up the pistol and started toward Khan. He stopped when the Pakistani held up his hand.

"But we're not in a movie. This bomb is real." He thumbed the toggle switch and a row of green LEDs flickered to life. "The Russians were generous in their original design. They gave their operatives an opportunity to escape, if they set the delay long enough." He slapped a large red button and the LEDs instantly changed to yellow and flickered, a steady beat as the reading incremented each second, counting.

"This, the Iraqi version, is more realistic. The mechanism provides sufficient time to place the device where it will be most effective when detonated and, in the Islamic tradition, allows the operator to become a martyr." He picked up the open suitcase, carefully balancing it as he stood.

Khan held the suitcase out in front of him like an offering. "Now you can leave this earth together with me, to be judged by Allah." He turned and carried the suitcase though the ragged hole and into the burial chamber.

Dark clouds flickered with muted hues as lightning streaked down to the far peaks, delayed peals of thunder in a soft timpani roll in the distance. Devon followed Khan into the dark chamber, suddenly brightened by an extended sheet of lightning just outside.

Khan slid behind the massive sarcophagus, shoved Devon's discarded briefcase aside and replaced it with the leather suitcase. "Stand back. In two hundred and ten seconds, our personal nuclear cataclysm will begin, sending us all to judgment." He smiled in the dim light. The yellow light from the LEDs flicked in Khan's eyes as the seconds counted down.

"I see, over on the wall, the picture you spoke of. There." Khan pointed at the fresco.

The image seemed to dance under the flicker of distant lightning. "If the man pictured is truly Jesus, He spoke only as a prophet, saving prostitutes and healing lepers. I bring to you salvation at the hand of the true God of us all." The blinking LEDs flashed from yellow to red. "Salvation will be mine, damnation yours, in one hundred and twenty seconds, only two more minutes."

"Jesus may only be a man, Pancho, but He was a man who taught love and compassion, not hate and death. Now stop the sequence!" Devon sprang toward the case and hammered the pistol, butt-first, into the metal faceplate, pounding at the controls.

"Get away," roared Khan. His spittle splattered against Devon's face. His fist came out of the dark and smashed against Devon's forehead.

Devon fell back, dazed, against the wall. He felt the chalky image smear under his hands as he pushed himself upright.

"You're defeated, Nash. Stand up straight like a good soldier and accept your fate." Khan's defiant voice boomed from behind the tomb where he stood with his hands across the case, protecting it from Devon's attack.

Devon stepped up to the tomb and faced Khan across the lights, flickering with each second. "Not me. Even if I die, my soul lives on, flying with the hawk. But no *Inshallah* for me. I want the others outside to live. You mock Christianity. You degrade my wife, my honor, you even mock the ways of my ancestors, the Lumbees and the other tribes, the Scots, the Irish, all of them.

"But those are only your words and my insignificant mortality. I can accept fault for not being perfect. But I love those outside more than life and I'll be damned if I let you kill them." Devon put the heels of both hands under the edge of the sarcophagus' marble top, planted his feet and pushed.

The heavy slab ground against the base as Khan stared across at Devon, hands still protecting the suitcase.

"Stop!" Khan screamed, snatching the suitcase up from the tomb lid.

Devon's shoulder joints both popped, loud in the small chamber. He clenched his gut and shoved, one final push. The sarcophagus lid began moving, slowly sliding toward Khan, first just millimeters, then the polished marble top suddenly flipped up and over and out of Devon's hands with a thunderous crash. Devon fell forward to stare down at a sightless skull lying peacefully in the bottom of the tomb, suddenly released from centuries of darkness.

Khan yowled as the marble top crushed him and the suitcase against the wall.

Devon scrambled around the tomb and dug at the broken rock, clawing to dig out the case. The LEDs continued to flash, half hidden in the dust and marble fragments. He threw chunks of rock aside until all that was left was the massive slab pinning the case and Khan to the rock floor. The case was bent into a distorted "V," still firmly lodged under the polished lid.

"Our time on this earth is over," gasped Khan, face twisted in pain, illuminated by the red LEDs as they clicked from triple to double digits.

"Then die alone, you bastard. May Allah deliver you straight down through this mountain, directly to Satan, your true master." Devon threw down the last crumbled bits of marble. When he turned, another lightning strobe imprinted the fresco in his mind, each tiny detail forever frozen in his memory, even after the cavern returned to darkness.

Devon walked out of the chamber into air that tingled with ozone as a lightning bolt arced into the slope, raising the hair on the back of his arms as the thunderous crash pierced the air.

In the distance, tall trees swayed, while overhead, the wind tore at the clouds, cleaving out patches of clear blue afternoon sky. The moon had risen early and glowed high in one of the clear patches, a floating Islamic crescent visible for a moment until the wind covered it with a dark storm cloud.

Devon walked toward the road, wishing he could hold Granwin once more before the detonation, tousle Arif's hair and show him how to whistle an American tune. Maybe Arif would have taught him to catch snakes. Devon stopped at the side of the slope.

Across the ravine, a white APC started down the steep incline toward the ford. Granwin and Arif stood below, waving up at him. Before he could wave back, the mountain thundered and threw him into the sky.

CHAPTER 38

Devon was flying, soaring far out over the ravine with the hawk, diving toward the water below. Was this his day of atonement for all his sins, his Yom Kippur and Ramadan? Was it to be his life, Granwin and Arif's, in exchange for the woman and child dead in the desert? Had he been so wrong all this time. Was he, not Khan, falling into the hands of Satan?

Sudden blackness and cold took his breath. Then pain brought him back to feel hands dragging him from the water. Was he now baptized? He blinked the water from his eyes and slowly focused on Granwin and Arif, staring down at him. The dried mud on Granwin's face cracked when she finally smiled, Arif's worried face close beside hers.

"Hey, Chief." Baker, leaning on a crutch, blocked the sun overhead. "You're a hard man to keep up with. What happened up there?" He motioned toward the mountainside. "We saw you up on the slope, then an almighty explosion. You came flying down, took one fine damn tumble down the mountain and ended up splat into the creek."

Devon shook his head, spitting out blood where he had bitten the inside of his cheek.

Granwin wiped the water from his face with a corner torn from her blouse. "Oh, Nash, but for the grace of God we'd all be dead."

Devon closed his eyes. Had he flown with the hawk or an angel? When he opened his eyes again, the first thing he saw was Granwin's cross, dangling from her neck.

"Birdi, come check him out." Baker backed up to let a woman in fatigues kneel beside Devon.

She dropped a bag by her side and pushed a mass of long hair back from her face, then began probing with her fingers, reviving the pain.

Devon looked down at his left arm. The skin was purple and the angle didn't seem right. Blood oozed from a break in the skin. But he could see, and feel, all over. He could feel the ache all the way to the roots of his hair.

Devon focused on the woman's pips. "Easy, Captain." He looked at her for a moment. The sun glared down, blurring his vision, but without the dirt-smears, her face rang a bell. "Birdi?" *But Birdi was a blond, wasn't she?*

Before she could answer, an APC in UN colors grumbled across the stream and to a halt, belching diesel fumes. A soldier in a blue helmet jumped down and trotted over. "You all right, Captain Flowers?" he asked. "Where the devil did these people all come from, the helicopter? What was the explosion?"

"Warrant Kendric, this is Major Devon, the man Captain Flowers was looking for. We really weren't expecting the others, but they're welcome." Baker motioned up the trail with his crutch. "Something blew up inside the mountain."

Devon reached out toward Baker with his good hand. "Bert, listen to me. This is very important."

"Easy, Chief. Just take it easy. Captain Flowers here is a Canadian nurse with the UN. She'll take care of you." Baker frowned and shook his head, trying to send some sort of signal. "We need to go. Warrant Kendric will clear the area."

"Games later, Bert. Khan triggered a suitcase nuke up there. I smashed it up pretty good before it exploded. Since we're alive, I reckon the detonation was a dud, but there's liable to be residual radiation. No idea how much, or if it was contained inside the mountain."

"Holy shit," muttered Kendric.

"After you blew up that damn reactor and scared the bejesus out of everybody, they sent me a Geiger-Meuller detector for my kit. I'll go up and check out the site." Baker limped over to the APC. "Kendric, have your boys drop the ramp and let me get to my bag."

At Kendric's shout, one of the Canadians grinned down at them from the top of the APC, nodded and disappeared inside the carrier. The ramp hit the ground and Baker limped inside. After a minute or two, Baker popped up on top of the carrier holding up a hand-held Geiger counter, pausing in each quadrant to read the meter. He waved the meter at Devon. "Normal readings here. We're not glowing yet."

He motioned up the road and yelled down at the Canadian. "Warrant Kendric, have your boys take me up top so I can check." He banged on the roof. "Come on, Sarg, get this damned rig going so I can see if we're hot or not." Retired Master Sergeant Baker had taken charge.

"Rasty," Kendric yelled at the soldier in the command hatch. "Take him up the hill and let me know what's going on." The APC slewed around the truck Arif had piloted down the mountain and clanked up the road.

"Is the radiation too high?" asked Granwin, cradling Devon's head in her arms as Flowers sluiced mud from his arm with a canteen of water.

"If Bert didn't detect any down here, we've got a chance the nuclear effects were minimal, or at least were contained in the mountain. Are you and Arif all right?"

Arif crowded close. "Chief, did you see? The water carried us all the way down here, knocked down trees, everything. I thought we would drown." His wide brown eyes inspected Devon's arm. "Ugh. Your arm looks ugly. Does it hurt?"

"Arif saved me, pulled me from the water. A true brave, today." Granwin hugged the boy to her.

Devon drifted away from the pain, focused on Granwin's eyes. Blue, gray, green, the sun was too bright and Flowers' probes too insistent.

Devon nodded toward the wrecked truck lying on its side. "I see you went like the devil."

Arif grinned. "Just the road was muddy or I would not have overturned. No one was hurt."

Flowers gently eased his head to each side. "Be still, Major, so I can see what happened to you. Where else do you hurt?" She probed around his hair, then his neck, then returned her attention to his left arm.

Devon shivered at the swell of pain when she wiped the dirt away from the open wound with a gauze pad. "Sweet Jesus, lady, go a little easier, if you would, please." Devon grimaced. "What kind of a medic are you? Last time I saw you was in Riyadh, behind a desk."

"Shush. I type and, in a previous life, plugged bullet holes as an ER nurse in Jersey City. So youse be quiet and let me do my job, Major," she said softly, turning on her old Jersey twang as she bent over him, probing his chest, gut and finally each leg. "You've got a compound fracture of the left arm and a multiple contusions, that much is obvious. Don't feel anything else broken, but with the fall you took, we need to be careful with your back."

She turned to Kendric, her mid-west neutral Canadian accent back in place. "Can you arrange transport back to the Israeli helicopter?" She dumped a bottle of iodine solution into Devon's open wound and loosely wrapped a field dressing around it. "I can stop the bleeding, but we need to get this man to a doctor. He should be in surgery."

Devon let his body sag. *No use being all tense now.* A nurse receptionist, a deacon—he and Granwin and Arif were all in good hands. A shadow swept across his face. *Hawk or crow?* Had to be the hawk, since all was finally well. In his mind, he floated over the valley, free from guilt and pain.

The Canadian Warrant Officer interrupted Devon's flight. "When the APC gets back, Captain, I'll run you back to the compound and the Israeli hello. Can you explain who the blazes these other people are? Is your demolitions man right? They're all from the crash? I wasn't expecting a crowd of strangers out in the middle of the Zone, much less a damn firefight. There's a hell of a lot more going on than you told me."

Flowers shook her head at Devon, cautioning him while she butterflyed the bandage around his arm, then loosely bound it to a splint.

"Oh, no. Nothing more than what we said. Mr. Baker is correct. Major Devon is vetted to the UN, as is the woman. The boy is the son of a UN employee. Get me and them out of your hair, and you can sort out the bandits. I have no idea why the armed men began shooting. Must be those Druze you mentioned."

Kendrick nodded. "Yeah, with a nuclear weapon." He shook his head and turned to watch the APC slowly returning down the slope.

The APC slid to a stop by the overturned pickup and dropped its ramp. Baker emerged and limped over to them. "Lots of rubble up there with a very low reading. Just enough gamma radiation to post warnings and keep everyone clear of the mountain for a while, but I think we're all clear."

Baker turned to the Canadian. "Warrant Kendrick, make sure your people understand there's residual radiation up there, and to keep everyone away until a proper survey can be made."

Kendric motioned two of the Canadians over and they eased Devon onto a stretcher. "You aren't going to stay and take care of that place up there, Mr. Baker?"

Baker looked down at his leg, still trailing bits of gauze and plaster, then over at Flowers.

Devon noticed she had a smile for Baker that she hadn't been able to muster up for him.

Baker grinned back at Kendrick. "Sorry. Captain Flowers has prescribed something else for me." He looked over at her for confirmation.

Flowers nodded. “Not the way the operation was planned, but results, Colonel Houston recently told me, results count, and the rest is just talk.”

Granwin and Arif lurched and bounced by Devon’s side for a short but tortuous excursion in the APC and on to the waiting Israeli helicopter.

One arm gripped tightly around Arif, the other around Granwin, Devon leaned forward as the helicopter lifted off.

Tears rolled from Granwin’s eyes as the helicopter banked away from the mountains and turned to cross a large body of water. “Is the Image of Christ gone forever, Nash?”

He pulled her head close to his. “I saw the fresco, just before the explosion. Any time you want, I’ll describe it to you. A family on the slopes, standing arm-in-arm overlooking the Sea of Galilee. A beautiful fresco, surely a painting of Jesus, his friends and family. I know you’ll remember the details better than I. Once in a while, you can describe it to me, to keep it fresh in your mind.”

She nodded, her damp hair still dripping onto his face as she bent over him. Her eyes were a deep blue, a reflection of the Sea of Galilee below them. “Should we tell others of the image?”

“I don’t know if it would be wise. People will just scoff if we can’t prove it.” He reached up to wipe away a tear from her dirty face. “*Inshallah?*”

She smiled and reached across so she could hold on to Arif. “Certainly. God’s will brought us to this place. As He will guard our way to a safe home.”

Arif leaned his face close. “Will I get to go with you?”

Devon held Arif’s hand. “Sure, buddy. We need you to take care of the kitten.”

“Like the one in the picture on the wall?”

“Yeah, just like that one, if a cat is what you want.”

“And a puppy, too.”

“We’ll think about it, scout.”

Outside the Plexiglas the harsh ground dropped away. Upward they flew. Like the hawk.

THE IMAGE OF CHRIST

BY
J. M. TAYLOR

Curious about the tablet?
Here is how it all began.

K H R I S T O S
YMJ NRFLJ TK HMWNXY
QNJX GJMNI YMJ LWJJS
BFYJW YMJ BFD YT YMJ
QNEMY YMJ BFD YT
JAJUGFXYNSL
HMWNXY XTR TK LTI
FSI KFYMJW XFANTW
TK HFJXFW UMNQNUUN
NS YMJ XMFITB TK
YMJ RTZSY TK YMJ
RTXJX QTAJ TK LTI
RFS BTRFS FSI HMNQI
FWJ UWTHQFDRJI YT FQQ

CHAPTER ONE

Galilee, 32 A. D.

Cyrus of Athena slowly shuffled up to Ajax.

Ajax paused, pestle and bowl of pigments in his hands, and bowed his head in respect before the old man as his father had taught him.

"You have a fine son, Telemond."

Ajax could barely understand the old man's words. Cyrus' breath held a hint of mint, faint disguise for the illness that even Ajax could smell, the aroma of an old man, dying inside. Ajax slowly looked up as Cyrus took Ajax's chin in his hand and peered at him through rheumy eyes. Ajax trembled in the grip of the old soldier, but returned his gaze as Cyrus sat on a stone bench.

"Child, aren't you pleased I brought you and Telemond to build my final place of rest?" Cyrus waved across the valley toward the distant Sea of Galilee and the narrow band of water that others of the valley called the River Jordan, and north toward the town of Caesar Philippi. "I, my father, and his father, have protected and cared for this valley and its people since our ancestors first rode as soldiers in Alexander's army. You know of Alexander, King of Greece and conqueror of the world, don't you, boy?" Cyrus held his scared arms up for the boy to see. "I have fought many battles with these old arms, but I am missing the greatest victory of all, a son." He reached out and patted Ajax on his shoulder, fingers light as bird feathers. "You be a good son for your father. You are his pride. I see it in your eyes, as well as his."

Truly, Ajax knew his father was proud of him, even though he sometimes moved a little slowly on his crutches. Ajax had worked hard in preparing Telemond's brushes and pigments. Eyes on the floor, he smiled, proud their work pleased their benefactor.

The engraved marble sepulcher had been complete for several days. Now Telemond worked when the light was clear on a landscape scene on the wall of the crypt, smoothing and cleaning an expanse of limestone while Ajax prepared the pigments for the fresco. Telemond had first sketched in the line of mountains between the Jordan River and the Mediterranean coastal city of Tyr, adding the rich greens of the Lebanon cedars and graceful date palms laden with fruit.

Ajax had carefully mixed the powders and today even added a few of the careful brush strokes under Telemond's supervision.

Cyrus stared at the evolving scene, then slowly climbed to his feet and shuffled back to the cave mouth. He paused, turned at the entrance. "You have done well, Telemond, you and the boy, well worth the expense of bringing you across the sea." He ran his hand over the smooth marble and waved at the fresco on the wall. "I will never be away from my beloved valley, even in death. The trees, the snow on the mountain, it is very peaceful."

Cyrus and Ajax worked for the remainder of the afternoon until a murmur of voices interrupted their solitude.

"Who is that speaking outside, son?" asked Telemond. They were almost finished for the day, and Telmond had begun cleaning his brushes.

When Ajax looked outside he saw a crowd, drawn by a strong voice speaking on the flowered terrace. He and Telemond joined the throng gathered to hear the man from Nazareth, the one they called the Messiah, the anointed one. Ajax sat with his father into the evening, long after the light had fallen too low to work inside the cave, listening to the gentle words of the man his disciples declared both a prophet and a healer.

Speaking in the Aramaic tongue of the valley, the Messiah spoke in parables, stories about devotion and compassion. He approached Ajax, who, while afraid, was drawn by the kind words about forgiveness and love of others. Others gathered around when the Messiah asked if Ajax understood faith. When Ajax replied that he did not know, the Messiah placed his hands on Ajax's head and in a soft voice told the crippled boy that with faith he could be strong.

And Ajax stood...and walked. Telemond propped his son's crutch inside the crypt, but Ajax never had to use it again.

Inspired by the healing of his son, Telemond worked the next day adding several figures to the fresco on the plastered wall of the crypt.

CHAPTER TWO

A cavern below Mount Hermon, 42 A. D.

Ajax took a deep breath and forced himself to continue down the narrow passageway, trembling at the silent darkness, almost faint with relief when he emerged through the waterfall.

In the years since his father crafted Cyrus' sepulcher, Ajax had married Persephone, one of Cyrus' granddaughters and, like Ajax, a Christian. The Roman feared a rebellion by the Christians, and solved their problem with more crucifixions of the men and selling the women and children into slavery. Weeping, Persephone had told him a fortnight before of the murder of her mother and aunts at the hands of the Romans when they refused to accept the bonds of slavery. With Persephone safely hidden with relatives in a small village in the Bekáa Valley, Ajax returned to the hillside overlooking the Sea of Galilee. Working from the inside where he would be hidden from the wandering shepherds, Ajax carefully sealed the entrance to Cyrus' crypt and Telemond's greatest masterpiece and crept out through the fissure leading to the waterfall.

Exhausted after his all-night task, Ajax looked back at the curtain of water, green as it tumbled down over moss-covered rocks and sparkled in the morning sun. He felt certain the cavern entrance and tortuous journey through the underworld to reach the tomb would remain hidden from the Romans and the wandering shepherds of the valley.

"Lorus," he said to his own son after many more years passed. "I grow old and can wait no longer." Ajax had feared this day because Lorus had never shared his devotion to the memory of the Messiah. "I must pass a sacred secret to you." Ajax told his son of his own miraculous healing and of the cave containing Telemond's fresco, guarded by the body of dear Cyrus.

Lorus was a Jew and had never accepted the old stories of the mysterious Messiah. But he dearly loved his father, and listened intently to Ajax's story of the miracle, his healing on the mountain-side. At Ajax's urging, Lorus traveled to the waterfall, found the entrance and, bundle of tapers in hand, made his way through the damp passageway to the tomb to see the fresco for himself. He returned from the cavern to confess to his father that upon seeing the holy fresco, he had knelt and wept, and now believed. So inspired was he by the revelations, Lorus was determined to commemorate the fresco's existence for others, but was afraid to expose his family to the dangers.

Christian artisans of the time had become adept at encryption and symbology; the most famous of which was the simple fish. Engraved on tombstones across the span of Roman rule, the simple sign of the fish identified a faithful Christian to other Christians, a symbol largely unrecognized, or at least ignored, by their prosecutors. Lorus described the path to the fresco, first in his native Aramaic, then transcribed to Greek, the language of his grandfather. It was a simple message.

"The Image of Christ lies behind the green water, the way to the light, the way to everlasting Christ, Son of God and father, savior of Caesar Philippi. In the shadow of the mount of Moses, love of God, man, woman and child are proclaimed to all."

Fearful of the Roman council ruling the valley, Lorus then encrypted the Greek words, substituting letter for letter following a simple substitution pattern. He selected a fine-grained slab of marble and spent an entire day polishing the slab until he could see his own face reflected in the stone. Then with a fine chisel he carefully engraved the encrypted words, polishing each facet of each letter, a silent memorial to his grandfather and the Messiah in hopes that one day the world would be safe for Christians to pray by the tomb. At the very bottom of the tablet he carefully engraved the symbol of the fish, the fine lines a hint to the words encrypted on the tablet.

Over the following years this holy relic was known as the Image of Christ, and was placed in a place of honor in the home of the eldest son. In the years of peace, when the Romans embraced Christianity, the family treasured it as a symbol of their devotion. In times of threat, it was carefully hidden away. During one of those times its meaning was lost to the family and the polished slab became just another piece of rock.

CHAPTER THREE

Damascus, 254 A. D.

The polished bit of marble lay in the corner of a distant cousin's house, so distant they considered themselves unrelated to the Greeks of the valley. Uncovered by Libby, the industrious wife of Petronius the grower of fruits, she installed the tablet in her kitchen the first year of her marriage. Covered with flour dust it lay unrecognized, engraved side down, as a base for rolling out bread and other tasks as children came and grew.

"Peatrie, leave the knife alone. You will cut yourself."

Despite the handicap of a badly stunted leg, Peatrie was a curious child. Libby watched her examine the pottery maker's pattern on a mug, set it back on the broad table, then slide her fingers along the flour dust. She picked up a corner of the tablet and peered at the underside. "Mother, what do the letters say?" she asked, running her fingers along the angular marks engraved in the marble.

More questions. "Ask your father," replied Libby. "Atronius studied with the priests in the temple; he understands the letters."

"Ah, my sweet girl, never you mind. It is just Greek gibberish," Atronius responded as he rinsed a pile of fresh dates, preparing them for the market. "The Greeks, even the ones in the village, they all believe they were the rulers of the world."

Atronius' frowned when the dates spilled through a hole in the old wicker basket used to carry the dates to the market. His frown immediately turned to a smile at Peatrie's giggle. "Now all that is left of the Greek empire are shopkeepers and evil-faced statues at the temple. I don't much like the proud ones who think they are still kings. Just wealthy they are, not wise." He peered at the basket and held out his hand. "Give me that piece of Greek stone." Atronius took the tablet from Peatrie and used it to plug the hole in the basket. "Now these Greek words are of great value." Atronius laughed at his joke and layered the dates with palm leaves, filling the basket to the brim. "Come. Help me take the fruit to the market." He handed Peatrie a small bag of figs, shouldered the basket and led the way to the town square.

Libby stood with her hands on her hips, shaking her head as she watched them walk side-by-side toward the town market, Peatrie limping as she carried the sack over her shoulder, her tiny hand engulfed by her father's. Libby would willingly give up the old stone to see her daughter and husband laughing together.

On the edge of town an Arab trader leading a string of mules stopped Atronius and Peatrie. After a few minutes of haggling, the trader strapped the date-filled basket on a complaining mule for the long trip to the Jordan River and eventually across the harsh Sinai. The trip took several weeks and the trader consumed many of the dates before the trader reached the mouth of the Nile River, enroute to the frankincense fields of the lower Arabia peninsula. The flour-coated marble tablet lay un-noticed under the dates until the trader emptied the basket in a produce stall in the Cairo market. There the tablet clattered to the hard-packed ground, the stone an unexpected weight in the bottom of the basket.

An old man pounced on the tablet and ran before the trader could do more than yell. Safe back in his warren of twisted alleys, the old man polished the marble tablet with his sleeve and a bit of spit. He laid it on a straw mat together with fragments of stone carved with strange symbols, birds and people with heads of animals, other oddities stolen from the graves around the Pyramids. He called out to anyone who passed to buy his collection, "Save an old man from starvation. Buy these precious stones. Healing, wealth will be yours, only if you take a stone for your home. Good luck can be bought here," he sang out, singsong in his call.

Origines Adamantius, a Christian philosopher, often strolled through the market. This day he paused at the old man's mat, inspected the odd pieces of rock, then bought the tablet for a single small coin, curious about the nonsensical words. He was a scholar, well versed in Greek and other languages, but the letters engraved on the tablet were clearly a secret message of some sort. Adamantius studied the tablet for several days.

"Ha," he finally exclaimed. "So simple, I should not wasted my coin or my time. But what do the words refer to, I wonder?" he mused. "Green water, a mountain." But one word was clear.

He scratched the letters over their encrypted counterparts across the top of the tablet.

"K...H...R...I...S...T...O...S."

CHAPTER FOUR

Cairo Museum, Egypt, 347 A. D.

Philo's back was tired. So much rubbish, all treated as treasures by the scholars. Heavy carved obelisks and ancient busts of people long dead lined the corridors of the Cairo Museum. Days like this, Philo was more than willing to set it all by the desert road and let the sands cover the stone as it had done for centuries, blowing up from the Sahara to the great sphinx and pyramids overlooking the Nile at Giza. Anthanasius, the Greek patriarch of Alexandria, had collected this great pile from shopkeepers, grave robbers and thieves all across Egypt. Now it was up to Philo to sort, clean, polish and evaluate the pieces scattered across the chamber of antiquities. He was so tired. He wiped the sweat from his brow and inspected both sides of the tablet. Simple marble, one side was defaced by angular engraved letters in the style of the old Greeks, like many of the pieces rescued and sent to Alexandria.

"Garbage." He spit on his sleeve and rubbed it across the slab of marble. No where could he see a sign of the hieroglyphs carved into the graves and great cities build by the rulers of the Old Kingdom. "Worthless," he muttered and threw the tablet onto a growing pile of rubble. He had no interest in garbled Greek inscriptions when so many magnificent Egyptian treasures had yet to be understood and protected from the Romans and others who came to Egypt only for treasure. The summer was too hot, the desert breeze filled with pestilence.

The tablet, unnoticed and unwanted, gathered the dust of centuries as empires waxed and waned, floods washed away the wicked, looters carried away the magnificent pieces and famines starved the innocent.

CHAPTER FIVE

Cairo, 621 A. D.

"Justin," the curator lay the gold mask aside and called out from the Room of Gold. "Please find something to stop the outer door from banging. I can't work with all that noise." The curator grumbled at the heat and returned to brushing the layers of dust from the gold mask.

Justin, a minor clerk in the Cairo antiquities building, picked through a pile of tablets and bits of carved stone, throwing each aside until he felt the slab of smooth marble. He had helped catalogue antiquities many years, enough to recognize the angular grooves forming the Greek letters. But he did not understand the words. Justine set the tablet aside and selected a rough square of stone taken from one of the lesser pyramids to prop open the door. A cool evening breeze blew across the room, bringing the damp air from the Nile, a welcome relief from the desert winds out of the west.

Toward the end of the long midsummer day Justine took the marble slab to an scholar on the other side of the building who, after a few moments of study pointed out the symbol of the fish and told Justine the tablet appeared to be a Christian relic, of no value to their studies of Egyptian Kingdoms past. "Trash," he said. "The Greeks, the Romans, their glory was only a pimple compared to the greatness of Egypt, even now. Go to the docks and listen. Sailors tell of lands across the Mediterranean invaded by barbarians from the wilderness, unworthy of scholarly interest. The important people of Rome and Athens, Caesar, Alexander and their like, are all are dead and forgotten, their armies defeated and palaces decimated. Even the great temples of Alexandria have been swallowed by the sea."

Justine, somehow intrigued by the old tablet, carried the piece to his home in the Nazlet el Simman quarter in the south of Cairo. His modest home stood on a slight rise where each morning the rising sun highlighted the Sphinx's aristocratic face watching over the Nile. Justine had prayed to the old gods, but they had not answered. His eldest son had died of the fevers, and Justine's wages were barely enough to buy food for a his wife and their daughters.

When he arrived home the light of the late afternoon sun still shown brightly into Justine's home. Before his evening meal he plastered the tablet into the entranceway at the exact spot where the long shadow from the tallest of the three pyramids fell. Over the following years, for one week each midsummer, only for an instant each day the tablet reflected the very last of the sun's rays. Whenever the sun glinted from the polished marble Justine closed his eyes and prayed on his knees in front of the tablet.

Perhaps the God of the Christians had listened. In the coming years his youngest daughter bore Justine's grandchildren.

He was happy.

CHAPTER SIX

Nazlet el Simman, Cairo, Egypt 808 A. D.

"Mosul. Dig that profane stone from the old wall. The mullah must not see a Christian relic in my home when he visits tonight."

Akmed seemed alarmed that he had forgotten the tablet, the Greek word "KHRISTOS" clearly scratched into the marble for a scholar like himself to recognize. Over the years Akmed had scrubbed at the words, but in the afternoon light anyone who understood Greek could clearly read the inscription. And then there was the fish. Blessed be to Allah, Akmed had no idea what other blasphemes were described by the Satanic words.

A new window allowing the breeze from the Nile to flow unimpeded through the home, a stone wall around the rear court; superficial changes had left the old mud and limestone dwelling much the same since the long forgotten Justine's death. However, following the spread of the Words of Mohammed out of Arabia and across the southern Mediterranean, the culture and basic beliefs of the community had changed dramatically.

Mosul held himself calm, swallowing back his rage as Akmed rapped him across the shoulder with his cane. He bowed his head before his master. Religion had not meant much to Akmed before, but his festering hate of Akmed and Islam grew with each day.

"Get on with it, man. I want the wall smooth before darkness and the cleric arrives." Akmed left to join his three wives, leaving Mosul to dig out the shiny marble tablet with its Greek letters.

Mosul hammered at the mud, loosening the straw and clay until he finally could pry out the tablet, leaving the marble no longer a finished rectangle but a ragged slab with chipped edges. A Coptic from the Christian quarter of Cairo on the east bank of the Nile, Mosul chaffed under his Islamic master. Partially to spite Akmed, Mosel secreted the tablet under his sleeping mat, a pillow for his head when he thought late at night about the legends of the Jews' flight from Egypt, and his own quest to escape. Summer passed and the next February Mosul took advantage of the wet winds to slip away. He walked to the Nile, then upstream toward the sprawling old city of Cairo and on to the docks where he found work as a stevedore. He slept in the bales of cotton at night after listening to the curious talk of the sailors. Their tales intrigued Mosul, stories from so many different lands and people.

One blustery day a whisper across the docks warned of a wave of clerics coming the next morning to cleanse the workers of their sins. That night Mosul sailed for distant shores, away from persecution by the followers of Mohammed.

Mosul carried the tablet with him wherever he traveled, his only material connection to Christianity as he sailed the North African littoral, following the old Phoenician routes. Along the Libyan coast he was taken by the fever and left by his shipmates at the Christian basilica at Leptis Magna, where Brother Jules cared for him until he died.

A practical man, Brother Jules discovered the tablet as he searched through poor Mosul's effects. Jules labored over the unfamiliar words, pouring over old scrolls as he laboriously tried to translate the encrypted and unfamiliar Greek to the Latin with which he was familiar. Several years passed before his understanding of Greek and the secrets of encryption allowed him to recognize the connection between the scratched name of Christ and the engraved words.

Inspired by his discovery and to escape the influence of the Arabs, Brother Jules shipped aboard one of the many trading vessels bound for Constantinople, with the intent of returning the tablet to the town identified in the encrypted words. Caesar Philippi had become a thriving seaport on the Palestinian coast south of Mount Hermon, built in the first year after the birth of Christ. Brother Jules braved rough winter seas and coastal pirates to reach the outer edges of the Syrian empire with barely his life, robes and the sacred fragment of stone. He died in the humble monastery at Caesarea Palistenae, satisfied he had returned the tablet to its land of origin. The tablet lay untouched in a side alcove, one of a very few holy relics watched over by the impoverished monks isolated in the land of the Muslims.

CHAPTER SEVEN

Berry, France, May, 1096 A. D.

Miriam turned from the window. The aroma of the May roses heavy in the evening air, teased by the buzzing insects to spread their petals and release their sweet aroma into the evening. "Jacques, must you go? My lord, please stay, oh please," she pleaded with her husband, already knowing the young nobleman had decided to join Pope Urban's call to the holy crusade.

Men of high and low standing had congregated around the town all spring, gathering horses and arms. Jacques had watched from afar until this very week when finally he joined the men of the province at the cathedral. Unable to hold back his feelings, Jacques had left Miriam's side to answered the call to arms issued by Peter of Amiens, full of fiery rhetoric after his recent return from the Holy Lands.

Jacques took her trembling hand in his. "My dear Miriam. The heathens have defiled Jerusalem, our holy city. You know I cannot stay here in France while others sacrifice so much. Even my love for you is overwhelmed by my duty."

She turned to the bedside table where she brought forth a finely carved wooden cross from beneath a scarf. "Carry this token with you, along with my love and devotion." Miriam held out the cross, candle-light glinting from the figure of Jesus worn smooth from years of prayer. "I suspected you would lead, not follow, the quest in the name of our holy Lord Jesus. I love you; I know your mind. Go, my dearest, with my undying affection."

"My darling." Jacques shook his head, "This cross was your mother's..." He paused, at a loss for words, fighting back tears. "... your grandmother's. How can you part with it?" He held the cross gently, the wood still warm from his wife's soft touch.

"It is not as precious to me as your return." She smiled in the soft candlelight. "Others demand you fight for the Church. Your only charge from me is to carry the cross. That way I know you will return, by the very grace of God safe back to my arms." She took the cross from his hand and placed it in a box, glittering with inlay filaments of gold and silver, and offered it back to her husband. "Let this box protect the cross as you keep yourself well. I will wait for you to embrace me again." A hint of perfume rose from the wood, a reminder of its previous use by Miriam to hold her scents.

"The box is beautiful, my dear, a fitting vessel for the cross. I will hold both as precious, a symbol of my love of God and you." He held the box to the light. "The word. What does it say?" he asked, illiterate as most men of his day who were not of the church nor artisans.

"You travel on a quest for the Son of God, so I asked the Greek in the marketplace to place His name on the box."

Jacques traced the inlaid gold letters, KHRISTOS, intertwined with tiny leaping silver fish. "The box and its cross shall never leave my side."

The mass of men, retainers and servants and camp-followers traveled across Europe and into Palistenae, only to be met with equal determination by the Turks. They fought on the very soil where Jesus walked, where the Muslims sought to desecrate all that was holy in the name of Allah and Mohammed.

October winds blew hot from the distant deserts as Jacques cantered his bloodied charger, urging the wounded horse toward the shadow of the cross. Jacques slid from his saddle, stumbled to the foot of the steps and lay his head on the cool stone, thinking of Miriam. Peace at last, he thought as the horse moved to the hillside and, ignoring its own wounds, began cropping the dry grass. The rhythmic sound reminded Jacques of home, his farmlands stretching to the horizon.

"Hello," a voice called from the stone battlements overhead.

"Miriam," he replied, thinking he had returned to his France and his beloved wife.

The monks carried him inside the monastery of Caesarea Palestinae, but he died before the night was out, to be buried in the catacombs beneath the chapel alongside the bones of a long-dead traveler. After a quiet prayer, Brother Peter honored the knight's memory by hanging his cross on the wall of the sanctuary and propped the empty box on the ledge beside an ancient tablet left by an traveler long before the Crusades.

Brother Francis picked up the aromatic box, puzzled that the box would have the same Greek letters inlaid into its surface as the stone tablet. "Brother Peter, may I use this box for the tablet? They both are blessed with the name of our Lord and Savior."

Given permission, he was chagrined when he realized the tablet was too long to fit in the box.

Handy with tools, Brother Francis first carefully etched a line across the bottom of the marble and broke off the bottom section with the symbol of the fish, leaving the words intact. He started to toss the segment with the fish in the trash, then stopped, aghast at what he had almost done. Instead of throwing it away, he slipped the fragment of rock into a fold in his robes, his own personal talisman. Now the tablet with the indecipherable words fit tightly in the inlaid box. He searched out several bands of copper and hammered them securely around the box. Thus sealed, the box sat for generations on the simple altar of the monastery, their single bit of treasure.

CHAPTER EIGHT

On the Damascus-Baghdad Road, 1917 A. D.

"Off your bloody arses," roared the Sergeant Major, and the bone-weary company struggled to their feet in the cool shade of the ruins. Until recently battered by an artillery attack, the ruins had once been a small monastery, a remnant of the disrupted flow of Christianity from Jerusalem across the world. "Don't let that bloody lot beat us to Damascus. We ain't gonna sleep all day while them buggers take all the glory, now are we?"

With a groan the British soldiers climbed to their feet. In the distance dark-robed Bedouins led by Lawrence trotted toward the sun, a great globe rising over of the distant hills. Shots echoed from the mountains as the Bedouins caught up with the retreating Germans and Turks.

Corporal Paddy O'Roark dusted off a wooden box and held it up to the morning rays of the sun to admire the gilt inlay. It was heavy with an engraved stone inside.

Private John Matthews leaned on his rifle waiting for his mate to get his gear settled, using any excuse to hang back a bit. "So now, Paddy. Since you're Catholic, you can just steal anything you want from a monastery without a bit of a worry God won't strike you dead?"

"Sot out, mate." O'Roark threw the broken bits of an old wooden cross back into the rubble and stuffed the inlaid box into his haversack. "You bloody Protestants ain't got no true feeling for what's holy in this world. If I leave this bit of Christianity here in these old rocks the heathens will steal it, sure as we stand here in God's glory. Now see here, you just leave it to me. I'll see the box gets to someone who can take care of it, by God."

"Oh, yes. Like you took care of Willie's Remington when that sniper smashed up his arm." Matthews looked at O'Roark's rifle with envy, shiny new in comparison to his battered Lee-Enfield.

O'Roark wiped a bit of dust from the sight. "This here piece of fine machinery needs a proper soldier like me to treat it proper. You're a grand Englishman, so you carry that fine old piece of English iron you better get slung over your bloody shoulder. Made in Eddystone, you tell me, in America? Right good English place that sounds." Gear finally settled, O'Roark led his mate out of the stone ruins and picked up the pace set by the Sergeant Major. "Hah! You might as well be carrying one of them old Spanish flintlocks the heathens wave over their heads." He grinned at Matthews, sweeping his hand around in a wide curve. "Barrel's so damn crooked I'll call you forward the next time we have to shoot around corners, I will."

O'Roark was true to his word, at least about the box. Like many of the Irish Catholic volunteers with the British army, he cursed with his mates but prayed before each battle. But today he couldn't shake it off; he had a bad feeling as they marched across the desert toward Baghdad.

"Get after them boogers," yelled the Sergeant Major, waving them up the steep road, and O'Roark and his squad scrambled after the desperate Germans. A bullet slapped the rock and O'Roark returned fire at a blur of dusty gray. His target staggered, then toppled over the side of the gray granite cliff.

"This bloody Remington, it do shoot nice, eh, John," crowed O'Roark.

"Don't stop to brag now, O'Roark. Only one left of this bunch," yelled the Sergeant Major. "Up there." He pointed up a steep road." You two kill the bastard, then join us back at the foot of the mountain." He waved O'Roark and Matthews after the German.

O'Roark scraped against the side of the mountain, away from the dizzying drop to the ravine below. He grinned at Matthews, crouched in a crevice in the rock. "Come on mate, our chance to be a hero." O'Roark led the way on up the steep climb. At the end of the road the German was gone, his rifle abandoned by a heavy wooden door set back into a narrow arched opening. The sun washed across a Christian cross carved into the keystone over the door.

O'Roark stopped in front of the door. "The booger has run into a monastery."

"You being the good Catholic, you roust the bastard," said Matthews.

O'Roark beat on the door and threatened the wrath of the mighty Imperial Army.

A voice called out from overhead.

O'Roark took a step back and stared up at a hooded figure looking down from a narrow window. "Open the damned door," he yelled, shaking his rifle at the monk.

"What a good Christian you are, mate." Matthews grinned at O'Roark. "Get on with it or we'll miss tea."

The monk adamantly refused to let O'Roark in until he left his rifle outside with Matthews. Once inside, O'Roark felt strangely at peace as the monk led him to the chapel where he knelt beside the trembling Boche. After they both took the blessing of the priest,

O'Roark left the inlaid box in the hands of the German and returned to rescue his Remington from Matthews.

"Come on, you bloody Protestant," he yelled, waking his mate from a solid nap in the shade. "The German sod, he ain't no soldier no more, he's a right monk, he is, robes and all. Here." O'Roark jerked his Remington from Matthews grip and tossed the Englishman the German's Mauser. "Go shoot yourself in the foot with this."

They trudged down the narrow road toward the road below, arguing the merits of the Remington and the Mauser until they once again joined the British column and their Arab allies chasing the fleeing remnants of the German-Turkish armies on toward Baghdad.

O'Roark should have taken the oath with the German.

A week later on the muddy bank of the Tigris a round ball fired from one of the ancient flintlocks struck Paddy O'Roark smack in the middle of the forehead.

John Matthews rummaged through his pal's gear, then spat in disgust when he discovered the inlaid box was missing from Paddy's haversack. He threw away the Mauser, figured it for bad luck, and took the Remington.

Back at the monastery in the Sinjar mountains, the heavy box with its golden leaping fish was carefully placed in a niche to gather dust and await the quest of another true believer.

J. M. Taylor - somewhere in the Saudi desert in the early '90s.

Taylor is also the author of the award-winning thrillers, GULF WINDS, MISSING STICKS and FLASH of EMERALD.

Combining his experiences as a paratrooper, nuclear weapons specialist and operations research analyst with travels in the Far and Middle East, Europe and the States, he packs a ton of adventure into action-filled page-turners.

Read more about Taylor and his books at http://johnmtaylor.com.

www.ingramcontent.com/pod-product-compliance
Lightning Source LLC
LaVergne TN
LVHW010051110826
845155LV00028B/288

* 9 7 8 1 8 7 9 0 4 3 0 7 7 *